It is the height of the Roaring Twenties – a fresh enthusiasm for the arts, science, and exploration of the past have opened doors to a wider world, and beyond...

In the emptiness beyond time and space alien entities known as Ancient Ones writhe hungrily at the thresholds between worlds.

In Arkham, the people feel in their bones that something is different. Something feels wrong.

A dread tide draws fear and terror along the Miskatonic River, and when it reaches Akham, nothing will ever be the same again.

Only a handful of brave souls with inquisitive minds and the will to act stand against the horrors threatening to tear this world apart.

Will they prevail?

ARKHAM HORROR™

The
NIGHTMARE
QUEST
of
APRIL MAY

The Drowned City, Book Two

ROSEMARY JONES

First published by Aconyte Books in 2025

ISBN 978 1 83908 312 9

Ebook ISBN 978 1 83908 313 6

Cover art by Martín M Barbudo.

Printed in the United States of America and elsewhere.

9 8 7 6 5 4 3 2 1

ACONYTE BOOKS

An imprint of Asmodee North America

Mercury House, North Gate,

Nottingham NG7 7FN, UK

aconytebooks.com

Dedicated with love to my biggest cheerleader and supporter, Phoebe aka Diane aka Mom!

PROLOGUE

The door banged shut. Harvey flew down the porch steps. Then he heard the door squeak open again behind him. His mother called out.

"Harvey Walters! Where are you going? School starts tomorrow."

"Ah, Ma," he said, not bothering to turn around. "I know more than the whole class already."

He did. He was first in his class. Knew more than any of the older boys, too. He also thought he was smarter than most of the girls. Although at thirteen, he was beginning to suspect that the girls would always know just a little more than he did.

Certainly his mother had an uncanny ability to guess where Harvey was going and what he was going to do next before the idea even occurred to him.

"Be careful going up that hill," she said behind him. He almost stopped to argue but he couldn't wait. This was the last night of freedom before school started. He couldn't waste it.

"Take a lantern," she called after him as he ran down the road, veering off into the field.

"Don't need no light. I want to see the stars." His bare feet crushed the brittle brown grass beneath his toes. Tomorrow he'd have to wear stiff shoes and scratchy socks. Tomorrow he would have his hair brushed down and a stiff collar attached to his shirt. Tomorrow his mother would insist on him looking "like a little gentleman" before sending him on his way to school.

But tonight, it was still summer. Which meant bare feet and the rest of his growing body barely covered by old overalls that he'd worn since June. His legs pumped harder, running as fast as he could, practically flying toward his destination.

Harvey crested the top of the hill and flopped down. The dirt was still warm under his shoulders. The scent of sun-scorched grass rose around him. Harvey looked up. Stars, nothing but stars, stretching across the sky and running down to the edge of the horizon. Like a bowl of stars upended over his hill, just for him.

And beyond those stars was something else, something enormous, looking down at his world.

Professor Harvey Walters snorted and woke to the smell of pipe smoke. He straightened in his chair. How many years? How many decades since he ran up a hill to wonder at the stars?

He reached for his pipe. Knocking out the ash into the brass tray that his housekeeper Mrs Fox left on his desk for just that purpose, Harvey bent over the book. Bits and pieces of string, a dried-out pen, letters from past students, and scraps of old notes lay scattered across his desk and his floor. The usual detritus of a day's work. He shrugged. Removing rubbish was why he had a housekeeper. But echoes of his mother's voice from his recent dream made him sigh and reach for the wastepaper basket. He scooped up all the trash and dumped it in.

Then Harvey noticed how stuffy the room smelled. He stretched and groaned, rising from his chair and crossing the floor to fling open a window to let a little breeze into his office. Leaning out, he peered at the night sky. The stars seemed dimmer than the days of his youth.

These days, too much haze hung over Arkham to see the night sky clearly. It smelled like rain was coming, with a cold, wet autumn to follow. Nothing like the crisp warm days that he remembered, ripe as apples and sweet as plums.

"Stop dreaming about the past, Harvey Walters," he told himself. "Get back to work."

With dreams still fogging his head, he rambled back to the desk. The book was a find. He doubted there was another copy anywhere on the East Coast. He knew a dozen occultists who would give their left arm to peek inside its covers. The fact that he discovered it in the half-burned trash of an estate sale on French Hill made him smile. The dingy little volume had been shoved into a box of cookbooks and sewing manuals by an inept auctioneer and so escaped the other bargain hunters.

Truth was that he'd almost forgotten about his purchase from the Fitzmaurice estate. After bringing it home, he'd shoved it into a bookcase in his study and turned to other more urgent research. But his new assistant had unearthed the book while cataloging his collection. Seeing it again stirred Harvey's interest enough to start reading the strange text after Sunday dinner. Especially when his assistant had plied him with questions throughout the meal about the unusual diagrams contained in its pages.

Puffing on his pipe, Harvey bent over his annotations. His last note was a simple sketch, a single eye, huge and unblinking, watching him just as he had once stared at the stars.

CHAPTER ONE

April May absolutely knew that she had the worst job in Arkham. And it was only Tuesday.

As the junior advertising salesperson at the *Arkham Advertiser*, her first duty every morning was to answer any complaints from the customers.

"Yes, Mr Perry," she responded to the fuming voice on the telephone. "I am looking at the ad right now. You are correct. The price is wrong. It does say two cents instead of twenty cents. But at least it brought a lot of customers to your store."

His comment was not one that April was likely to repeat to anyone.

"I am sorry, sir," she continued, holding the earpiece a little further away from her ear. "We can certainly run a correction in tomorrow's newspaper."

More muffled yelling made her sigh. "No, we can't replace the ad in today's newspaper. It's already been printed."

Continued shouting indicated that the angry hardware store owner was not pleased by this information.

"Of course, today's advertisement will be free. In fact, the whole week will be free!" April set down the phone to pull the memo pad toward her. She quickly scribbled instructions for the correction needed. A second memo to accounting gave Mr Perry a week's credit. She dropped both sheets into the wire basket for outbound messages. Picking up the phone again, April found that Perry's shouting had dropped to a dull mumble of general complaints about the state of the world and the carelessness of newspaper people in general. Judging it safe to end the conversation, she wished him a pleasant morning and hung up.

"Did you give away a week's worth of ads?" said Simon Phillips, the most senior salesperson on the staff. He leaned over the counter where April stood. While most ad salespeople roamed the city, April stood ready to take orders from anyone who walked into the newspaper's office. She thought at the start that she would prefer being in the office and not calling on customers, but she had not reckoned on the telephone. She had come to dread its ringing bell.

"I had to credit Mr Perry." April looked over her notes. "It was the third time that a price was wrong in his copy." She didn't add the obvious, which was that these mistakes frequently occurred because Phillips tended to scribble instructions in handwriting nearly illegible to everyone in the office. April pointed this fact out during her first week of work and it had nearly been her last week. Nobody, she was informed, liked college girls who tried to show up hardworking guys like Simon.

April had not, in fact, finished college. Instead, after only one year, she decided she hated school and left. Which was why she was working for the *Arkham Advertiser* in advertising rather than earning a degree at university as her mother wanted. Or working for her Uncle Tito's grocery, which is what her father would have preferred.

But she swept floors in Uncle Tito's store throughout high

school. She could list working in a grocery store as not a job that she wanted. Nor did she think about training as a nurse, as her Aunt Bernila suggested. She volunteered a few times at the clinic where Bernila worked and found the job involved too many bodily fluids. So April said a firm "no" to the suggestion of attending a nursing school.

"Try to sell an ad rather than give one away if you want to earn accounts of your own." Simon liked giving obvious advice but at least he was a distraction from making lists of jobs that she didn't want. So April just smiled and nodded at him.

"I will be out most of this morning, meeting with my clients." He grabbed his mail from the wooden slot marked with his name and stuffed it into his pocket, heading for the door.

The phone rang again. April sighed and picked it up. "A lost dog? Yes, you can place an advertisement. The cost is ten cents a line, seven words per line. The minimum charge is twenty cents per day. We count all ads as two lines."

The caller objected to the fees, but April stayed stern. She had just given a week of advertising to the hardware store owner. "No, ma'am, we do not offer a free service for lost pets."

More arguing ensued but the owner finally agreed to spending one dollar on her beloved Fritzie.

After some editing to make the owner's description of her German Shepherd fit into two lines, April filed the order for five days running under "Strayed or Stolen." Glancing at the current edition of the newspaper's classified advertisements, she noticed the "Strayed or Stolen" now covered more than two columns. Many dogs, a few cats, and even one cow were listed. Arkham seemed to be suffering from an unusual number of lost pets.

April turned back a page to "Help Wanted – Female" and ran her finger down the listings of jobs. Nothing new there. She picked up a pencil and began doodling cats and dogs on the edge of the page. With a couple of quick strokes, she added a dancing cow.

A man rapped on the counter. April stepped up on her box to better look him in the eye. At barely five feet tall, she was smaller than most people, so she kept a wooden box behind the counter to stand on when customers came in. Not that many did. Located in Arkham's Northside, the neighborhood surrounding the newspaper's offices was mostly factories and warehouses. This man looked like he might be one of the factory bosses, dressed reasonably well in a brown suit.

"How can I help you?" April asked.

"I need to sell my twin beds," he said. The gentleman was very tall, so April still had to crane her neck to see his bearded face. "The wife said we'd sleep better with twins. And that it was fashionable, too. Don't care about fashionable. I admit I do sleep better without her snoring in my ear and putting her cold feet on mine."

This, thought April, was one of the reasons that her job was difficult. People felt the overwhelming need to explain their decisions. Why they wanted to sell something or why they wanted to buy it. What an object once meant to them or how much they disliked it and needed something new. If they'd only told her just what they wanted to say in their advertisement, fourteen words minimum, she could enter their transaction so much more efficiently. But she never could summon the nerve to tell anyone to stop. So she listened.

"The beds are almost brand new," the man went on. "So I think fifty dollars seems reasonable." He looked slightly embarrassed. "But I'd probably take forty."

"Yes, sir. We can add 'willing to negotiate' to your copy." April pulled out a fresh form. She marked the ad to go in "For Sale – Furniture, Used" and waited for the rest of the information.

After a moment, the man stopped contemplating the ceiling. "Well, how much then?"

"Fifty dollars, is that what you wanted?" asked April, thinking he'd already settled on a price for his beds and wondering why he was asking her how much to charge.

"Fifty? For a little ad?" His outrage could be heard all the way across the building. A couple of reporters looked up from their typewriters in the bullpen to stare at April.

She sighed. "Fifty dollars as the price for the beds in the advertisement. Do you have a phone number that someone can call? Or would you rather they send a note? We can include your address. The cost of the ad depends on how many words we use."

"There's a phone in my office that they can call." He gave her the number of a nearby cannery and mentioned he was one of the supervisors.

April composed the advertisement in fourteen words, including phone number, and even managed to slide in the description "nearly new." She excelled at keeping the words to a minimum, cutting away the overly long descriptions and highlighting only the most interesting bits. It was something of an art.

Mr Deane, the owner of the twin beds, read the copy over twice, grunted, and then counted out four quarters.

"If the beds don't sell in a week, would you like an option to renew? We offer a discount for a second week." April counted the quarters into the cash box tucked by the phone.

"A week is long enough." Mr Deane sighed. "We're sleeping in the guest room on the old bed tonight. Maybe that will be enough to end these nightmares. The wife says we could always keep the twins for visitors. But if they sold quickly, we could buy a new mattress for our bed."

He stomped out of the newspaper office. April dropped the ad order in the wire basket. The phone was silent. She stepped down from her box and snagged the tall stool that she used during a slow period. April flipped through the pages of the newspaper, but she'd already read everything interesting. A glance around the office showed nobody looking at her. The door to the editor's office remained closed so Doyle Jeffries was probably on the phone with the publisher. Later in the day, Doyle would prop the door open and start yelling about deadlines.

A glance behind her showed the desks where the advertising people sat were empty. Simon would be on his way to lunch with one account or another. Cyril, who drew the illustrations for the advertisements, wasn't in yet. He preferred working at home, dropping off his assignments toward the end of the day.

She was rather envious of Cyril, both for being able to work at home and because he spent the better part of the day drawing. April enjoyed art classes best in school, but knew there was no career for someone like her. If she could do anything that she liked, and be paid for it, she would love to be an artist for the pulp magazines. Painting pictures like the ones found on the covers of *Amazing Stories* or even *Weird Tales*. Or, in the wildest of her dreams, painting the cover picture for the *Saturday Evening Post*.

April reviewed the mail one more time, but she'd already sorted all the payments from the new orders. She slid her fingers toward her pulp magazine hidden under the past issues of the *Advertiser*. She had time to read the conclusion of "Wastrel" by Gordon Young before lunch.

The phone rang so she abandoned the pulp under the pile of newspapers. April picked up the receiver and flipped to a fresh page in her order book.

"*Arkham Advertiser*, how can I help you?" She hoped it wasn't another lost dog. Those stories were too sad.

"Hi, April, it's Nella." Her friend's cheerful voice made April smile.

"Hello, and you're not supposed to call me at work." April dropped her voice and glanced around. Nobody was paying attention to her.

"I'm not supposed to use the phone at work for calls either. But they're all in a meeting. I've finished typing up the new policies and sorting the morning's mail." Nella worked at a marine insurance office two blocks away from the Advertiser. "Want to go to lunch?"

"I shouldn't." April kept trying to save money. Nella spent every penny that she earned almost as fast as she earned it. As soon as they moved to Arkham, Nella bobbed her hair, bought makeup, and began her transformation from small town girl to fashionable flapper.

"Just a hot dog from the cart. It's a nice day. We can eat outside," Nella wheedled.

Deciding a hot dog was much more exciting than the crackers in her handbag, April agreed.

"Oh, good." Nella sounded relieved. "I need a walk. And a cheerful conversation. I had the worst nightmares last night."

A slight cough at the counter caused April to raise her eyes. Marcus, one of the typesetters, nodded at her. April passed him the basket of completed classified ad forms. "Thank you for your call." She hung up, knowing Nella would understand that somebody was listening. They often ended or started calls with absurdly formal phrases as phones were not for personal use.

By noon, April was eager to escape the newspaper office. The fog of cigarette smoke rose to the ceiling but failed to muffle the clatter of typewriters. Outside, the air felt crisp, a tinge of cold under the sunshine marking the end of summer and the start of autumn, although a mound of purplish clouds to the east did threaten rain.

A short walk brought her to the hot dog cart, where her friend was already ordering for both of them. Extra mustard for Nella, plenty of sauerkraut and pickles for April. Clutching their hot dogs, they maneuvered through the lunch crowds to the small park where they often ate together. Tucked between two taller office buildings, it wasn't an official park, rather a leftover garden from the time before Northside had been overrun with factories and warehouses. An iron gate kept it private, with keys going to the tenants of the two buildings flanking its sides.

Nella long ago appropriated her company's key, since nobody else in her office seemed to know or care about the little park. April and Nella hurried to their favorite bench. Juggling her hot dog in one hand, Nella pulled out a bottle of soda from Schoffner's General Store, the shop nearest their boarding house. She also withdrew a pair of waxed paper cups from her enormous handbag. Nella favored a satchel style of purse that always reminded April of a doctor's case. April never knew exactly what Nella carried in her purse, but her friend frequently had food or drink stashed away in it.

"Here's to lunch at the Ritz!" Nella said as always, pouring out their drinks.

"Cheers," said April, toasting her friend as was their tradition. They'd been best friends since kindergarten, with Nella usually leading the way in their games. Unlike April, Nella never considered going to college. She searched for an office job as soon as high school was done.

Nella certainly looked like an efficient secretary. With height and shoulders to carry off styles which overwhelmed the smaller April, Nella looked smart in her dark blue two-piece sailor dress. The pleats on the skirt would have wrinkled in five minutes on April but Nella was clever with an iron and starch. The wide sailor collar and jaunty bow set off her creamy skin and rounded features. Nella's auburn curls were neatly clipped in a style similar to Clara Bow or Betsy Baxter, two Hollywood stars that they both adored.

Unfairest of all, Nella had a sprinkling of freckles across her nose, which made her look absolutely American. April never understood why Nella bought creams to fade her freckles or powdered her nose to hide them.

Then again Nella often said she didn't understand why April complained about her height or lack of figure. "You look like a flapper or a movie star in those straight little dresses," Nella assured her whenever they went shopping for patterns and materials. Both were experts with their needles, although unfortunately too different in size and style to be able to swap dresses easily.

After a few sips of cherry soda, Nella sighed. "It's almost too cold for soda. I should have brought coffee, but I couldn't think how to carry it."

"We need a thermos," April said. She wondered how much one would cost and if it would be worth it for warm coffee at lunch.

Nella nodded. "We could fill it from the pot in the dining room. If Mrs Garcia agrees."

They munched their hot dogs in companionable silence while considering the ways and means of transporting coffee for lunch. Would it be stretching their landlady's rules about tenants being required to provide their own lunch? Mrs Garcia frowned on egg sandwiches and other attempts by tenants to create lunch from the breakfast table.

"I didn't see you this morning." April reached the end of her hot dog but still had some bun left. It was something that happened every time and she was never sure why.

When April and Nella first moved to the boarding house, they'd shared a room to save money. April found it a lot like living at home with her sisters, except Nella was even messier. With both now having jobs, they had secured separate rooms on the same floor. April enjoyed the privacy of having a neat little room of her own. These days, April usually met Nella at the breakfast table. Then they rode together on the trolley to their jobs. But if Nella overslept, April never waited for her. On those mornings, Nella would barrel out the door, still doing her hair and makeup as she ran to catch the streetcar. April hated to start her morning in such a rush.

"Oh, I missed breakfast entirely!" said Nella, taking a big bite out of her hot dog. "And barely made it to the office before Mrs Lanigan." The widowed Mrs Lanigan was the terror of Nella's office, in charge of all the typists and a strict watcher of the clock. "In fact, she was late, too. Almost five minutes. Which is extraordinary. I not only had time to hang up my hat but also roll a piece of paper in my typewriter before she loomed over my desk."

April giggled. Nella could paint vivid pictures of life in the office with only a few words. April wished she could do the same, but she tended to think of what to say hours or even days after the moment had passed.

"How was your morning?" Nella refilled both their cups from the soda bottle.

"Same as always. Mostly lost dogs." Two more ads had been called in by frantic owners of a dachshund and a beagle. "And a man who wanted to sell his twin beds for giving him nightmares."

"I'd sell my bed if it would stop the nightmares," said Nella. "I kept dreaming that I was drowning. Water rising all around me and something with eyes swimming around me. Hideous huge eyes, watching me squirm."

"Ugh." The bulging eyes of dead fish always disturbed April as a child, perhaps because she had been short enough to be face to face with the fish in the boxes while her mother shopped in the fish market. She felt there was something alien and grotesque about a fish's eye.

"Should I sell my bed? Would that make me sleep better?" Nella mused as she finished off her hot dog.

April shook her head. "Your bed belongs to the boarding house. You can't sell it." She wished avoiding nightmares was as simple as switching beds. But in her experience, strange dreams happened wherever somebody slept. Even when she shared a bedroom at home with her two sisters, April frequently experienced odd dreams. But as her mother often said, the only sensible thing to do was to forget her dreams in the morning.

A squirrel ran out from under a bush and across the lawn to them. April threw her remaining hot dog bun to the furry beggar. The squirrel stood on his hind legs to nibble the bread in a way that made April smile.

"Oh, don't encourage it!" Nella brushed the crumbs off her skirt. "We'll have the pigeons descending on us next."

April gathered up the paper cups and the hot dog wrappers, shaking out her own skirt as she trotted to a trash can.

"Do you want to go dancing on Saturday?" Nella asked.

"Maybe," April waffled. "We went last Saturday. I was thinking of doing something else." What, she had no idea. She liked dancing but going out every Saturday was expensive.

"There's a new Lon Chaney playing at the Palace starting Friday," said Nella. She adored horror movies and never missed a Lon Chaney picture.

"I hate monsters," said April, who always went to these movies with Nella and then spent half her time cowering with her hand over her eyes. Still, going to the movies was less expensive than Nella's original plan.

"He plays a policeman and a vampire in this one!" Nella said, ignoring April's protest. "You know I love mysteries. And it's set in London! You want to see what London looks like."

Someday soon, they planned to cash out their savings and take a trip to Europe. Ever since April read Kate Douglas Wiggins' books about Penelope's adventures in England and Scotland, she had wanted to take such a trip. Nella had fallen right in with her plans, buying her travel guides and maps every birthday and Christmas. They'd made endless lists together about places that they could go. London, of course, and Paris, because everyone was going to Paris. So far, they'd only gotten as far as Arkham, only a day away from their hometown by train, but that was something. They were out on their own, living as career women in a boarding house, and not staying home waiting for some man to marry them.

Aware that she wouldn't have had the courage to board the train to Arkham without Nella nudging her, April said, "I suppose we could go see the Lon Chaney picture on Saturday. But then I want to pick the next one. Chaney gives me nightmares!"

"We haven't been to a scary picture in ages. So I suppose you didn't have any nightmares last night," said Nella as they left the park.

"You're wrong." April paused, thinking hard about how to describe her strange dream last night. As much as her mother advised her to forget her dreams, April always recalled them with strangely vivid clarity. "I saw the man again."

"The angry one?" said Nella.

April nodded. "I keep thinking I know him. He's shouting at me. I'm supposed to be doing something. I know it's important. But I just don't understand him."

"Sounds like a dream about your office," said Nella.

April thought about this for a moment but disagreed with Nella's suggestion. The man shouting in her dreams definitely wasn't Simon or anyone she knew. "No, it's not the newspaper. It's a place like nothing that I've ever seen before. The buildings are twisted, huge, and terrible." Yet at the same time the drowning city in her dreams felt like Arkham, the streets nearest her home and her office, in the muddled way of dreams.

"How can a building be terrible?" Nella asked.

"I don't know," April admitted. For as long as she could remember, dreams haunted her nights. Sometimes she stood on a stony mountain, high above a desolate country. Other times she walked through cities in ruins. Once she met a talking cat, and it was exceedingly polite. Dreams often inspired her art during the day. Nella loved the watercolor of the talking cat that April gave her for a birthday present. But the nightmares of the last few days were different.

"But whenever I start to dream about the tower, I am terrified. There's something hideous hiding there. I know it." The tower had appeared every night for the last three nights. Sometimes April glimpsed shapes converging on the steps of the tower. Beautiful women like the *aswang* of her mother's stories, with long tongues stretching out of their mouths to suck away a person's blood.

The only thing which made these recent nightmares bearable was every dream ended as soon as the man arrived. Tall, dark-haired, and oddly dressed in robes of burnished gold. April tried to describe him to Nella but couldn't find the right words. So she drew a picture and Nella pronounced him "a real heartthrob."

Sometimes he appeared masked in her dreams, but she still knew it was the same man. He would shout and she would wake up, trying desperately to recall his words. But all she could remember was the strangeness of the place and an overwhelming feeling of dread, as if something had followed her from the nightmare to her home.

"Look at the time!" Nella twisted her wrist around to show off a new watch but also that lunch was over. "I have to run or Mrs Lanigan will catch me away from my desk!"

April waved goodbye to her friend and headed back to her office, grateful that nobody at the *Arkham Advertiser* was so strict a clock watcher.

Once settled behind the counter, April sorted through the afternoon mail deliveries as well as some orders dropped off by the other salespeople. The phone rang.

"*Arkham Advertiser*, how can I help you?" April asked.

"I'd like to place an advertisement," said a woman with a crisp, clear voice.

April hoped that it wasn't another lost dog. "Yes, ma'am, will this be a display ad or classified?"

"Whatever you think best," was the response. "But I want it to be noticed."

"Display advertisements are the most visible," April said, perking up a little. Selling a large display ad would make up for having to credit the hardware store earlier in the morning. "Is this for a business?"

"In a way." The woman paused. Then she resumed. "I need you to make up an advertisement for a scientific study. I'm looking for volunteers with the right symptoms. I will provide free treatment. As long as they are suffering from nightmares."

CHAPTER TWO

After the saleswoman from the *Arkham Advertiser* ended the call, Carolyn slid off her glasses and pinched the bridge of her nose. She hoped the advertisement would work. It was unconventional to try to find patients this way. Carolyn was certain one or more of her colleagues would even judge it ghoulish. Others would dismiss it as "what can you expect from a woman?"

Very few people wanted to discuss their nightmares with a doctor, even if the doctor was a psychologist. Or maybe especially because the doctor was a psychologist. She knew her very profession made her suspect in many people's minds. Not only a woman but also "not a real doctor" according to most. Added to this were the very unflattering portraits of the profession in almost every form of popular media. The movies and the pulps nearly always showed her profession as the villains of the story. Even the Philo Vance mysteries didn't do much to dispel the image of psychology as a rather strange profession occupied by odd individuals.

Also, the stigma surrounding depression and other forms of mental illnesses survived, despite the best efforts of her profession. The most enlightened medical doctors often had a hard time acknowledging the mind could create such trauma that it could impact the body's health. Thankfully Dr Roger Mortimore at St Mary's was not only willing but actually eager to refer patients to her.

Twelve new patients since Monday morning, all suffering from nightmares, and the most peculiar nightmares at that.

Peculiar and fascinating. She drew her journal toward her and looked at the notes already written down. Carolyn had long believed the key to healing the mind might lie in the dreams of her patients. However, dreams were highly individual. If she could classify their nightmares, those most traumatic expressions of the dreamer, in a far more detailed way than Freud and Jung, then she might find a cure for their sleep deprivation. She could revolutionize the treatment of the mind and the body, for Carolyn believed the health of one directly impacted the health of the other.

To find twelve people suffering from such similar nightmares was truly a gift.

A twinge of guilt immediately accompanied her excitement. She had become a psychologist to heal people, not to write papers to promote her place in the history of her profession. But the possibilities of these twelve cases with their peculiar similarities was extraordinary.

"I wonder if Jung or Freud ever suffer from such doubts," Carolyn mused out loud. Then she dismissed the thought immediately. They, and many other psychologists and psychiatrists, would not hesitate to document their analysis of such dreams and their conclusions. Often, she wished the members of her profession would write less. So much had been published after the war that she always felt behind on her reading.

Still, it didn't stop her from desiring to add her theories to the mix.

But she needed to know how widespread these recurring

nightmares were. Carolyn suspected her current patients were only the tip of the iceberg. The newspaper ad might be an unusual approach but one which could yield results. If her research led to others being treated in a more humane manner than many current "cures" for mental illness, then she should not hesitate at all.

If only she could summon up more energy. After the last patient, Carolyn was relieved to see her calendar was free of any more appointments. If there was a response to the advertisement, she needed to spread out the sessions more. Performing hypnosis on twelve patients in less than forty-eight hours turned into the exhausting equivalent of a marathon and probably, no, certainly, was not the best practice. A mild but persistent headache made her rub her temples.

Her own failure to sleep, or rather to fall into a deep sleep full of dreams troubled her greatly. And she hadn't sought any help or even admitted the problem to Roger, not after he had sent so many patients to her. "Physician, heal thyself," Carolyn muttered.

"Dr Fern, did you want me?" Barbara Darro stood in the doorway of her office.

"Just talking to myself," said Carolyn. Not everyone called a psychologist "Doctor", but Carolyn had a PhD hanging on her wall and was used to the application from her work at the Arkham Sanatorium. She appreciated Barbara's recognition of her academic and professional achievements.

"Occupational hazard. Thinking out loud," she said to her secretary.

After some very trying cases, Carolyn planned to spend more time traveling and writing this past year. But the work to be found in Arkham intrigued her. When the opportunity came to sublet the office, Carolyn couldn't resist. Barbara came with the office for a very modest salary. The luxury of having a secretary to type up notes, manage billing, and even arrange to have Carolyn's name stenciled on the outer office's door – it was a dream come true.

She felt enormously lucky to have encountered Barbara and her boss on the boat back from London. Augusta Palmer, the psychologist who formerly occupied these offices, had received an exciting offer from a West Coast college to teach. To meet another woman who sought to heal minds was rare. One who taught and was in the position to encourage others to follow in their footsteps was rarer still. Even if she had not enjoyed Augusta's companionship during the voyage, and their long discussions on how to best heal or, at the very least, offer solace to those afflicted, she would have been hard pressed to find any reason not to temporarily take over her practice.

The position was ideal, Carolyn told herself. A ready-made private practice already established in a city which held so many possibilities. She might even find such work preferable to being attached as staff to an asylum or hospital. But if she disliked private practice, the temporary nature of the arrangement would allow her to leave gracefully and resume her work at the Arkham Sanatorium. Or perhaps to return to travel and writing.

But Carolyn hoped to work more with Augusta, a woman she liked, when the psychologist returned to Arkham.

Augusta was one of the rare practitioners who acknowledged that not all forms of mental degradation could be healed. Nor could "mental illness" be completely free of subjective standards set by the doctor.

"For too many," Augusta said one night on the boat, "being mentally healthy means being exactly like the treating physician. Which means anyone who deviates from the physician's definition of normal is automatically diagnosed as suffering from lunacy."

"Careful," Carolyn joked. "If you include those sentiments in your lectures, you may be labeled as a champion of Anti-psychiatrie, rather than a teacher of psychology."

"I am not sure those Germans are wrong. Are we to ignore the testimonies of Beers, Grant-Smith, and others?" With a clarity that surprised her in reflection, Carolyn recalled how angry Augusta had sounded as she named some prominent patients who had testified on abuses encountered in asylum care.

"No, of course not," Carolyn had countered. "I prefer psychology over psychiatry because I do not believe drugs and surgery are the answer." Indeed, the abuses Carolyn had observed at the asylums where she had worked deeply disturbed her. Following some unsettling incidents, she decided to abandon the use of drugs, even the mildest forms, in her treatments. While she wasn't a member of the Nature Cure movement, she did find their descriptions of conventional treatments as "combative medicine" far too close to home. Many times at the asylums, it seemed as if the doctors waged a war on madness rather than sought to help their patients.

"You believe in hypnosis, don't you? That's your method." Augusta smiled at her in a way that still warmed her to remember now. "A manipulation of the unconscious."

"I have been able to help others through hypnosis, but only with their complete consent," Carolyn confirmed. "I think hypnosis offers extraordinary potential to heal."

"So you don't sedate your patients into accepting your hypnotic suggestions?" Augusta asked.

Carolyn winced. She had used such a method. However, the sedative concoction proved less than ideal and even yielded some disturbing results. She now kept the syringe and vial of sedative for very different reasons.

"I think you are right, Carolyn," said Augusta. "Hypnosis

may prove to be far more powerful than you suspect. With the right technique, we should be able to change dreams and their dreamers."

When Augusta's teaching assignment came to an end, she hinted at combining their resources and expanding the practice. Carolyn believed a partner so closely aligned to her sympathies and interests would be ideal.

In the meantime, Carolyn had an extraordinarily efficient Barbara to keep the office organized.

"Are you ready to review the files?" Barbara asked.

"Yes, thank you!" Carolyn put her glasses back on. She held out a hand for the files that Barbara proved so adept at keeping. Her typing was exceptional. Carolyn knew there would be no mistakes in the folders. The only mystery was why Barbara remained attached to this small practice and didn't seek employment elsewhere.

However, judging by the streaks of silver running through Barbara's brown hair, perhaps she found it difficult to find another job. From the few comments Barbara made, Carolyn gained the impression the woman was somewhere near sixty. It was strange to think the militant suffragettes of the last generation were now old enough to be grandmothers.

"I have finished the case notes." Barbara handed the stack of folders, all organized according to the patient's last name, to Carolyn.

"You are a marvel." Carolyn believed in speaking truth and being complimentary whenever possible. Why shouldn't good work be rewarded with courtesy? She set the stack on her desk for further review.

"Is there anything else?" Barbara wore her outside coat, a clear signal that she was intending to leave. "My sister needs my help."

Carolyn shook her head. "Nothing more. I'll write up my notes for the hospital." Unfortunately, her theories amounted to very little yet. But Roger thought the nightmares didn't exactly qualify as illness, at least not that he could treat. If she could give Roger a clearer answer as to why so many people were suffering from nightmare-induced insomnia, it might lead to a breakthrough. Numerous cases had been reported from a variety of medical practices around Arkham in the last few days. All said their patients were literally too scared to go to bed.

Which reminded Carolyn that she meant to ask Barbara to call Arkham Sanatorium and ask if they'd seen anything similar in their patients.

"Are you leaving soon?" Barbara asked.

"I'll stay a little longer to finish these and then go to St Mary's," Carolyn replied.

Barbara fetched her purse from a hook by the door. As always, she seemed to lack any curiosity about Carolyn or her patients. Which, Carolyn reminded herself, was an attitude to be admired. A secretary who gossiped about patients would be disastrous for the practice and the practitioner.

Barbara pulled her tan leather gloves from her purse. The woman dressed always in shades of dark green and brown, eminently practical. At one point, Barbara said that she disliked shopping and preferred to buy several skirts or shirts in the same style to avoid unnecessary trips to the store. That and a complete lack of personal items in the office rather summed up Barbara's personality. As bland and efficient as the typewriter gleaming on her desk.

Such an oversimplification of another's personality made Carolyn shift uneasily in her chair. She wasn't usually so quick to judge or so judgmental. Thinking back to Barbara's recent statement, she realized this was the very first time that she'd heard the woman had a sister.

"I hope your sister is well," Carolyn said, getting up from her desk and following Barbara into the outer office.

"My sister will be fine. I need to find a dog for her. I will see you tomorrow morning." Barbara opened the outer door and stepped into the corridor. "I set the latch. All you need to do is pull the door tight to lock the office when you leave."

"Of course." Carolyn started to ask what type of dog, but Barbara was already down the corridor and heading into the stairwell. Shaking her head, Carolyn returned to her desk. Apparently, Barbara had a sister and the sister wanted a dog. So now she knew something about her secretary.

With a muffled sigh of exasperation, she realized she had forgotten to ask Barbara to call the Arkham Sanatorium. Her own lack of sleep was catching up with her. However, Barbara could make the call tomorrow, Carolyn decided. A better use of her own time would be to review the case notes.

Carolyn studied the dozen folders neatly stacked on her desk. All the patients sent to her from St Mary's by Roger. Twelve people who she knew far more intimately than Barbara for all she had met them only once in this office. Their fears, their night terrors, and their pain, all neatly recorded and bundled away in a manila folder. Ridiculous to think that a person could be reduced to words on paper, but that's what she had to do. Record precisely what they told her and hope to find an answer to their problems in their own words.

Something was infecting Arkham's residents. Not a virus, although she knew one or two doctors at St Mary's had theories about underlying physical causes of these dreams. But no virus could lead twelve people, all from different households, to dream the same nightmare in the last forty-eight hours. Yet here it was.

The dream began in some type of woods, often described as a jungle or a forest, then the dreamer saw a tower or a tall structure (one man called it a steeple), and a masked man. The same basic elements reoccurred in each dream, but the actual terrors encountered during the nightmare varied widely – that, Carolyn decided, was the individual trying to remake the dreamscape into something that their mind understood, much as witnesses to an accident might all perceive different elements of the event. So she believed the accounts of slithering serpents, creepy dolls, aggressive arachnids, and other common terrors could be easily traced to the patient's own phobias.

One and all, these patients needed a way to remake their dreamworld into a more welcoming place where the fears of the daylight hours could be contained or even cured.

During these sessions, Carolyn reluctantly turned to the work of Hereward Carrington. She met him in Copenhagen once. While she found him rather strange, she couldn't deny his theories about dream control felt uncommonly appropriate to her current cases. She'd urged her patients to try his methods of keeping conscious control until falling asleep to better remember their nightmares and control them.

Carolyn modified his ideas to give permission for the patients to call upon the masked men to end their dreams.

Two of her Monday patients contacted her this morning. Both confirmed the details they recalled did improve. One felt that he was able to summon the masked man to dismiss the snakes and allow him to escape his dream. The other patient, a woman, also recalled an abrupt end to her nightmare about fires surrounding her. She too credited the masked man for it. A result which pleased Carolyn enough that she considered corresponding with Carrington about it if the rest of her patients reported similar results.

She was impatient to see these two patients again and hoped to hear from the other ten before the end of the week. The latent content and symbolism of the dreams recorded in her files were extraordinary. Carolyn could admit her fascination with these dreams to herself. Each one so weirdly strange and yet specific in their detail as if the dreamers had visited another world and encountered beings there who remained remarkably consistent in their descriptions.

Also, there was another thread running through these dreams, a similarity to the stories told by another private patient of hers. Although Josephine Ruggles had left Arkham for Paris recently, Carolyn could never forget all she had learned about dreams from her. This knowledge was carefully chronicled in her own private journals that she had no intention of publishing. Not unless she wanted to be laughed out of her profession.

Carolyn pulled down various monographs and journals on Augusta Palmer's well-stocked shelves. The other doctor had exactly the type of books that Carolyn would want in an office. Thumbing quickly through the literature, she searched for comparable cases or a possible cause for a group of dreamers to manifest their fears and insecurities in a similar manner to her twelve patients. She sought confirmation of her theory that a natural occurrence created the same psychological reaction in several patients. Never mind the fact that the first treatment she had tried came from the writings of Carrington, a man obsessed with psychical development and what he called "supernormal phenomena."

Through her window, Carolyn heard the clamor of ambulance bells. St Mary's was just around the corner from her office, which made the location perfect for her current needs.

Another ambulance followed the first, bells clanging, and charged up the street to St Mary's. Two so close together! Carolyn repressed a shudder. The days of the influenza pandemic were long over. These dream-haunted patients were certainly not a harbinger of another epidemic. Perhaps two women had gone into labor at the same time and needed to rush to the hospital for a happy event.

Just as she often advised, Carolyn held to her imagined scenario rather than create a conjecture about possible disasters leading to ambulances racing across the city. New lives arriving, and not more sleepers sickened by their nightmares, Carolyn told herself firmly as she shuffled her files again and sought answers in the neatly typed notes.

The phone rang in the outer office. With a stifled exclamation, Carolyn remembered Barbara was gone and went to answer it.

"Roger," she said as the voice on the other end identified himself. "How can I help you?"

The request was sharp and almost angry from the doctor. Obviously he also had suffered from a long day of demands on his time.

"I already planned to stop at the hospital on my way home," Carolyn promised. More people arriving with complaints about nightmares and worse than before? What could it mean?

As she hung up the phone, the feeling of unease engendered by the ambulance bells increased. Suddenly the office seemed less like a haven for her work and more like a trap, holding her prisoner to a monstrous wrong.

Quick to dismiss this odd fancy, Carolyn gathered her things and resolved to use some conscious suggestions on herself. She needed more sleep. Sleep without worries.

CHAPTER THREE

The advertisement for nightmare sufferers requested by Carolyn Fern wasn't quite as large as April hoped. However, the psychologist was a new customer. She noted this information on the order. At the end of the month, the advertising salespeople earned extra for new clients. With luck, this would offset the whole debacle with the hardware ad. If she did receive a bonus, April vowed it would go immediately into her savings for the European trip.

"How's it going?" Minnie Klein leaned over the counter.

Happy to be interrupted from her mental calculations on how much she needed to sail to Europe with Nella, April smiled up at the photographer. Minnie was one of the newspaper's friendlier staff.

"Any good stories in the classifieds?" Minnie asked. While the other reporters tended to rib Minnie about her obsession with the classifieds, she claimed that she once captured photos of a bootlegging operation based on a few obscure ads about buying farm equipment. Another time, the photographer told April, she prevented a medical student from selling a set of skulls.

"He claimed they were just plaster models," said Minnie. "But they were the real deal. Taken from storage at the university. He tried to sell the lot at Halloween as decorations."

April shuddered when she heard the tale. "Why would the university have skulls?"

"Very good question! I asked the provost the same thing." Minnie winked. "Never had a phone slammed down so quickly! So I went to campus the next day. By then they'd decided the wretched skulls were left over from an anatomy class. But I'm not sure that's the full story. Every single one had a hole drilled right through the top. I tried to talk Doyle and Rex into investigating it, but Doyle just ran my picture with a short squib under it about real life Halloween horrors. Here today and fish wrap tomorrow, that's the story of my newspaper career."

April told Minnie about the twin bed man, but she shook her head.

"Nightmares are no good." Minnie tapped the camera slung around her neck. "You can't take a photo of a dream."

April almost mentioned Carolyn Fern's request, but that was just dreams, too. So she told Minnie about the lost dogs.

Minnie pursed her lips. "Maybe. If I could find one and reunite it with its owner. People love puppy pictures. Give me the descriptions."

So April wrote out the information including the neighborhoods where the dogs were last seen.

"I'll keep an eye peeled." Minnie gave a jaunty wave as she set off toward the bullpen where the reporters gathered. Doyle popped out of his office, yelling for the evening mockup.

"Deadlines!" shouted the editor. "We have deadlines! Every single day! Where's my copy?"

As the bullpen slid into the usual afternoon chaos, April went back to answering phone calls. A lady dropped by the office to place an advertisement for a new dress shop. When April showed her Cyril's drawings of shoes and hats for other merchants, the customer asked about having the same done for her dresses. April even sketched out a few ideas on her own notepad.

"It sounds expensive," Mrs Hanover fretted. "Just outfitting the shop has cost me more than I budgeted."

"We can work out a payment plan," April promised.

"Well, I don't know. But I will think about it." Mrs Hanover nodded to her. "You have been very helpful. I do appreciate it. People can be so pushy whenever you want to talk about business. I called somebody else about advertising. He kept going on and on about how much I should spend. But he didn't actually listen to me, if you know what I mean."

Simon, thought April, always talked over people. To Mrs Hanover, she said, "I would love to see your dresses. Cyril and I could come to the shop. Then we could draw up some ads for your approval."

Mrs Hanover smiled. "What a sensible plan. After we are open. I don't think I can make one more decision until then. Really, all I want to do now is go home and sleep soundly for one night. This opening has been giving me nightmares all week long! I keep dreaming the shop has flooded and the mannequins all turn into mermaids who swim away with my dresses."

"We would be happy to visit you later." She wrote down the address of the shop and promised to follow up when it was convenient for Mrs Hanover. April almost told the tired shop owner about Carolyn Fern's advertisement, but she wasn't sure if mermaids absconding with dresses counted as a nightmare.

"Well done!" April spun around at the comment to find Columbia watching her. Columbia Goadby had joined the newspaper recently although April couldn't exactly remember when. By now, it seemed like Columbia had always been at her desk, just behind where April stood at the counter.

Doyle Jeffries called Columbia's position the "office manager" which seemed to cover a number of jobs. All of which Columbia handled with stunning efficiency. Suddenly ad orders were invoiced promptly, files were filed into the correct cabinets, and office supplies were actually to be found in the supply closet. In an office where everyone's desk was buried under stacks of newspapers, either their own *Advertiser* or local rivals, Columbia's desk stood like a polished island of orderliness with nothing on it but her typewriter and two wire baskets for inbound and outbound mail. By the end of each day, the wire baskets would be empty and ready to be filled again the next day.

Columbia made April a little nervous. Whenever she looked around from her place at the counter, Columbia seemed to be watching her. Old enough to be her grandmother, Columbia reminded her of the more disapproving matriarchs in her old neighborhood. The rich ones, because Columbia was always flawlessly turned out in outfits of green and brown. Her brown hair had one perfect stripe of white running through it, which made her seem even more imposing.

Once or twice Columbia made comments that made it clear she listened to April's conversations. While overhearing things was hard to avoid in a big office like theirs, April never met somebody who so openly admitted to eavesdropping.

"You handled Mrs Hanover in exactly the correct manner," Columbia said.

April ducked her head, unsure of what to say. Compliments always confused her. She couldn't agree without sounding boastful. But ignoring it sounded rude too.

Also, it worried her that Columbia had listened that closely to her conversation.

Columbia smiled, a faint but definite smile. She was not a woman given to large gestures or much warmth. "Take credit when you do something well. I'm afraid women like us must stand up for ourselves. It's the only way you can advance."

"Well," April started to tell Columbia about how little she wanted to advance in advertising when the phone rang.

Picking it up, April heard an agitated Nella on the other end of the line. "April, are you there?"

Columbia nodded goodbye to April and moved toward her desk. April hissed into the phone, "Nella, I can't talk. It's busy here." A glance over her shoulder showed Columbia seemed preoccupied with files but the woman was still too close to carry on a conversation.

"Oh, April, I don't know what to do." Nella sounded as if she was trying to whisper and cry at the same time. "Mrs Lanigan collapsed right over my desk! They called an ambulance. And the police!"

"I'm coming." April didn't hesitate. She never refused a cry for help from Nella and she never would. Nella's distress was clear on the phone. If her best friend needed her, April would be there. She dropped the receiver back in its cradle and hurried to Columbia's desk.

"I need to leave," April told the older woman. "All the orders are done and in my basket waiting for pick up."

"Very well," said Columbia, rolling a blank piece of paper into her typewriter.

Surprised that the office manager was so agreeable about her leaving, April promised to come in as early as possible in the morning.

Glancing at the clock, Columbia said, "It doesn't matter. It is past three. Nothing new could go in the evening's newspaper. You can write up any orders for tomorrow's newspaper when you arrive. I'll listen for the phone." Then she began typing, clearly intent on finishing her own work in a timely manner.

"Perhaps you can have an early night. You look tired. Go to bed as soon as you can."

"Thank you!" April grabbed her coat and hat from the wall hook, slung her purse over her shoulder, and ran out the door. She forgot Columbia's peculiar instructions to go to sleep as soon as she left the building.

At Nella's office, April found a confused group of people milling around the desks in the outer room. Even one or two of the managers had left their offices to stand with the typists and salesmen. Nella was on the bench usually reserved for waiting customers, crying into her handkerchief while another older woman patted her shoulder. A police officer stood in a corner, quietly chatting with a gentleman who April thought was the head of this particular office.

"Nella, what happened?" April walked up to her friend.

"Oh, it was awful." Nella swallowed back her tears. She clutched April's hands tightly in her own. "Mrs Lanigan collapsed right across my typewriter as she was pointing out a missing comma. She fell on me!" Nella's voice rose to a near shriek. Several people in the office winced.

"Poor thing." The other woman straightened up, subtly shifting Nella toward April. "It wasn't your fault, Nella. Mrs Lanigan has been complaining for days that she couldn't sleep. It was exhaustion, plain and simple, which caused her to faint. I heard the ambulance people say so."

April sat down on the bench, shifting to hold Nella with one arm. Most of the time, her friend was strong. People expected that of Nella. As a girl, she'd always been the tallest in their class. Also the girl with the biggest laugh and the loudest voice. But sometimes, like now, Nella would collapse when faced with an unexpected upset. Nella would feel awful about making such a fuss when she calmed down. But right now, she would need April to be the sensible one and keep her from falling apart in public.

"But why the police?" April asked the other woman as she patted Nella on the arm.

"Eusapia Whately, most people call me Pia." Pia reached across Nella to shake April's hand. "The police are here because Tom panicked when Nella started screaming. He called everyone, including the senior partner at lunch." Nodding at the well-dressed gentleman talking to the policeman, Pia continued. "That's why Mr Humphries is back from his club and talking to the police."

"April, I want to go home. I don't feel very well." Nella did look a little green, although April guessed Nella was more embarrassed about screaming in the office than nauseated.

"That's an excellent idea," said Pia, gathering up Nella's coat and bag from the hook where they hung. She thrust them at Nella. "You go home and don't worry. I'm sure they'll close the office early. Mr Humphries said so."

With a few more pats and even a discreet shove, Pia herded them out of the office. Nella must have made a scene, April thought as they exited the building. Unlike herself, Nella could shout. April always rather envied her ability. April could never yell without stopping and apologizing, even when her youngest sister borrowed her favorite dress for a school dance and brought it home with a torn hem.

They walked to the corner to wait for the streetcar. Nella kept fidgeting with her bag, opening it and clasping it closed with a click. "I was a bit hysterical," she admitted. "But Mrs Lanigan fell on me. It was awful."

"I would have screamed too." April pointed down the street when she heard a trolley bell ringing. "Look, there's the number three coming." The number three stopped less than a block away from their boarding house in the Rivertown neighborhood. "We'll be home soon."

After boarding the trolley, they slid to the back, so Nella could continue telling her story to April without the other passengers in the front overhearing them.

"Mrs Lanigan had been complaining about not sleeping, although she didn't say why," Nella said. "I told her about my nightmares. She wasn't sympathetic. She said dreams were no excuse for being late to work."

"Perhaps she wasn't feeling well." April herself had very little patience with other people's complaints when she was sick.

Nella sighed. "As if five minutes matters. I'm the fastest typist in the office, and Mrs Lanigan knows it. I do more when I'm there than anyone else. So why should anyone care if I arrive a few minutes late? I get my work done. I was so tired and Mrs Lanigan made me so mad. Then she fainted and I did nothing. I'm not a very nice person."

April hugged her friend. "You are a nice person! You always listen to my complaints. And you never laugh at my pulps." April's addiction to pulp magazines was well known at her boarding house. Occasionally the others would tease her about her horrible choices in literature.

"Why shouldn't you read what you like?" Nella's indignation flared up and then died. "No, I was terrible when Mrs Lanigan fell over. I just flew out of my chair screaming. Did you know she has a glass eye?"

April shook her head.

"She does. All the office knows about it. It's no secret. Her glass eye popped out when her face hit my typewriter. Then it rolled across the desk toward me. It was just like my nightmares. This thing staring up at me!"

Nella started to cry again. April fished a handkerchief out of her purse and pressed it into Nella's hand. Nella blew her nose and wiped the tears off her face. Then she tucked the handkerchief in her own pocket. "I'll wash it and iron it for you," she promised April.

"Don't worry about it." April hugged her friend. "Let's go home. Maybe Mrs Garcia will make us a cup of tea."

When they reached the boarding house, they circled around the back to use the kitchen door. Boarders were supposed to go in and out through the front, but everyone knew the easiest way to find Mrs Garcia was to start in the kitchen.

Their landlady was sitting at the kitchen table, drinking her coffee and reading the Spanish newspaper.

"You are home early," she said. Looking more closely at Nella's reddened eyes and nose, Mrs Garcia added, "Are you sick?"

Nella shook her head while April explained what had happened.

"People are getting sick all up and down the street," said Mrs Garcia. "The other ladies say so." There were five boarding houses on Flotsam Street, all big houses now filled with "paying guests" rather than large families. April knew most of Arkham considered the Rivertown neighborhood one of the worst in the city, but their little street, tucked up near French Hill, still clung to the remnants of respectability. At one time, these houses had been as fancy as those on French Hill.

All five boarding houses were run by widows, women who had lost their husbands in earlier wars or during the influenza pandemic. They ranged in age from "old enough to be your mother" to "old enough to be your grandmother." Mrs Garcia fell into the latter group. The "ladies," as the entire street called them, met regularly in each other's kitchens and knew everything happening on Flotsam Street. After determining that Nella wasn't running a fever by the tried-and-true method of slapping a hand on her forehead, Mrs Garcia pronounced, "What you need is a nap."

As Mrs Garcia believed all the world's ills could be solved by a nap, April wasn't surprised by this advice. She was startled to hear Nella agree.

"I'll go lie down now," Nella said, heading toward the stairs. "Maybe I can catch up on my sleep."

Mrs Garcia settled back in her chair and rattled her newspaper. April took the hint. Mrs Garcia cooked for all her boarders as well as supervising the two women who came daily to do the heavier chores. She deserved her time alone with her coffee cup.

April, however, didn't need or want a nap. She wouldn't have minded a chat with Nella, but her friend had looked exhausted. After a moment's consideration, April went out again and knocked on the basement door set next to the kitchen door in the back courtyard. The garbageman who lived in the basement set out to work every morning before dawn. She thought it was now late enough in the day for Lefty Googe to be home. If he was, she could at least grab some new reading material, which would be a nice distraction from the disasters of the day, although the fluster around the hardware store advertisement seemed very long ago.

"Coming!" Lefty's shout sounded through the door, as did his heavy footsteps on the basement's wooden stairs. When he popped open the door, April saw he had changed out of his garbageman coveralls. Instead, he wore a heavy flannel shirt and overalls.

April read in the newspaper that Babe Ruth resembled "toothpicks attached to a piano." Herman "Lefty" Googe once played ball professionally and even earned some press as "the Ozark's answer to Babe Ruth." He certainly looked like the Bambino with perhaps even broader shoulders and a more rounded belly. And possibly less hair on the top of his head. A halo of salt-and-pepper curls, closely clipped, circled his head, running from ear to ear.

"April, this is a pleasant surprise," rumbled Lefty, "did you come for *Radio Beasts*?" Lefty obviously had started his evening reading as his reading glasses were propped on top of his bald head.

Like April, Lefty loved the pulps. Many people on his route knew it. They kept their magazines separate from the other garbage so Lefty picked up stacks of *Argosy All-Story Weekly* and other pulp magazines. He enjoyed sharing his finds with a kindred fan of weird fiction. Recently, Lefty talked enthusiastically about *Radio Beasts*, the exciting sequel to *The Radio Man* by Ralph Milne Farley. He had been given nearly a year's worth of *All-Story* and passed the slightly battered but still readable copies to April as soon as he finished an installment. April liked *The Radio Man* stories even better than Virgil Gray's stories in *Tales from Nevermore*. Although Gray was a local writer, and a favorite of Lefty's, April found Gray's stories often disturbing and too close to actual nightmares in their descriptions.

"Nella was sick so we came home early," April explained as she followed Lefty down the basement stairs, although it probably would have been more accurate to say Nella had been frightened out of her wits. All in all, it had been a very strange day.

Unlike the other boarders, Lefty lived in almost a complete apartment in the basement. At the bottom of the stairs was a small sitting room, lit by narrow windows along the ceiling. Covering one wall were the bookcases that Lefty scrounged on his garbage run. These overflowed with the books and magazines that he brought home. His bedroom and a small bathroom were tucked behind a dark velvet curtain, discarded long ago from a fire-ravaged theater. The rest of the apartment was equally furnished with Lefty's finds from his garbage runs.

Most of the furniture was hidden under the books and magazines that Lefty brought home and couldn't bear to throw away, even after he was done with a story.

Lefty once told April that he'd become addicted to reading in the boys' home where he grew up. One of the Catholic priests who ran the place stocked the school's small reading library with adventure stories, in hopes of encouraging the boys to read. Even after Lefty left the home to play baseball, he never lost the habit.

A big, deep chair with a standing lamp filled up the corner nearest the bookcases. A heavy oak table and a couple of wooden chairs took up the rest of the space. Lefty kept an electric kettle on the table and a hot ring for heating up pots of soup. He'd even found and repaired an electric toaster, although April couldn't imagine who would have thrown away such an expensive appliance. But Lefty claimed the rich of French Hill frequently discarded the most amazing items.

"Tea?" Lefty asked as he settled into one of the wooden chairs. A mismatched bunch of china teacups were stacked on the shelf almost directly above his head. "Just brewed a pot."

April nodded. Lefty swung around and grabbed a cup off the shelf. Tenants weren't supposed to cook in their rooms, but Mrs Garcia ignored what Lefty did in the basement. Lefty poured out a cup and shoved it toward April. The dark mahogany brew filled the mug. Lefty chuckled at the face that she made on the first sip of his bitter offering. He slid a sugar bowl toward her along with an intricately wrought silver spoon.

"Oh, that's pretty," April exclaimed, twisting the spoon to the light so she could make out the pattern of daffodils twined around the brightly polished handle.

"Found it a few days ago. Tarnished but not enough to warrant throwing it away," said Lefty. "Don't know what house that came from. But I thought I'd hold on to it for a bit." Like most garbagemen, Lefty made money selling things he retrieved from the trash to local antique and junk dealers. But if he thought something was thrown out by mistake, he made a habit of knocking on the back doors and checking with the owners. One woman broke down in tears, Lefty told April, when he handed back her wedding ring. She'd lost it in the garbage by mistake, just as Lefty had thought.

April ladled sugar into her tea and told Lefty about her day. He shook his head over her account of Mrs Lanigan's fainting and Nella's screaming reaction.

"Glass eyes aren't strange," he said. "I've found a few myself. There's a market for them."

"Ugh," said April.

"Odd about the dreams though. I've been hearing about nightmares all along my route." He chugged back his cup and refilled it from the pot.

"Have you had nightmares?" April asked, not willing to share anything more about her dreams. Lefty was a good twenty years older than her, closer in age to her Uncle Tito. Things she felt comfortable discussing with Nella, April would never mention to Lefty.

"Nope. I don't dream. At least, I don't remember dreaming." Lefty stretched out a hand to snag a pile of magazines. "Here's the issues that I promised."

He plopped the magazines in front of April. Her eyes lit up at the sight of the giant ants attacking the Radio Man on the cover of the top magazine in the stack.

"Oh, this does look good!" She scooped up the magazines and thanked Lefty for the tea.

"I'll keep an eye out for those lost dogs," he promised as April headed back up the stairs. "Mutts like nosing around the garbage bins."

Outside, April circled around the house to enter properly through the front door as Mrs Garcia preferred. A peek in the front parlor showed it was empty, so April grabbed the nearest chair to the window. She picked up the first magazine and was soon lost in the Radio Man's adventures on Venus. She completely forgot about lost dogs and nightmares.

Then Ollie Pinkser arrived home. The middle-aged Black woman plopped herself into the seat next to April. She was dressed in her nurse's uniform, the starched white cap pinned to her hair. The long-sleeved button down top with wing collar and belted skirt still looked crisp but Ollie was visibly wilting into her chair.

"What a day!" Ollie exclaimed. "So many people coming in and complaining about nightmares and being afraid to sleep! The doctors couldn't keep up with all the new patients. I've never seen anything like it."

CHAPTER FOUR

April preferred bathing in the evening. For one thing, she could read in the bath without people banging on the door and telling her to hurry up.

The chatter at dinner was all about nightmares. Everyone seemed to be suffering from lost sleep. Nella's story of Mrs Lanigan's faint lasted through the pork chops and mashed potatoes. Ollie's tales of the crowds at the hospital soured dessert, even though Mrs Garcia had baked a devil's food cake.

Nobody mentioned influenza but the specter hovered over them. Everyone in the room had experienced death in the last pandemic, either friends or family. It was a time that April tried very hard not to think about. As a child, she could remember the ghastly spectacle of adults hidden behind cloth masks. The whispers behind closed doors about how the illness was progressing through their town. Of being forbidden to play outside the house or visit the neighbors (a rule that she and Nella had broken more than once with considerable guilt on April's part).

A subdued group of tenants left the dinner table. Mrs Garcia vanished into the kitchen to supervise the washing up by Ada and her daughter Cleo, the pair who helped all the boarding house owners with their cleaning. The others trooped into the parlor to play the nightly battle of bridge. Nella was an avid player and generally partnered with Ollie if she was home. Mr and Mrs Sullivan, the residents of a two-room combination in the attic, always partnered with each other. The elderly couple played cutthroat bridge, so conversation was minimal as Nella and Ollie struggled to hold their own. Lefty, as usual, headed back to his apartment and his current magazine as soon as dinner was done.

Sally McMillan, who would play bridge if Ollie wasn't available, took over the easy chair nearest the brightest lamp. Sally crocheted every evening, a seemingly endless number of booties and baby hats to be sent to relatives and friends. She even made Christmas scarves for all the kindergarteners that she taught at the local school. Everyone up and down the street would drop off odd ends of yarn for Sally's projects, who then made each item out of a lovely collection of colors. Ollie often took Sally's creations to the child patients at St Mary's. Sally frequently knitted specific toys at Ollie's request, including a small puppy that was particularly popular.

With everyone occupied, it was a perfect time for April to slip away to the upstairs bathroom. She didn't want to hear about any more nightmares or sick people. Already convinced that she would have nightmares herself, April decided a long soak in the bath was the best remedy for a troubled night ahead.

April turned the taps on and dumped more bath salts than normal into the tub. The steam rose, filling the room with the scent of lilacs and blotting out April's worries. She arranged a stool next to the tub with her pile of pulps and a hand towel to keep her fingers dry. In all her years of reading in the tub, she'd never lost a book or magazine to the water.

April pinned her hair up to keep it out of the water. She'd wash her hair on Friday, or maybe she'd finally go to the hairdresser and get it bobbed on Saturday. Nella nagged constantly about April's long braid being old-fashioned. But if anyone else said anything about her hair, Nella switched sides and defended April's looks. That's what friends were for, Nella would say, keeping you on your toes and knocking down your enemies. It had certainly been their relationship since they first met in a kindergarten sandbox.

Comfortably settled into the clawfoot bathtub, April picked up the first magazine and turned to the latest installment of *The Radio Man*. She decided to ignore the big worries and the small decisions needing to be made. April willingly plunged into the world of *The Radio Man*, all giant insects and strange encounters on Venus. Eventually the hero overcame every obstacle encountered by using his scientific knowledge.

April set aside the last issue with a small feeling of satisfaction. Now that she knew what happened to the Radio Man, she'd go back through the magazines and read the other stories. But she'd nearly wrinkled into a prune. The cooling water propelled her out of the tub. She drained and cleaned the bathtub, and wiped the lilac-scented steam off the mirror before brushing her teeth. Sounds of the card game breaking up could be heard through the floor. April gathered up her bath bag and magazines, whisking across the hall into her own bedroom.

Nella called out a good night as she passed April's room. April could hear Nella and Ollie still chatting about the evening's game, and the possible ways of revenge against the triumphant Mr and Mrs Sullivan, as they proceeded to their respective rooms.

Snuggled down in bed, April read as long as possible, unwilling to turn out her light or try to go to sleep. All the talk of nightmares today rattled her. She usually didn't fear her dreams, but the nightmares of the last few nights felt even more real and disturbing. Still, when the casement clock downstairs finally bonged its midnight chimes, the magazine slid out of her fingers. Her eyes closed even as she thought about turning off the lamp.

A strange world engulfed her. She stood on a path of silvery sand. Enormous, twisted lichen, grown to the size of oak trees, rose along the side of the path. The lichen blocked her view at first. But as she moved down the path, she could see the glimmering white tower between the green-gray trunks. A clicking sound filled the air. With the awful logic of a dream, April recognized the sound of giant ants.

April began to run down the sandy path, which twisted and turned. Sticky pale webs hung from the branches of the lichen. With a terrible certainty, she knew if she left the path, she would become entangled in these webs and food for spiders. So she stayed on the path even though it was obvious she could not hide from the ants pursuing her.

A glance over her shoulder showed the ants driving a trolley down the path, which was now as wide as a road in Arkham. The ant behind the wheel used its two front legs to steer. Another hung out of the back door, where the conductor usually rode, clashing its mandibles. In one skinny leg, it held a green umbrella over its head to protect it from the spiders above.

April whirled around and ran for her life. Convinced capture by the ants would trap her in this dream world forever or worse, she sought to escape.

Always before her was the tower. Behind her was the terrible metallic racket caused by the pursuit of the giant ants in their monstrous machine. Why she needed to reach the tower, she didn't know. But she felt an overwhelming compulsion to stand on its steps.

Above her, something buzzed like a bee. April looked down,

afraid to look up and see what creature flew overhead. A glass eye lay on the path in front of her.

April scrambled to a stop. She reached for the glass eye, intent on pocketing it before Nella saw it. It rolled a little further away. April pursued it without even wondering why she was so intent on capturing the glass eye when Nella wasn't there. Dogs barked all around her as the cries from the giant ants rose to a scream.

April made another lunge for the glass eye. But she felt as if she was moving through molasses. The air was heavy, sticky, holding her back, almost holding her down, although she remained upright on the path. The sensation became more painful as she struggled to move her arms.

If the eyeball rolled away, April simply knew Nella would find it and be frightened all over again. So she crawled toward it, pushing against the heaviness in her arms and legs as she struggled to remain upright and moving forward. Her early terror of the ants was forgotten as she struggled to overtake the glass eyeball.

Suddenly the masked man blocked her path. Draped in golden robes, an ornate gold mask covered the upper half of his face. He shouted and waved his arms, ignoring the glass eye rolling between his feet. Almost peeved that her sometimes rescuer was nearly standing on the object of her pursuit, April toppled toward him.

She woke up with the lamp shining in her eyes. A glance at the clock showed it was past three in the morning. With a sigh, April collected the pulp magazines spread across her counterpane and stacked them on the bedside table. She felt overwhelmingly tired. After considering getting out of bed and going in search of a glass of water, April decided it was too much effort.

Clicking off the lamp, April slid as far down under the covers as she could go. Curled into a small ball in the center of her bed, she remembered bits and pieces of the nightmare which woke her up.

When she barreled into the masked man, she was sure he had said two words. A phrase that was actually intelligible.

"Dream lands."

That was what she had heard. For some reason, the phrase made her curl up into an even tighter ball under the covers. For she was certain his words were a warning about something horrible about to happen.

CHAPTER FIVE

The newspaper office felt even more chaotic than usual when April arrived at work the next morning. Even for a Wednesday, the notorious middle of the week, everyone seemed more harried than normal. April felt rushed. She had waited through breakfast for Nella to appear, wanting to tell her friend about the extraordinary dream of the night before (although she planned to leave out any mention of the glass eyeball).

But Nella failed to appear. Finally, April went to Nella's room and banged on her door, only to hear her friend groan and beg for another hour of sleep. After persistent knocking, Nella came to the door. "I will send a message to the office," she promised April. "I'll tell them I'm sick."

"But you'll lose a day's wages," said April, knowing how quickly Nella spent her salary and how little she had left at the end of the month.

"It will be worth it," said Nella, leaning against her door jamb. Her fashionable bobbed hair was a tangled cloud around her pale face. Her expensive cold cream still clung to her cheeks. Deep circles, dark as bruises, ringed her eyes. Her freckles seemed more obvious than usual, given her pallor. "I barely slept last night. Every time I fell asleep, I dreamed of the tower and the seawater rising all around me. I couldn't move! I was just frozen in place waiting to drown. It was horrible. I won't go to work until I get some rest. It wasn't until a few minutes ago that I slept without any dreams. Then you woke me up!"

"I'm sorry," April said. "Shall I call your office and explain when I get to work?" Mrs Garcia had not installed a phone yet, but the tenants could go across the street to Mrs Alba's house to make calls as long as they left change in a jar by the phone. If April made the call from her office, it would at least save Nella a nickel.

"Would you?" Nella said. "I only want to go back to bed."

"Of course!" April had never seen her friend look so pale. Perhaps a day in bed would be a good idea. "Can I bring you anything?"

"No, just sleep. Sleep without any dreams." Nella stifled an enormous yawn behind one hand.

"I'll let Mrs Garcia know." April knew their landlady would check on Nella during the day. For all their strict rules and the gossip which ran between the five boarding houses, the landladies of Flotsam Street took care of their own. Mrs Garcia, champion of naps, might even know a remedy to help Nella sleep.

April promised to visit Nella as soon as she returned from work. Her exhausted friend waved her goodbye with another giant yawn, going back into her room and shutting the door firmly behind her.

As tired as she was, April didn't want to lose a day's wages. So she finished breakfast with an unusually somber boarding house crew. Lefty was already gone to his job, but Ollie poured herself a second cup of black coffee while complaining to Mrs Garcia about a troubled night. "I barely slept. Now I'll be on my feet all day today at the hospital," Ollie sighed. "I don't know how I'll stay awake."

Looking around the newsroom, April saw everyone looked a bit like Nella and Ollie, simply exhausted. Minnie and another reporter were slumped in their chairs, almost dozing at their desks.

Columbia caught April as she checked the mail in her basket and said, "Keep your coat and hat on. Simon's sick. Somebody needs to take these proofs to his clients."

The manager thrust a stack of papers into April's hands. "The names and addresses are at the top of each page," Columbia said. "Just have them sign or initial where it is marked. It's a new rule. Nobody is happy about giving refunds. Including Simon."

April nodded. It seemed only fair that she ran this errand as she instituted the last refund. However, she glanced at the counter, wondering who would cover her work. "What about the phone?"

"I will listen for the phone," said Columbia. Unlike the rest of the newsroom, Columbia seemed as organized and efficient as always. She gave no evidence of being tired. Rather, she had the appearance of a woman who slept soundly without any emotional dreams at all. Certainly, giant ants would not chase her throughout the night.

"I need to type up some memos about office procedure and timecards," Columbia remarked. "The timecards are simply a disaster, especially the ones filled out by the reporters."

"I can sort the mail when I return," April promised. Columbia simply nodded and waved her away, already walking back toward her desk and leaving April feeling oddly relieved. Somehow, she realized that it was important to do what Columbia wanted. Although yesterday April might have called Columbia a colleague, today she was very aware that Columbia occupied a place above April in the hierarchy of the newspaper. Upsetting your direct supervisor was not a good way to retain your job, as she frequently told Nella.

April made a quick call to Nella's office, explaining that her friend was sick. Luckily it was the sympathetic Pia who answered the call. Mrs Lanigan was still at the hospital, Pia said, "and the office is all sixes and sevens anyway. Tell Nella not to worry. We will manage without her today."

While Pia's favorite phrase was "not to worry," April worried for Nella. Her friend was on her third job in less than a year. Nella's somewhat lackadaisical approach to arriving on time never went over well in the offices where she worked. "Although," Nella once remarked to April, "the insurance office where the manager timed everyone's break with a stopwatch in the name of efficiency was ridiculous." Nella also grew bored with office work and left her jobs as soon as somebody started fussing at her. Luckily Nella excelled at typing, a skill in high demand. If she lost or left her current job, perhaps April could find Nella a place at the newspaper.

While mulling possible work that Nella could do, April gathered up the advertising contracts. Her purse was too small to hold the paperwork, but she found a large folder in Columbia's well-stocked supply closet and slid the pages inside it. As April left the office, she paused on the sidewalk to check the addresses. Included with Simon's orders was the mockup of the ad ordered by Carolyn Fern. That address was the furthest away from the office, and her client as well, so April decided to start there and work her way back to the *Arkham Advertiser*.

The bell sounded from the trolley rolling down the street. For a moment, April recalled her strange nightmare. But this trolley was driven by a completely ordinary man, not a giant ant, so she shook off her momentary fear. Dreams were only dreams and could not harm her, but April resolved to read no more pulp magazines after midnight.

She caught the trolley on the corner, which deposited her practically at the door of the building that she wanted. Checking the names in the vestibule, she found the correct floor and office number. Heading up the stairs, April came out on the third floor where a row of oak doors with frosted glass windows stretched down the long hallway. The pine floors were scrubbed and polished. The place looked almost academic, or at least as if important business was conducted behind the doors. April noted a dentist, a doctor, and a lawyer all had practices on the third floor. She began slowly walking down the hall, checking the brass numbers above the doors. The fourth door had "Carolyn Fern" in gold paint on the frosted glass as well as a list of letters after her name to denote her degrees. April knocked.

"Come in," could be heard through the glass.

April opened the door. The small windowless room inside contained a desk, a rolling chair, a typewriter, and a green-glass-shaded lamp. A rag rug lay under the desk, possibly because the floors would be cold in a building like this. A couple of straight-back chairs were arranged against the wall. Another half-open door obviously led to the outer office with a window. Pale sunlight pooled through the second door, a square of light upon the polished floor.

"Can I help you?" A short plump woman turned away from an oak filing cabinet tucked in the corner. She looked to be in her early sixties, with heavy streaks of white in her brown hair. She wore a very simple tan dress with a slightly darker green cardigan pulled over it. Something about it reminded April of how Columbia dressed. Very neat and well-tailored, and she wondered if the two women patronized the same dress shop.

"I have a proof from the *Arkham Advertiser*." April held up her handful of papers. "I need Carolyn Fern's signature."

The woman nodded and called out, "Dr Fern, there's a young lady from the *Arkham Advertiser* to see you."

"Thank you, Barbara." A tall, slender woman appeared in the

doorway of the other office. She nodded at April and motioned for her to follow. "Please call me Carolyn."

"April May," April responded with a quick handshake.

"That's a pretty name," Carolyn remarked.

"I was born in April," she explained, "and my father thought it sounded very American to name me for the month… and in English." Her mother, of course, had been furious when she'd seen the birth certificate. She had picked out at least one saint's name and her grandmother's name, both of which she later insisted on being used for her younger daughters. Nor had her father considered how his surname would sound when combined with April. Throughout her younger school years, April had been teased frequently about the combination. And nobody ever thought her family were Americans.

In fact, the only other person who had ever reacted to her name by saying "That's pretty" was Nella. As they'd both been in kindergarten at the time, April had almost forgotten about it until today.

Carolyn paused in the doorway of her office. "Do you like your name?" she asked. Apparently, April's slight reaction to her earlier comment had caught her attention. Something about the woman made April think she missed very little.

April shrugged when Carolyn asked if she liked her name. "I guess," she finally said. She certainly never spent her time doodling nicknames on pieces of paper like Nella, who had long ago sworn her best friend to never reveal her actual name. Nella disliked her true name and had used Nella since she was old enough to write it down.

"I don't want to be called anything else," April told Carolyn.

"It's good to know who you are," Carolyn responded. "So many of us struggle to accept who we are or what we can be."

"But you know exactly what you can do," April said, glancing at the diplomas displayed on the wall of the office. Carolyn Fern was obviously a woman who had found a career that suited her.

"I probably doubt myself as much as anyone," said Carolyn. "That's why I became a psychologist. To understand why I had those doubts. And to help others resolve their problems."

It was rather discouraging to learn that a woman of Carolyn's education and position would still have any doubts in her life. April hoped when she was thirty, she would know exactly what to do in every situation. As Nella often said, "By the time we are thirty, we will be extraordinary."

Oh well, they had ten years to figure it out, April thought.

Carolyn's office was bright and airy with two windows. A heavy oak desk took up one end of the room. Bookcases lined the inner walls. The leather chairs in this room had deep seats and thick cushions. April could imagine sinking into one with a book and never wanting to leave. A fuzzy wool blanket lay across the back of one leather chair.

Carolyn caught April's inquiring look around the office. She patted one end of the wool blanket. "Some of my patients grow cold. It's easier if a person feels comfortable while talking. Warmth conveys a feeling of comfort," she said, walking to the desk. "Far too many believe a patient should suffer deprivation as a part of treatment. I believe the opposite."

April nodded. She had never met a psychologist before and wasn't very sure what they actually did.

However, she knew her job. April put the sheet of paper showing Carolyn's advertisement on the desk. Carolyn adjusted her heavy glasses to read over the ad.

"This appears fine," she said, taking a pencil from a bronze cup decorated with an interesting geometric pattern. She initialed the proof and handed it back to April. "When will the ad run?"

"Starting with this evening's edition," April answered.

Carolyn nodded. She was a tall woman or, like many people, considerably taller than April. Dressed in a beautifully tailored shirt and skirt, she had a fashionable flare that Nella would admire. Her dark red hair was held away from her thin face in neatly marcelled waves. April rather wished she could achieve the same waves, but her heavy black hair worked best in a simple braid coiled on the back of her head. At least the mass of hair made it easy to pin her hat on when she went out.

"Is there something else you need?" Carolyn was sorting through some papers on her desk, but the glance she gave April seemed kind.

"I was wondering about your research," April admitted. "What are you trying to learn?"

"I want to understand more about nightmares," Carolyn said. "I've had several patients suffer from poor sleep due to frightening dreams. To help them, I need to know more about what is causing those dreams."

"Would you be able to cure them if you knew more?" April wondered if she should tell Carolyn about Mrs Lanigan fainting yesterday, Nella's reaction and subsequent nightmares, or the other complaints that she'd heard in the boarding house. Maybe even mention the giant ants invading her dreams. Something was going on and somebody, preferably somebody with a medical degree, needed to investigate. April supposed a psychologist was like any doctor or nurse. After all, Carolyn talked about having patients.

Carolyn shook her head. "I don't think anyone can stop nightmares from occurring, but I do believe that I can help patients better manage their dreams," she said.

"How?" Then realizing her questions might be a little strange coming from an advertising saleswoman, April added, "I have friends who are suffering from nightmares. Perhaps I could send them to you. If you're not charging anything…" She trailed off, wondering if the last query was rude, but the ad implied Carolyn's services would be free. Also, April wished she could better control her own dreams and almost volunteered herself for Carolyn's study. But how could she explain the giant ants driving trolleys to such an elegant woman? Better that she inquire for Nella, who would find it fascinating to be the subject of psychoanalysis.

Carolyn smiled. "My services are free, just as the ad describes. I'm doing this for research and to help as much as I can. I have seen an increase in illnesses caused by poor sleep, which does seem linked to nightmares. But I need to see more people to understand what's happening."

April nodded. She was still a little unsure of how doctors discovered cures and wanted to be certain that Carolyn's methods were safe. There'd been talk in the boarding house of "experiments" done at St Mary's and the Miskatonic University. Ollie once worked for a doctor who ran a sanitorium outside Innsmouth with truly strange ideas of how to treat nervous patients. It was Ollie who often warned against doctors more interested in cures than patients.

"You don't make people drink seaweed?" asked April.

"Seaweed! No, I don't," Carolyn exclaimed. "Psychologists rarely prescribe drugs or invasive treatments. Most recently I've become interested in the work of Émile Coué. He used conscious suggestions to help people."

"How would that help?" April asked.

"Coué had patients suggest to themselves how they would feel better each day when they took his medicine," Carolyn explained. "He found such practice made the medicine more effective. Since then, others have tried the suggestions without the medication. I think one could apply the same technique to nightmares. The right series of suggestions could influence the subconscious mind and promote more peaceful dreams."

"It seems too simple," said April and then felt slightly embarrassed to be contradicting a woman with so many certificates on the wall. Still, she persisted. "If you can talk yourself out of a nightmare, why wouldn't everyone just do that?"

"You could not talk yourself out of the situation once you begin dreaming," said Carolyn. "Nightmares evoke strong emotions in the dreamer. These fears can overwhelm the dreamer and cloud their ability to think clearly. The suggestions are what you tell yourself before you go to sleep, which may give you more control within the dream or even prevent the nightmare from occurring."

April remained unsure but she decided to discuss Carolyn's offer of free therapy with the residents of the boarding house. Perhaps it would help Nella. Ollie was certain to have an opinion too. April trusted the nurse when it came to medical matters.

Carolyn grabbed a notepad and scribbled a few words on it. She ripped off the page. "Have your friend try this," she said, handing the note to April. On the page, she had written: "Nightmares have no power over me."

"Have her say it several times before going to sleep," said Carolyn. "If it helps at all, please have her come to see me. I can do more if I know the specific fears of the dreamer. There's hypnosis as well. I use that in conjunction with conscious control."

"You hypnotize people?" April asked. She thought of the stories that she'd read about how hypnosis gave the practitioner control over the subject and shuddered. She and Nella once lied to April's mother about *The Cabinet of Dr Caligari* when it played at their movie theater. They had told her that it was a film for children. April still remembered how frightening it was to walk home through the dark streets after seeing it.

"Only if they are willing," said Carolyn as if she read April's mind. Just like the hypnotist in the last *Weird Tales* that she read. He was a mind reader and a murderer!

"It is important that the patient trusts in the process to achieve good results. I would never force anyone to undergo hypnosis," Carolyn continued while April cataloged in her head how many evil hypnotists appeared in the stories, which gave her real shivers.

"I couldn't do it," April admitted, still thinking about how Caligari caused Cesare to murder several people at his command. Better to suffer nightmares than become a sleepwalking killer! And wasn't Caligari a doctor in an insane asylum, treating people much as Carolyn might? Or had he been a patient dreaming that he was a doctor? As April recalled, the ending of the movie was rather strange.

But the woman regarding her so calmly didn't seem to have the maniacal demeanor of Caligari. Shaking herself free of her morbid thoughts, April thanked Carolyn for signing the paperwork and let herself out of the office.

April couldn't stifle a small sigh of relief, however, when she reached the sidewalk. It was generous of Carolyn Fern to offer free treatment. But didn't Uncle Tito always say to never trust a stranger who comes bearing gifts?

Sifting through the remaining contracts, April realized she needed to start walking if she was to visit all the businesses listed in one day. Another of Uncle Tito's favorite sayings was "a walk is as good as an aspirin to clear the head."

Perhaps by the end of the day, she would decide whether or not taking up Carolyn Fern's offer was a good idea. It would be wonderful to be free of the nightmares, but not if the cure was more horrible than her troubled dreams.

CHAPTER SIX

Some people might believe being a garbage collector was the worst job in the world, but Lefty enjoyed his route and the people on it. He didn't love garbage. It smelled. And the cans felt heavier every year as he tipped them into his truck. But there were worse jobs. He knew all about terrible jobs as he'd taken several over the years. Factories! He hated working in factories.

Best job in the world? That was easy. Baseball. Except it hadn't been a good job for him. He'd made a lot of mistakes in those days, most stemming from believing what other guys said about him being another Babe Ruth.

Still, he would never regret the time spent playing the greatest game ever invented. Even had the uniform and glove tucked in the back of his closet to remind him of those glory days. As for his favorite bat, it rode with him under the bench of his truck. Not everywhere he went was safe, and there were some strange creatures to be found in the back alleys of Arkham. But his Louisville Slugger tended to discourage interference.

Not that he needed the bat today. The neighborhood where he was collecting garbage was one with neat green lawns in front of nice homes. The cans were always lined up in the delivery alleys that ran behind the houses. He grabbed the metal can sitting outside a gate leading to the backyard of the house. Heaving it over his head, he dumped the contents in the back of his truck. A few years earlier, it would have been a horse and cart. Lefty knew some of the older guys missed their horses who plodded along their routes with them. But he loved Pequod, his sturdy truck with the Packard engine. He'd even painted the name across the hood of the truck, mostly to discourage the other guys from borrowing "his" truck. Never mind the supervisor claimed all garbage trucks belonged to the company. He understood Pequod and, although he never said it out loud, Pequod understood him. "Don't you, my beauty?" said Lefty with a friendly knock on Pequod's back end as he swung the empty garbage can over his shoulder and carried it back to its place in the alley.

"Is that you, Lefty?" a voice called over the fence.

"Oh, hi, professor," Lefty said as he set down the homeowner's garbage can. "How's the roses?"

"Still alive, although I am never certain why." The gate swung open to reveal Harvey Walters standing beside a tangle of rose bushes which climbed all over his back fence. Although late in the season, the pale pink roses still bloomed. It wasn't the first time that Lefty found Harvey in his backyard regarding his roses with some perplexity. He once claimed the roses simply appeared in the garden following a "strange series of events that not even I fully comprehend." Since then, the rose bushes spread joyously throughout the yard. Every week the tangled bushes seemed to take over more space. The roses burst into bloom in early June and looked to stay blooming well until the end of the year. Periodically, Harvey threatened to take the shears to the bushes, but Lefty had never seen any evidence of pruning in his garbage or backyard.

"How are you?" Harvey turned away from the roses to chat with Lefty.

"Can't complain," Lefty replied.

"Oh, certainly you can complain. It would be almost un-American to fail to complain about something," Harvey said. "I, for example, do my best as a grumpy old man. I complain constantly about inheriting money and being saddled with the responsibility of managing it. I further complain about being encouraged by my academic colleagues to spend my inheritance on buying a house and retiring. At the same time, if I met a man who complained about his good fortune in such a way, I would complain about him!"

Harvey had moved into the neighborhood a few months ago. He had quickly become Lefty's favorite customer. His housekeeper, Mrs Fox, was a good-looking middle-aged widow. Lefty may have admired her hanging out the laundry in the backyard, but he hadn't worked up the courage to talk with her. The professor, however, was an easy man to befriend, eager to chat whenever he saw Lefty.

"In addition, I complain in the morning to Mrs Fox about the temperature of my coffee, in the afternoon to my assistant Ira about his unfortunate habit of rearranging my bookshelves, and in the evening to whatever deities might be listening about the indignities of indigestion after eating too much cake." Harvey smiled at the end of his recitation, somewhat undercutting his claim to be a grumpy old man.

Lefty chuckled. The old man had a wicked sense of humor. "Can't complain about cake," said Lefty. "Mrs Garcia made a very fine devil's food cake last night."

"Ah," said Harvey. "I prefer angel's food to devil's food, but there's no denying that Mrs Fox makes an excellent chocolate ganache when she is in the mood. As wonderful as it was, three slices weighed very heavily on my stomach by midnight. I spent a good part of the night pacing the house, trying to convince my digestion to let me sleep."

"I slept like a baby," said Lefty, "and I had seconds of dessert."

"Ah, injustices of youth!" said Harvey.

"You're the only one who calls me young," said Lefty. "I won't see forty again. I don't think of myself as a young man."

"Wait until you can say the same about passing sixty," retorted Harvey. "But you slept well last night, I gather."

Lefty shrugged. "Same as always. Turned off my light and fell asleep. Woke up at dawn. Haul garbage cans up and down alleys all day and you'd sleep better too."

Harvey tilted his head, looking a little like a heron picking through the mud of the riverbank. "My doctor claims that I should stop eating cake and drinking coffee in the afternoon," he said. "At least your suggestion does not include curtailing my intake of cake. Still, you've suffered no nightmares this week?"

"I don't dream," Lefty admitted. He knew most people didn't believe him when he said that. A doctor once told him everyone dreams but not everyone remembers their dreams. "Least not that I remember," he clarified to the professor.

"Mrs Fox claims there's been a number of nightmares suffered all up and down the street. She hears things." Harvey dropped his voice. "People gossip over the back fences. Can you imagine?"

Lefty grinned and shook his head at Harvey leaning against the gatepost to talk to him. "No, I cannot imagine that," he said.

"Still no nightmares?" Harvey persisted.

"None at all," Lefty reassured him. "Although some of the folks on Flotsam Street mentioned nightmares." There had been all kinds of chatter at the table last night, including a long tale from April's friend Nella, but Lefty tended to let such gossip wash over him.

"Flotsam Street? Is that in Rivertown?" Harvey half turned away, worrying at the petals of a rose.

"Well, the neighbors say that Flotsam runs at the bottom of French Hill. The garbage company says it is part of the Rivertown route. Doesn't matter much to me. It's a nice street."

"It used to be a nice neighborhood, Rivertown," said Harvey. "But that was one or two floods ago." He bent a stern look at Lefty. "And no jokes about Noah's Ark. I don't go back quite that far. But the flood of 1874 convinced a number of the wealthier families in Rivertown to move further up on French Hill."

"No jokes about Noah, professor," said Lefty, dusting off his hands and preparing to go. "And I doubt you remember 1874."

Harvey chuckled. "I was a boy then, but I do remember reading about the floods that year. There was a whopper down in Mississippi, too. Fascinated me then, fascinates me now. All that water and destruction. It's almost as if there's a reason for it. If we could figure out how to predict natural disasters! I am convinced the ancient druids knew a great deal more than we did. There are very interesting texts about celestial events prior to flooding. Why, I found a fascinating book at an estate sale which suggests one could even control floods through animal sacrifice … or perhaps floods are needed for animal sacrifice. I'm still working out the translation."

"Floods happen. Just bad luck." Lefty knew once Harvey started on his book collection, he could talk all afternoon. As much as he enjoyed a gab with the old man, he had work to do. "Neighborhoods like Rivertown bear the worst of it being closest to the river. Doesn't take a genius to figure it out."

"I still maintain you are a philosopher among garbagemen," said Harvey. "And a far more entertaining conversationalist than Ira."

"Who?" said Lefty. This was the second time the old man mentioned an Ira. Lefty certainly didn't know everyone who worked with Harvey, but the professor liked to gossip. Lefty had an odd feeling that he'd missed something significant, although he couldn't say why.

"Ira, my assistant," said Harvey. "Oh, you wouldn't have met him yet. He started recently. The most irritating person. He keeps rearranging my books! I should shove him into the garden to organize these roses instead."

Based on Harvey's grumbles, Lefty expected Ira would be looking for a new job soon. Or perhaps not. Harvey's bark was definitely worse than his bite.

"Wait, I almost forgot, we have some more magazines for you." Harvey walked to the back porch and picked up a bundle of magazines. Lefty took the stack from him, noting with pleasure the latest edition of *Adventure*, some copies of *Tales from Nevermore*, and several others. The *Adventure* magazine featured a robust man lowering himself by means of a stout rope into a large cave. A pair of red eyes gleamed from the shadows below.

"Looks like a good story," Lefty said. "Caves! Now if I ever had nightmares, it would be about being trapped underground." As a boy, he'd gone into a cavern once. It had been a dare among lads to see how long they could last without a light. He had never been so happy as to have the lantern lit again and be led out. The irony of living in perfect comfort in a basement did not escape him, but his basement had some windows and the sound of people walking overhead. It was not like being trapped under miles of dirt in a cave.

"The ancients also tied caves to weather. *Sed pater omnipotens speluncis abdidit atris.* Jupiter hid the winds in dark caves according to Virgil. I remember being very taken with exploring *speluncis*. Even proposed we form a society and call ourselves *Fraternitas Speluncis*. Almost every town has a cave system.

Kingsport, Innsmouth, and Arkham," Harvey said. "We did make an expedition to your neighborhood."

"Are you talking about the Black Cave?" Lefty only knew of the one cave in Rivertown.

Harvey nodded. "Some say it runs the length of Arkham, more like a series of passageways carved out by the water than a single cave. Of course, there are a few at Miskatonic University who believe all the caves in the region are connected."

"I wouldn't go near the Black Cave these days if I was you," Lefty warned the old man. Rivertown's cave was on the southern edge of the Miskatonic River and a popular drop spot for bootleggers. A number of men in Rivertown made a little money on the side hauling barrels and crates out of the Black Cave on dark nights. Lefty had been approached once or twice about the use of Pequod since he parked it every night in the company's Rivertown yard. He managed to sidestep such requests by claiming the garbage company would notice if the truck went missing from the yard one night. No money was worth going into the Black Cave. And when the river rose, it was said the cave flooded. One or two bodies had been hauled out of it to the graveyard, although it was unclear if they died of natural causes or meeting someone intent on protecting a stash.

"You are probably right about the Black Cave. Cave exploring is also a young man's hobby. But there used to be some very interesting pictographs in one of the far passages. I sketched them into a notebook... but where did I put that notebook?" Harvey sighed. "Ira has probably filed it away somewhere. He's a very efficient person." The last sentence did not sound like a compliment.

"Good luck finding it," said Lefty. "And stay out of the Black Cave."

"I have no time for exploring," Harvey said. "I am studying a little book about dreams and nightmares right now. You said you haven't had any lately?"

"No nightmares. At least, not for me."

"Interesting. Interesting. I've suffered a few dreams this week, but nothing I would term as terrifying. But Mrs Fox claims hers were horrifying. I wonder why," Harvey said.

Conversations with Harvey were often like this. Intriguing, but he had work to do and Harvey obviously had thoughts to think.

Calling out a goodbye to Harvey, which the man acknowledged with a wave of his hand, Lefty climbed back into Pequod. He dropped the magazines on the seat next to him, intent on reading *Adventure* during his lunch break. Then he set his truck rumbling to the next stop.

By mid-afternoon, Pequod was nearly full. Lefty finished emptying the garbage cans behind the Palace Movie Theater, including cans of old film and many crumpled lobby posters. Harry Callum, the theater's owner, had apparently cleared out his basement. Lefty even spotted the tattered remains of a Sydney Fitzmaurice "nightmare picture" poster in the trash. It had been years since he'd seen a Fitzmaurice picture. He preferred pulps to movies. The adventures in the magazines contained more terror and entertainment than flickering shadows on the screen in his opinion.

Climbing back into Pequod's cab, he spotted April May trudging down the sidewalk toward him.

"Hi, April," Lefty called, wondering what she was doing so far from her office.

April's always slightly worried expression lightened when she saw him. "Hello, Lefty," she said.

"What are you doing downtown?" he asked. She worked in the Northside and rarely left the newspaper's offices as far as he knew from her conversations with Nella and the rest of the boarders during meals.

"I had to take advertisements around for the clients to sign off," April said. She sighed, lifting one foot and then the other off the sidewalk. "It was more walking than I expected. My feet ache."

"How many more stops do you have?" Lefty said.

April pointed to the theater. "I just need to show Mr Callum his ads. This is the last one."

"Go on. I'm due a break. Once you're done, I'll give you a ride back to the *Advertiser*." Once he collected all the garbage, he dropped it off in the Northside yard and then drove the truck back to Rivertown, ready to start all over again in the morning. The boss might not be fond of him giving a friend a lift, but what the boss man thought about Lefty's handling of his route was his problem, not Lefty's. Not many men liked hauling garbage and the turnover was high. Lefty showed up every morning, finished his route in record time six days a week, and even kept Pequod running without much fuss. So nobody bothered him about the items he took home (they all did it anyway) and he regarded giving his friends the occasional ride in Pequod the same way. A well-earned perk of the job. April gave a relieved smile from where she stood, hanging on to the handle of the door and chatting through the window. "A ride would be wonderful. If it doesn't take you out of your way?"

Lefty shook his head. "Nope. I'm heading back to the incinerator." He'd given April and her friend Nella a lift home a few times as they worked fairly close to the incinerator yard on the edge of Northside. "I'll drop you off and then go deliver my load."

"I'll be as quick as possible!" April ran up the steps of the Palace Theatre.

Lefty leaned back in his seat, fishing out the copy of *Adventure* magazine that he had been reading. Since April was sure to be back in a few minutes, he turned to the "Wanted – Men and Adventurers" column. Not that he had any plans to leave Arkham or garbage collecting. The job suited him, letting him work alone at his own pace as long as the cans were emptied and the trash burned at the end of the day. Still, a man could dream of big game hunting or serving as a bodyguard to a princess in some far-off country.

Less than ten minutes later, April climbed into his cab. "That's everything," she said with satisfaction, ruffling the papers in her lap before sliding them into a cardboard folder. Lefty changed gears and set Pequod toward Northside.

"Been a long day?" asked Lefty.

April sighed and nodded. "Too much walking," she said. "If I do this again, I need to wear better shoes. And there was a lot of talking to strangers."

Lefty glanced at the young woman. He suspected she was a bit shy around strangers. Even around folks that she knew, April kept quiet and sat in the back of the room when she could. Unless it was her friend Nella. The two together could sound like a flock of starlings over the breakfast table, although it was usually Nella who led the conversation.

Still, he hoped his daughter, wherever she lived, was like young April. Always kind and full of imagination. A reader, too. "Have you seen this one?" he asked, taking his hand off the wheel to toss the copy of *Adventure* into April's lap.

"No," she said, flipping through the pages as they bounced back toward Northside. April wasn't as big a fan of *Adventure* as he was. Lefty knew she preferred magazines like *Argosy* and the new *Amazing Stories*. And he failed to persuade her that the stories of Virgil Gray in *Tales from Nevermore* were the best. Still, with the *Adventure* to examine, April was paging through the magazine to see what the issue contained. She enjoyed reading almost everything, an addiction that Lefty understood all too well.

A dog darted across the street. Lefty slammed on the brakes, throwing out an arm to catch April as she jerked forward.

"What was that?" April asked. Her papers slid off her lap and cascaded around their feet.

"Dog," said Lefty. Ignoring shouts from drivers stuck behind him, he searched for the animal. A small shape darted off the sidewalk into a nearby alley. From the brief glimpse that he got, the dog looked like it had been limping as it ran away.

"April, are you in a hurry? I might have clipped it," Lefty said. He pulled over to the curb.

"Oh, poor thing," April said. She gathered up her papers. Hopping out of Pequod's cab, she left the contract folder and magazines piled on the seat. "I can help you look for it."

Lefty reached under the seat for his Louisville Slugger. Going down alleys in this part of town, even in the afternoon, could be dangerous. He wondered if he should discourage April from following him. He didn't want to frighten his friend, but he didn't like the look of the shadows gathered in the narrow space between two old factories. "It might take some time," he warned. "Especially if the dog is scared."

"Don't worry," April said. "We're close to the *Advertiser*. I can walk to the office from here. Let's see if we can find the dog first."

But the minute they entered the alley, Lefty wanted to send April off to her office immediately. The afternoon sun slanted into the alley, highlighting a faded sign covering one wall, but leaving the end of the alley in deep shadows. One side showed H. B. Young Manufacturing painted across the brick. The other side was a pile of rubbish. A deep rumble of machinery echoed through the space, which smelled of oil and coal. A tarry muck pooled in the corners.

Working out where they were in his head, Lefty guessed the alley ended on the riverbank. A lot of factories built in this part of town backed onto the Miskatonic River. From the smell of dead fish and sulfur, he bet this one did too.

"Maybe you should go back?" Lefty waved April to the center of the alley away from the muddy water trickling sluggishly through the gutters. There had been a spattering of rain before dawn, and puddles lingered in the shadowy alley. Lefty shifted himself so he and the Louisville Slugger were between April and whatever might come out of the shadows.

"I'm fine," April said, picking her way around the puddles. "Look, down there, behind the crates."

Wedged into the center of a pile of broken boxes, a white poodle peered out at them. It looked like a plump pampered dog and not much past the puppy stage. Panting softly, its pink tongue lolling out, the small poodle shivered in its hiding place.

"Oh, poor thing." April whistled softly and snapped her fingers, trying to lure the poodle out.

"Careful," Lefty warned. He eyed the broken boxes. "There's nails and splinters. Let me try to grab it." He laid down his bat and crouched as close as possible to the dog. The poodle backed further into the crates. It was definitely a pet, wearing a fine scarlet leather collar. "Come on, come out. I've got a sandwich for you in the truck."

The dog whined and scrambled out of Lefty's reach. The poodle's tremors turned into a frantic shaking of its whole body.

From the far end of the alley came a low, guttural moan. The sound vibrated through the ground under Lefty's knees.

Picking up garbage in all weathers and all parts of Arkham, it wasn't the first time that Lefty had heard or seen something...

call it strange… hiding in an alley. It was why he carried his Slugger.

"Go on," he said to April, "you go back to the street. I'll get the dog."

As he crept closer to the poodle, he heard a splash. Something was stirring in the river. Such things usually came out in the night or the earliest misty mornings, well before any people were stirring or machinery in the factories was booming. Would this creature be so bold as to slither into an alley in broad daylight? Lefty had a feeling that he wouldn't like the answer.

The moan from the end of the alley sounded again. Lefty reached for his bat and hauled himself upright, trying to pinpoint the source of the noise.

Ignoring his advice, April came up behind him, whistling and calling to the dog.

"Get back," he said again.

Then a trio of river rats raced down the alley, running for their lives. Matted fur and slightly greasy from frequent swims in the Miskatonic River, they flowed toward him. Lefty hefted the bat. Rats and garbage went together, but he never saw the creatures so terrified. The rats completely ignored him, barely swerving to avoid a collision as they sought to escape the rising moan behind them.

Whatever was coming out of the river, it sounded both mournful and hungry. The guttural growl rose into a keening wail, as if the sound itself was trying to claw its way out of the shadows.

CHAPTER SEVEN

Lefty shifted his stance so he remained between April and whatever moaned at the end of the alley. It also meant she could no longer see the poodle. But she heard a scrabbling of claws come from another pile of garbage.

"What's that?" April spun around. She searched the shadows for the source of the new noise. Two or three long brown bodies went hurtling past her feet. Their muddy, naked tails swished from side to side. April jumped out of the way.

"Rats! They are running away. Go back to the truck!" Lefty hissed. Even as he spoke, April spotted the trio of river rats scrabbling up a drainpipe. In a flash, they vanished.

At the sight of the rats, April almost left the alley. She hated rats. But then the poodle whimpered again, a sound laced with pure terror. Spurred by concern for the dog, April slid around Lefty's broad form to try to see the poor dog. They couldn't abandon the dog. It might be injured.

Then, from the inky blackness further on, emerged a glistening tentacle. Glowing with an unnatural light, the almost feathery feeler groped along the ground.

"Is that a snake?" April's voice rose a couple of octaves,

but she didn't scream. As usual, her inability to yell like Nella weighed on her. Instead, like Lefty, she almost whispered. Why, she didn't know. But she had a feeling, similar to her nightmares, that making noise might attract unwanted attention.

"Maybe," said Lefty in a tone of voice that actually said "no, it's not but if I tell you that you'll scream."

Which she wouldn't, but Lefty didn't know that she reacted to fear with silence rather than screaming.

April was fairly sure that it wasn't a snake. But she also guessed that Lefty was hoping whatever it was would leave them alone. The tip withdrew into the shadows. Determined to rescue the poodle before the strange "it is not a snake" returned, April edged forward as quietly as she could.

The moaning sound from the end of the alley started up again. The poodle's nerve broke. With a high-pitched yelp, it darted between Lefty's legs for the street. The big man swore, teetering in place but never taking his eyes off the river end of the alley where the moan rose in volume.

The poodle's fuzzy legs were a blur as it dashed toward the street. It ignored everything around it. The little dog barreled toward the alley's entrance, obviously intent on escaping from whatever rose from the river behind it.

Just as quick, April grabbed at its collar as the puppy went dashing past her. "No, you don't," she said, hauling the poodle close. She lifted it off the ground in a firm hug. Someone once told her that if you gripped a dog hard enough, it would calm it down. Or maybe they told her never to grab a running dog. Either way, she felt relief when the poodle sagged in her arms with a throaty whine.

"April, get out of here," Lefty shouted as the tentacle appeared again. But April froze, unable to move, her heart beating as frantically as the whimpering dog clutched in her arms.

The tentacle went straight up in the air. Lefty swung like he was trying to hit a baseball over the back fence. Connecting with the glowing feeler or whatever it was, he slammed it back into the pile of broken crates. Something screeched and the tentacle withdrew, an inch-long nail thrust through it. The nail made a hideous scraping sound along the alley's floor as the feeler recoiled back into the shadows.

Lefty waited for a moment. A splash sounding like a large body hitting the water echoed through the alley. Then he turned and shouted at April. "Go on, get out of here," he said. Happy to leave now she had the dog, April whirled around, running toward his truck, with Lefty close behind her.

Back on the sidewalk, people were still going in and out of the buildings. The cars and trucks rumbled past. Nobody seemed to notice them.

April leaned against the cab, cradling the puppy in her arms. The smell of garbage rising from Pequod's bed seemed almost comfortingly normal. Lefty continued staring back at the alley, but nothing followed them.

She took a couple of deep calming breaths. She couldn't have seen what she just saw, could she? But it wasn't a dream. Not this time. She had a shaking poodle clutched in her arms. The sun was beating down on her head. The smell of oil and gasoline competed with the pungent garbage, with the muddy whiff signaling the river was just on the other side of the buildings.

She thought of the stories that Minnie told in the newsroom. Of things seen but never fully understood. Things which eluded the reporters, but they were sure that they could catch in the next story, the next photograph.

"Do you know what that was?" she finally asked Lefty as he turned his gaze from the alley and toward her.

The big man shrugged. He opened the cab door and slid his

baseball bat under the seat. "Not exactly," he finally said. "But it wasn't good."

April nodded. She stayed plastered against Pequod's hood. Never mind it was a garbage truck. It was solid and warm against her back. She wasn't courageous or resourceful like Minnie. She sold ads! Over the telephone! She didn't venture down dark alleys seeking monsters. But she had rescued the dog. Feeling a little better, April examined the poodle more closely. The puppy gave a friendly bark and licked her nose.

"I don't think it's hurt," she told Lefty. "There's a name on the collar too."

"Yeah? What is it?" Lefty leaned over to take a closer look at the poodle's gleaming red collar with its engraved name tag.

April giggled. "Valentino. I guess the owner is a fan of the movie star."

Lefty chuckled too. He sounded as relieved as she was to be discussing the silliness of a dog's name and not whatever lurked in the alleys of Northside. "That's a big name for such a little guy." He climbed up to the cab. "Hop in. I'll take you to the *Advertiser*."

"What was that?" April asked again as the truck put some distance between them and the alley. She might not be a reporter, but she could try to tell the story to Minnie when she got back to the *Advertiser*. Minnie might want to come back and try for a picture. April only hoped that Minnie wouldn't need her to point out the alley or ever go down it again. Once was enough.

"Maybe it was a snake," Lefty replied.

"But you don't believe it was a snake?" April never heard of a snake which glowed. Not outside the stranger stories of Virgil Gray. But she could imagine many other things that it could be. Which was probably why she shouldn't read so many weird fiction pulps. She hoped Lefty had some nice westerns or romances in his current stack.

"Stuff comes out of the river, but usually not now." Lefty was keeping his eyes on the road and not looking at her. She had a feeling that he wanted to tell her the truth but still not everything that he knew. She understood the feeling. So she kept quiet and listened. "We don't have problems in the middle of the afternoon. Most of us garbagemen know things show up in the alleys but only at the very start of the run. In the winter, when it's still dark in the morning, that's when you get things hiding in the corners."

For Lefty, it was a long speech, but April sensed the man was as shaken as she was by the encounter.

Beside him, April scratched the dog's head, lost in her own thoughts. Lefty had never talked about the possible dangers of his job. At least not to her. When they chatted, it was about the imaginary terrors encountered in the pulp magazines.

But Arkham did that to people, she knew. Made them quiet about events and creatures which were hard to explain, much to the frustration of the reporters at the *Advertiser*. But folks who lived in the poorer parts of town knew about the dangers of the night. They mastered the art of ignoring it. Because they also knew the terrors of losing a job and speaking up could make trouble in different ways.

April was fairly adept at forgetting squirming things herself, although so far her encounters had only been in her nightmares. But that was largely to keep her mother from worrying. When she was very small, she'd talked about things that she'd seen in dreams, including the talking cat (which hadn't been frightening at all). Her mother had dragged her to church three days a week for months afterwards when her siblings only had to go to mass on Sunday. As she grew older, the night terrors had retreated. At least until this last week.

"What should we do with Valentino?" April asked as she petted the puppy panting on her lap.

"I could drop him off at the pound," Lefty said.

April frowned. The pound wasn't the best place for a dog. But Valentino's owners might find the poodle there. Then again, they might not.

"Oh, don't!" April said. "Take him home. I'll check the lost dogs column at the paper. We can find the owners ourselves."

"How will Mrs Garcia feel about that?" Lefty pulled up to the curb in front of the newspaper building.

"Please! You can take Valentino into the basement. She'll never see him." April knew Lefty had a soft heart. At the sound of her voice, Valentino gazed at the pair of them with a big-eyed look of entreaty.

"All right," Lefty grumbled. "But one night only. Then if we can't find the owner, we take the poodle to the pound."

"Thank you!" April hopped out of the cab, grabbing her paperwork as she went. "Be good, Valentino."

The poodle heaved a sigh. Then Valentino curled into the smallest ball possible on the truck seat, tucking his head under his tail.

"Been a hard day?" she heard Lefty ask the dog as he crashed the gears and maneuvered into traffic. "Stay out of alleys. You'll be a lot happier."

CHAPTER EIGHT

At the *Advertiser*, April discovered everyone seemed more awake. At least Doyle Jeffries was standing in the middle of the office yelling his usual refrain: "Deadlines! I need copy now. Not tomorrow!"

April swung by her spot at the counter, dropping the signed-off contracts into the basket on Columbia's desk. The office manager was not there, although a stack of perfectly aligned file folders marked "accounts receivable" showed she had completed her main tasks. By the phone on the counter, April found an equally neat pile of messages and new ad orders. Flipping through them, she spotted a few more ads for lost dogs, but none matched Valentino's description. She resolved to go down to the *Advertiser*'s morgue in the basement as soon as possible. She wanted to see if the newspapers stored there would yield any clues.

Glancing around the office, April spotted Minnie typing madly at her desk. When April approached her, she thought she heard Minnie respond to Doyle's latest shout, "Deadlines! Ha! Am I a secretary now?"

Minnie ripped a page out of the typewriter and thrust it at a copyboy rushing past. "Send that to composition now!" she ordered.

"Doesn't Mr Jeffries need to see it?" asked the copyboy. April couldn't remember the teenager's name. Ed? Matt? He was a new hire, very new, brought in by Columbia to keep the reporters and editors from wasting time running changes to the composition room in the basement where they set the type for the day's newspaper. April had a vague feeling that he had started yesterday, although that couldn't be right. Columbia had been around longer than that. Hadn't she?

"Doyle has seen it!" Minnie barked over the din of the newsroom. "I just typed out his changes. Move!"

The kid ran for the stairs. Minnie slumped in her chair. "Hi, April, how's your day going?"

"Strange," admitted April, dropping into the chair by Minnie. From where she sat, she could keep an eye on the counter and listen for the phone. It wasn't exactly where she was supposed to be, but she figured nobody would care or notice. And her feet hurt after a day of tramping around Arkham.

At April's response, Minnie perked up. She straightened out of her slump over the typewriter. "How was your day strange? What did you see?"

April chewed her lip, considering how much she should tell Minnie. The more she thought about the incident in the alley, the more like a dream it seemed. Glowing tentacles, briefly glimpsed, didn't make a good story, she decided, at least not the type that Minnie wanted to write. But she could tell her about the dog.

"I may have found one of the lost dogs," she finally said.

"Oh," said Minnie, relaxing a little. "Well, that's nice. I was hoping for a bit more blood, guts, and possibly ghosts."

April widened her eyes, shaken out of her own tired stupor by Minnie's response. "Ghosts?" she squeaked in surprise. "Why would you think of ghosts?"

"Because that's all I dream about these days," Minnie admitted. "Night after night, I dream a ghost is walking through my bedroom. He's trying to tell me something. A story, the biggest story, the one that will land my name on the front page."

"Seems like a good dream," said April, thinking of the night terrors suffered by Nella and herself.

"Not when your pillow explodes into a pile of fish guts and blood comes raining down from the ceiling," said Minnie.

April shuddered. "That sounds horrible."

"It is the worst." Minnie tapped idly on the question mark key of the typewriter. "Because I never hear the story. I could put up with the guts and blood if I could hear what the ghost was saying. But tell me about the dog. Can we take a cute reunion photo with its owner? Doyle would probably print a dog picture on the back page." The back page was devoted to "domestic stories" as Doyle put it. Mostly it was recipes and write-ups of community picnics and church socials. Every now and then, they would run a tale about a clever cat saving its owner from a domestic disaster or a good dog finding a lost child. These were particularly popular to judge by the letters received.

"I don't know who the owner is," April confessed. "But it's a poodle puppy named Valentino. I'll check the papers and see if I can find a lost dog advertisement to match."

Minnie nodded. "Let me know when you find the owner. I'll bring along the camera."

"Copy!" bellowed a voice right behind them. Both women jumped in their seats.

"Do you know we are on a deadline?" said Doyle, striding up to Minnie's desk. "Where's my copy?"

"Already being done, boss," said Minnie. "I gave your changes to Ed to run to the composition room."

Ed! April resolved to remember the teenager's name.

Everyone told her that memorizing people's names was essential for getting ahead in business.

"I was talking to April about a possible story for tomorrow," Minnie said. "Something heartwarming. The *Advertiser* reunites a lost dog with its loving owners."

"Lost dogs!" After making a modified bellow, Doyle twisted his mouth into something like a smile. "Actually, that's not a bad idea. People like a good dog story. It shows we help in the little ways as well as report on the big stories. Demonstrates the civic value of newspapers."

"It might also sell a few more ads," April suggested.

"Ads! We're in the business of reporting news, not selling ads," said Doyle with a fine disregard for the newspaper's name and how everyone's salary was paid.

Minnie, however, grasped April's idea. "Yes, if we can prove that an ad in the *Advertiser* resulted in a found dog, it will encourage others to buy ads when they lose a dog. We should put a bit from the original ad in the story, just to show how the newspaper helps reunite pets with their owners."

"There's been a lot of lost dogs recently," April told them. "More ads than usual, I think."

"That's speculating like a reporter, young April," said Minnie, lightly punching April's shoulder like the other reporters pummeled each other when they came up with a good headline or a lead for a story. "She has good instincts, doesn't she, boss?"

Doyle harrumphed. "Lost dogs aren't a story," he said. "Dogs run away all the time. Corruption in city government or sea monsters in the Miskatonic River. Those are stories."

"Sea monsters?" April squeaked again, thinking of the moaning cry at the end of the alley. Then she ducked her head, thinking that Doyle was eventually going to remember that she wasn't a reporter but only the most junior advertising salesperson, who was supposed to be standing at a counter on the other end of the floor and answering the telephone when it rang.

Doyle just shrugged, apparently unperturbed by April's question. "Rex got a call that something large was seen moving up the river. Probably a lost whale. But the fishermen who called said that it glowed under the water."

"Glowing creatures!" yelped Minnie. She leapt from her chair, grabbing for her camera bag. "And that rat Rex went looking without me? Where did he go? How are you going to run a story like that without photos!"

"He headed to the Rivertown docks," Doyle said. "You know the district. There were some men fishing the Miskatonic, not far from the Black Cave, and they started telling stories when they came back in."

"On it!" yelled Minnie, already grabbing her hat and coat from the wall hooks.

Doyle just shook his head as Minnie sprinted out the door. "Good instincts," he said to April. "But hasty too. We need to finish today's paper." Then looking slightly puzzled, he asked April, "Are you new? When did you start?"

Realizing that Doyle had also failed the task of memorizing people's names and positions at the newspaper, April made some noncommittal sounds as she moved back to her usual spot at the counter. Doyle had already turned away and was shouting at a hapless reporter. "Are your deadlines tomorrow? No! We need to finish this today! Type faster!"

Eventually the windows rattled and hummed as the big presses in the warehouse next door sprang to life, printing out the evening's edition. Rex and Minnie were still out. April hoped they found a great story but no river dwelling monsters. She had had enough of those.

All around her, the remaining staff grabbed their hats and coats, chatting with each other as they headed out the door.

Columbia reappeared from whatever errand had taken her from her desk, which reminded April that she had meant to ask Minnie when Columbia had started at the newspaper. It bothered her that she couldn't remember something as simple as that. Or when Columbia had become her direct supervisor even though April had answered to Simon when she first started. But that was before Columbia began taking over their department, April realized, and spending so much time watching April.

At her desk, Columbia quickly flipped through the contracts collected by April. "Very good," she said as she placed her hat just so upon her head and pulled on her coat. She collected a large brown handbag from her bottom desk drawer. "I need to help my sister, but I'll be back tomorrow."

With a final nod, she left too.

April glanced around the newsroom. Other than Doyle in his office, still shouting at someone on the phone about deadlines and delays, the place was deserted.

Her feet ached and she longed to go home. But glancing at the clock on the wall, April realized she had time to visit the morgue and then catch the later trolley back to the boarding house. She had promised Lefty to try to find Valentino's owners as quickly as possible.

Still puzzling over Columbia, and why the woman seemed so much a stranger when she worked in the same office, April headed for the stairs.

In the basement of the building, the rumble of the presses was much more evident. There was a tunnel which ran between the basement of the office building to the warehouse where the newspapers were produced every day. The sound carried, echoing oddly through this area. The roar of the big machines covered the tap of her footsteps as she turned and went down the hallway to the morgue. Left unlocked at all hours so reporters could do research when the mood struck, the big room was a vast cavern of filing cabinets.

The scent of newsprint and dust clogged her nose. By the door was a battered oak table piled high with newspapers and clippings. Smitty, who maintained the files of the *Arkham Advertiser's* old stories, was already gone for the day. But his desk had a good lamp on it. April switched it on, glad she didn't need to search in the shadowy spaces in the back of the morgue. The bare bulbs hanging over the filing cabinets barely provided enough light to see the years etched on the front of the drawers.

The newspapers and clippings on the long oak table interested her the most. One pile was a month's worth of recent newspapers, looking as if they'd just come from the print room and never been opened. These would be every edition printed during the week. Smitty would file two copies under the date in cabinets. Additional copies would be clipped, with stories sorted by topic and filed into a different set of cabinets. Obituaries was the cabinet closest to the door, because it was the one most frequently used by the reporters, according to Minnie. She had given April a tour of the morgue when April first started at the newspaper, even explaining how all big newspapers called their storage room for old issues after a place that storied bodies.

"It's because all the dead words are buried here," joked Minnie. But April thought the space as creepy as an actual morgue.

Besides the newspapers in the various filing cabinets, clippings of stories were logged in big ledger books filling the bookcase behind Smitty's desk. Minnie had pulled one down and shown April how to look up a reference. Next to the piles of uncut newspapers on the big table, April spotted the smaller stacks of clippings that Smitty had already made and was going to log before filing. Beside these were other folders stacked under sheets of pink notepaper with topics written on them like "1918 – The Great Flu" and "1923 – French Hill Fire". One simply said "Nightmares, Any Mention". These were probably research work requested by the reporters, who would call down to Smitty during the day if they didn't feel like grubbing through the file cabinets themselves. April wondered who was writing about nightmares.

Grabbing a handful of old unread newspapers from the table, April settled into Smitty's chair, quickly flipping through the pages to the classified advertisements at the back. Ads were not logged by Smitty so the best way to find the ad that she wanted would be to read through the actual newspapers.

Other than the swish of the pages turning under her hands, it was deadly quiet. Even the presses sounded muted and far away in this dusty tomb filled with the *Arkham Advertiser's* past.

Going back approximately three weeks, April found her vague belief that the lost dog ads started increasing recently was correct. The paper went from barely half a column of ads at the beginning of the month to nearly two full columns of owners desperate to find their pets in the last two days. But none of the ads described a poodle named Valentino.

April recalled the puppy's plump sides and fairly clean fur. Valentino hadn't been living on the streets for weeks. The dog's general good appearance suggested he had only been lost recently.

Looking through the newspapers of the past week, April found no mention of a poodle. Which, as she thought about the orders that she'd placed, made sense. She couldn't remember talking to the owner of the lost poodle. Discouraged, she flipped the pages again. In Sunday's newspaper, she suddenly spotted a small display ad asking for information about a white dog named Valentino!

"Why didn't they just call it a poodle?" April muttered as she searched for a notepad and pencil on Smitty's desk. Imprecise language in ads annoyed her. Since it was a display ad, although very small, it must have been one of Simon's orders. Which explained why she'd missed it. She rarely checked his ads unless they caused angry phone calls. This one might even have been filed on the weekend, when she wasn't at work.

April tore the ad out of the newspaper as neatly as she could. "Anyone in here?" called a woman from the doorway. "Smitty, you still around?"

Startled, April twisted in Smitty's chair. Inga Blohm stood in the doorway, her mop and bucket dangling from one hand. As broad as she was tall, her tangle of white hair was skewed up in a bun that nearly hit the top of the door frame. Inga trundled through the hallways every night while sloshing water before her in her never-ending battle with dirt and dust. Some of the reporters speculated the old Swedish woman dwelled in the basement like a troll, only emerging at the end of the day. Crack a joke like that, warned the others, and the next time that Inga caught you in the office, water would cascade over your shoes no matter how new and highly polished. Simon had been particularly perturbed by having Inga swing her dirty mop across his feet.

As April generally tried to leave the office as early as possible, she'd only run into Inga a few times. She knew Minnie liked her.

"It's just me, April May," she called, clicking off Smitty's desk lamp and tucking the ripped-out ad in her pocket.

"*Ja*, the quiet little one who sits by the phone. What are you doing here so late?" asked Inga.

"Some research," said April. "I'm helping Minnie with a story."

"More about the sea monsters?" said Inga.

"No, about a lost dog. Wait, how did you know about the sea monsters?" asked April.

Inga plunged her mop into her bucket and gave it a good swish. Pulling it out, she plopped the frayed yarn head on the floor and made broad strokes, sending a small tidal wave of water toward April's shoes. April sidestepped quickly, judging she was still on Inga's good side when none of the water hit her.

"Everyone was talking about Jack Valko seeing a glowing creature swimming up the Miskatonic this morning. But I think the dogs are the better story. You tell Minnie that."

"All right." April edged toward the door, trying to avoid the ever-growing lake of Inga's cleaning. Then, because she had to ask, she added: "Why are the dogs a better story?"

"Because they are all running away," said Inga with another swipe of the mop under the oak table. "Dogs are loyal. Dogs don't run away. Cats might leave just because the wind changes or your neighbor serves tuna on Thursday night. But it takes something big to frighten away a dog. Something they don't understand. If they are running away. Could be that someone is stealing the dogs"

April hesitated in the doorway. If she was Minnie, she'd know a dozen questions to ask. She'd know the right questions to ask. But she wasn't a reporter. She was just a junior ad salesperson who had found a lost dog. And, glancing at the clock on the wall, a junior salesperson who needed to run if she wanted to catch her streetcar.

"I'll tell Minnie what you said!" April shouted over her shoulder as she rushed for the stairs.

"You do that," Inga rumbled after her. "It might not be too late. Not yet."

CHAPTER NINE

At St Mary's Hospital, Carolyn Fern found the morning's chaos was settling into the evening's muddle. Patients were still being admitted. Carolyn overheard one nurse ask a doctor if it was time to set up beds in the corridors.

The nurses walked with quick efficiency through the hallways. Starch fairly crackling from their white aprons, they strode beside orderlies pushing gurneys laden with sleeping patients. One thing Carolyn noticed was the eerie silence. The complete lack of sound, even moans or snores, from the sleeping patients sent a prickle down her spine. This wasn't normal. Only the staff made any noise, and they seemed to be holding their comments to the barest whispers.

"Carolyn," said Head Nurse Sharon Greenberg, "can I help you?"

The nurse's normally sunny smile seemed dimmed. Carolyn judged her as tired as the rest of the staff, something that she'd never thought she'd see. Sharon was known throughout the hospital for her unflagging good spirits and kindness toward the patients.

Only yesterday afternoon, during Carolyn's final visit of the day to the hospital, Sharon still moved with purpose through a tour of the wards, stopping at a number of beds to say a few words of cheer to worried patients or their families.

"I received another call from Dr Mortimore," Carolyn told Sharon, still worrying about the other woman's obvious fatigue. "Apparently a few of my patients have been readmitted to the hospital. The nightmare cases."

Sharon sighed. "They're all here, Carolyn. And fast asleep like all the rest."

Startled, Carolyn protested. "Not all of them!"

"We referred twelve patients to you," said Sharon.

"Yes, I was treating them at my office. None had any symptoms which would indicate the need for further medical intervention," Carolyn said.

Sharon shrugged. "That may have been true then. But they are all … well, I'd describe them as catatonic. We've been unable to wake any of the sleepers." The last sentence was almost whispered. Sharon looked around and said in a more relieved tone, "Oh, here's Dr Mortimore. He can explain."

If it was possible to say the unflappable Sharon took to her heels, then Carolyn would have to describe the head nurse's quick escape down the hallway as pure flight.

Carolyn couldn't believe what she had heard was true. Not all twelve of her patients! There was nothing about them to indicate such a drastic change in their condition in less than twenty-four hours. Her own doubts nagged at her. If only she wasn't so tired, but she was sure she had not missed signs of another ailment. It was nightmares and insomnia plaguing her patients, nothing which would cause such a dramatic physical response.

"Roger," said Carolyn as soon as he approached her. "What is happening?"

"I hope you can help us," Roger Mortimore replied. Unlike

Sharon, Roger always looked tired and overworked. As the chief physician and head of patient services, furrows in his brow seemed as standard as his impeccable white lab coat. But this Roger seemed even grayer and more aged in only a few days. As he stood next to Carolyn, his gaze still roamed up and down the hallway. Carolyn could practically see him counting hospital beds in his head. His hands were wrapped white-knuckled around his clipboard.

"How bad is it?" Carolyn found herself as unwilling as the hospital staff to speak above a whisper. Could it be a new outbreak of influenza? Another year of death like 1919?

"I don't know." Roger's voice sounded strained and anguished. "Carolyn, did you give any drugs to your patients?"

"What? No, of course not!" she replied, indignation causing her voice to rise. A few staff turned their heads. "You know my methods with these patients. Hypnosis, with their consent only, and some verbal techniques for directed dream control."

"Come in here." Roger shifted one hand to her elbow and practically dragged Carolyn into an empty office. It was a tiny night nurse's station, just a single desk and chair, but it had a door that closed. Roger clicked it shut.

"Could it be the hypnosis? A delayed suggestion keeping them asleep?" Roger's questions peppered her.

Carolyn shook her head. "Impossible! Our sessions explored their fears so they could cope with the emotions generating their dreams." Even as she spoke, the doubts returned. But she had specifically eliminated the sedative from these sessions. After her experiences with Josephine Ruggles, she wanted to make sure her patients retained as much conscious control as possible during a hypnosis session. She even gave each patient what she called an "escape sequence" allowing them to end a session if their revisiting of their nightmares grew too stressful.

"Then nothing to cause them to fall into a deep sleep?" Roger looked disappointed. Obviously he had been hoping for a quick answer.

"Of course not." Carolyn reviewed each session in her head. Due to the number of patients seen over the last two days, she had not been able to spend as much time as she would have liked with each of them. No more than half an hour under hypnosis, a few minutes discussing possible methods of dream control, and then the next. Barbara had ushered one in and one out with the precision of a drill sergeant. Carolyn planned to spend a longer time with each one at a later date. She disliked the rush of seeing one patient after another, the only drawback so far to her private practice.

"I conducted a short hypnosis session with each one," she told Roger. "We concentrated on their nightmares and the fears which created their associated insomnia. As you asked, I worked with them so they could resume their normal sleep patterns."

"Carolyn, we can't wake the sleepers," said Roger. "Nothing works on them. Smelling salts, light stimulation. God help me, I even slapped Mr Gravsmore as hard as I could."

"Roger!" Carolyn was shocked by his admission of unmedical behavior.

"The man's an ex-pugilist. I doubt I hit him harder than any of his opponents. It certainly didn't disturb his slumber. He is sleeping peacefully like an oversized baby." Still, Roger was obviously upset by the incident.

"Gravsmore?" Carolyn thought for a moment. With slightly guilty relief, she realized she had not treated anyone called Gravsmore. She would remember a boxer, even a retired one. "That's not one of my patients."

"No. They are coming from all over the city. Uptown, French Hill, and Southside predominantly but there's not a neighborhood without some representative here." Roger flipped through the lists on his clipboard. "It started early this morning when family or friends failed to wake them. The patients are still being brought in."

No wonder the staff had looked upset when she had arrived at the hospital. Carolyn could not ignore the uncanny resemblance to early days of the flu pandemic, a time that Carolyn hoped would never come again.

"What could be causing it?" Carolyn hadn't realized she speculated out loud until Roger responded.

"I have no idea. I thought it might be a variation of African trypanosomiasis, sleeping sickness, but there's no symptoms of a parasite. No bite marks. No swollen lymph nodes in the armpits or groin." He paused, a quick wash of color coming and going on his face.

"Roger," Carolyn said. "I am a medical professional. You can say groin to me. Surely you discuss groins and all other body parts with the nurses."

"Of course! But they're in uniforms with caps and aprons. They are not in street clothes looking like..." He paused.

"If you say my mother or my sister," Carolyn said, "I will hit you. And then we'll have to schedule at least an hour of therapy for both of us. Possibly more. I will have to see what Freud suggests."

"Bloody Freud. Bringing sex into everything." Roger shrugged. "Of course, you're right. You're a medical colleague. You are also the only person that I know who has a connection with twelve of the patients admitted today. I was hoping it would turn out to be as simple as you recommended some tonic to them, and they recommended it to their friends."

Carolyn shook her head. "No. But it is not a bad theory. It could be something they ate or drank. You said many of the patients were from Southside or French Hill. Could it be something in the water supply?"

"Or a shared cook like Typhoid Mary spreading this from one house to another?" Roger countered. "Possibly. But there's no real connection that we've found. Except they are all well off, if not wealthy. Exactly the sort to have family or servants call an ambulance and have them admitted to the hospital."

Carolyn knew her twelve patients, all of whom were happy to pay her fees to cure their nightmares, came from similar backgrounds. It was why she'd placed an advertisement in the newspaper promising free treatment. To attract a broader clientele and gain a better understanding of why so many were apparently suffering severe nightmares.

If what was happening was a natural disease. That thought popped into her head and was distressingly difficult to dislodge.

"So you think this may be spreading through Rivertown and other areas?" she asked instead.

"Most likely. We have had one or two from the poorer neighborhoods," Roger answered. "We won't see as many of those patients until their families have exhausted every other alternative. It was the same in 1919. Nobody there wants the expense of a hospital stay if they can avoid it."

"But don't you provide charity care?" she asked.

"Certainly, but you'd be surprised how few want to ask for it. They'd rather hold on to their pride and pay what they can." Roger shook his head and frowned. "I hope they don't leave it too late. We lost so many that we could have helped during the influenza pandemic. I don't want to even speculate on what's happening in Dunwich or Innsmouth. Those communities could have the dead piling up in the street before they would even admit there is a problem."

"Some people fear bringing medical attention to their

community will cause an even greater problem than the disease itself," Carolyn agreed. There had been some unsavory stories even about St Mary's in the past. She knew a fear of doctors was not entirely unwarranted. But she also knew that Roger sought to do as much as he could to help his patients. Even if his bedside manner might leave them feeling a little like a specimen under a microscope.

"There are days when my patients seem to suspect we are still prescribing bloodletting and mercury," he muttered.

"First do no harm." Carolyn winced even as she said it. The last thing her frustrated friend needed was more platitudes.

"But how can I do good, Carolyn? When I don't even know what I am treating?" After his outburst, Roger visibly drew himself together. "If you can't help me, I must return to the lab. Perhaps the latest batch of blood samples will yield some clues as to what we are facing."

Roger swung about and let himself out of the office, striding down the hospital corridor. Nurses and orderlies drew out of his way. And, of course, the sleeping patients took no notice of the agitated doctor rushing past them.

Carolyn followed Roger into the hallway. She considered going in search of Sharon to learn more about the most recently admitted patients. But as she looked around the busy corridor, she thought the answers that she sought wouldn't be found at St Mary's.

Roger was right. They needed to find the common link between the sleeping patients. Could the cause be found in their nightmares?

Because she doubted it could be found in the blood samples that Roger had in his laboratory. She needed to examine her files again. Something her patients revealed, either in their conscious state or under hypnosis, something that she had missed but would be in those exceedingly neat notes typed up by Barbara. The answer lay there and not in a test tube. Carolyn was sure of this, if nothing else.

As Carolyn left the hospital, she decided to return to her office. Time, Carolyn was convinced, was quickly running out. Who knew how many more would succumb to this strange sleep while they searched for a cure?

CHAPTER TEN

Running out of the *Arkham Advertiser* building, April saw her trolley rolling away from the stop. Despite her shouting and arm waving, it jingled on, leaving her alone on the deserted street.

Glancing in her purse, April found that she didn't have enough money for a cab. Nobody she knew owned a car. Lefty would have returned Pequod to the garbage company's lot in Rivertown by now and walked home. He wouldn't have access to the truck until morning.

Doyle and Inga might still be in the building but the thought of going back inside and begging money for the cab sent April walking toward the train station. While she knew both were kind enough to help her, the embarrassment of admitting she had so little left until the next payday stung her. She shouldn't have bought so many lunches with Nella. Or treated herself to a sandwich from the deli when she was out collecting contracts.

Besides, the train station wasn't too far. There were other buses and trolleys that left from there. One of those would take her close enough to home.

As she walked through the neighborhood, April wondered why it was so quiet. Usually, delivery trucks rumbled through the district at all hours. Either picking up from the river warehouses and factories or dropping off supplies. She knew there were even a few speakeasies in the neighborhood. Minnie talked about going into those, trying to nose out a story or a drink.

But if anything was open, April didn't see it. Or hear it. The streets were eerily still. The sun had set. The twilight glow in the sky meant it really wasn't night yet. Even after sunset, the incandescent streetlamps made walking in this area perfectly safe, April reassured herself. But she still scurried past the darker openings to the alleys, the memory of that strange afternoon encounter with the glowing tentacle never far from her thoughts.

The clang of a distant trolley bell made April hurry in hopes of spotting the streetcar. But she turned the corner to see only the hulking silhouettes of warehouses looming on either side of the street. The chemical smell of the nearby textile factories mingled with the strong stench of fish processing plants nearer the river.

Sharp pains ran up her heels. A day of walking around Arkham was making itself felt in April's feet and the backs of her legs. She just wanted to go home and collapse into the boarding house's big tub.

April reached another crossroads and considered the best way to proceed to the train station. If she continued straight ahead, it meant a few more empty streets of factories and warehouses closed for the day. A short cut through the tenements which clogged the neighborhood near the train station might take less time. But ever since she'd started at the *Advertiser*, she'd been warned away from the area, especially at night. Nella and she had ventured down there one lunch break, discussing how taking an apartment so close to their jobs would save them money and time. The apartment they'd viewed had been horrible. A tiny, nearly windowless set of rooms in a grimy brick building. As they'd stepped back out onto the street and viewed the laundry lines stretching between the wrought-iron fire escapes, along with the pong of boiling cabbage drifting from open windows, they had decided Mrs Garcia's clean, fluffy beds and wholesome meals made far more sense than a room within walking distance of their offices.

But the area at lunchtime had been full of people. Children playing stickball in the street. Men in overalls heading back to jobs with their wives or girlfriends striding beside them as they went to their own work. She'd liked the liveliness of grandmothers sitting out on the stoops, calling to the kids in a half dozen languages and commenting on all the other passersby to each other.

Opting for the way which would put her among crowds and take the least time, April chose the left-hand road.

An unsettling stillness pervaded this block as well. Though the streetlamps provided small puddles of light, April felt a distinct chill as she walked down the shadowy street. The sound of her heels seemed unnaturally loud.

April stopped. She still didn't see anyone else on the streets. No grannies or mothers hung over the fire escapes shouting at the children to come home and get ready for bed. No young men clustered on the corner, smoking cigarettes and discussing in loud voices all the things they planned to do when they were paid on Friday. Nor were there any young women equally gathered on opposite sides of the street, ignoring the young men throwing boasts like roses at them. April had grown up in such a neighborhood. In this hour after supper, a bit of relaxation and fun entered the place as people took a moment for themselves after a day of hard physical labor.

But there was nobody on the streets. The doors of apartment buildings were shut tight. Looking up, April saw curtains drawn across each closed window. Not even a cat or dog slinked among the garbage cans set by the curb for tomorrow's pick-up.

It was as if the whole street had barricaded itself against the oncoming night.

The complete emptiness spooked her. Something about the buildings stirred memories of her nightmares. Suddenly she felt as if a glance would reveal a distant tower. More distressing, the feeling that something horrible loomed over the city took hold of her. But this was ordinary, everyday Arkham, not some alien world where a trolley driven by ants would run her down. Also, there was no masked man dressed in robes of gold to chase her away.

Much to her own embarrassment, April found herself looking over her shoulder just to make sure there was no mystery man standing in the road. Of course, there wasn't.

However, a short distance away, she spotted a watchman's hut outside a junkyard. The lighted window indicated someone was there. She crossed the street, intent on asking what had happened. Could there have been some accident at one of the factories? What had caused such a complete absence of people? Through the dirty glass of the window, she saw the watchman tipped back in his chair. The man appeared to be asleep. Although April rapped and called through the glass, he never stirred.

An unmistakable chugging sound grew steadily louder in the distance. April heard the harsh blast of a train's whistle as it pulled into the station. She left the watchman behind as she hurried toward the sound, the pain in her feet almost forgotten as she ran toward a station full of light, sound, and, she hoped, people.

CHAPTER ELEVEN

During the long trolley ride back to the boarding house, April observed that the rest of Arkham seemed as strangely deserted as Northside. The odd air of anticipation, of waiting for something to happen, pervaded the empty streets. Again, April was reminded of her recent nightmares, of the persistent feeling that whatever horrors she encountered were nothing compared to the horror to be found just beyond the tower in her dreams.

When she got off the trolley, the rain began to fall. Just a few drops, not hard enough to get truly wet. Still, April hurried down the block.

With some relief, she entered the boarding house, which smelled faintly of dinner. The usual group of boarders were gathered in the parlor. But as soon as she stepped through the door, April realized something was wrong. Mr and Mrs Sullivan sat on the sofa, clutching each other's hands. Ollie was huddled into the chair by the window. Most unusually, Mrs Garcia occupied the opposite chair. Like Ollie, she sat slumped in her chair, seemingly drained of all energy. Strangest of all, Lefty occupied a straight-backed chair in the corner of the room that was rarely used. He held a newspaper in his hands, but he didn't appear to be reading it. His reading glasses were hooked into the top pocket of his overalls.

"What has happened?" April asked as she stepped into the room.

"April! You're home!" Ollie pulled herself out of her chair. The nurse's warm brown eyes looked her over. April realized that she was undergoing an inspection for possible injuries. Ollie must assess her patients in the hospital in the same way. "Thank goodness that you are all right!" Ollie said, confirming April's supposition.

"I missed the trolley," April said. "So I walked to the train station and took the later bus here." She almost mentioned the eerily empty streets, but everyone looked so worried that she didn't want to upset them further. She was home and safe, that was all that mattered. She'd discuss it later with Nella.

"So good you are back," murmured Mrs Garcia. "There's a plate in the kitchen for you."

Her statement shocked April. If boarders missed a meal, they needed to find their own food outside of the house. That was one of Mrs Garcia's most cherished rules. If she'd saved some dinner for her, then something must be terribly wrong.

"What has happened?" April asked again.

"It's Nella," said Ollie. "She won't wake up."

April shook her head, confused. People didn't just fall asleep and stay asleep, not healthy strong people like Nella.

Mrs Garcia nodded. "Sally too. Nothing we do will wake them. They sleep like the dead." She crossed herself. "But they are still alive."

"What can we do?" April said. Ollie was a nurse. Surely she had answers. "Should we call a doctor?"

Ollie sighed. "I am not sure that will help. We have been seeing patients like this all day at the hospital. None of the doctors have the answer." The last sentence came out very softly for Ollie, who often had a nurse's cynical opinion of the infallibility of doctors but sounded more scared than April had ever heard. It was Ollie's reaction which finally frightened April, who had never seen the Black woman look so distressed.

"We could still take them to St Mary's," rumbled Lefty in his corner.

Ollie shook her head. "There are almost no beds free. I think it would be better to leave them here." For all her grumbling about her job, Ollie often spoke with immense pride about the modern facilities of St Mary's. April couldn't believe what she was hearing. Ollie was advising them against going to her cherished hospital.

Although looking equally troubled, Mrs Garcia agreed. "Better we care for them in their own rooms," she said. Then she added, "It's the same in the other houses. Two or three of the boarders stay asleep, no matter what anyone does. And Mrs Alba also does not wake up." The latter was one of the ladies who ran a boarding house and a good friend of Mrs Garcia.

"But there must be something that we can do." Even as she said it, April felt hopeless and empty of ideas. She was absolutely exhausted by her day. Her feet hurt. She wanted nothing more than to sit down in the kitchen and eat whatever dinner Mrs Garcia had saved for her. Then she wanted to take a hot bath and go to bed. Well, actually, she was a little afraid to go to bed. She wondered if she could sleep upright in a chair in the parlor. She wondered if that was why everyone else was huddled in the room now.

But most of all, April wanted to talk to Nella about everything that was happening. Nella couldn't be asleep. She wouldn't leave April all on her own to handle whatever was happening. April might be the one who saved her money. She might be the sensible one who went to work on time and stayed in a job (no matter how much she disliked it). But Nella was the one who made plans. Nella was the one who always knew what they should do next. She really needed to talk to Nella.

Although Ollie was practically swaying on her feet, she muttered something about checking on Sally and Nella. Mrs Garcia asked if she needed any help, but the tired nurse just shook her head. "There is not much we can do," she said. "I only hope they are having sweet dreams instead of nightmares."

April snapped up her head, the last word catching her attention and distracting her from her worries about Nella. "I met a woman today," she said. "A doctor of sorts, a psychologist. Carolyn Fern."

A brief smile lit Ollie's face. "I know her," she said. "She consults at the hospital. A decent woman." Which from Ollie was heartfelt praise.

"We could call her," April said. This was something that she could do. Much better than just sitting in the parlor and worrying about what came next.

Mrs Garcia looked troubled. "A doctor would be expensive," she said. "Better we find a *bruja*, a healing woman." If naps and chicken soup did not cure whatever ailed their tenants, the landladies of Flotsam Street often broke out various herbal teas. The most powerful concoctions were created by Mrs Alba, who was regarded as something of a white witch as far as April could understand their rapid Spanish explanations. But Mrs Alba was among those fast asleep, which meant Mrs Garcia must be suggesting finding someone else in Rivertown or even outside the neighborhood. Which would take time.

"Carolyn Fern was offering to treat patients with nightmares for free," April said, recalling the ad placed by the psychologist. "Perhaps she will come here," she suggested, even though she recalled the ad had been for patients to be seen at her office. Despite April's fears of hypnosis, the doctor seemed like a nice person. April wasn't sure what Carolyn could do if the patient was asleep, but trying something would be better than nothing.

"You could still see if there is a *bruja* able to help," she told Mrs Garcia.

Their landlady nodded. "It is best to fight," she said, quite unexpectedly. "Better than sitting still and suffering from despair again." The shadow of 1919 lay across her face. April had heard the number of dead in Rivertown during the flu pandemic had been extraordinary. Some people even said that the nearby Christchurch Cemetery had expanded its borders to accommodate all its new residents. But then others said all of Rivertown was built on graves, an attempt by the early residents of Arkham to carve out livable land near the river. It was a part of the neighborhood history that April preferred not to think about.

Mr and Mrs Sullivan raised their heads. The couple nodded at Mrs Garcia, like two wind-up dolls in absolute accord.

"We have a little money," whispered Mrs Sullivan.

"We will help pay for whatever medicine is needed," added her husband.

Lefty stirred in his corner. "We will all help," he said. "Mrs Garcia is right."

"So who will make the call?" asked Mrs Garcia.

"I will go to Mrs Alba's tonight and use the phone there," said April. "It was my idea."

"Do you need a nickel?" asked Mrs Garcia, who would know exactly how much Mrs Alba charged for phone calls.

"No, I have one," April said. At least she was still in her coat and hat. Better yet, she was doing something. As Nella always said, you had to keep moving to get ahead. Although Nella usually used that phrase as an excuse to quit a job that she didn't like.

Delaying dinner, April went across the street to find the subdued residents of Mrs Alba's boarding house also huddled in the parlor, whispering about what they should do. When April told them that she was calling a doctor, they still looked worried.

"There are only three of us awake," said one thin girl, who looked slightly younger than April, not yet out of her teens. "I work nights at a café downtown. The others have to go to work too. What if she calls back? I can't stay here. I'm the only waitress on the midnight shift."

April reassured them that she would have the doctor call her at her workplace. "I am sure she is not in her office, but she must have an answering service. Do you need help here?"

"Mrs Chiebek has only one woman asleep at her house. She's sending a couple of her boarders to sit with Mrs Alba and the others."

"Then if Carolyn Fern calls here, they can run a message to us. I will leave a note by the phone," April said. "But she probably won't call back until morning. I will be at the office then."

The thin girl pleated her dress between nervous fingers but finally nodded. She was new to Flotsam Street and April didn't know her name. "Perhaps it will help." But the young woman didn't sound hopeful.

"I'm sure it will," April said with more confidence than she actually felt. But if she sounded as if she believed it, perhaps this waitress would feel better. "I'm April May. What's your name?"

"Frieda," she said with a faint smile. "I don't like it much. Most people call me Freddy. I've used that since grade school, although my father hates it." April guessed Freddy changed her name during the war. Most kids with German sounding names did so, to avoid being teased or bullied.

April dropped a nickel in the jar. Then she called the operator, asking for a call to be put through to Carolyn Fern's office. As she suspected, the doctor paid for an answering service. When a calm voice asked for a message, she nearly collapsed with relief. April tried to be as concise as possible, very aware of a stranger writing down her words, and hung up wondering if

Carolyn would be able to make heads or tails out of her garbled sentences.

After promising Freddy that she'd tell her as soon as she heard anything, and leaving a note by the phone just in case Carolyn called Mrs Alba's house, April went home. As she crossed the street back to Mrs Garcia's house, she noticed lights shining in the parlor windows of the other boarding houses. She wondered how many were sitting up, discussing what to do, and how many were fast asleep in their beds.

April slipped back into the entry with a sense of relief that they had done something.

Ollie came down the stairs, shaking her head when she saw April. "No change at all," said the nurse in a dispirited tone of voice.

April told her about the phone call and Freddy's worries. Also that Mrs Chiebek had one woman asleep but was sending her boarders to help at Mrs Alba's.

"I'll go over there and check on Mrs Alba," Ollie said, "and visit Mrs Chiebek."

"Thank you!" April replied. "I hope Carolyn Fern calls back tomorrow."

"If not, I can look for Carolyn at the hospital," said Ollie. "I've seen her there a couple of times since Sunday." Ollie's twelve-hour shifts ran from Sunday to Friday, with Saturdays off. Ollie often said this schedule was far better than the twenty-four hours on duty that she experienced before the war. Ollie also made five dollars a day at St Mary's, which she was scrupulously saving to buy her own house in the future. She hoped to rent rooms to teachers, like Sally, she told April.

April sighed. "I wish I could think of something else to help. Can I sit with Nella? Will that be all right?"

"Of course. You can sit and talk to her. Maybe she'll wake up if she hears a familiar voice," said Ollie. "It certainly can't hurt."

But April had a feeling that Ollie's reassuring words were for herself and not because April had suddenly discovered a cure. After all, they must have tried talking to Nella and Sally already. She couldn't see either Ollie or Mrs Garcia staying silent in such a situation.

"I'm glad to hear there's only a couple of people asleep at each boarding house," Ollie said. "I was worried there would be more than that."

As the nurse spoke, a boom of thunder shook the house. Then they heard it, a torrent of rain falling outside, striking the street almost as hard as hailstones. Mrs Garcia came out into the hallway.

"If the roof leaks now," she said, "I will scream."

Lefty followed her out of the parlor. As usual, he appeared calm and able to deal with things, like April's Uncle Tito. "I'll check the attics," Lefty said, "and the basement. I'll stop any leaks I find."

"There are buckets at the top of the attic stairs," said Mrs Garcia in the tone of one who knows that disasters come not only in pairs but sometimes entire crowds.

Lefty nodded and headed toward the attics.

"Now you," said Mrs Garcia to April, "come into the kitchen and eat something. We do not need more sick people in this house." And she clapped a hand to April's forehead, to test for a fever. Not finding any sign of heat, she seemed pleased. "Then you will have a wash and a nap. Then it will be morning. We will survive this." The last came out as something of a growl for Mrs Garcia. "We always survive on Flotsam Street."

April followed her militant landlady into the kitchen for her long-delayed supper.

CHAPTER TWELVE

It wasn't until the next morning that April remembered the poodle. Like the rest of the house, she was up well before dawn, having slept only briefly while curled up in a chair in the parlor. She remembered Lefty passing through the room once or twice on his patrol of patching and stopping potential leaks, but he was not there when she awoke. Mr and Mrs Sullivan still occupied the center of the sofa, leaning against each other, their hands intertwined. Both were snoring very softly with their heads on their chests.

Ollie was the only one who had gone up to her bed. They'd all been a bit relieved to hear her walking between her room and the others all through the night, checking on Nella and Sally. Once or twice, she crossed the street to Mrs Alba's house and then circled through the other houses before returning home.

Outside April could still hear rain coming down but at least the thunder and lightning seemed to be over. The booms and brilliant flashes of light had continued well past midnight, helping to keep everyone in the house awake. Except, of course, Sally and Nella. April would have gladly had the thunder continue if it had woken the sleepers.

April found Mrs Garcia and Ollie in the kitchen. Mrs Garcia was cracking eggs into a frying pan while Ollie sipped coffee from a large mug. At the sight of April, she nodded to the kitchen chair next to her. Today it seemed breakfast would be in the kitchen rather than the dining room where the boarders usually ate.

"How is Nella?" April whispered to her. Something about the atmosphere of the house, with its sleeping residents, kept her from speaking loudly. She'd slipped upstairs once or twice in the night to peek into Nella's room, but hadn't had the courage to go in. Her old fears of doing the wrong thing when somebody was ill washed over her. Better to leave the nursing to Ollie, who knew how to properly take care of someone. But now April felt terrible about not spending more time upstairs and trying to help.

Ollie seemed to have caught the subdued mood of the house as she whispered back the same answer that she'd given all night. "No change. Sally is still asleep too." The last came out as a pained whisper.

Looking closely at the Black woman, April thought she saw tears in Ollie's eyes. Exhaustion was grinding them down. April longed for another hour of sleep, but she had to go to work. She needed the money. Besides, Carolyn Fern might return her call. The psychologist might have the answers that would solve all their problems.

"The rain is worse," observed Mrs Garcia, glancing out of the window over the sink.

Welcoming the distraction, April went to the kitchen door and opened it, mostly for the fresh air to blow away the tired cobwebs in her brain. The boarding house's small backyard looked like a sea of mud. Glancing at the door of the basement, she noticed Lefty had rolled a number of burlap bags and stuffed them along the edge of the door.

Mrs Garcia joined her on the back stoop. "We have a little

water in the basement. It ran under the door and down the stairs," she said. "Lefty came up for a mop about an hour ago. Now he has a rake and is checking the drains on Flotsam Street. Then he will go for his truck."

She gave the entire litany in the tired voice of a woman who fully expected a plague of locusts to descend upon them next. Then Mrs Garcia turned back to the kitchen and her place at the stove. She lifted the cast iron frying pan from the counter to the hot stove.

Brightening slightly, Ollie said, "Maybe Lefty can hang on to the truck for later. They'll probably be passing out sandbags before the end of the day." She spoke like a woman happy to be making a suggestion rather than reporting grim news.

Mrs Garcia gave an affirmative grunt as she flipped the eggs from the frying pan onto a warm plate.

"Sandbags?" asked April. With a start, she remembered Valentino and wondered how the poor poodle was doing in a damp basement. "Why would we want sandbags?"

"If the river is rising," Mrs Garcia said, "then this street floods. Especially on a day of bad luck like this."

Flotsam Street was near the river and directly downhill from French Hill, April knew, but she hadn't thought of floods.

"Some say that's how the street got its name," added Ollie. "Things wash up here when the floods come. But it hasn't happened in years."

"If it is not too bad, we can stay here and sandbag the basement doors," Mrs Garcia said.

"And if it is too bad?" April asked, thinking of Nella and Sally fast asleep in their beds. Of Mr and Mrs Sullivan exhausted by a mere night of sitting up with the rest of them. Of the other four boarding houses full of sleeping residents.

"If Lefty can keep the truck today, it will be no problem. It is a big truck," said Mrs Garcia.

Ollie nodded. "Exactly what I was thinking."

"It is a garbage truck," April protested.

"The rain will wash it clean," Mrs Garcia responded. "We will wrap the sleepers up in blankets to keep them dry and warm."

"If we have to evacuate. But I think it would be better to stay in the house," said Ollie. She grabbed the small notepad and stubby pencil that Mrs Garcia used to make shopping lists.

"Here's some ways to keep the sleepers comfortable," Ollie said as she scribbled on the pad. "I agree it's risky to try to move people in Lefty's truck, but if you have to, you can. Just be sure to keep everyone as warm and dry as possible if they need to be moved. There's extra shawls and scarves in Sally's room, in that trunk where she keeps her knitting. Bundle everyone up with those. There's probably enough for the whole street."

Ollie handed the list to Mrs Garcia, who tucked it into her apron pocket. "I need to go to St Mary's before the trolley stops running," Ollie said. Storms, snow, or just a very bad day of ice often stopped the service in their neighborhood. April knew what it was like to hike several blocks up French Hill in search of a trolley or bus still running. French Hill, unlike Rivertown, kept its trolley service unless the entire city was shut down. It helped to have a neighborhood of rich people close by. Their streets were always plowed and salted first.

And, April thought, any flood waters probably wouldn't reach French Hill. They could go there if things got worse.

Lefty came splashing through the backyard. Wrapped in an old oilskin coat and wearing a battered sou'wester hat, he carried the wooden rake that Mrs Garcia used to keep leaves off the lawn in the autumn.

From the doorway, Mrs Garcia called, "What do you think?"

Lefty shrugged. "It is not bad yet. I cleaned the grates at both ends of the street. The water is going down the storm drains."

"But the river?" asked Mrs Garcia

"The Miskatonic is well below its banks. It is running fast but nobody seems too worried. The talk was all about the sleepers at Schoffner's," he said. Davy Schoffner's General Store served as something of a Rivertown club. There was always a group gathered around the potbelly stove in the back of the store, ostensibly to play checkers. In truth, they came to drink cheap coffee from the pot Davy kept warm on the stove and exchange news about the neighborhood.

Most of the potbelly stove club lived in the tumbling down brick rowhouses closest to the river. Compared to those, the boarding houses on Flotsam Street were as fancy as French Hill. And far safer. Fire had ripped through one row near the general store not more than a year ago, leaving behind a new set of empty lots overgrown with weeds.

Lefty stepped into the kitchen to lean the rake by the back door. "I might need it again," he said. "But I have to finish moving my books higher on the shelves. April, can you help me?"

April nodded and trotted down the basement stairs on Lefty's heels, glad to have something to do. She would need to leave soon for work, but she was due far later at the *Arkham Advertiser* than Ollie needed to report to St Mary's. And April was beginning to sympathize with Nella's attitude. On a day like today, what would it matter if the most junior advertising person was a few minutes late? It wasn't as if she could wake the sleepers by taking another classified ad order. Besides, she really wanted to pet and possibly hug the puppy that they rescued. That was something that she had accomplished, even though it seemed weeks ago rather than just yesterday.

The basement smelled a little damp but there was no sign of water on the floors. Lefty had rolled up his rugs and set them to dry on the counter where he normally kept his dishes. Books and magazines had been pulled from the lower shelves and stacked on the table or chairs. In one crate full of newspapers, also put as high as possible on the table, was Valentino. The puppy's nose rested on the edge of the box, but his ears flicked forward when April went to pet him.

The dog was mostly asleep, probably still exhausted from his earlier adventures, thought April.

"You should take Valentino upstairs," said Lefty.

"What will Mrs Garcia say?" April scratched the poodle under the chin. The little dog gave a contented sigh. "Do you think the street will be flooded?"

"I hope not," said Lefty. "But there was some water down here this morning. It would be safer if you took Valentino."

"I'll take him to the office," April decided. "Minnie can grab a picture with the owners." She told Lefty how she had found an advertisement listing a dog which sounded like Valentino but had forgotten all about it when she arrived home. "I was so worried about Nella. I'm still worried about Nella. I forgot all about poor Valentino." She scratched the dog again. The poodle sighed.

"You'll need something for a leash." Lefty rummaged around in one box, finally pulling out a long cord. "This should do. If you can leave now, I can take you both in Pequod to the *Advertiser*. You will have to walk with me to the truck yard."

"Oh, that would be easier than trying to take Valentino on the trolley or inside the house!" said April, dashing back up the basement stairs. "I will be ready to go in ten minutes."

Back inside the kitchen, she told Mrs Garcia that Lefty would give her a ride to work. Ollie had already left for St Mary's.

"What about the doctor you called last night?" Mrs Garcia asked.

"I left the number of the *Advertiser*," said April. "Carolyn Fern should call me there. If she calls Mrs Alba's phone, there's a note and someone will come to you with a message. If Ollie sees Carolyn at the hospital, she will tell her about Nella and Sally."

All contingencies covered, she paused. "But will you be able to cope, Mrs Garcia?"

Mrs Garcia shrugged. "Two people sleeping. Two people left to feed. That is not hard. Mr and Mrs Sullivan will help me keep an eye on Sally and Nella. I will be fine. As long as you take the dog with you."

April froze. "What dog?"

"The one that Lefty carried into the basement last night." Mrs Garcia gave her a bland look. "When you are talking on the basement stairs, I can hear you." She stamped her foot on the kitchen floor and the boards wobbled a little. "The stairs are right below these. Also, the dog barked every time there was a clap of thunder."

"I am sorry," April said. "It is a lost dog, but I think I know how to find the owners. We just needed some place to keep poor Valentino last night."

"It was a bad night for anything to be lost and outside," said Mrs Garcia. "No harm was done."

"Thank you, Mrs Garcia, you are the best landlady in all of Arkham," said April.

Mrs Garcia waved away the thanks but added, "Be careful. I do not like this rain."

"Oh, it will stop," April promised. "It always does."

But Mrs Garcia seemed unconvinced.

As April left the backyard with Valentino, she spotted her landlady watching them from the kitchen window. The poodle resisted the idea of venturing outside in the rain, but finally succumbed to a bit of bacon waved as a lure. Now Valentino bravely splashed through the puddles. April waved goodbye to Mrs Garcia. Her landlady still looked very worried. The rain continued to fall.

CHAPTER THIRTEEN

Carolyn Fern barely slept. When dawn came, she was already up and groping for the coffee grinder in her tiny kitchen.

Thunder and her own worries kept waking her the night before. By midnight, she gave up and turned on the light. Then she started on the mystery novel beside her bed. Augusta Palmer gave it to her on the ship with a slightly caustic recommendation. Augusta's name was written in a neat script at the front of the book, with a note "To Augusta, with love from her sisters."

The novel served as a distraction from the medical records of her patients, which refused to yield the answers that she needed. She had reviewed the stack of folders that she'd fetched from her office until her eyes crossed. Carolyn couldn't stand to read her patients' accounts one more time. There was no rational reason that healthy people should be so overcome by their night terrors as to slip into a coma-like state. Her perusal of the reference materials frustratingly failed to reveal any answers as well.

Carolyn hadn't stayed in the office building as long as she planned. As it had earlier in the week, the walls of the office kept closing around her. Something felt terribly wrong there. So she brought her files home with her, something that was sure to upset the neat Barbara if she didn't return them in the morning to the proper cabinets. At least she made it home before the storm started.

Despite the foul weather, she probably should have stayed at the office. But the silent floors, the lack of people in the other offices, disturbed her.

Which, whenever she thought about it rationally, rather annoyed her too. After all, she wasn't like the ninny in *The House of Dr Edwardes* who stayed in the isolated asylum clearly run by the inmates as people were murdered around her. Who thought up such ridiculous plots?

Augusta Palmer had passed the mystery to her after finishing it. Carolyn vaguely recollected the other woman telling her that it clearly showed all the prejudices against their profession and their patients. "The majority of the practitioners at the asylum are incompetent or outright villains," she said with a laugh. "Even the vaunted Dr Edwardes makes you question the sanity of the profession. Who would go off on vacation and leave the most newly hired doctors in charge? And install a gate which can lock everyone out of the asylum, so you're forced to use a ladder to return to your place of work?"

"Well, I suppose if everyone did the rational thing, then there wouldn't be much suspense," Carolyn said.

"I can forgive the descriptions of the doctors, but the lunatics are worse," replied Augusta with some heat. "As if the inmates lack the ability to have practical thoughts at any time. It's the worst kind of tripe, depicting the chief lunatic as a homicidal maniac intent on currying favor with some supernatural power. This one was particularly taken with Satanic rituals and able to pass himself off as a doctor!"

"Then why read it?" asked Carolyn.

"Oh, it is always good to know how the public perceives us," said the other woman. "If only to be able to counter their fears with our rational behavior."

But after only an hour of reading, Carolyn gave up. She flipped to the end, and then sighed in exasperation at the resolution of the novel. Of course the ninny fainted and had to be rescued. Augusta was right about the gate, too. It was a ridiculously complicated way to "guard" the patients and the general public. She was also correct about the portrayal of the patients. Some of them might be called clinically insane, but a number seemed to be simply frightened men and women, unable to cope with a highly unusual situation. Only one could actually be called a homicidal maniac and he was the most unrealistic of the bunch.

For some reason, this reminded her of another conversation with Augusta Palmer, when the woman abruptly asked her, "Do you consider yourself sane?"

"Yes." Carolyn didn't hesitate. Her pride in her mind had carried her through many trials.

"But how do you know?" Augusta asked. "By your own diagnosis? By the judgment of others? I assume Lizzie Borden considered herself sane. But would a woman who chopped up her stepmother be judged sane by others?"

"Wasn't she acquitted?" asked Carolyn, who vaguely remembered reading something about the case after Borden's death. Borden died not far from Arkham and a recounting of the famous trial appeared in the back pages of the *Arkham Advertiser* shortly afterward.

"Well, she was a clever witch," said Augusta. "She and her sister inherited all the family money. But they couldn't stifle the nursery rhyme. Forty whacks for thirty-five years of living in a grand style even though she was shunned by the neighbors. I can think of worse fates. So would you call Lizzie sane or insane?"

"I would have to interview her," Carolyn said. "Many times," she added more firmly. "A diagnosis of insanity is not something to be done lightly."

"How very reassuring," said Augusta.

Determined to relax, Carolyn got out of bed and examined her own bookshelves. She pulled out every book that she had on dreams and sleep, some so old as to qualify as antiques. Then she returned to bed, propping herself up on the pillows to read.

Once or twice, she felt as if she was about to slip into a dream, only to find herself blinking at the flashes of lightning visible through the edges of her bedroom curtains. Eventually she gave up on all pretense of research, dropping the books in a heap on the floor. Carolyn thought of the sedative and the syringe in her dresser drawer. Perhaps sending herself into a trance state would enable her to find an answer.

Where she would find herself or her answer after using it, Carolyn dared not hope. She slid out of bed again and crossed the room. But to her confusion, she found the bottle of sedative was nearly empty. She had no memory of using it recently. In fact, she was certain it had been full when she brought the bottle home from the sanatorium.

The headache of the last few days increased, as did her frustration with her own memory. Could she have been mistaken about the number of doses remaining when she brought the vial home? Had she used it on herself and forgotten? Carolyn stared into the dresser mirror as if it could reveal the answers that she was almost afraid to find. The world revealed by Josephine's dreams still called to her. The knowledge of the human psyche that it could reveal always tempted her. But had her obsession begun to cloud her good judgment? Carolyn rolled the cool glass vial between her fingers, shaking it and holding it up to the light. One dose left. Did she want to use it tonight? Previous attempts had been less than satisfactory. She had achieved the deep trance that she desired but the steps, the pathway, and, more importantly, what lay beyond had eluded her.

Reluctantly Carolyn replaced the bottle in her drawer. With so little left, it seemed a pity to waste the last dose on a night nearly gone already. That the emptiness of the bottle alarmed her, she strove to ignore.

Rather, she told herself, it would be better to wait until she had more time and, with luck, Augusta to work with her. From their discussions on the ship, Carolyn believed Augusta would be sympathetic, even enthusiastic, to learn more about the journeys the mind could take in a dreaming hypnotic state. Carolyn wished she could remember when Augusta was scheduled to return to Arkham. She needed to ask Barbara when she saw her next. Barbara would know the answer.

As if Barbara's name was one of the hypnotic commands that she gave to patients, Carolyn felt herself relax. Tomorrow would see the discovery of a solution, she was sure. Back in the order and calm that Barbara created in Augusta's office, she would find a way to help her patients.

Returning to her bed, Carolyn finally fell asleep only to be instantly awakened by her alarm clock's jangling bell. She lay in bed trying to recall her dreams but found there was frustratingly nothing to remember. No impressions at all, which was strange, as she was usually a vivid dreamer.

After she dressed and made her usual breakfast of black coffee and an apple, she pulled the patients' files open one more time. Her next reading of her patients' dream accounts preoccupied her through two cups of coffee. She noted all her patients described a tower, but Carolyn felt this was a red herring. It was not the tower which was important. More intriguing was the number who talked about something lurking behind the tower, which gave her the feeling that she was searching for "who" rather than "what." With the vexatious tendency of dreams, none of her patients clearly described what they believed was so evident in the moment.

But her review of the files in the light of morning, or her cups of coffee, gave Carolyn an idea to take to the hospital as she went to inquire about her sleeping patients.

As she gathered her belongings, Carolyn noticed the drawer of her dressing table was slightly ajar. Mindful of the sedative stored there, she clicked the drawer closed. It wasn't until much later that she remembered the nearly empty vial and the fear it engendered.

CHAPTER FOURTEEN

As they drove from Rivertown to Northside, April noticed the city seemed unusually subdued. Even as early as it was, she expected to see more people abroad. Factory jobs started soon after dawn. Where were the workers?

Perhaps it was the unrelenting rain, but the streets were nearly bare of pedestrians. Only a few cars went splashing by. April saw, as she clutched Valentino to her lap, there were no dogs or cats anywhere. Strange that the lack of animals should be so evident in these industrial neighborhoods, but she could remember seeing sly tomcats slinking around garbage cans or stray dogs running along the edge of the road. Now there were none.

The empty streets troubled April with echoes of recent nightmares. But her dreams involved woods and paths or eyeballs rolling about, she reminded herself. Not rain-washed buildings no matter how sinister the familiar streets now seemed. As she kept repeating to herself, it was simply a dismally wet day.

"I wish the rain would stop," she said to Lefty.

He just grunted as he turned the heavy garbage truck down an unfamiliar side street. If he was worried about the state of the streets or the water now overflowing the gutters, April thought he would surely say something. That he was silent was a good sign, she told herself.

Or perhaps not, she thought, glancing at the heavy creases visible on his brow as they came up to an intersection which resembled a small pond.

"I'm going to take a shortcut through there," he said to April, nodding at a side street. "We should be at your building in a few minutes."

In this stretch, the road ran alongside the Miskatonic but there was no standing water in the road. The muddy river was still well below the banks, but April couldn't recall ever seeing it moving so fast. She said as much to Lefty.

"Must be raining even harder upriver," he said with a glance at the rushing water.

"Will Flotsam Street flood?" April asked, voicing the worry which seemed small next to the problem of Nella and Sally still asleep in their beds. Except if the street flooded, how would they get help for the sleepers? Where would they go?

Lefty chewed his lip, taking his time to answer. April had a feeling that it was like their encounter in the alley. That he was trying to figure out what to say without frightening her.

"I'm not a screamer," she said out loud. But what she meant was she'd rather know what was going on than be frightened by the thoughts that neither of them cared to talk about.

A corner of Lefty's lips quirked up in a faint smile. "Nah, you're not a screamer," he said. "You're a sensible young woman. Brave too."

This compliment had the usual effect of leaving April even more tongue tied than usual, but Lefty didn't seem to notice.

"Everyone thinks the river will stay below flood levels during the day," he said.

By everyone, April guessed he meant the potbelly stove philosophers of Schoffner's General Store.

"But if the Miskatonic keeps rising at its current rate, they think it will crest after midnight. Then Arkham will flood," he said.

April looked out of the truck's windows, trying to imagine the streets full of water. How bad could it be? She'd never been in a flood and she didn't know what to expect. She definitely felt unprepared.

As if he could hear her thoughts, Lefty said, "Don't stay late tonight. Come to the yard and I'll give you a ride home." By the yard, he meant the grim incinerator where Arkham's garbage was turned into black smoke every night. April had been there a few times and found it a sinister place.

"I will meet you there," she said.

"Good," said Lefty. "I will wait for you."

His curt instructions told April more than he was saying. He was worried about the potential flooding, and it wouldn't be safe to be on the streets alone. She curled her fingers into Valentino's collar. The little dog wiggled on her lap and aimed a lick in the general direction of her hand, possibly still smelling slightly of bacon.

Lefty took a hard right and then another left, bringing them back to the street running in front of the *Arkham Advertiser*'s main entrance.

"Will someone be there?" he said with a nod at the doors.

"Always," said April, sliding out of the cab. "They never lock the doors because people come and go at all hours."

"Take care," Lefty said. "I have to start my rounds."

"I will be fine. We'll find Valentino's owner today. Perhaps Dr Fern has received our messages. She might know how to wake Nella and Sally," April said, trying to put as much positive energy as she could into her statement. Despite Ollie's reports of so many sleepers at the hospital, April wanted to believe the calm professional woman that she'd met only yesterday would have the answer to their problem.

"I hope she can help," Lefty responded in an unconscious echo of April's own thoughts. Then with a wave, he started up Pequod again and rolled down the street, heading toward his first garbage pick-up of the day.

CHAPTER FIFTEEN

Although it was still very early in the morning, and well before visiting hours, nobody at the hospital seemed surprised to see Carolyn there. From what she saw and overheard, the staff either stayed the night or returned as quickly as they could.

At St Mary's, Carolyn saw the nurses setting out oil lamps in special niches and tables along the halls. The lights flickering overhead indicated this was a sensible precaution.

"I don't know what we will do if the electricity goes out," said one young nurse to an older one instructing her on how to trim the wick and light the lamp if necessary.

"My dear girl," said the older nurse, "if Florence Nightingale and Clara Barton could nurse by lamplight, so can you! After all, we didn't have electric lights at St Mary's until 1892."

"But I wasn't even alive in 1892!" cried the young nurse.

The older nurse shook her head. "Well, I was. The world will not end if we lose electricity for a day or two."

Looking skeptical, the younger one continued down the hallway, setting out lanterns and matches where instructed.

Carolyn searched for Roger. She found him uncharacteristically alone, leaning against a wall. Looking at his drawn features, heavy dark circles under both eyes, she shoved him toward a white painted chair meant for waiting patients.

"Sit down," she said, "before you fall down."

"What?" Roger shook his head as he sank into the empty chair. "Carolyn, when did you get here?"

"Just a few minutes ago," she said. "It's barely morning. But I couldn't sleep."

"They've been coming in all night," Roger said, his head sinking into his hands. "More and more sleepers. But there's nothing wrong with them. No signs of trauma. No fever. Strong regular heartbeat. It makes no sense at all."

"Have you had any dreams?" Carolyn asked, still preoccupied with the accounts that she had read during the night.

"Other than the nightmare that I am currently living?" Roger shrugged. "I haven't slept, not really slept for days. No dreams." Then he shook himself alert. "Why?"

"You sent those twelve patients to me because their dreams were overwhelming them," said Carolyn. "Perhaps that is what happened. Their dreams have ..." She broke off, unwilling to put her hypothesis into words. For a scientific man like Roger, it was unlikely he would agree with her.

"What are you saying? Their dreams have put them to sleep?" Roger looked baffled.

"We need to know more about what people are experiencing in their dreams. Are there any other patients who talked about their dreams to you? To the staff here?" Carolyn asked.

"Probably," Roger admitted. "But I do not recollect any specifics. You would have to examine their files. But what are you thinking about?"

"An entanglement of the threads of thought." Carolyn recalled the dusty books on dreams and sleep that she'd struggled to read last night. As a cure for insomnia, she felt Waller and Cox were the perfect antidote. But nothing current could explain this strange epidemic that gripped Arkham. So she had pulled out books that she had bought as curiosities years ago from Sweets and Nephew in Boston. Those last century explanations of dreams and nightmares stirred something in her memories.

"Cox says the dreaming brain wanders among worlds of its own creation – crowding into an hour the events of years – doing, saying, seeing, hearing, and feeling more than we do awake. What if those dreams are truly overwhelming our sleepers and leaving them caught in what Cox calls an entanglement of the threads of thought?" Carolyn pulled out Barbara's neat files. As she looked at the notes that she scrawled last night, she felt as if some pattern was there, teasing her as she tried to see it.

Even as she spoke to Roger, Carolyn could feel the beginning of a theory engulf her. It felt like a wave of knowledge, curling just out of sight, but ready to rush in.

"We all experience dreams," said Roger. "And we all wake up. Except now."

"Of course," Carolyn said, still pursuing the uncurling idea in her own mind. She almost had it, but then a nurse stopped and spoke to her.

"Dr Fern?" said the Black woman. "Can I have a word?"

"Yes, I am sorry," said Carolyn, turning to the nurse. "Have we met?" She looked familiar but Carolyn could not recall a name.

The nurse shook her head. "I know you by sight, but I don't think we have ever worked together. I'm Ollie Pinkser. You know my friend April May."

Carolyn nodded, recalling the shy young lady who visited her office yesterday. Still, Carolyn thought, the young woman had the nerve to overcome her shyness to ask questions about her treatments for nightmares. To Ollie, she said, "Yes, the *Arkham Advertiser* saleswoman."

"Yes, that's April. She said you were looking for people suffering from nightmares. Well, our whole house, we all live at the same boarding house, has had terrible nightmares recently. And now two people won't wake up. They seem to be fine, but they are fast asleep. Like the people here."

"I don't know if I can do anything to help. I need to find dreamers who are still awake." Carolyn wondered if April May was one of the ones who did not wake today.

When she asked about April, Ollie shook her head. "No, April is fine. A little scared, like all of us. It was her best friend, Nella, who is one of the people asleep at our house. The other is Sally…" The nurse stopped abruptly, clearing her voice with a soft cough. "Sally is a teacher. The whole street loves her, she's so kind and good with the children."

"I am sorry," said Carolyn automatically, aware of Roger still slumped in his chair. She needed to see the hospital's files. There had to be something there. But the chance of talking to a dreamer who was still awake also held possibilities.

"Do you know if April had nightmares last night? Did you?" she asked Ollie. "I need to interview dreamers. We might find an answer there."

Ollie looked troubled. "Some nightmares might be too private to share," she said. Carolyn thought the nurse might be talking about herself.

"But you could ask April. She does have some fancy dreams. She draws wonderful pictures based on them. Nella showed me one or two," Ollie continued. "April called your office last night."

"I haven't checked my messages yet. It's still early," Carolyn said. Barbara usually reviewed the messages and gave Carolyn what she needed to know. She should go to the office as soon as she finished at St Mary's. "I need to talk to my secretary, but I will try to find time to visit."

"Mrs Garcia's house is on Flotsam Street, right at the bottom of French Hill," said Ollie. "Look, I must go. Anything you can do, it would be appreciated. Everyone is so worried."

Carolyn searched her pockets and pulled out a small memorandum book, writing down the directions. "I will go there as soon as I can," she promised the nurse.

"April and Lefty would have left for work after I did," said Ollie, "but Mrs Garcia will still be home. There are four other boarding houses on Flotsam Street. They all have sleepers but there are still people awake too. Most would be at work by now, but they will be home early in the evening."

Carolyn nodded. Flotsam Street wasn't in a rich neighborhood. The residents would not want to miss a paid day of work. As Roger feared, they would also be reluctant to come to the hospital. It would be better for her to go there.

"If I come around supper time, would most people be home by then?" Carolyn asked.

Ollie nodded. "Maybe an hour or two after, around seven, would be a good time to catch them."

Carolyn agreed. With luck, there would be enough people awake and willing to talk about their dreams that she could find the common thread that she was sure must exist.

After Ollie left, Roger said, "Flotsam Street is in Rivertown. It's not the safest neighborhood, especially at night."

"She said it was near French Hill," Carolyn reminded him.

"The bottom of French Hill is Rivertown," said Roger. "It's cheap housing, which is why a number of the nurses live there, but it is not the best place."

"Then perhaps St Mary's should pay their nurses more," said Carolyn.

"I have made the same argument to our board more than once," Roger said. "But their reply is if the women are willing to work for the salaries we offer, why should we offer more?"

"Remind me to increase my charges to St Mary's," said Carolyn as she walked toward the door.

"Where are you going?" Roger sounded almost forlorn.

"Back to my office. I need to make some notes before I go to Flotsam Street." They were all exhausted at the hospital and soon emotions would boil over in strange ways. Even the most iron-willed might crack into sentimentality. Carolyn recollected the days of the pandemic, when entire households waited in dread to learn the fate of loved ones.

Barbara was not in the office when Carolyn arrived. Checking her wristwatch, Carolyn was surprised to see that it was still so early in the morning. She felt like she had been at the hospital for hours. The clouds and rain made for a murky light outside and it was impossible to tell the position of the sun. It could be an hour after dawn or nearly noon. Her much more reliable watch told her that it was barely 8 AM. She recalled the scanty breakfast that she'd eaten at home, nothing more than a cup of tea and an apple. She could seek out some decent coffee and something more substantial.

But as she set the files on her desk, she had to examine the whole lot one more time.

As she inspected the files, Carolyn read again the description of the masked man who woke her patients before rocks fell, fire engulfed them, snakes struck, or creepy dolls did something unspeakable. The entrance of the man to rescue them might be blamed on popular fiction. Carolyn detected elements of popular pulp stories and silent movies in several of the dreamers' accounts. Still, the consistency of how the man was described was a particularly intriguing detail. These descriptions were so alike that she could practically create a portrait of the man described.

As she sketched out the drawing, a crude but practical attempt to stir her own brain into defining exactly what this man represented to the dreamers, her own memories stirred. Carolyn had a sinking feeling that she knew who the man was. But he was an impossibility, one she tried very hard to forget. Worse than Carrington, the dream walker, as she had described him in one of her journals, defied every scientific and rational explanation.

But hadn't she seen the impossible herself? Wasn't the Dreamlands and its guardians what she sought when she picked up the syringe and plunged herself into a trance? Simply because she did not fully understand what she saw yet, that didn't mean she wouldn't find an answer that would fit into her beloved science of psychology.

Carolyn pulled out her address book. Ever since the case of Josephine Ruggles, she made it a practice to record the names and phone numbers of those who, like Carolyn herself, had experienced unusual encounters around Arkham. She flipped through the pages slowly and paused on one name at the very end of her book. If anyone knew anything about dreams and travelers found within dreams, it would be Harvey Walters.

Of course, the old professor would give the most unscientific and completely irrational explanation for what was happening... and the identity of the masked figure appearing in people's dreams. Harvey Walters never met a phenomenon that didn't have an occult explanation.

But he also possessed an exceptional memory for obscure texts and unusual explanations of the world. While she doubted the occult could be blamed for the nightmares experienced by her patients, perhaps Harvey could give her greater insight into what the dreamers believed they saw. And Harvey, unlike Hereward Carrington, resided in Arkham.

Carolyn went to the outer office. Barbara had not arrived yet. So Carolyn picked up the phone and requested a connection from the operator. When she heard the old man on the line, she said, "Harvey? This is Carolyn Fern. I wonder if I could come and talk to you about nightmares?"

The answer sounded gruff, but Carolyn caught the intrigued note in Harvey's voice.

"Yes, two o'clock today would be fine," she replied. "Yes, I'd love to have coffee with you and your assistant. No need to change your routine for me."

She gathered her own coat and hat. Carolyn took a quick glance at the tin of shortbread that she kept in the office for her own pangs of hunger. But no, that wouldn't suit Harvey's tastes at all. It didn't appeal to her either. She wanted something more substantial. She would stop by the bakery for a slice of orange honey bread and pick up something to take to Harvey. A small cake should appeal to the old man.

Then she would go back to the hospital and see if there was anyone awake willing to talk about their nightmares.

As Carolyn started to leave the office building for the bakery, she spotted Barbara crossing the street. As usual, her assistant walked with a measured pace. Today her neat ensemble included a stout green umbrella to keep off the drizzling rain. Carolyn was relying on a not very sturdy hat to keep her dry. Perhaps she should go back to her apartment for an umbrella.

She waited in the entryway for Barbara. The woman gave a little nod when she saw Carolyn standing by the mailboxes.

"You are early, Dr Fern," she said.

"And I'm out again," said Carolyn. "I need to run some errands. I may have lunch at the hospital." If she was going to see Harvey, she suddenly thought of a few more questions she wanted to ask about the newly admitted patients. "Then I'll be visiting Harvey Walters. After that, I will be going to Flotsam Street."

Barbara looked slightly peeved. An odd reaction, thought Carolyn.

"I have heard Harvey Walters is not the most rational gentleman," Barbara said. "Not somebody that I thought you would associate with."

"We have met a few times," said Carolyn, surprised to hear Barbara voice such an opinion, or any opinion at all. Mostly the woman was unnaturally quiet about her likes and dislikes.

Barbara must have also thought she had said too much. Instead, she reverted to her usual quiet manner. "I must not keep you from your errands," she said. "I will sort the mail. There's one or two files to be completed as well."

"Thank you, Barbara, I am sure you will do whatever is necessary," said Carolyn. Looking through the glass door at the street outside, she grimaced. "Oh, I should have brought an umbrella. It's raining even harder."

"Take mine," said Barbara, handing the green umbrella to her.

"What will you do?" said Carolyn.

"I have another in the office," said the ever-efficient Barbara.

Of course she does, and I can't even remember where my umbrella is in my apartment, thought Carolyn.

"Please take this. I know you will return it," Barbara said, pressing the green umbrella into her hands.

Carolyn thanked her and promised to call later in the afternoon to see if there were any messages.

On the stairs leading to the sidewalk, Carolyn unfurled the dark green canvas. As she lifted it over her head, she noticed the strangely carved handle. Although the hook at the end was as smooth as any umbrella, tentacles entwined the shaft, creating patterns reminiscent of waves and anchors rather than any particular creature.

Carolyn twirled the handle slowly. Both strangely entranced and repelled by the carving, she tried to find a head attached to the tentacles. Surely the carver meant to portray an ordinary octopus or squid. But rather than the shape she expected,

Carolyn found an eye at the very top of the shaft, where it would have been covered when the fabric panels were closed. Inlaid into the wood, it was a large and round disk of mother-of-pearl etched in such a way as to suggest a pupil staring out at the world revealed by the simple act of opening the umbrella.

Shuddering slightly at this grotesquerie, Carolyn lifted the umbrella higher so the eye was well out of her line of sight. Then she went in search of a snack for her and a cake for Harvey Walters.

It wasn't until she was standing in line at the bakery that Carolyn remembered Barbara had left the office yesterday to search for a dog. Which had something to do with her sister. Carolyn wondered if Barbara had been successful and resolved to chat with the woman when she saw her next. Her assistant was more than an operator of the filing cabinet and typewriter. Barbara was obviously a woman with strong opinions and unusual tastes in umbrellas. As her boss and an empathetic human being, Carolyn felt she should try to find a connection that went beyond the banalities of small talk.

Certainly, Barbara had been far more chatty when they had been on the boat. At least Carolyn thought Barbara had taken part in the long conversations with Augusta. She vaguely recollected Barbara saying many things to her. To her vexation, she couldn't remember exactly what Barbara said. But Barbara's words had been a crucial part of the discussion, she recalled, outlining exactly how to make the practice succeed.

Then the bakery clerk asked what she wanted. Carolyn turned her attention to the cakes in the display and forgot about Barbara's instructions again.

CHAPTER SIXTEEN

April persuaded a sleepy Valentino to follow her into the offices of the *Arkham Advertiser*. She considered a few weak excuses for bringing the dog to work as they climbed the stairs to the offices. With luck, she'd find Minnie before anyone asked her why she had a poodle in tow. If Valentino became one of Minnie's stories, nobody would question the dog being there.

But Minnie wasn't at her desk. In fact, almost nobody was in yet, except Doyle Jeffries looking as tousled and tired as if he had slept in his office. He leaned against one of the proofing tables, flipping through pages of a recent edition and cradling a cup of coffee in one hand. At second glance, April thought Doyle wore the same shirt and tie as yesterday, lending some evidence to her theory that he slept at the *Advertiser*.

Fixing his bleary gaze on April, Doyle said, "At least someone is here early. We may be putting out extra editions before the end of the day. Can you phone City Hall? We need their plans for flooding. Ask if they expect the river to crest. Better yet, ask them when they expect the river to crest and what they mean to do about it. Don't let them put you off with any old bromide. We want hard news."

Startled that he'd noticed her and apparently not Valentino now curled and sleeping at her feet, April responded, "I'm in advertising."

Doyle shrugged. "I've seen you on the phone. You know how to use it?"

"Of course!" she said. "I take orders for classifieds." She thought that might jog his memory.

"Perfect," said Doyle. "Call City Hall. Ask what they will do if the Miskatonic rises to flood levels. Take notes. Give the notes to Minnie or whoever gets here first. We're on deadline. I want a story." He strode back into his office, muttering loudly as he went. "Deadlines. Why does nobody remember about deadlines?"

April started to call him back. But he looked exhausted. Suddenly she did not want to simply write ads about lost dogs. As there was nobody else in the office, she could make a call for Doyle. But she wondered who would be at City Hall so early in the morning.

To her surprise, the phone was answered, although the woman on the other end of the line sounded as tired and irritable as Doyle.

"Willa Murgatroyd here," said the woman. "How can I help you?"

April asked Doyle's question about flood plans.

"Well, I have no idea what Mayor Kane has planned," the woman responded. "I am in charge of the archives. I don't know why the operator rang my phone."

"Oh," said April. "I just asked for information on city plans. I suppose she thought that was what I meant."

"Probably," said Willa, her voice sounding a little less snappish. "Are you new at the *Advertiser*? You should have asked for the mayor's office. Not that I think anyone is here yet. City Hall was nearly deserted when I came in."

"It's empty here as well," April said. Something about talking to someone on the phone seemed almost comforting. As if everything was going back to normal. Although a glance at the empty desks surrounding her mocked that idea. She never knew the office could be so quiet.

"It's an odd day," said Willa. She seemed as reluctant as April to end the call. Perhaps an empty City Hall was as depressing as a deserted newspaper office. "I thought the *Advertiser* never slept. I think it's on your masthead."

"The editor doesn't," said April, stoutly defending Doyle to her surprise. "He is here all the time." She could just see a bit of Doyle through his open office door. For once, he was silent, not yelling at anyone on the phone. April shifted a little and looked closer. Doyle appeared to be leaning back in his chair. From where she stood, he seemed to be asleep. "Well, he stays here all hours."

If Doyle was asleep, like Valentino curled up at her feet, then April was the only person awake in the office. Possibly the entire building. The thought made her feel worse.

To distract herself, she asked Willa, "What about the history of past floods?"

It was the type of question that Minnie would ask, April thought. And it would keep Willa on the phone. She certainly didn't want to sit in a silent office waiting for Minnie to appear. Already the entire morning was taking on a nightmare feeling. She was also terrified that she might fall asleep like Doyle and not wake up.

"Past floods?" said Willa, interrupting April's desperate thoughts. "Of course we have documents pertaining to past floods." She sounded almost happy to have questions to answer. "An entire river runs through Arkham. Although there has been no serious flooding since 1874."

"Tell me about the flood of 1874," said April. She pulled closer the notebook that she used for taking ad orders and picked up a pen. She could give the information to Minnie as soon as she arrived. Glancing at the clock, April hoped it would not be too long before other people returned to the office. The rain streaking down the windows and the light snoring coming from Doyle's office combined to make her feel like the last person left awake in Arkham. A dreadful drowsiness was creeping over her. But if she slept, she knew the nightmares would return. She was also convinced any terrors encountered in her sleep would be worse.

April needed to hear Willa talking, if only to keep herself awake.

"Please tell me about the flood," April asked again.

"It was in the spring of the year. The river spread over its banks, creating a lake nearly five miles long. Let me fetch the files. Don't hang up."

"I won't!" April promised.

There was the click of the receiver being set down on the desk and silence on the other end. April arranged a notepad by the phone, ready to take answers from Willa as soon as she returned. She did feel a little like a reporter and wondered how difficult a job it would be. Doyle seemed to think she could do part of it. April picked up a pencil and began to draw Valentino in a boat, rowing valiantly across a rushing river. On the shore, a talking cat waited under an umbrella for the poodle to land.

"Here it is," Willa's voice came back through the receiver. "In 1874, almost every Rivertown residence was flooded to the second floor. Northside suffered serious damage as well. In some cases, houses were washed away. The mayor at the time sent an appeal to the state and federal government." Willa paused for a moment. "Ah, here is the mayor's report to the city council. He states that they received 585 barrels of flour, 218 sacks of flour, 54 barrels of crackers, 13 half-barrels of crackers, 239 barrels of meal, 41 boxes of crackers, 79 barrels of pork, 23 barrels of beef, 76 barrels of beans, and 41 barrels of potatoes to help those in need."

April abandoned her drawing and asked Willa to repeat the numbers, although she wasn't sure how Minnie could use this particular information. She wondered why there were so many crackers and why the crackers came in so many different types of containers.

Willa clucked over something else that she was reading. "Here's another letter from the mayor of Arkham to the mayor of Boston, stating that they are experiencing an unprecedented time of intense misery."

"Even with the aid received?" asked April. Crackers apparently weren't enough, even in a variety of containers.

"Yes," said Willa. "It's an odd letter. There's a reference here to the problem of the Black Cave. He requests people from outside the city be sent to help clear the area."

"Oh, I know the Black Cave, that's in Rivertown." The Black Cave had something of a reputation for a bootlegger's hangout, although April knew people also went on exploring hikes during the day. The cave system was said to extend almost completely under the neighborhood. Nella once talked about taking a picnic to the cave, except both Mrs Garcia and Lefty had been adamant it was not a safe place to go. To April's relief, Nella had dropped the idea.

"What was the problem in the cave?" April asked. Minnie had run off yesterday looking for reports of sea monsters seen from the docks of Rivertown. She wondered if something like that had been found in the Black Cave, something large enough that the mayor needed extra men to remove it. This type of information might be more useful than the number of crackers received in relief. At least more intriguing. People liked reading about monsters to judge from some of the discussions that she overheard between Doyle and the reporters.

"Oh, how horrible," said Willa. Paper rustled on her end of the line. "They found dozens of dogs in the cave. All drowned. The poor animals must have been swept in there by the floods. The mayor writes the discovery of these lost pets brought unprecedented misery to an overburdened population. He lacked volunteers willing to enter the Black Cave to remove the bodies and requested that Boston send stalwart and unimaginative men." Willa paused again. "I wonder why he specified unimaginative? That seems an odd choice of words. Perhaps this transcription is incorrect."

April stopped writing when Willa began talking about what they found in the Black Cave. She was sure nobody would want to read about drowned dogs. She certainly didn't want to hear more about such a disaster. The poor animals! Swept into the Black Cave by flood waters, unable to escape. If she thought about it too hard, she knew what her next nightmare would be. Looking down at Valentino, April bent and scratched the sleeping poodle's head.

"Thank you," she told Willa. "I appreciate your help."

"Of course," Willa responded. "If you need anything else from the archives, I will be here all day. Please call Mayor Kane's office for current information. However, you might want to wait an hour or two."

"I will," April said. She hung up the phone. The office was still frighteningly empty except for Doyle sleeping at his desk. She wrote up the information that she received from Willa in her best handwriting and walked the sheet of paper across the room to Minnie's desk. Then she walked slowly back to the counter.

Fidgeting there, she wished the phone would ring. Even an order for a classified ad about a lost dog would be better than staring at an empty room.

The door swung open. Much to April's relief, Columbia entered. In one hand she clutched a large green umbrella, slightly unfurled and dripping wet. Columbia carefully placed it in the umbrella stand by the door. She glanced at April and then at Valentino asleep at her feet. Columbia exclaimed, "Where did you find that dog? That's the one I purchased for my sister."

CHAPTER SEVENTEEN

Harvey Walters liked the cake that Carolyn Fern brought to his house. It was a proper angel food cake, not one of those overly rich devil's food cakes that had become so popular. After his recent experiences with Mrs Fox's chocolate ganache, this white fluffy cake was sure to be much easier on his stomach too. Enough to justify an extra slice or two.

"Coffee or tea?" he asked Carolyn once they'd settled in his office.

"I'll have what you're having," she said. She smoothed her hair. Carolyn had left her hat, coat, and dark green umbrella in the hall to dry.

The rain seemed worse in Harvey's opinion. More a gullywasher than the usual Arkham drizzle. He might even call the downpour a proper frog strangler before the end of the night. It was definitely an excellent day to stay in his study and entertain guests.

"Doctor says I should stick to tea in the afternoon," said Harvey. "On the other hand, who wants to live forever? Especially if you're half asleep. Ira, ask Mrs Fox for a pot of coffee and have her cut up this cake too." Harvey handed over the cake box to his assistant, who headed toward the back of the house to confer with Mrs Fox on coffee, cups, and whatever else was needed to make a decent tray for an afternoon break. Mrs Fox was a great believer in "having a little something" in the afternoon and she'd enjoy a slice of cake too, in the kitchen.

"He's new," Carolyn commented to Harvey as his assistant left the room with no more than a nod.

"Graduate student," Harvey explained. "He's working on an advanced degree." To his chagrin, Harvey couldn't remember what the man was studying. He was fairly certain that they discussed it, but Ira was such a dull person that Harvey forgot their conversations almost as soon as they happened.

Tall, thin, and with irritatingly thick brown hair kept under strict control with a sweet-smelling pomade, Ira always dressed in the same navy-blue suit, crisp white shirt, and conservative striped tie in shades of dark green and olive. He tidied away all his paperwork and notes into neat file folders as soon as he was done with them. Harvey couldn't imagine working on a desk that didn't have a teetering pile of books. Ira apparently couldn't work for five minutes on anything but a desk polished bare of all accessories except his old-fashioned fountain pen and a square of blotting paper. Ira also had imposed a ruthless sense of order on Harvey's overflowing bookcases over the past few days. Having all his books arranged in alphabetical order by author's name was still slightly distressing. Although Ira had unearthed one or two rather interesting volumes that Harvey had forgotten that he owned.

"Does your assistant have a name?" Carolyn asked.

"Ira Erastus Palmer," Harvey said.

"How odd," said Carolyn. "I rented an office from a Dr Palmer. I wonder if they are related."

"Common enough name," said Harvey, unwilling to admit

that he had no notion if Ira had family in Arkham. He had been impressed with himself that he'd remembered the boy's middle name. Only Ira wasn't a boy, he was almost thirty, but he still seemed unbearably callow to Harvey. He also thought the young lady now occupying the visitor's chair in his office wouldn't appreciate being called a young lady or a girl. She might be older than Ira. But she was definitely younger than Harvey, decades younger.

He dismissed those depressing thoughts and asked Carolyn what she needed from him. "You didn't come here to discuss my boringly efficient assistant," he said with a quick glance toward the door. Ira was still in the kitchen, so he was safe to be a bit of an old grumbler. Not that Ira would be insulted by being called efficient... or even boring. Harvey rather thought Ira prided himself on being as bland as possible. Why, he had no idea. Harvey preferred people to remember him and acted accordingly.

"I wanted to talk to you about dreams," Carolyn said. "More particularly, nightmares."

"There's been a plethora of bad dreams plaguing people," said Harvey.

Carolyn raised her eyebrows.

"I don't spend all my time buried in occult books pursuing cosmic mysteries," Harvey said. "Besides, Mrs Fox gossips over the poached eggs and bacon. Every breakfast I hear the news of our neighborhood, if not all of Arkham. She is far more reliable than the *Arkham Advertiser*, at least when it comes to the dreams troubling her and her lady friends."

"Her lady friends?" Carolyn asked in what Harvey felt was a disapproving tone.

"What am I supposed to call the friends of Mrs Fox? The women who she chats with over the back fence when she is hanging out my drawers to dry," Harvey muttered. "Who are hanging their laundry in their backyards."

Carolyn seemed a little startled by his statement. Harvey wondered if he should apologize for the mention of unmentionables. Except it was the 1920s and presumably she was not shocked to learn that men wore underpants, which needed to be laundered and hung out to dry on a weekly basis.

"So the women are gossiping about nightmares?" said Carolyn.

Somewhat relieved that she was only interested in nightmares and not anything else, Harvey nodded. "A number of ladies are suffering from frighteningly vivid dreams. Including Mrs Fox. And not just the ladies. I heard from one of my former students that his nightmares were so terrible that they were causing him to sleepwalk."

"How about yourself?" Carolyn asked.

"I don't remember many of my dreams anymore," confessed Harvey. "Don't sleep much either. One of the trials of old age." In fact, the dream on Sunday was the only recent one he could recall. And that had been less a dream than a memory entangled in his drifting thoughts while he rested after dinner. He did not, no matter what Mrs Fox said, fall asleep every night after supper while reading in his study. He simply closed his eyes for a short time to gather his thoughts.

Ira appeared in the doorway with an overladen tray complete with the silver coffee pot, beautifully plated slices of angel food cake, the sterling forks, and the good china cups. Mrs Fox obviously meant to make the best impression possible on Harvey's visitor, possibly to encourage her to return. Mrs Fox often muttered that he was turning into a regular hermit, which was untrue. He went to New York not long ago and even attended a party. He dined at least once a week with what friends he had left on the Miskatonic University faculty. It wasn't his fault so many of them had disappeared into the Antarctic or suffered other untimely ends. Having passed sixty himself, Harvey had little patience for men who met their doom while still relatively middle aged.

Actually, he had little patience with most people. But he couldn't blame his attitude on age. He'd always found people uniformly less interesting than the mystic secrets hidden in his books.

Harvey waved the tray over to his desk and poured out coffee for the three of them. Ira took his cup and withdrew to his smaller, pristine desk in the corner of the room. When Harvey offered him a slice of cake, Ira shook his head, possibly from fear of crumbs marring his desk's unnaturally clean surface.

Carolyn stared at the generous slice of cake and the large cup of coffee which Harvey took for himself.

"I might have some suggestions for improving your sleep," she said, taking a much smaller slice of cake and pouring milk in her coffee.

Harvey grinned. "I find the early hours of the morning are an excellent time for research." He then carved out a big bite of angel food cake with his fork and popped it in his mouth. He followed that with a large swig of black coffee. Already his mood was improving. Doctors be damned.

"So, what do you know about nightmares?" she asked.

"Historically dreams come in two forms," Harvey replied. "True or false, and both types were thought to emanate from an otherworldly source such as a supernatural intelligence or divine place. The gates of horn and ivory in Homer's *Odyssey*, for example."

"But nightmares?" persisted Carolyn.

"A word derived from the Old English *night* and *mara*, the latter being a malicious imp which walks on people's chests to induce terrifying dreams," Harvey said. "Of course, your medical colleagues once theorized that nightmares were simply the byproduct of digestive disorders during sleep."

"John Waller's treatise on the subject stated every derangement of the digestive organs could create frightful visions. Which may have led Dickens to having Scrooge blame his ghosts on a piece of undigested gristle," Carolyn murmured.

"Exactly," said Harvey. "Waller discounted all supernatural sources for dreams." He was impressed that Carolyn had read Waller. Not many people studied early nineteenth century medical texts. He owned a copy himself. After all, how could he resist a title like *A Treatise on the Incubus, or Night-Mare, Disturbed Sleep, Terrific Dreams and Nocturnal Visions* when it was offered in one of those cunning little catalogs Sweets and Nephew mailed him on a regular basis.

"I rather like Waller's hypothesis," replied Carolyn.

"But so many cultures believe differently." Harvey had been a bit disappointed by Waller. Much too much emphasis on diet and far too little on the incubus, in his view. "Can they all be wrong? The ancient Egyptians believed a person's *ba* or spirit could leave the body and travel within dreams. An idea which nearly every ancient culture shared in some form or other."

At this point Harvey was well aware that he was showing off, but Mrs Fox was right. He didn't have as many visitors as he used to. Certainly, none who brought him cake. The very least that he could do was throw out some glittering trivia, much like a magician conjuring with smoke and mirrors.

"Bram Stoker claimed his creation of Dracula was the result of a nightmare after a supper of dressed crab," Carolyn countered.

"Some occult theorists suggest dreams contain ciphers which will reveal the destiny of the soul," Harvey responded. The nice thing about Carolyn was that she was a woman of considerable intellect. She spent time in the library at Miskatonic University, practically prowling the stacks where Harvey spent his time. In fact, that's where they'd met and noticed some mutual interests in their piles of books.

Besides, Carolyn actually could keep up with his references and match him line for line. He didn't have to stop and explain himself as often as he did with many young people. Harvey was fairly sure that Ira had never read Stoker. Too sensational and last century, Ira would say.

"Nightmares may indicate an exceedingly unpleasant journey ahead," Harvey added. "I used to dream about lost luggage… and I never took a train trip that ended well."

"That can be explained as a manifestation of perfectly normal anxieties. Possibly a form of hodophobia," Carolyn said.

"Is there really a name for fear of travel?" Harvey said.

"Of course," she replied. "There's a name for every terror that we experience. If a state of mind hasn't been classified yet, it will be. We are in a new era of psychology, the beginning of a century when the science of mental life, both its phenomena and their conditions, will be recorded, cataloged and–"

"Cured?" interrupted Harvey in a harsher tone than he had intended. But several of his colleagues had been threatened with the madhouse in his younger days. Harvey himself had learned what was safe to discuss around others and what should be spoken to a select few only. Or as one friend liked to say, "Do what you want, just don't scare the doctors."

"Do you think all mental states should be treated as an illness? Must all nightmares be vanquished?" he asked Carolyn.

"Now you're straying into the realm of philosophy," Carolyn said, "and not science. But yes, I think nightmares should be cured if they are causing harm to the patient."

She glanced at Ira, sipping his coffee and making notes on some book that he had open on his desk. He certainly wasn't contributing to the conversation. In fact, he had said very little to Carolyn since she arrived. Which surprised Harvey. When he was a younger man, he would have been working very hard to impress a woman like Carolyn. In fact, he still tried very hard to impress any of the ladies who were willing to listen to him ramble about his favorite topics. Then Carolyn turned back to him and Harvey forgot about Ira's peculiarities.

"Are there any cures for nightmares in your occult texts?" Carolyn asked. "Or must we default to Waller's sensible suggestions?"

Harvey sensed that Carolyn didn't care what the answer was. She's drawing out the conversation, he thought, like a woman discussing weather or fashion at a dinner party. What does she really want to know? But he indulged her and himself by relating some of the more outlandish nightmare cures that he knew.

"Chaucer and Shakespeare both give charms within their works for dispelling nightmares," he said. "Look to the Miller's tale or Mad Tom in *King Lear*. Quite the most effective was said to be Pliny's decoction but it requires the tongue, eyes, liver, and bowel of a dragon. I'm not sure if St Mary's stocks dragons' parts."

Carolyn smiled. "Probably not."

She fiddled with her coffee cup and glanced again at Ira, who set his own empty cup down on the saucer placed squarely in the middle of his desk. Obviously, the polite chitchat was to continue until they were alone.

Harvey waved at his assistant. "Ira, can you ask Mrs Fox to set back dinner an hour? This cake is so good that I'll have another slice now and enjoy my roast later."

Ira nodded and rose. "I'll tell her and then make some phone calls if you don't mind," he said. The phone was in the hall, set up in its own little niche, and making calls would keep Ira out of his study. So Harvey said that would be perfectly fine.

"My sister needs help. We found a lost dog." Ira seemed to feel an explanation was needed for using his employer's phone. Not that Harvey minded. Ira had made other calls in the last few days. In fact, his one enthusiasm seemed to be the possibilities of the telephone for quick communication.

Harvey was old-fashioned enough to prefer the letter for more serious exchanges and thought the telegram was perfectly adequate for anything that needed to be sent quickly.

"Take as much time on the telephone as you need," Harvey said to Ira.

Carolyn stirred in her chair. Harvey nodded to Ira, who shut the door behind him as he left the room.

"I keep hearing about dogs," said Carolyn. "And sisters."

"Is it important?" asked Harvey. Even as he asked, something tickled his memory. The burned book that he bought on French Hill. There had been something in it about dogs which Ira had asked him to translate.

Interrupting his train of thought, Carolyn said, "I think dreams can tell us a great deal about an individual. But this current outbreak of nightmares makes no sense to me."

Harvey heard the underlying note of uncertainty in her last statement. She started to speak again, then shook her head and said, "Oh, it is all ridiculous. How can I find a scientific reason for these incidents if I look to unreasonable explanations, the supernatural? Too many people already believe psychology is just another form of hocus pocus."

"Then why come here?" Harvey said. "I do appreciate the bribe. But you know my views." He sank his fork into the angel cake and took another enormous bite. Indigestion was a problem for another day... or at least another hour. "I'm all hocus when I'm not pocus." The joke failed to draw a smile from his visitor.

Carolyn still sat silent.

Harvey leaned across his desk and fixed his gaze on Carolyn. "Go ahead, voice your unreasonable suspicion," he said. "I am sure I can answer in even stranger terms."

"Have you ever heard of twelve people having the same nightmare on the same night?" she said.

Now that Ira was gone, she was ready to discuss the real problem, Harvey thought.

He leaned back and closed his eyes to better turn his thoughts inward. Decades of research scrolled through his thoughts and a few of his own darker dreams.

"Not exactly," he finally admitted. "There's works recounting sybils or druids who dreamed together, conjuring similar prophecies. Some believed a collective dream granted considerable power to influence the future. Have you encountered twelve people dreaming the same nightmare?"

"Remarkably similar dreams at least," said Carolyn. She sipped her coffee as she considered her next words. "You must keep this to yourself. I am perilously near the edge of betraying their confidences by saying this much. But all of my patients on Monday and Tuesday dreamed about the same place and, even more unlikely, all had their nightmares ended by a masked figure appearing in their dream."

"It goes without saying that I'll tell no one, not even Ira, about this. Describe the place and the person – is it a person? – who interrupts their nightmares," Harvey said.

"The place is easy," Carolyn replied, setting down her coffee cup and leaning forward. "A tower, very tall and thin, almost a spire on the horizon. Sometimes they are far away from it. Sometimes they are close enough to see it clearly and even people gathering on the steps leading to a great door. There's other details but those vary wildly. I believe the variations are more indicative of their subconscious fears than anything else. Those fears and the monsters evoked remain very individual. But before they are overwhelmed by the embodiment of their fear, they encounter a man, dressed in ornate robes and masked in gold. Then they wake."

"Gold, not yellow robes or a silver mask?" Harvey asked, thinking of a magical experiment on French Hill that had gone disastrously wrong a few years earlier.

"A golden mask," replied Carolyn. "They're all certain about that."

"Well, that's a relief," said Harvey, crossing one nightmare possibility off his list. "What else do they say about this masked savior?"

"The descriptions of the man vary, as you might expect from twelve people, but still all mention he is tall, dark haired, and relatively young," Carolyn continued. "Except one boy, who was only sixteen, and he described the man as old. But his description may reflect his perspective of anyone over the age of twenty."

"I can make a fairly good guess at who it might be. And I doubt he would be pleased to be called old." Harvey looked more closely at Carolyn. "Didn't you meet him once or twice?"

Carolyn sighed. "You are going to tell me that it is Luke Robinson, aren't you?"

"Probably," said Harvey. "But why come to me if you already know the answer?"

"Because I was hoping the answer was something else," Carolyn admitted. She fidgeted in her chair, finishing off her slice of cake but leaving a puddle of coffee to cool in the bottom of her cup.

Harvey remained silent. Luke was a disturbing character. Even he was not sure where the man lived or rather how he lived.

There were a few people who suggested Luke was a phantom of dreams. But Harvey was completely certain the man was real. And, since he was, Harvey was also a little jealous of Luke's access to glorious knowledge of the type only the most obscure texts documented in arcane and vague language.

Carolyn obviously had much deeper reservations about the gentleman.

"If I admit that Luke Robinson can appear in my patients' dreams through some actions of his own, I certainly can't explain how he does it," she finally said. "Which makes my theory that he might be a catalyst for these nightmares less than easy to propose to the doctors of St Mary's."

"Well," said Harvey, thinking of his own encounters with the man, "if he is causing a multitude of nightmares, I doubt his intention is to harm anyone. He's always struck me as a good man." There were those in Arkham who were careless with certain old magics, as Harvey was painfully aware, and who counted human life as cheap. But Luke Robinson never did anything that would indicate he was one of their number.

"I hope he means no harm. I would like to ask him if I could," Carolyn said. "If I could only access the Dreamlands–"

"So you do think these nightmares are occurring in the Dreamlands?" Harvey interrupted her and then apologized. But any mention of the Dreamlands was a cause for considerable excitement.

He rather assumed that was why Carolyn wanted to discuss Luke, who apparently had unlimited access to the Dreamlands. But he'd also noticed in earlier conversations with Carolyn that she was very reluctant to discuss this fabled and terrifying dimension which certain philosophers and mystics claimed existed beyond the waking world. Although she once or twice mentioned some of the bizarre creatures and landscapes said to exist there, she deflected Harvey's questions about the origins of her knowledge with claims of patient confidentiality.

"I am reluctantly entertaining the theory that this may have something to do with the Dreamlands," Carolyn said. "But I would much rather find a more scientific answer. Or failing that, discuss this with Luke. If only I could find a way to reach him!"

"Presumably in your dreams." Harvey meant it as a joke, but Carolyn looked even more disturbed.

Carolyn mumbled something like, "I have tried but nothing happens."

Then she straightened in her chair. Her expression became what Harvey might have labeled her "doctor face." Concerned, intelligent, and not giving any weight to any superstitious nonsense. She obviously was serious about wanting a scientific answer.

Harvey wished he had one for her.

"I was hoping that you had a practical suggestion," Carolyn said. "An address? Here in Arkham?"

"Outside of dreams, I haven't the least idea of how to contact Luke. You can't pick up the telephone and ask the operator to put you through," Harvey said. "But if he is appearing in your patients' dreams, I would say you are correct in diagnosing these nightmares as more than an expression of their fears."

"What are these nightmares then?" Carolyn asked.

"True dreams," Harvey answered. A theory was starting to form in his head, one involving dreams and warnings, and it made him wish the nightmares were simply the product of indigestion. "Someone, most probably Luke, is trying to send us a message from the Dreamlands."

"The terrors experienced in their dreams are overwhelming my patients," said Carolyn. "So much so that they have reached a point where they cannot regain consciousness. Something, someone, is preventing them from doing so."

"Then it's not just a message," Harvey said, abandoning his cake with considerable regret. Going to his newly organized bookshelves, Harvey ran his hand over the spines of his crumbling volumes and cursed slightly when the book he was seeking wasn't where he used to keep it.

Recalling the name of the religious order listed on the manuscript he wanted, Harvey wandered a few feet over and found the crumbling codex wedged between two authors whose surnames began with the same letter. Most probably moved there by the ever-annoying Ira. "Alphabetical! It's a terrible way to organize," Harvey muttered. "Why not by age? Subject matter?"

Flipping open the book, he read out loud the passage contained within, automatically translating from the medieval French to English. "Before the great flood engulfed the town of Letourneau, a number of citizens experienced nightmares which left them prostrate and unable to leave their beds. Nearly all spoke of a terrible tower looming over them and a sea creature of gargantuan size rising up behind that. In the days following the destruction of Letourneau, the survivors expressed their regret in not heeding their own dreams and abandoning their town to its fate."

Carolyn asked, "How does this relate to the nightmares of my patients?"

"This is a listing of true dreams drawn up for the King of France," said Harvey. "Prophetic dreams, recorded by a group of medieval monks trying to prove which type of dreams came from angels and which from devils. The nightmares recounted by the dreamers of Letourneau sound very much like what your patients are experiencing."

Carolyn looked thoughtful. More than thoughtful, Harvey decided. He waited in silence as she turned over some idea in her head.

"Waller cites Aurelianus," she finally said, "who claimed nightmares were once an epidemic in Rome, killing a great number of persons in their sleep. But Waller doesn't describe the dreams or if the patients suffered the same dream. Could it be a virus or an outside agent causing a form of mass hysteria?"

"Mass nightmares? You still wish to blame a germ for causing a dozen people to have the same dream? Why not the Germans experimenting with sleeping gas?" Harvey made no attempt to hide his sarcasm. Really, scientists and medical professionals would go to any lengths to avoid the simplest answer to an unusual phenomenon: it was magic!

"Perhaps something like convulsive ergotism," Carolyn replied in a way that reminded Harvey very much of a boy whistling to keep up his courage. As he once whistled to himself exploring the Black Cave as a very foolish young man.

"A food or water contaminant creating hallucinogenic effects," elaborated Carolyn. "Is this too extraordinary an explanation? When we are faced with an alternative of a man who somehow travels in the dream world whose physics defy explanation?"

Harvey thought of his recent dream of his boyhood and the shadow looming over him. Was that caused by a bit of moldy bread, like St Anthony's Fire in the Middle Ages? "The virus seems like a more far-fetched explanation," he said to Carolyn. "When the simpler one would be these are messages from our friend Luke. We know he has some unusual abilities."

"I'm not sure that the doctors at St Mary's will accept your explanation," said Carolyn. "I'm not sure that I want to believe it. I'd rather deal with a virus. But the situation is growing dire at St Mary's. It began when they saw an influx of people suffering from sleep deprivation. People who are afraid to sleep because of their nightmares. They referred those people to me. I was supposed to help them." With the last sentence, her voice broke with unexpected desperation. "All of my patients are now unconscious and cannot be awakened. I even had Roger questioning if it was my use of hypnosis which caused it."

"Do you think hypnosis would have such an effect?" Harvey doubted it himself, but he also knew that Carolyn's practice of hypnosis had some unusual features.

"Absolutely not." Carolyn grew flushed. Anger swept her unnatural depression away. "Besides, twice as many patients have been admitted with the same symptoms and absolutely no encounter with a hypnotist."

"As far as you know," said Harvey.

Carolyn deflated as quickly as she had roused. "As far as I know. And I now believe I know nothing. How can this be happening?"

Before today, Harvey would have called Carolyn Fern the calmest woman that he ever met. This Carolyn looked close to breaking.

"Does frightening people into a comatose state sound like Luke trying to send a message?" she pressed.

"If the nightmares are not messages from Luke," said Harvey, "perhaps the nightmares are like the visions experienced by the villagers of Letourneau. Warnings. Luke may be intercepting them, rather like a man cutting in on a party line."

"I don't think this is a case of crossed wires at the switchboard," Carolyn argued.

"Maybe not. We need to know more to understand what type of disaster is brewing." Harvey looked down at his manuscript, hoping for just such inspiration.

Carolyn nodded. "I do agree. We need to understand this, although I'm not at all certain we are dealing with premonition of a disaster. And there's been no talk of gigantic sea creatures… except…"

While he considered himself about as psychic and sensitive as a cucumber, something cold touched the back of Harvey's neck. "Except what?"

"My patients also talked about an overwhelming presence, a being indescribably large whose very gaze sapped their will and caused them to be frozen in their dream. Just moments before their individual terrors appeared and the man in the golden mask arrived to rescue them," Carolyn said. "But that is as nonsensical as the scary dolls and the overabundance of spiders that they experienced."

As Carolyn talked, Harvey stirred the papers on his desk. He knew he had read about a great power in connection with some ritual or other which involved dreamers. Something full of fishing references, rather like the strange prophecies of those medieval French peasants. Which of his books contained this vital piece of information?

"Did the dreamers who perceived the giant whatever react any differently than the others?" Harvey asked, flipping through his own notes, trying to recapture the idea which teased his brain.

"Those eight who gave me the most vivid descriptions of the entity behind the tower could also be characterized as the people most terrified by their dreams," said Carolyn.

A fragment of his earlier dream returned to Harvey, the sense of a gigantic eye peering down at a boy on a hill, a presence as cold, distant, and unknowable as the stars. He found his notebook, the one bearing the circle diagram, similar to the drawings in the odd little book from French Hill. His auction find did talk occasionally about dreams but far more about augury and a most gruesome kind of sacrifice as well. He wouldn't bother Carolyn with such information. That wasn't what she needed.

"Still, I think the best idea would be to find a way to talk to Luke. As far as I know, the simplest method would be to find a dreamer who can carry a message from us to Luke," said Harvey. "Perhaps make this a hypnotic suggestion so the next time they dream of snakes or fire and the man arrives to save them, they give him the message?"

"I thought of that. But all of the dreamers that I examined are now unconscious and in the hospital," said Carolyn. "I cannot give them any instructions."

"Can't you place yourself into a dream state?" asked Harvey, who had some recollection of Carolyn discussing the difference between self-hypnosis and certain trance states with him over dinner once. "I would offer myself for hypnosis except…"

"Except what?"

"Oh, hypnosis always fails spectacularly with me." Harvey could place himself in a trance. But, for very sensible reasons, he had convinced his brain years ago to resist hypnosis. Unfortunately, his brain never let him undo this suggestion. There had been other times when he rather wished he could experience whatever Carolyn's patients experienced.

Carolyn frowned and then said, "I have been trying a few techniques for autohypnosis. But I have not seen the Dreamlands or Luke."

"Perhaps we could use Ira?" Then Harvey shook his head. "No. I am certain the man cannot dream. He's a soulless creature."

"Because he alphabetized your bookshelves?" Carolyn smiled, relaxing a little.

"And refused to eat a slice of cake," said Harvey, sure Carolyn would agree with his impeccable logic. "But what you need is an artistic soul, able to journey to the Dreamlands and return." Artists frequently slipped into the Dreamlands without knowing it. Look at the work of the Surrealists, a bunch of Dreamland travelers to go by the strange paintings they produced.

"All the patients at the hospital are fast asleep," Carolyn

repeated. "If they encounter the masked man in their nightmares, they are now as unreachable as Luke."

"Is there anybody still awake?" Harvey said.

"Perhaps. I received a message from a boarding house on Flotsam Street. Some are asleep, like the patients at the hospital, but there are others awake there. Certainly, the woman who left the message was awake a few hours ago. Her message sounded as if she is also suffering nightmares," she said. "If she has seen a masked figure, do you think she could make contact with Luke again?"

"Most probably," said Harvey. "Start there. See if you can send a dreamer to Luke. While you are on Flotsam Street, I will do what I do best."

Carolyn looked puzzled.

"Research!" Harvey cried in a loud and boisterous voice. He strode back to his bookshelves and pulled various volumes down. He peeked over his shoulder at Carolyn. Good, he had made her smile again. The woman seemed to have the weight of the world on her shoulders.

Harvey dumped the books in a satisfactorily messy pile on his desk. "I will find some answers for you."

CHAPTER EIGHTEEN

April wanted to be delighted that Valentino could be reunited with his owner. But she felt oddly reluctant to hand the dog to Columbia.

Valentino seemed oblivious to the newsroom, tightly curled in a poodle ball of napping under the counter most of the day. The poodle enjoyed a brief walk at noon and a shared hot dog with April before promptly falling back to sleep.

Now Columbia was prepared to leave the office and planned to take the dog with her. After her initial recognition of Valentino, she seemed happy or at least unperturbed to leave the dog with April throughout the day. Nor did Valentino seem terribly excited to see Columbia. At their first encounter, the puppy whined and pressed against April's legs. Although April did not think a woman so neat and pragmatic would mistreat a dog, she couldn't imagine Columbia as a pet lover. She certainly didn't look like the sort of person that would tolerate the messes that came with dogs (as April had discovered during her noon walk with Valentino). But perhaps Columbia's sister was different. After all, she said the dog was for her sister.

April wished Minnie was back. But while other staff came

trickling into the office throughout the day, muttering about a night without sleep, Minnie and Rex remained absent. While it wasn't unusual for them to go off for a few days in pursuit of a story, April worried about river monsters with glowing tentacles and rising waters.

When April pointed out her notes on past floods that she'd left on Minnie's desk, Doyle had grunted and collared another reporter to send to City Hall. "And don't come back until you have a quote from Mayor Kane!" said Doyle to the man as he shoved him out the door.

To April's anxious and softly spoken question about Minnie's whereabouts, Doyle simply shrugged his shoulders. "She and Rex know how to take care of themselves," he said. "But it better be a whale of a story they bring back. I need everyone on this flood. Somebody needs to drive out to Kingsport and see what's happening between here and there. Can't let the *Gazette* get a jump on us."

But a little later, when Matt came up from the presses, April overheard the two men talking about what they would do if the water rose in Northside. "Get the plates ready," Doyle said, "and call the *Gazette*. If we flood, we'll need to print at their plant."

When Matt passed her at the counter, April asked what Doyle meant.

"We're lucky. Both the *Advertiser* and the *Gazette* use Hoe's. Installed around the same time," said Matt. At April's blank look, he explained, "We both use the same type of printing press, so I can take the plates for the *Advertiser* and run them on the *Gazette*'s equipment. We've done it before, although the other way around. When there was trouble in Kingsport, we printed the *Gazette* for a few days."

"And they'll let us do that? Print at their plant if we're flooded out?" April said.

"Of course," said Matt. "They may try to steal our stories or scoop us, but we are all in the newspaper business together."

Now as the clock ticked toward the end of the day, Columbia declared her work done. She put on her tan raincoat, took up her green umbrella, and asked for Valentino.

She also thanked April for finding her sister's dog.

"I didn't know you have a sister," said April.

Columbia's eyebrows raised and her eyes widened. "Most people do have siblings," she said in the flat tone of voice which indicated April had just made a very foolish remark.

"Of course. I have four sisters." Which was one of the reasons April lived in Arkham in a boarding house, which during any hour of the day was a calmer place than her home full of sisters, cousins, and aunts, to say nothing of her mother. She started to tell Columbia about this but one look at the woman's blank face made it very clear that Columbia wasn't interested in April's tangled family history.

April's embarrassment increased. She admired Columbia. At least, she told Nella once or twice that she admired Columbia. Mostly Columbia's calm and collected speech, her incredible orderliness in how she handled tasks, and her amazingly efficient handling of all problems as soon as they arose seemed like traits April should admire.

So why didn't she like Columbia very much?

Perhaps because Columbia was so cold as well as efficient.

If Nella, for example, spotted the lost dog of her sister – and given Nella's youngest sister's general flightiness, any dog of hers would be lost – then Nella would be full of questions and exclamations and general hullabaloo around the dog.

Columbia made no exclamations and gave no explanations about how Valentino had ended up in an alley on the north side. She simply claimed the dog. Columbia said nothing except the poodle was purchased for her sister. Then she ignored the dog and April for most of the day. Only when her work was done did she declare she was leaving with Valentino.

Now she simply stared at April and waited, calmly, for an agitated April to hand Valentino's makeshift leash to her.

Which April would, of course, do. Except April very much wished that Nella wasn't asleep at the boarding house, Lefty wasn't halfway across Arkham on a garbage run, and Minnie wasn't missing from the office. She even wished Doyle would stop disappearing into his office for another nap and start yelling about deadlines.

Because the whole moment felt strangely like a dream. For no sensible reason, April almost expected the door to open and the man in the golden mask to appear. Perhaps even to shout some cryptic warnings.

Instead, to April's profound relief, the phone rang.

"I am sorry," she said, turning her back on Columbia's increasingly unnerving stare. "I should answer this."

"Is this April May?" The woman on the phone wasn't as good as the man in the golden mask but April recognized the voice of Carolyn Fern as somebody who would have the answers that April lacked.

"Yes, I am April," she answered quickly. "Oh, thank you so much for calling me back."

"I met your friend Ollie at the hospital." Carolyn sounded tired but everyone today had sounded tired, more tired even than the day before. "She said there were people at your boarding house who could not wake up."

"Yes, two," April confirmed. "My friends Nella and Sally."

"Is there anyone there who is awake now but has suffered from nightmares in the last few nights?"

Recalling conversations over the past two days, April

confirmed everyone at the boarding house had suffered from disturbed sleep. "Except for Lefty," she added. "He says hauling around garbage cans leaves him too tired to dream."

"But has anyone dreamed about towers and a man wearing a golden mask?" As Carolyn voiced her question, April noticed Columbia turning away. Apparently content to let April finish her call before claiming Valentino, Columbia was now sorting methodically through the files in her desk drawer.

Distracted, April asked Carolyn to repeat her question.

"Has anyone dreamed about a tower or towers? Have they mentioned a man wearing a golden mask appearing in their dreams?" The voice on the phone sounded far more urgent than April recalled. Carolyn had struck her as a very calm and even warm individual. This woman seemed almost desperate.

April blinked at the oddity of the questions and Carolyn's intense tone. Then she said, very slowly, "I have dreamed about the man in the golden mask." A glance at Columbia showed she was still looking at various papers and probably not paying attention to the call. Although it was hard to tell with Columbia. April quickly added, "How did you know about him?"

"Oh, good. Then I want to talk to you." Now Carolyn sounded jubilant. Which seemed an even stranger reaction to April. "How soon can we meet? It's very important. I want to know everything you remember about the man. Did he help you in your dream?"

"Yes," April admitted, pressing the phone as close to her ear as possible. She didn't think Columbia could hear both sides of the conversation, but she definitely didn't want to say anything more that would attract the woman's attention. Masked men and giant ants were not something that Columbia would understand.

"I am at work," April said, thinking that sounded very sensible and like she was having an ordinary conversation, although a bit personal for work. "I can be home by six. We eat then so I am free by seven."

Carolyn seemed dismayed by her answer. "But it would be best for us to meet as soon as possible."

April shook her head then realized Carolyn could not see her over the phone. "No." As much as she wanted to help Nella and Sally, she didn't like the insistent tone in Carolyn's voice. It disturbed her. Also, she wanted to wait a while to see if Minnie reappeared. Minnie would know what to do about Valentino.

At least Minnie would insist on going with Columbia to take a picture of Valentino at home. Which would greatly soothe April's nagging feeling that she was abandoning the poodle to a dire fate.

Except looking over at Columbia, a woman of the same age as her grandmother, feeling so afraid seemed a wrong response. Not that her grandmother couldn't be terrifying if somebody misbehaved. But she'd never hurt a dog or cat (chickens went into the pot and couldn't be treated as pets, as April learned to her sorrow quite young). In fact, her grandmother would take a broom to anyone who teased or harassed a puppy.

"Could you possibly come a little earlier? I have a car. Should I pick you up at your office?" Carolyn's voice recalled April to their conversation. "Or could you come to my office? You know where it is."

Why did she dread meeting the doctor?

Was she afraid of everyone these days?

April took a deep breath. Why shouldn't she meet Carolyn Fern? After all, she had called her in the first place. If it would aid Nella and Sally, she wanted to help. But she also wanted her friends close by. Going to Carolyn's office seemed like a bad idea.

"Perhaps I can be home by five," April compromised. "I have a friend nearby who is driving me home." She was glad Lefty had already planned to give her a ride. He would be nearly done with his garbage run by now and headed to the incinerator. Lefty had asked her to leave work early too. "Very well. I will be there then and explain more when I see you." Carolyn made a brief goodbye and hung up.

With reluctance, April hung up her receiver. She wished Carolyn had explained now. Which would have given her an hour or more to worry about whatever Carolyn wanted, but she could worry with knowledge about whether or not what she was worrying about was worth worrying about.

That thought left her more confused than before. And she still needed to return Valentino to Columbia.

Columbia returned to the counter with a piece of paper. "Here's a copy of the ad I placed when my sister lost the dog," she said.

Surprised to receive any explanation from Columbia, April looked at the paper. It was the order for the ad that she had found in Sunday's newspaper. The one which so blandly described Valentino as a lost white dog. The style certainly seemed like something Columbia would write. It also explained how the ad was placed without April seeing it. She didn't work on Sunday. Columbia must have phoned it in. There were staff there during the day to take such orders and the ad had run in the last edition of the day. But she must have paid extra too. A rushed ad on a Sunday, a display ad, cost more than a regular classified ad. Columbia obviously wanted to recover the poodle.

If somebody worked so hard to find a dog, they wouldn't hurt it, April told herself, not admitting that Columbia scared her a little. There was something about the stare. Or perhaps the way that she clutched her green umbrella as she pulled it from the rack and held out her other hand again for Valentino's leash.

"I am glad Valentino is found," April said, handing the leash to Columbia while she tried to convince herself that she was doing the right thing. As Columbia rearranged her things, she handed the umbrella to April to hold for a moment.

The umbrella had a very strange carving on its handle, and April had twirled it one way and the other as she gave Columbia a number of unnecessary messages for Valentino's owner and wished the puppy an unhappy goodbye.

"Minnie wanted to take a picture for a story," April said, casting another forlorn glance at Minnie's empty desk. "Perhaps your sister could come to the office? Or we could take Valentino's picture at your sister's home? I can arrange it just as soon as Minnie comes in. If you wanted to wait, Minnie could go with you." Assuming Minnie would ever return to the office! April was starting to feel a bit desperate about her too. At the same time, a glance at the wall clock reminded her that Carolyn Fern would be arriving soon on Flotsam Street. She needed to go. But she hated abandoning Valentino.

Columbia frowned. It was a very slight frown, barely a downturn of her lips, but April stepped back. At Columbia's feet, Valentino gave an uneasy whine, which made April wince in sympathy.

"We don't like publicity," Columbia said.

Which was a very odd statement for a woman who worked at a newspaper.

But then Columbia, April thought as she handed back the green umbrella, was a very odd woman.

April hoped she'd done the right thing by giving Valentino to her boss. But she still wanted to snatch the puppy back as Columbia led the reluctant poodle out of the door.

CHAPTER NINETEEN

To her relief, April found Lefty immediately at the garbage company. The day crew was leaving and the night crew was coming in. Both groups lingered in the yard, exchanging bottles and muttering comments about the never-ending rain. Behind them the great roaring furnaces of the incinerator burned with a startling hiss as the water dripped down the chimneys and blew through the open doors. The trash loaded on the groaning conveyer belt was drenched but still moved with slow precision into the incinerator building.

Despite the pouring rain, the fire won, and Arkham's debris was released into the air as thick inky clouds of black smoke. A sickly-sweet odor laced with a metallic tang permeated the yard, the scent of Northside intensified and refined by fire. Behind the hulking brick building containing the furnaces, the barges waited, floating high on the rushing river. The ashes and anything which wouldn't burn were cleaned out of the ovens after they cooled. Yesterday's residue was already piled behind the building and waiting to be shoveled onto the barges by the night crew. Then Arkham's burnt garbage would be dragged out to sea and its final resting place beneath the waves.

April found the place intimidating. The clanking unseen machinery within the incinerator building, punctuated by the occasional hiss of escaping steam, sounded eerily like one of her nightmares.

She ignored the bottles wrapped in paper sacks being passed from man to man. Tonight would be a terrible night to do an already brutal job, rolling wheelbarrow after wheelbarrow of ash and debris down the wharf to the waiting barges. Those who drove the trucks and gathered garbage around the city were the lucky ones, as Lefty once told her. The night crew would be wading in yesterday's cold ashes and be up to their knees in burned trash by midnight as they spread the filth evenly across the holds of the barges. So if one man passed another a bottle for a quick nip against the night's cold, she recognized it as an act of kindness.

"No Valentino?" said Lefty when April approached him. He slung a bundle of tarps and ropes into Pequod's truck bed. The rain sluiced off his sou'wester and coat.

"We found Valentino's owner." April corrected herself as soon as she said it. "Well, somebody who knows the owner found me. Columbia, who works at the newspaper. She is taking Valentino home to her sister."

"That's good news, isn't it?" Lefty hadn't missed the worry in April's voice.

April sighed. "I suppose so. There's something about her. I thought people would be more excited to be reunited with their pet. But she was so cold."

"Perhaps because the dog belongs to her sister, not to her?" Lefty opened the door of the truck and motioned April to climb up into the cab.

"Yes. That might be it." April hopped on the truck's running board and jumped into the dry cab as quickly as she could. The rain beat a hard tattoo on the roof over her head. If anything, the rain was growing worse. She regretted leaving home without a sturdy umbrella like Columbia's. If she did admire anything about Columbia this night, it was the sensible umbrella. She'd been very aware of the green umbrella during her last conversation with Columbia.

April could have used just such an umbrella today. During the brief walk between the newspaper's offices and the garbage company, her once stylish cloche hat wilted and now clung limply to her head.

Relieved to be out of the rain, April blotted herself dry as well as she could with a handkerchief. Lefty leveraged himself up and behind the wheel with a distinct squelch. The water ran off his oilskin coat to pool on the floor of the truck.

April pulled off her soggy hat and set it on the bench seat between them. The tires hissed over the wet pavement. As they turned out of the yard, the reflections of the streetlights gleamed in the puddles.

"It looks worse," April said.

"They're moving all the trucks out of the Rivertown yard and Northside." Lefty gestured over his right shoulder. "The river is rising. It may be over the embankment by morning. Everyone is sure now that both neighborhoods will flood."

Dismayed but not surprised by Lefty's information, April twisted in the seat and peered out the back window. A line of trucks snaked out of the garbage yard, although most turned in a different direction once they cleared the garbage company's gates.

"They were talking at the office about what to do if the presses flood," April told Lefty. "Everyone seems to be expecting trouble."

"We're driving as much equipment as possible to higher ground tonight." Lefty chuckled a little. "I told them I'd park

Pequod on French Hill after I picked up something on Flotsam Street. So I'll take you all the way to the door."

April pictured a garbage truck left on French Hill in front of one of the stately mansions. She muffled a small giggle at the thought.

"Really I'm planning to leave Pequod on Flotsam Street until morning," Lefty said. "If we have to leave quickly, we can load the back with everyone who needs help, including the sleepers."

It was the plan discussed over breakfast. Alarmed at the thought, April looked over the wet streets. "We won't need to evacuate, will we?" she said. For some reason, she expected the water to come no closer than the front door of Mrs Garcia's house. Flotsam Street might be cut off from the rest of the city by a flood … but actually destroyed by rising waters? The impact of that she hadn't comprehended until now.

"I don't know, April." Lefty heaved a sigh. "I have never seen the river so high. The water's almost over the wharf. They were arguing in the yard about the barges. Some of the captains want to tow them down river now, rather than waiting for them to be loaded. But the bosses want to load first and then let them go. Either way, it's going to be a bad night."

Inside the cab with the rain fogging the windows, April felt a bit ashamed of her own fears. People would be facing much worse tonight than a few nightmares.

"Hey, did you have any luck with the doctor? Can she help Nella?" Lefty's voice was hearty as if he was trying to cheer them both up.

"Yes! Dr Fern is coming to the boarding house." April squirmed on the seat, trying to catch a glimpse of the world outside the truck cab to judge how far away they were.

Lefty cranked down the passenger window on his side to swipe at the windshield with the manual wiper. "Sorry," he muttered as the wind and the rain invaded the cab.

"It's fine." April huddled down into her coat, still pinning her hopes on Carolyn Fern finding a way to help Nella and Sally. That would be a solution to at least one problem. April also tried very hard not to think about the grim statistics recited by Willa Murgatroyd this morning. But she did remember her comments about the destruction and despair wrought by the flood of 1874. All those poor dead dogs in the Black Cave! At least Valentino should be safe now with Columbia and her sister.

Pequod inched along as Lefty navigated the rainy streets with grim determination. Neither of them spoke again until April spotted the lights of Schoffner's General Store.

"Almost home," she breathed.

Lefty's shoulders dropped about an inch as he gave a relieved grunt.

They turned onto Flotsam Street. The downpour continued. All the boarding houses had lights burning in nearly every window. It should have looked like a holiday, but somehow the lights gleaming in the wet night seemed more like a beacon, calling the lost and storm-tossed to a temporary haven.

As soon as Lefty came to a full stop, April was out of the cab and racing up the steps to Mrs Garcia's front door. Inside she found everyone waiting for her in the parlor, including Carolyn Fern.

Everyone except Ollie.

"Where's Ollie?" April asked after she greeted Carolyn. She wanted the nurse there, as Ollie would know more about medical treatment than her. April was almost certain that Carolyn would be helpful. But she trusted Ollie's judgment as a nurse more than her own when it came to the health of Nella and Sally.

"Ollie phoned Mrs Alba's," said Mrs Garcia. "They sent Marco over with the message. The nurses are all staying at St Mary's tonight."

"This storm is causing problems," said Carolyn. "So as many

as can stay will do so. It's better than the doctors and nurses going home and being trapped there when they are needed at the hospital."

"Unless somebody needs them at home," said Mrs Garcia.

"How is everyone?" April asked, hoping for some good news.

Mrs Garcia had none to offer. "No change. Those who were asleep are still asleep. Everyone else is drinking coffee and afraid to go to bed. And it's still raining."

April knew this summary covered the entire street, not just Mrs Garcia's house.

"I went to the store." Mrs Garcia confirmed her thoughts. "It's the same everywhere in Rivertown. Too many people asleep, too much water falling from the sky."

A knocking sounded on the front door. "More bad news," predicted Mrs Garcia.

"Genevieve came by." Lefty had shed his coat, hat, and wet boots in the hallway. Still dressed in his blue coveralls, he escorted the tall young woman who lived at Mrs Iskander's boarding house into the parlor.

April liked Genevieve. She was a jolly gal, fun to be with, and had invited Nella and April out a few times. Which April had not told Mrs Garcia, as Mrs Garcia disapproved of Genevieve's boyfriend, a member of the Drowned Rats.

The local gang took small boats on the river to run errands which rarely occurred during the day. Mostly the Drowned Rats stayed near the docks of Rivertown and away from Flotsam Street, although Mrs Alba was supposed to have a nephew in the gang.

"Sol and his friends plan to clear the drains throughout Rivertown. The water is backing up into several houses by the Miskatonic," said Genevieve. April knew Sol was her young man and the friends were probably the Drowned Rats. "They want to know if you need any help."

Mrs Garcia pursed her lips. A kindness was a kindness, even if it meant beholding to the Drowned Rats or Genevieve. "Lefty swept our drains this morning," she said. "But ask them to check the big storm drains at the top and bottom of the street."

"Will do, Mrs Garcia!" Genevieve turned to go.

"Genevieve, tell them to come around to the kitchen door when they are done. I made sandwiches earlier and there's too many for us to eat," Mrs Garcia added. "I'll have hot coffee, too."

"You're the buzzing best, Mrs Garcia." Genevieve gave them all a cheerful wave. "They'll clean the drains after they pull their boats out of the river. Sol plans to move the boats as high as they can. But they'll be around soon."

The little dinghies and canoes used by the Drowned Rats could slip between the pilings of a wharf when they wanted. But the river roaring through Arkham right now was like nothing April had ever seen. She knew the Drowned Rats hid their boats when the law came through Rivertown. But this sounded like they anticipated a different type of trouble.

"Everyone is expecting a flood then." Lefty grunted as Genevieve let herself out to tell the other boarding houses help would be coming from the Drowned Rats. "We should keep an eye on the street tonight."

"Who wants to sleep? I must go make more coffee now. And more sandwiches. Sol and his friends will eat an entire loaf and still be hungry." Mrs Garcia looked at Carolyn Fern. "For a doctor, what you propose sounds like dangerous magic. But it is April's decision."

With that troubling pronouncement, Mrs Garcia left the room.

CHAPTER TWENTY

April looked at Carolyn Fern. "What did Mrs Garcia mean?"

"It's not magic." Carolyn appeared ruffled. April guessed Mrs Garcia had made a few of her more pithy comments before April arrived. "As I told you earlier, I use hypnosis to help people resolve problems."

"But you can't hypnotize sleeping people, can you?" April asked. Of course, in *The Cabinet of Dr Caligari*, the murderer Cesare slept while under Caligari's control. She wished she didn't remember the movie so clearly. Obviously being scared half to death at the age of thirteen stuck in a person's head. But April kept telling herself that Carolyn Fern was not Dr Caligari. She wouldn't do something to Nella and Sally that would hurt them. Or turn them into irrational killers.

"No, of course not," said Carolyn to April's relief. Then she looked around at the other people in the parlor. "Is there some place where we could speak more privately?"

Lefty looked up from the paper he was reading when Carolyn spoke. But then he looked at April as if to say it was her decision. Mr and Mrs Sullivan were paying no attention at all to the conversation. The couple had moved a small table near the window and were playing some version of two-handed bridge to distract themselves.

"Nobody will be in the dining room," said April after a moment's consideration. She thought Carolyn might want to ask her some personal questions about Nella and Sally. Although she could have told Carolyn that everyone knew everyone's business when you lived in a boarding house.

But as soon as they entered the dining room and Carolyn shut the door to the hall, she made a much more startling request. "I would like to hypnotize you."

Much to April's consternation, her startled "Why?" came out as a squeak. She sounded as if she was a child again instead of a sensible working woman of twenty. Although she might have expected this when Carolyn asked her questions about her dreams.

"You have been having nightmares similar to the other patients that I treated. Nightmares which involved a tower and a man in a gold mask." Carolyn confirmed what April feared. She wanted April as a test subject, just like the doctors in the pulp stories.

"Well, yes." April wondered if she should push past Carolyn and leave. Or perhaps she should stay and hear what she had to say. Again, she told herself, Carolyn was not an evil mastermind who escaped from a madhouse. She was a doctor trying to help people.

"I was so glad you said you had seen the man in the golden mask," said Carolyn. "Your dreams may be the key we need to understand why others are having nightmares and cannot wake. If I can hold you in a hypnagogic state, where you are suspended between wakefulness and dreaming, we can work together to control your dream and find the answers we need."

April had no desire at all to be hypnotized. Also, it was Nella and Sally who were asleep. She doubted hypnotizing her would help them. She expressed her doubts to Carolyn.

"These repetitive nightmares are overwhelming so many people. Together we can break the cycle. I know we can." Carolyn's forceful tone wasn't hostile, but it was unnervingly direct as if she was trying to quash every fear April held.

The intensity of Carolyn's gaze as she locked eyes with April felt as overwhelming as the nightmares. More so, if April was being honest with herself. It was as if Carolyn's stare could discover and dissect every uncertainty hidden within April's mind.

April squirmed, backing up a step or two until she bumped into the dining room table.

"I'm not sure…" she began. Except she was sure. April was absolutely certain that she didn't want to be hypnotized. She started to speak, wanting to explain that this was about Dr Caligari and not her personal opinion of Carolyn.

But as soon as April mentioned the movie, Carolyn grimaced.

"That's nonsense," she said. "A ridiculous story made up by people who don't know a thing about how hypnosis is used in a responsible practice. You might as well say that you're afraid of hypnosis because of *Dracula* or *Trilby*."

April adored both books. And thought they were a fairly good excuse to be worried about hypnosis.

Carolyn went on, cutting off her objections before April could voice them fully.

"I am no Svengali. You have nothing to fear," Carolyn said.

"I just don't want to lose control of my mind," April responded.

"But you won't lose control. It's a myth that hypnotists can make you do something against your will," Carolyn responded. "Your most basic beliefs and desires cannot be changed. You want to help, so your actions under hypnosis will help."

"Perhaps somebody else would be better. I can talk to the other boarders on Flotsam Street. Ask them what they've seen in their nightmares," said April, aware she was failing miserably at being brave. But Carolyn's arguments dismayed her more than persuaded her. If only she could have a little time to think this over.

Carolyn had no patience with her hesitation.

"We cannot wait. You are the only person that I have found who has experienced these nightmares involving the man in the golden mask who remains awake. We must proceed." Carolyn drew a sharp breath. Her voice came out a bit louder. "This is vital. I must know why–"

"What are you doing in my dining room?" said Mrs Garcia from the doorway which led to the kitchen.

Preoccupied with Carolyn's speech, April had completely missed Mrs Garcia's entrance. But she was delighted to see her sturdy landlady standing there, matching Carolyn Fern with a gaze as steely and determined as the doctor.

"We are having a private conversation." While completely factual, the statement from Carolyn was absolutely the wrong thing to say to Mrs Garcia as April could have told her, if anyone allowed her to slip in a word edgewise.

As it was, Mrs Garcia snapped back, "My dining room is a place for eating. Not for foolish talk. I am preparing to serve a meal here, as I do every night at six. I still have tenants who need to eat. Also, I have a crew of men coming to my back door for sandwiches after dinner."

"Mrs Garcia, I do not think you understand," Carolyn began.

April winced.

Puffing up like one of April's aunts when Uncle Tito said something foolish, Mrs Garcia looked Carolyn up and down with one comprehensive flick of her eyes.

"I understand. I understand you are a doctor who wishes to make our April dream terrible dreams." The way Mrs Garcia said "doctor" sounded as if she was pronouncing a curse. April was a little flattered to be called "our April" as Mrs Garcia rarely said such things unless boasting about her tenants to Mrs Alba and the other landladies.

"Hypnosis is a perfectly safe technique which will help–"

But Mrs Garcia was not going to let Carolyn regain control of the conversation. "If it is so safe, then why did you need our April?" Again her accent turned "safe" into a highly questionable if not downright dangerous trait. "Why do you not practice this safe technique on the patients in the hospital? Why do you come all the way across Arkham to Flotsam Street to plague us?"

"I am not plaguing…" Carolyn stopped and blinked. April guessed she was counting to ten in her head. It was a technique April often used when dealing with her aunts and mother when discussions grew heated in two languages simultaneously.

"Mrs Garcia, I mean no harm to anyone." Carolyn's voice was the epitome of reason.

"Help the patients in the hospital so our Ollie can come home." Mrs Garcia looked almost smug after making this verbal jab. April could feel the control of the room, never truly in doubt, was now firmly in Mrs Garcia's work-reddened hands.

"The patients in the hospital are all asleep. I cannot hypnotize them." Carolyn stepped back, like a fighter trying to recover from an unexpected blow.

April could guess Carolyn was struggling to maintain her calm. She could sympathize. Which was part of the problem. She liked Carolyn. Rather, as with Columbia, she admired Carolyn. She wanted to be like those women, to be so comfortable and calm in themselves that they could take charge and make things happen. But the very thought of submitting her will to someone else, to allow them to control her dreams, even if it would help Nella, simply terrified her. No matter how much she admired Carolyn for becoming a psychologist, how could she trust her?

Mrs Garcia all but snorted at Carolyn's admission that there was nobody at the hospital to be hypnotized. Actually, Mrs Garcia did snort, but in a very landlady specific way developed from confronting tenants trying to wiggle out of certain rules. "How many of them did you hypnotize before they fell asleep and could not wake up?"

"Only twelve." Carolyn practically snapped the answer. Then she was silent while the last two words lingered in the air.

"Better our April not be the thirteenth." Mrs Garcia rested her case.

Carolyn cast one last appealing look to April.

"It is your choice," said Mrs Garcia to April. Then she pointed at Carolyn. "It is not her wishes that we consider." Another very Mrs Garcia grimace at April. "I cannot decide for you." Although it was obvious Mrs Garcia had opinions. "You must do what you think is best."

With all her fears confirmed and the bulk of Mrs Garcia at her back to give her courage, April crossed her arms across her chest. "I don't want to be hypnotized," she said.

And then, because she was April and couldn't stand to upset anyone, she added, "Isn't there any other way that I can help you?"

"I am afraid not." Carolyn looked resigned, which made April feel worse.

"I want to help," April repeated.

"I am going back to St Mary's," Carolyn said. "If you change your mind about hypnosis, you can find me there."

April followed Carolyn into the hall, trying to think of a way to secure the doctor's help without undergoing hypnosis. Carolyn put on her hat and coat.

"Don't forget your umbrella," said Mrs Garcia from the dining room doorway. Carolyn pulled a handsome green umbrella from the stand by the door. Unlike Columbia, she kept hers tightly furled until she stepped outside.

"Please, if you change your mind, call me," she said. "I will be at St Mary's all night." Then she opened up the umbrella, revealing the same oddly carved handle as April had seen on Columbia's umbrella. They must all come from the same store, April thought, but she couldn't remember seeing anything like these umbrellas advertised in the newspaper.

After Carolyn left, April turned to Mrs Garcia. "Now what will we do?" For Nella and Sally were still fast asleep upstairs and April didn't know how to wake them up.

"We eat dinner and then we make sandwiches," said Mrs Garcia. "You help me cut the bread."

CHAPTER TWENTY-ONE

Mrs Garcia's prediction that Sol and his friends would eat all the bread proved true. They devoured the equivalent of three loaves, and all the cheese in the house went into the first round of sandwiches. After the cheese disappeared and a few young men still looked sadly hungry, Mrs Garcia sighed, pulled a tub of peanut butter and a jar of jelly from her pantry, and made those childish sandwiches with April's help.

The Drowned Rats resembled their name, with everyone dripping wet. So they stayed in the kitchen, gathered around the big central table, wolfing down the sandwiches and drinking every cup of hot coffee that April poured.

As they ate, the Drowned Rats reported the condition of the streets ("wet") and the state of the river ("rising"). But their wholesale clearance of the neighborhood drains did seem to be working. So far none of the streets held standing water and most houses were dry.

"The city is going to start distributing sandbags," said Sol, Genevieve's boyfriend and apparent leader of this small group. "The mayor sent stacks of sandbags to Schoffner's General Store. Mr Googe is making drop offs around the neighborhood with his truck. We'll help you ladies with your sandbags as soon as he gets back to Flotsam Street."

Mrs Garcia raised an eyebrow at the suggestion that she couldn't sandbag her own house, but she handed Sol another sandwich.

It took April a moment to realize that Sol was talking about Lefty and Pequod. She wasn't used to thinking of her friend as Mr Googe. But he was nearly twenty years older than the Drowned Rats so she shouldn't have been surprised that Sol called him Mr Googe. After all, she only called Mrs Garcia by her last name. In fact, she wasn't even sure she knew her landlady's first name.

"Can't you sandbag along the riverbank?" asked April, thinking that stopping the water there would be the best idea. She had some vague memory of her father and uncles doing this when she was very young, when a nearby river threatened to overrun their hometown.

Sol shook his head. "It would take more supplies and more people than we have. The best we can do is stop the water from going under the doors." He shared with April their plans to barricade basement doors and windows, especially at the more necessary places like Schoffner's and St Stanislaus Church.

"But will that be enough?" she said.

Sol shook his head. "Not nearly. Too many houses and warehouses right along the Miskatonic. Christchurch Cemetery will have floating coffins by morning."

April shuddered.

"Aw, it's not so bad," said Sol, who had grown up in Rivertown. "Father Iwanaki will bless any that come up with the waters and have them buried again. He's already making up a roster of volunteer gravediggers to help."

Mrs Garcia slapped her forehead. "Father Iwanaki! I forgot. We put together a basket for him earlier. From all the landladies of Flotsam Street. You boys take it to him. He will be at the church all night, in case any need refuge."

Sol nodded. "Will do, Mrs Garcia. We're heading there next to clear the drains."

Then he turned back to April with a wicked gleam in his eye. She could understand why Genevieve was so taken with him. He was a tease, but in a way that made a gal smile.

"But the graveyard isn't the scariest place to be in a flood," he said, dropping his voice to a mock whisper. "When the Black Cave floods, you never know what secrets will wash out."

"Probably a few boxes of rum," grumbled Mrs Garcia as she pulled the basket from the pantry and plopped it on the table in front of Sol. The rest of the gang was gathering up their coats, putting on their hats, and gulping down their coffee. The last few peanut butter and jelly sandwiches disappeared into hungry mouths.

"Not any contraband in the Black Cave," said Sol with great confidence. "At least not since ten o'clock this morning."

"The Drowned Rats cleaned it out," Mrs Garcia said with a shake of her head.

A few of the men gathered around the table chuckled and clapped each other on their backs.

"Mrs Garcia! How could you say such a thing?" Sol grinned. But he also didn't deny his crew had cleared the Black Cave of any bootlegger booty before moving their boats out of the river. His voice dropped back to an ominous whisper and his friends all leaned in to hear the rest of his story. "But I'm talking of the great flood of 1874, when they found the Black Cave full of…"

"Dead dogs," said April, suddenly remembering the conversation with the lady at City Hall. It was a horrible thought.

Sol reared back from her. "Yeah," he said, with the disappointed huff of a storyteller robbed of his last line. "Dozens of dead dogs, my grandpa said."

"That's bunk," said one of the Drowned Rats, looking far more upset than April. "Dogs are too smart to get caught in the Black Cave."

"Nah," said another. "They might go in there. Didn't we hear something barking this morning?"

The first one appeared dismayed by his friend's comment. "I told you that we should have gone all the way to the back."

"There ain't no luck going too far back in the Black Cave," said the second. "You know. It's not safe to go beyond the Eye."

"What's the Eye?" April said, intrigued by this small exchange.

Wrestling back the story and returning to being the center of attention, Sol grabbed the pad and pencil Mrs Garcia kept on the kitchen table for writing notes to the dairyman. He sketched a round circle with a dot in the center. "That's the Eye," he said.

"How do you know it's an eye?" asked April. "It could just be a circle. With a dot."

"Because everyone calls it the Eye. It's a couple chambers back from the entrance," said Sol. "It's been there since my grandfather's day."

"The grandfather who saw the dead dogs?" asked the first Drowned Rat. "How did he know they were dead? Maybe the dogs were sleeping." He looked very proud of this explanation.

"No. It was in a letter from the mayor," April assured him. "Dozens of dead dogs had to be taken out of the Black Cave. Nobody wanted to do it."

The Drowned Rat gave her a look like she'd killed his dog. "I am going to have nightmares now," he muttered, tossing down a half-eaten peanut butter and jelly sandwich.

"You were having nightmares before," said the unsympathetic Sol. "We all are."

"About towers and a man in a golden mask?" April asked eagerly. Perhaps she could persuade one of the Drowned Rats to undergo hypnosis with Carolyn. Which would relieve her guilt about refusing the psychologist's request.

"Nope," said the Drowned Rat. "A man in a golden mask sounds like something from *Weird Tales*. Mr Googe loans us his magazines. Those are good stories with no dead dogs." He glared at the other Drowned Rats, who wisely kept their mouths shut. "I wouldn't mind a dream like that."

Although pleased to meet another fan of the pulps, April was disappointed to learn they weren't dreaming about the tower and the masked man who so fascinated Carolyn. "What do you dream about?"

"Well," said the Drowned Rat, thrusting out his chest a little.

"Hey, look, a doll is finally taking an interest in our Joey," muttered another one.

"Shut up," said Joey to the mutterer. He cleared his throat and smoothed down the front of his jacket. "I dream about the river. And boats. And the Eye."

"Just like all the rest of us," said Sol. "Ever since someone repainted the Eye."

April took another look at the drawing on the notepad. She had seen that very design somewhere else and recently. If only she could remember where. She certainly had never dared enter the Black Cave. No matter how much Nella nagged it would be an adventure.

"Repainted the Eye?" she asked Sol.

He shrugged and nodded. "It used to be very faded. Just a few faint lines. I knew it was there because my grandfather pointed it out. It's supposed to be bad luck to go beyond it."

"So you never went past the Eye?" April said.

"Nah. Never needed to. It's a long way back. Some professors from the university paid my grandfather to show it to them. But they were upset when they saw it. Said the Eye was too modern. Probably painted in their lifetime."

"Probably they thought your grandfather painted it," said Mrs Garcia, reaching around him to collect up the dishes and dump them in the sink. At a glare from her, a couple of Drowned Rats started rinsing off the plates. "I remember your grandfather. A prankster and a smuggler." Then she shrugged. "But not a bad looking man. He liked to flirt with all the girls. I remember dancing with him once or twice before I married Mr Garcia."

"Not denying Granddad liked his jokes," said Sol. "But he always claimed the Eye was there when he was a boy. But on Sunday, somebody painted over it. Or rather repainted it then."

"Sunday? How do you know they did it on Sunday?" April asked.

"Because it was a newly painted Eye on Sunday night." Sol didn't elaborate on what they were doing in the Black Cave on a Sunday. But April could guess. Bootlegging business.

"It was very faded on Saturday, same as always. When we went back on Sunday, it was a very obvious bright green circle with a dot in the middle." Sol pulled his cap out of his back pocket and put it on his head.

"Green?" said April. She had seen something green and with a circle like this. But what?

"Emerald green. They probably bought the paint from Schoffner's." Sol looked around. The dishes were cleared. The coffee was gone. He picked up the basket for Father Iwanaki. "We better stop lollygagging. Lots left to do tonight."

Mrs Garcia slathered the last two heels of bread with butter and thrust them at Sol.

"Go," she said. "Locusts may descend next. But at least there will be nothing for them to eat."

"Thanks, Mrs Garcia." Sol's voice was a bit muffled as he

crammed both pieces of bread into his mouth at the same time. "You're the buzzing best."

"Genevieve already told me about my buzz." Mrs Garcia waved the Drowned Rats out the door. "Be careful near the river," she said as they trooped outside. "Your grandmothers have had enough sorrow. Come home safe tonight." She closed the door and turned back to her almost empty kitchen.

"I think I'll go sit with Nella," said April, not knowing what else to do. She didn't want to think about her argument with Carolyn Fern or dead dogs. The eye that Sol had drawn on the notepad seemed to glare up at her, almost as if it heralded even greater trouble.

Mrs Garcia fetched flour, shortening, sugar and yeast from her pantry. She put all the ingredients in the middle of the table in a very straight line.

"You sit with her," said Mrs Garcia. "I will make the bread for tomorrow." She thumped down the big metal hand-cranked mixer next. According to Mrs Garcia, she had been making bread with this particular mixer for more than twenty years. April grew up with a similar mixer in her house and had sore arms just from looking at it.

But still she offered to stay and help.

Mrs Garcia waved her away. "I mix," she said. "It helps me think. If my thinking makes me mad, I will knead too. Maybe even pound this dough." She glared at the ingredients on the table. "If only the rain would stop. And our girls would wake up."

"I know, Mrs Garcia, I know," said April.

April stopped in the parlor to check on the Sullivans, telling them that Mrs Garcia was pounding out bread in the kitchen. They just nodded like old-fashioned china dolls and kept their eyes on their cards. She hadn't the heart to ask the old couple if they had had any nightmares involving a masked man.

Upstairs, she found Nella's room was unusually tidy. April

guessed Ollie or Mrs Garcia had folded up all the clothing and even straightened the dresser scarf. Nella's cosmetics, the little china doll which held her rings, and the carved lacquer box that April gave her last Christmas all stood in a neat line on the top of the dresser. The Kewpie doll which Nella won at the county fair when they were both sixteen looked especially forlorn on her bedside table.

Or perhaps it was just April who felt wretched, looking down at Nella in her bed. Even her messy curls had been combed in the neatly waved bob that she always struggled to achieve. That would have been Ollie's touch, thought April, noting Nella's face had also been washed clean of the freckle fading cream that she so adored.

The sleeping Nella looked too much as if she'd been laid out for a funeral, April decided. She reached over and deliberately scrunched up Nella's bangs. Then she dragged her chair over to the bed.

"Nella," April said, reaching under the counterpane and clutching her friend's hand. "You have to wake up. There's something happening. Something awful. You love horrible scary things, like Lon Chaney. You always said so. You wanted an adventure. I don't. Please wake up."

Holding her hand, April told Nella about her strange day. About the streets running with rain, and the river creeping ever higher on its banks, and abandoning poor Valentino to Columbia's care.

"I think that was a mistake," April whispered to Nella. "I don't know why. But I wish I hadn't given the dog to Columbia. Valentino is just a puppy."

She talked, and talked, more than she ever told Nella when they were both awake. Because Nella had been the one who told stories about everything and could talk to everyone. April had been very content to bob along in Nella's wake, doing whatever she suggested. Like moving to Arkham after they graduated from high school. And getting jobs. And being flappers (well, pretending to be flappers as April still hadn't bobbed her hair). Going out with dashing girls like Genevieve to dance in speakeasies.

Nella made it possible for April to feel like a real American, even though she had a slight accent picked up from her mother and her aunts. Even though her skin was browner and her hair blacker than all the other girls in their high school. Even though her entire family came from the Philippines, a country that nobody in the United States apparently ever heard of because everyone always asked if April was Mexican.

Most importantly, though, Nella didn't care about any of that. She even accepted that April didn't want to bob her hair (well, she grumbled but she accepted). Nella didn't try to make April into anything except what April wanted to be.

Nella was a true friend.

"And we have such plans. We are going to see London and Paris," whispered April, so tired from talking that she could barely hold her head up. So she withdrew her hand from Nella's limp one, and folded her arms on the counterpane. She put her head down and let herself take a deep breath.

Then April dreamed of green umbrellas, a tower, and the man in a golden mask. Everywhere she looked in her dream, she saw the eye. But it was no longer a circle with a dot. The eye was huge and staring straight at her, a terrible green monstrosity like something dredged from Arkham's garbage resting at the bottom of the ocean.

More horrible still, she knew the eye was able to see all the way to the bottom of her soul.

CHAPTER TWENTY-TWO

It was well past visiting hours, but the hospital lacked the customary feel of night duty. A jittery tension still remained among the staff, who were constantly peering out of the windows and whispering to each other about the steady onslaught of rain. With most of the day nurses staying on and adding to the conversation, the place had an unusual buzz of gloomy anticipation.

Carolyn remembered wandering the silence of the night wards at one asylum, checking on patients as a very young psychologist, still trying to earn the trust of the disapproving French doctors. An American! And a woman! How horrified they had been when she started work at the Chateau and how hard she had to overcome their initial resentment.

But that assignment had been a very long time ago. She could no longer remember the names of those disapproving doctors. Just the long shadows cast by the snowcapped Alps, looming outside the windows, and the queer iron gate at the end of the drive, which could only be operated by one switch inside the asylum. It all felt like someone else's memory or even a book that she had read.

Even as she thought this, Carolyn became convinced she was remembering a story. Not her own life. Just somebody else's suggestion of what a psychologist might experience.

This disassociation with her own memories was growing worse, Carolyn recognized. If she wanted to diagnose herself, she would chalk it up to lack of sleep and frustration. The argument at the boarding house with the landlady rankled, far more than it should. She was used to setbacks. Any woman who pursued a career in medicine, especially medicine of the mind, needed to have the skin of a rhinoceros, one of her early mentors had said.

But she'd also been an idiot. The nurse, Ollie, had told her to go after supper. That would have been easier on the landlady rather than interrupt her plans for serving dinner. Carolyn knew April May had her doubts about hypnosis. She'd thrown both women on the defensive. She should have expected some hostility and handled it better.

Oh, be honest with yourself, Carolyn decided. April May was terrified of hypnosis. Instead of listening to her and discussing her fears, Carolyn had talked down to April, tried to push her into being hypnotized, and completely forgot everything she knew about persuading people. Trying to make somebody feel guilty was the worst possible way to bring about a positive outcome.

When had she become such a poor practitioner of psychology? She felt as if her head was suddenly stuffed full of cotton wool, with all the little cues and signals that she was so used to interpreting concealed from her. Blocked by an underlying core of anger and despair so foreign to her nature. She almost felt as if there was someone else in her head, a Carolyn that she didn't like very much.

Everything had been going so well. She had the private practice that she had wanted. Now she seemed set on confirming everyone's fear of overbearing psychologists rather than actually helping them.

She was lucky, Carolyn knew, to find such quick acceptance in Arkham. Her first work in the town at the Arkham Sanatorium led to numerous professional friendships. She'd encountered so many cases which improved her understanding of dreams. Her use of hypnosis continued to yield stunningly good results, despite the popular prejudice against her technique. Even her shipboard friendship with Augusta Palmer brought about an established practice, a well-run office with an efficient secretary. Professionally, she was very close to achieving every goal that she had set for herself.

So why was she so upset because one young woman was afraid to be hypnotized?

Then Carolyn passed an open doorway and saw the six beds within the room, each containing a sleeping patient, a patient who would not wake. Her answer lay there. These people needed her help. She needed answers to help them. Even answers like those Harvey Walters proposed.

If she could only think of another way to reach Luke Robinson than hypnotizing April May!

"Carolyn, there you are." Roger strode down the hall. "Thank you for coming in. We will need all the assistance we can get before the night is over."

"Are there more sleeping patients?" Carolyn supposed when this was all over, they'd have to find a more scientific term to describe their patients. Something long, involving Latin probably, but for now "sleeping patients" worked.

"Yes. Fewer people are coming in this evening than earlier in the day, but I think that's the rain. People are very reluctant to leave their homes if they don't have to. But the switchboard has had numerous calls. We are advising them to keep their loved ones as comfortable as possible in their own beds. For now, at least."

Exactly how April's friends were being cared for, thought Carolyn. Perhaps Mrs Garcia wasn't entirely wrong.

"Any change in the patients already here? Have none woken up?" Carolyn was fairly sure that Roger would have spoken out immediately if that was true. But she had to ask.

"Nothing has changed. So far this sleep is not life threatening," he said, "but if it continues past seventy-two hours, we may need to take more extreme measures."

"Like what?" Images of water immersion, electric shocks, and other horrors of asylum life flashed briefly across her tired mind. Even the bloodletting so beloved of nineteenth century doctors. Surely St Mary's would not resort to such horrors?

"I have one young idiot advocating cranial surgery." Obviously Roger agreed with her views of the more extreme ways of "healing" the brain. "Dr Marheswaran has made some much more sensible suggestions."

"Marheswaran?" Carolyn couldn't place a face with the name.

"Brilliant woman. She joined us recently. I should introduce you." Roger paused. "Actually, I thought you had met. Last month. That dinner at the university?"

Carolyn shook her head. "I was traveling last month." Although the answer didn't feel right as soon as she said it. Was it last month she met Augusta Palmer on the voyage home? Normally she had a perfect memory for dates. Didn't she?

The sheer volume of work over the past few days, the number of patients that she'd seen in her office since the beginning of the week, had been unusually high. It was taking its toll. It seemed extraordinary now that she'd managed to hypnotize and then counsel twelve people in less than two days.

Roger was still talking about Dr Marheswaran. "Apparently

there's passages in an Ayurvedic document about treatments for patients resembling logs of wood, which she takes for coma or prolonged sleep. Various forms of herbal stimulation are placed on the tongue. The rubbing of the skin with a hairy fruit. Anyway, it's much safer than drilling into someone's skull."

Carolyn followed Roger into his office. He pointed to a long table overflowing with paper running the length of one wall. "There's everything we could collect about our current patients. The lab tests are inconclusive. Nothing out of the ordinary. If you can find anything, anything at all, I would be grateful."

"I wish I could consult with Augusta Palmer," Carolyn muttered out loud, turning over the pages of the files piled high on the table opposite Roger's desk. So many people admitted in the last twenty-four hours. She didn't want to call what was happening a pandemic, but it had all the hallmarks of one, given how rapidly it had spread through the city. Carolyn remained convinced there must be a clue for all of this to be found within their dreams.

How she wished she could persuade April May to undergo hypnosis! If only the silly Caligari movie hadn't put such a fear of hypnosis in people. Although she could also blame *Dracula* and *Trilby* for the public's confusion of hypnosis with supernatural powers.

The calm and sensible Augusta Palmer might know how to overcome the fears of the people on Flotsam Street and truly help them. Certainly, their discussions on the voyage from London revolved around the stigma surrounding their profession and how best to alleviate the fears instilled by such popular trash as *The House of Dr Edwardes*. Perhaps she should try to phone Augusta Palmer. Barbara must know how to reach her. Try as she might, Carolyn could not recall the name of the college where Augusta was teaching.

Behind her, Roger gave a grunt. "Why would Augusta Palmer's case interest you? We know the cause of her coma."

"Coma?" Carolyn whirled around to face him. "What are you talking about?"

"Augusta Palmer." He opened up a drawer and pulled out a file. "I just saw her on my rounds this evening. Such a sad case. Insulin induced coma but the sanatorium's doctors could not revive her with the glucose shots."

Carolyn was baffled. Experimentation was being done with insulin, but the treatment was highly controversial. A patient underwent a coma caused by insulin, only to be roused hours later by shots of glucose. "Why would Augusta subject herself to such a treatment?"

"I suppose she agreed to it. She had been a hopeless case, according to the files sent over to us. Undergone dozens of treatments with no improvement. In fact, according to their notes, this was something of her last hope." Roger looked at her oddly. "Haven't you been working at Arkham Sanatorium? Of course, you probably don't know all their residents."

Carolyn recalled one patient's description of their recent nightmare being like sinking into a vat of molasses. Stuck, unable to move, almost unable to breathe. But she wasn't experiencing a nightmare. She was in control of her mind.

"I know Dr Augusta Palmer," she said to Roger. "This cannot be the same person. The woman I know is a psychologist like me. She's older, approximately sixty."

"Our patient is sixty-three. But there's no mention in her files of her being a psychologist," Roger said.

"Is she still here? At St Mary's?" If Carolyn could see this Augusta Palmer, she could prove to herself that it was not the same woman. No matter what Roger claimed.

"Yes, of course. We have been hoping she'll come out of the

coma naturally. In fact, like our other patients, there's no real reason Augusta Palmer remains unconscious. We knew the cause of her coma so the glucose should have worked to revive her. I just never associated her with the others because she came here almost two days earlier than our first sleeping patient. She went into her coma on Saturday night, I believe. Yes, her file shows a Sunday morning admission. Our sleeping patients first began arriving on Tuesday evening. Do you think there might be a connection?"

"I need to see her." Carolyn started out the door, unwilling to explain anything else to the puzzled Roger who followed her. But he conducted her to the room with almost no comments, as if aware how frantically her heart was beating as she peered at the pale woman lying motionless in the bed.

It could not be the Augusta Palmer that she met on the boat from London, Carolyn told herself. Except try as she might, she could not remember exactly what Augusta Palmer looked like. Older than her. With a warm voice and comforting manner. They had sat together several times. Discussed the care of patients. Why couldn't she remember the woman's face? Just an impression of thick brown hair streaked through with gray, beautifully styled, or had it been? Carolyn also had a brief flash of memory, a plain braid drawing hair back from a well-washed face and a woman in drab robes, almost like this patient with her braided hair. Although the blankets were drawn high on her chest, Carolyn glimpsed a drab hospital gown covering her sturdy frame. But Augusta was stylishly dressed as appropriate for the public areas of the ship every time that they met. She had given Carolyn a mystery novel. Why then, when Carolyn looked at this woman on the bed, did she both know and not know her?

"It's strange," Carolyn said as she gazed at the patient.

"What?" Roger looked up from the chart.

"How much she looks like Barbara." Carolyn backed up a little, scrutinizing the woman in the bed. "My assistant. Only she was Augusta Palmer's secretary first."

"I don't think they would let a patient at the sanatorium have a secretary," said Roger. "Of course, it might be one of their new forms of treatment. Rather like occupational therapy."

"Don't make jokes about my profession." Carolyn still gazed at the sleeping woman. The patient did look like Barbara. Or Barbara looked like her. The color of her hair. Something about the shape of her nose and chin. Carolyn wondered what color her eyes were. Then she realized that she couldn't remember what color Barbara's eyes were.

"Does she have any family?" Carolyn asked. "Next of kin?"

"No one listed," Roger responded. "Which is sadly common for the patients coming from the sanatorium."

Carolyn nodded. Many families were often ashamed of relatives suffering from mental illness. Some treated the better sanatoriums and asylums as places to send their unwanted family members and forget about them. Some doctors even advertised this as a benefit. Send your mad sister or daughter or wife out of state and nobody would ever hear about her again. Another reason Carolyn wanted to start a private practice that would let people remain with their families, safe in their own community.

"Who brought her to St Mary's? Was there a referring physician?" she asked Roger.

"Yes, of course." He flipped through the papers. Then he paused, a strange look coming over his face.

"Roger, I'm not asking you to breach any confidentiality. Surely you can at least tell me who sent her to St Mary's. I need to talk to them. Understand who this woman is."

"But that's it," said Roger. "Two people came with her in the ambulance. A nurse and…"

"Who was it?" Carolyn snapped. Because her heart was sinking. A memory stirred. Not a memory of a ship. A memory far more terrifying. Clearer than any memory or dream over the past few days, she remembered sitting in a swaying ambulance as it raced through the early dawn streets. Clutching the hands of the patient who would not wake up.

"You were with her," said Roger, turning the file so she could see her own signature scrawled across the admission papers.

Then she and Roger spoke at the same time and said exactly the same thing. "Why didn't I remember that until now?"

CHAPTER TWENTY-THREE

As April watched, every giant ant pulled a green umbrella out of a holster strapped to their sides. The ants unfurled these umbrellas, cowering beneath them, to hide from the eye. A mass rose behind the tower, blotting out the sky. This colossal shape seemed as organic as the dead fish stinking on the slabs down at the docks. A suggestion of trailing limbs resembled the squid and octopus that her relatives insisted were delicious when cooked with vinegar and soy sauce.

April had always shied away from eating anything with multiple legs and fins as a child. But her disgust then was nothing compared to the dread she felt as she struggled to understand the shape looming behind the tower. It turned its head from side to side, independently rotating eyes apparently able to see the entire world with its sweeping, condemning glance.

April felt herself dwindle. She had always been the smallest in her class. Wherever she went, she struggled to be seen and heard. Now as the gaze of the gargantuan monstrosity raked across her, she became as insignificant as the ants huddling under their umbrellas. Just a tiny particle in a vast universe which did not care if she existed.

A weight fell upon her.

"April, wake up!" Mrs Garcia's voice buzzed in her ear. Her landlady shook her shoulder.

April blinked, groggy, and unable to immediately remember why she was slumped over Nella's bed.

Mrs Garcia heaved a huge sigh of relief. "I thought we would be putting you in a bed too," she admitted.

"No." April shook her head, remnants of the nightmare still clinging to her thoughts like the vast spiderweb in her dream. If the world could tip sideways in a moment, then her dream world had slid from a place of ordinary terrors to incomprehensible horrors. Talking cats and giant ants were one thing. What loomed behind the tower was something different, something that she did not want to remember but feared that she could never forget.

April glanced out Nella's window. It was still dark and streaks of rain ran down the glass.

"What's the time?" April asked.

"Still evening. Not even nine o'clock. I finished the loaves. But we are out of eggs. Can you go to Schoffner's? Sol said that the store will not close before midnight."

In times of emergency, Davy Schoffner kept his store open all evening. Far more important than City Hall to the residents of Rivertown, the general store served as the place to exchange news. Despite the rain, the thought of a brisk walk to Schoffner's and back appealed to April. She needed to clear the dreams out of her head, especially the most recent one.

Promising Mrs Garcia that she'd be ready to leave in a few minutes, April returned to her room for stouter shoes and a warm coat. After some consideration, she put on a thick wool scarf that Sally had knitted last Christmas. Wound around her head, it should keep her hair drier than any of her cloche hats. And was far less likely to be spoiled by the rain.

In the entry, she found Lefty in conversation with Mrs Garcia.

"Shake a leg, April," said Lefty. "I'm heading back to Schoffner's for another load of sandbags. Flotsam Street is done, but Sol needs more up at St Stanislaus Church."

"I could walk." April looked out the open front door. The rain pounded even harder on the steps. A ride with Lefty suddenly seemed far more sensible.

"Go with him." Mrs Garcia pressed the egg money into her hand. "Two dozen and tell Nathan to check my eggs before he packs them up."

"Yes, Mrs Garcia." April hurried to Lefty's truck, hopping inside Pequod's cab as quickly as possible.

Lefty followed a few minutes later. "How are you?" he asked as he took his place behind the wheel. "Mrs Garcia said she found you asleep upstairs."

"I was sitting with Nella. But I only fell asleep for a few minutes, I think." April remembered talking to Nella for a long time. The dream couldn't have lasted more than ten or fifteen minutes by her calculations. So why was it still so clear and terrifying in her head? "I dreamed about green umbrellas and giant ants."

"What?" Lefty was distracted by the rain, peering through the windshield and driving as slowly as possible down the wet streets. While Pequod rode higher than a normal car, he told April that water was now collecting in more low-lying streets, especially at the crossroads.

April described her most recent nightmare, leaving out the enormous creature peering down at her. The ants were strange enough. She lacked the words to describe whatever it was that blotted out the tower and almost overwhelmed her before Mrs Garcia shook her awake.

"Isn't that Farley's story? *The Radio Man*? All the ants carry umbrellas in their holsters instead of the weapons that the hero expects." Lefty was concentrating on driving through the dark streets so he didn't look at her. But the sheer normality of his voicing the type of questions they usually batted back and forth made April breathe a little easier.

"You are right!" April remembered the peculiar descriptions of the ant-men carrying green umbrellas to protect themselves from the rays of the Venutian sun. "But I keep seeing green umbrellas everywhere today."

"Probably because it's raining," Lefty said as he backed Pequod so the rear of the truck faced the entrance of Schoffner's General Store.

"I suppose," April said, but she remembered the strange carving on the handle on Columbia's umbrella. And how similar Carolyn's umbrella had been. Both also reminded her in a peculiar way of the eye in Sol's sketches and, even more disturbing, the one glimpsed in her recent nightmares.

Despite the lateness of the hour, a number of people, both men and women, were gathered under the store's striped awning. Below the windows displaying the latest merchandise, the sidewalk was full of sandbags. Several men stepped forward to help load the back of Pequod with practiced swings of their arms. These dock workers were used to heavy bags. The truck was filled before April finished purchasing the eggs inside.

As April suspected, the potbelly stove conference was in full swing at the back of the store, with the elders of the neighborhood offering their opinion to the youngsters about whether or not the river would crest over its banks.

"Not yet," predicted one old gaffer, pulling a corn cob pipe out of his mouth. "Storm is worse to the west. It will be another day or more before the Miskatonic crests. You'll hear the water coming like a freight train. That's how it was in 1874."

"I don't think it was the water you heard," said an equally

wizened old woman. She chewed her own corn cob pipe between her teeth. "It was dynamite."

"Dynamite!" yelped Nathan, Schoffner's teenage clerk. Then realizing he'd jostled the eggs, he apologized to April and checked them again.

"Dynamite. Mawmaw is right. They blew it right near the mouth of the Black Cave," the gaffer said. "To clear a log jam. Or so they said."

"That's what they said." Mawmaw and the gaffer exchanged a look which cast some doubt on "they", whoever they might be.

"Was that when they found the dead dogs in the Black Cave?" April asked. Nathan yelped again but the eggs were safely packed for Mrs Garcia.

The two oldsters stared at her.

"We don't talk about the dogs," said the man.

"It's bad, bad luck," said the woman.

Then they turned back to their friends and began cheerfully speculating on when the river might flood downtown Arkham. April took the eggs and rejoined Lefty in the truck, more troubled than before.

"Back to Mrs Garcia or do you want to ride to St Stanislaus with me?" Lefty pulled Pequod away from the sidewalk with a wave at the crowd. A couple of dock workers rode in the back on top of the sandbags. He would leave them at St Stanislaus to help the Drowned Rats and Father Iwanaki barricade the church as best they could.

"St Stanislaus," said April, thinking it wasn't fair to the men riding in the back to leave them out in the rain any longer than necessary. Not that the rain seemed to bother them.

When she said as much to Lefty, he just chuckled. "They work outside in all weathers. Same as me. But it is kind of you to think of them."

"I just don't want to go back to the house yet." April looked at the eggs carefully wedged in the cab at her feet. "I don't want to fall asleep again. The eggs will keep."

"Fair enough." Lefty picked up speed as they went past Christchurch Cemetery.

The roads in this part of Rivertown seemed drier. April hoped the big graveyard wouldn't flood. Sol's stories of coffins floating out of the graves made her shudder.

At St Stanislaus, Father Iwanaki and groundskeeper Leonard Cohen joined Lefty and the other men in unloading the sandbags. April waited in the cab, still thinking about green umbrellas, eyes, and all the uneasy feelings stirred by the conversations at the general store. As always, she wished she could discuss this with Nella. But Lefty would have to do.

When Lefty swung back into his end of the bench seat, she blurted out, "There was an eye!"

"An eye? Like a glass eye?" Lefty obviously recalled April's earlier story about Nella's encounter with Mrs Lanigan's glass eye.

"No." April described Columbia's umbrella as she had seen it in the newspaper office. "On the piece of wood below the hook of the handle."

"The shaft." Lefty was almost as fond of crosswords and word games as he was of pulp magazines.

"Yes. It was a circle with a dot in the middle. Carved on a piece of shell and set into the wood. It caught the light." She could see it so clearly in her memory. As clear as some of her dreams. "Carolyn's umbrella had the same type of shaft. It's odd. If it's a new fashion in umbrellas, stocked at the department store, we usually run an ad." April paid attention to the fashion ads that Cyril drew and often copied his designs onto her own notepad, just to practice sketching clothes, shoes, and, yes, umbrellas.

April recounted what Sol had told her about the painting in the Black Cave and his grandfather's memories of 1874. And what Mawmaw had said about not talking about dead dogs.

"Dead dogs?" Lefty looked more troubled by this part of the story than the frustrating appearance of green umbrellas in Arkham.

"A woman at City Hall knew about the dogs too." April regretted ever hearing that story. But the tale kept coming back in so many odd ways. At the entrance of Flotsam Street, Lefty slowed Pequod. In a thoughtful voice, he asked, "April, would you mind making one more trip tonight?"

"No, of course not." As bright and welcoming as the lights of their boarding house were, she still dreaded going home and falling asleep. She now knew what was waiting for her in her nightmares. She wasn't certain Mrs Garcia could wake her in time if the colossal eye gazed upon her again.

"I think you should tell all this to a man I know." Lefty swung the truck around. "Harvey Walters may not understand his roses. But this type of story, he'll know what to do with."

CHAPTER TWENTY-FOUR

Harvey was pontificating at dinner. He knew he was, because Mrs Fox was practically asleep in her seat. Ira poured himself another glass of wine. Sometimes having a head full of knowledge was a problem. Even Harvey grew tired of hearing himself drone on about the symbolism of certain patterns found in diverse occult practices.

But Ira had asked a question and Harvey, as always, couldn't stop himself from giving a complete answer. It began with the quaint little book that he'd bought at the auction on French Hill. Finding it on top of the pile of papers that he'd been examining for Carolyn, Harvey finally discovered the bit he remembered about harnessing the power of dreams. It wasn't a cure for nightmares, but it indicated some interesting possibilities.

After Ira returned from making some more phone calls in the hall, he noticed the open book on Harvey's desk. "So you have translated this?" Ira asked, leaning closer to the page full of symbols drawn in spiky sharp shapes. Additional strange *vesicae*, those interlocking circles beloved of scientists and occultists, filled the opposite page. "It's taken days."

"All finished. A neat little puzzle." Harvey picked up his

notebook and flipped it open to show Ira the work that he'd done since Sunday night. Had it been only Sunday when Ira found the book and handed it to him? It seemed like he'd been working on it for weeks. He certainly hadn't taken many breaks from his task, other than a brief interlude of cake and coffee with Carolyn. And the earlier discussion of roses with Lefty when he picked up the garbage. And, of course, his regular meals. Really, Ira had no call for complaint. He'd been working very hard indeed. And, the thought spiked briefly in his head, why should he be concerned with Ira's approval? After all, the man worked for him! Didn't he?

"Several passages are similar to the Pnakotic Manuscripts, but with enough differences to be intriguing." Harvey flipped the charred pages as he talked to Ira. "The writer seems to have recorded bits from a number of tomb or temple carvings. A dash from Egypt, a dollop from Macedonia. A peripatetic man. And perhaps not even a man. This part" – he pointed to script written under the *vesicae* – "appears to have been written by a woman. One who spoke French as her second or third language." The notes were in French but the grammar, as Harvey explained to Ira, was almost too precise. Rather like someone who had learned the language later in life.

"So what does it say?" asked Ira, who apparently lacked French along with his other failings. Harvey wondered why he had ever agreed to take the man as an assistant. He had a vague recollection of someone asking for a favor, but he couldn't remember who.

"It's about a series of sacrifices, rather distasteful, which need to be made in order to set in motion an intricate cosmic clockwork. The Pnakotic Manuscripts contain such rituals, although with less specific detail. It is all about attracting and holding the attention of an indifferent god. Or it could be translated as stealing a shadow of the god. There's a bit about creating a net of dreams to siphon power to the high priestess.

Then, as in the Pnakotic, the god is described here" – Harvey flipped back a few pages – "as a being of such incomprehensible greatness that it can only be understood by the dreaming minds of an entire temple. So care must be taken to protect the priestess from being overwhelmed. The rituals are most unusual. Not what I have seen in other manuscripts."

"In what ways?" Ira asked.

And Harvey was off and running, unable to stop himself from diving deep into what he knew about fragments of texts discovered in the most obscure corners of the world. Any number of these had made their way to the Miskatonic University's library, which was one of the great attractions of Arkham as far as Harvey was concerned. Many spoke of a time before time and how to attract or even command entities beyond human comprehension. A few spoke about these rituals as being meant to both protect and empower a select few. Although with a good many sacrifices along the way, if Harvey was guessing correctly at the subtext of selecting the least of the temple to perform certain ceremonies. But none boiled down to these odd step-by-step instructions of various sacrificial rites for various circumstances as the little book on his desk.

The whole book rather reminded Harvey of a collection of recipes once cherished by his mother, a book passed down from her grandmother, full of notations and additions by other women of the family. It ranged from how to bake a cake to the proper care for woolens in the summer. As a boy, he'd been fascinated by his mother's housekeeping book, as she called it. He practiced reading with it as she cooked or cleaned. Perhaps that was why this little smoke-stained book had landed in a basket of cookbooks. Some bored auctioneer had glanced at it, seen a miscellany of notes apparently written in a woman's hand, and tossed it with other battered relics of the kitchen shelves.

It was rather a good thing that it hadn't gone to a cookbook collector. He doubted they would have been as intrigued as he was by the oddly precise description of how to cut a dog into nine parts to attract the attention of a waking god and distract the god from the priestess carrying out another ritual in another place. Even Ira looked a little nauseated when Harvey turned to that page and explained what the drawing of the dog with the arrows and dashes meant.

Harvey was surprised by his assistant's reaction. Such stuff was fairly common, if not so precise, in ancient manuscripts. Surely Ira studied animal sacrifices as part of his work at the university? Although, once again, Harvey was aware of the nagging frustration of not remembering precisely what Ira did study when he wasn't at Harvey's house.

"Are you going to eat tonight, Mr Walters?" asked Mrs Fox from the door, interrupting Harvey's internal grumbles. "I have held supper as long as I can without the roast drying out completely."

A glance at the clock showed it was getting very late indeed. So Harvey invited Ira to join them for dinner.

As they walked toward the dining room, they discussed Harvey's translations and continued talking about it over supper. Well, to be completely honest, Harvey lectured Ira for a steady forty minutes on the similarity of the symbols in the book and those he had seen years ago in the Black Cave. He couldn't recall if Ira had said anything other than "please pass the wine." The young man had poured himself a second and then third glass of wine, much to the surprise of Harvey and Mrs Fox. Both liked a glass with their dinner, but Ira generally stuck to water or tea in accordance with the laws of the land.

A knocking on the door interrupted Harvey before he could delve into probable relationships to the *Al Azif*, a tome which

Harvey did not believe was another name for a more infamous grimoire and a far more intriguing volume in its own right.

"I'll answer it." If Mrs Fox looked relieved to be leaving the table, Harvey didn't comment on it.

"More visitors, Mr Walters," she said when she returned. "Shall I bring what's left of the cake into your study?"

In other words, would they be so good as to depart the dining room so Mrs Fox could clean up and leave for her own home.

"Dessert in the study would be excellent," said Harvey, leading the way.

To his surprise, he found his garbage man and a young lady waiting for him. Ira sidled around him, clearing the papers from Harvey's desk so Mrs Fox could lay down the tray of cake and coffee.

"I hope you'll join us," Harvey said to Lefty and his friend. "Otherwise I will be forced to eat it all. Mrs Fox would not approve of such greediness."

The young woman gave him a shy smile and accepted a plate of cake from Ira. She looked to be the age of his youngest students. Barely out of her teens and into her twenties, Harvey guessed. Cups of coffee were passed around.

"I'll get the dishes started," said Mrs Fox, closing the door of the study firmly behind her.

"That means you need to keep us busy and out of her hair for twenty minutes," said Harvey to Lefty. Ira sat a little apart from the group with the pile of papers from Harvey's desk piled on his own. Harvey noticed his assistant still had his glass of wine and sipped from it as he looked over Harvey's notes.

With a shrug, Harvey turned from his contemplation of Ira to ask Lefty how he could help him.

"It's not me, professor," said Lefty. "My friend April has some questions. I told her that you're the smartest person I know and would probably have the answers."

"How can I help you?" Harvey said, thinking with Carolyn's visit and now Lefty and April, his neighbors would be gossiping for months over the clotheslines. He rarely entertained. It was rather pleasant, he concluded, taking a bite of cake as April told him about the dead dogs found so long ago in the Black Cave and how she kept seeing things from her dreams in Arkham. Like a green umbrella. But she didn't know how it all tied together.

She also spoke of her recent confrontation with Carolyn Fern. Harvey was a little disturbed to hear how badly the encounter had gone. He didn't know a more empathetic soul than Carolyn. But what intrigued Harvey most was how April described walking down a silvery path through woods and encountering the man in the golden mask who interrupted her dreams. Harvey strongly suspected this young woman had a great if unrealized talent for navigating the Dreamlands. Such people were rare, but exactly what they needed to contact Luke.

Strange how controlling dreams and sacrificing dogs kept cropping up in his translation work too, Harvey thought, but before he could mention it and perhaps bore a new audience, April continued her story.

"I know it all sounds like a story from the magazines. Circles painted in caves, masked men in dreams, my friend unable to wake up." April looked at him with hope in her eyes. "Do you know why this is happening? Carolyn Fern thinks I can help. I don't want to be hypnotized, but I do want to help my friends."

With regret, Harvey put down his cake. "I don't have a rational explanation. My explanations, while logical to me, would sound much worse than any story that you read in the magazines. I've spent my life studying occult rituals and ancient histories which talk of beings older than the stars. Such stuff has not earned me a reputation as a purveyor of rationality."

"But you're a clever man," said Lefty. "What do you think April should do?"

"Sadly, I think she should do what terrifies her." He turned to April and tried to be as reassuring as possible. "Carolyn is right. Your nightmares could be key to understanding why the sleepers are caught in their dreams. Your actions could help your friend."

"What do you mean?" she asked.

Harvey wondered if he could explain Luke Robinson in a way that would not make him sound as if he needed a psychologist's treatment too. Better April should work with Carolyn, who would strive in all things to be as rational and reassuring as possible, even as she sought a way to enter the Dreamlands through April May's nightmares.

So he urged April to give Carolyn a second chance.

"Carolyn Fern is a good woman. And an exceptional healer of the mind. I have known several who benefitted from her methods, when their encounters here in Arkham grew too much to bear." Harvey leaned forward in his chair. "I truly believe no harm will come to you if you allow her to hypnotize you."

April still looked uncertain.

Harvey considered the alternatives. There were spells that he could cast which could send April May from his study directly into the Dreamlands, but the potential for harm was far greater than Carolyn's methods of hypnosis. He would not risk another, especially such a courageous young woman as April May.

When he said as much about her bravery, April looked startled. "But I'm afraid of almost everything." She barely spoke above a whisper so that Harvey had to strain to hear her.

"I am certain of your courage," he replied. "Only someone who struggles valiantly would be seeking aid for a friend in a stranger's house. It is the very definition of courage to do what makes you afraid. I promise Carolyn would never hurt a patient.

You can trust her to do all she can to end your nightmares and wake your friend."

There, thought Harvey, I can pontificate for a purpose when I need to, and I only borrowed a little of my speech from Mr Baum's *Wizard of Oz*. While Harvey spent most of his time reading ancient tomes, he liked to relax with Lewis Carrol's *Alice in Wonderland* or Baum's earliest Oz volumes.

"Well, what do you want to do, April?" Lefty asked.

"Perhaps we should find Carolyn Fern." April placed her uneaten slice of cake back on the tray. "She went to St Mary's. At least she said she was going there."

"I have a phone. Ira can call and confirm Carolyn is at the hospital." Harvey nodded to his assistant, who left the room to make the call from the phone in the hall.

"But what about the eye on the shaft of the green umbrella?" April said, returning to their earlier discussion. "Lefty said you might know what it means. I can't understand why Sol's drawing looks so much like the carving on the umbrellas."

"Can you show me exactly what you saw on the umbrella's shaft?" Harvey pushed a piece of paper and a pen toward her.

"The whole bit about dead dogs in the Black Cave seems more than an accident, at least according to what April heard. And it sounded like something you would know about," added Lefty.

Considering his recent dinner conversation about animal sacrifices, Harvey couldn't deny Lefty's assessment. Could the dogs found in 1874 have been evidence of such a ritual? Wicked magic wasn't unknown in Arkham, but Harvey couldn't think of any cults active at that time who would have done such an evil spell.

April got out of her chair. Leaning over Harvey's desk, she drew a perfect circle of an eye surrounded by writhing vines or tentacles. With a second quick sketch, she drew the shaft of an umbrella, indicating how the carvings had appeared on it. Then she drew the same circle as Sol had seen it in the Black Cave.

"You have some talent." Harvey examined the sketch. The one showing the umbrella's shaft reminded him of something which he had seen recently.

"I like art," said April. "Nella and I were planning to travel to Paris. We even talked about studying art there."

"You should do that." Harvey pulled the paper closer to him, looking at the sketch. Where had he seen this type of shaft before?

April reacted very strongly to his casual statement. "You think I should study art?"

"Why not?" Harvey glanced up from the drawing in his hands. April looked astonished.

"Because everyone in my family says there is no future in being an artist. It is not a real job. And women can't be artists anyway. They can only be teachers, nurses, or clerks." She gave this litany with the sad conviction of a child who had heard it too many times from the adults around her. What were people thinking that they would achieve by throwing up such barriers? Harvey was thankful as always that his mother never told him no when he wanted to go exploring. Look where her support had gotten him. A bachelor professor of occult arts who had few living friends and a number of horrific memories.

Perhaps his life wasn't the example that he should give young April.

Leaning back in his chair, Harvey made a pronouncement, one he had spoken to a number of female students and assistants, and one niece being teased by her overly confident sisters. "You can be whatever you want to be. It may be harder for you, because so many men can be obtuse fools when it comes to a woman's wisdom and abilities. A great number of women, too, seem to find pleasure in confining their sex to very small spheres of domesticity. But you should never let them define you."

"See," said Lefty to April, "I told you that he was the smartest man in Arkham."

Harvey tried not to preen, even after April gave him a shy smile and a nod.

Ira popped his head around the door to confirm Carolyn Fern was at St Mary's Hospital and would wait for April there.

"We should leave now," said Lefty. "The streets aren't going to get any drier."

Harvey glanced out the window. It was too dark to see much, but he could make out the steady downpour. Hear it too. "Still raining, I see." Frog strangler indeed.

"It's going to be a long night, especially near the river," Lefty replied. "They're expecting flooding in Rivertown and Northside, at least. You shouldn't have much trouble here. You are well away from the Miskatonic."

Harvey shook his head. "The basement floods if it rains hard enough. We may be bailing it out tomorrow." Well, he would deal with any water in the morning. Tonight he had a much more intriguing mystery to solve. Perhaps he should check Paschal's diary. Ira would have placed it under P.

"Thank you, Mr Walters," April said to Harvey. "I think you're a very smart man. And kind as well."

Ira escorted his visitors out the door. Still glowing a little from their praise, Harvey bent his considerable attention to April's drawing of the umbrella shaft left on his desk. What did it mean?

CHAPTER TWENTY-FIVE

This time, crossing Arkham by garbage truck was even slower. Although the streets were empty of pedestrians, a number of cars and trucks carried people on official business. Others were speeding to less than legal endeavors.

Twice Lefty pulled over so ambulances and firetrucks could go ringing by. Once a police car nearly clipped them as it barreled through a stop sign. As evidence of their serious business, they continued on with only a wave of the fist at Lefty from the driver.

The next car running a stop sign was a powerhouse of chrome and gleaming red paint, bigger than a hearse. The car roared past them.

"Might as well take the stop signs out," grunted Lefty.

Two more trucks barreled after the big car. The blur of red in the lead swerved around a trolley and sharply turned south. The two trucks followed, narrowly missing a lamppost as they chased the leader around the corner.

"Bootleggers. Moving the hooch," Lefty said. "If Arkham floods, at least there will be drinks somewhere dry tomorrow."

"I thought you didn't drink," said April, remembering a

few conversations when they were exchanging magazines and commenting on the foibles of the heroes.

"I don't. Not much. The booze wrecked my ball game and my marriage," said Lefty. "Tea and a good book is a better way to spend your evening."

"I wish we were reading tonight," she replied as the lights of St Mary's Hospital swung into view.

They pulled up to the entrance of the hospital. "You still don't have to do this," Lefty said, shutting down Pequod's rumbling engine. "No matter what the professor thinks. If you don't judge it's safe, you say so. I'll take you home."

"My leaving now won't help Nella," said April.

"I'll come with you," Lefty offered as April continued to stare out the window at the imposing hospital entrance. "Maybe Dr Fern can hypnotize me instead."

"But you don't dream," said April after they left Pequod parked where it wouldn't block any ambulances headed to St Mary's. They climbed the stairs to the hospital's big double doors. "Carolyn told me that was important. She needed a dreamer who dreamed about the tower and the man in the golden mask. Mr Walters practically said the same thing."

More importantly, Mr Walters had told her that she had courage. She wanted to believe him. He was a comforting old man, the way he took what she said seriously. Maybe even a little inspiring, as she recalled his astonishing speech about how she should try to become an artist.

"Just because I don't remember my dreams doesn't mean I didn't have them," said Lefty as he pulled open the hospital door and waved her in.

April giggled a little at his statement. Here was a very good friend who also tried to support her. "No," she said out loud as her nervous giggle died in the vastness of the hospital's entry. "I can do this."

At the hospital desk, they asked for Carolyn Fern and were directed to an office on the third floor. When they found it, Carolyn was working at a bare wooden table surrounded by sturdy white painted chairs. The walls were bare except for a notice about what to do in case of fire. A narrow window overlooked the back of the hospital.

"Thank you for coming," said Carolyn, standing up to shake hands with Lefty and April. "They use this room for meetings during the day. We won't be disturbed."

The woman in the office had changed in the few hours since she'd left Flotsam Street. Carolyn Fern was no longer the calm individual that April remembered from their first meeting. Nor was she as intense and driven as she had been at the boarding house.

This Carolyn seemed distracted although grateful to see April.

When Lefty still offered to be hypnotized despite April's rejection of the idea, Carolyn declined his request. "It won't work," she explained. "You must have conscious memories of the dream. Those memories will lead us deeper into what the unconscious mind experienced. From there, I hope to meet a guide who will tell us how to bring the sleepers back to full awareness."

"A guide?" April questioned.

Carolyn nodded. "I believe the man in the golden mask is trying to give us information on how to end these nightmares. This person may be a manifestation of your unconscious mind. A way of telling you, literally, how to wake up when the dream threatens to overwhelm you."

"But if it's April's mind telling April how to wake up, how does this help the other sleepers?" Lefty gave her the look of a man who had read many mysteries and knew a fishy explanation when he heard it.

April couldn't disagree. She also felt something was missing from Carolyn's explanation.

"Harvey Walters had an alternative explanation," Carolyn said very slowly. "One I do not like to credit but so much evidence indicates that it may be true."

"We visited Mr Walters," April said. "He suggested we come here."

"He said to trust you. But he didn't say much about this," Lefty said. "Only that you would explain."

Hearing Lefty voice her own doubts, April felt bold enough to add her own questions. "Tell me everything about the man in the golden mask before you hypnotize me. Everyone keeps saying this is my choice, but how can I make a choice if I don't know what is going on?"

Carolyn sat down in one of the chairs. She gestured for Lefty and April to join her around the table. She fiddled with her glasses, adjusting them on her face and then sweeping a section of her hair behind her ear.

"Harvey thinks the man appearing in the dreams might be Luke Robinson." Carolyn looked at them as if she expected a reaction. "I suspect he is right."

April shook her head. "I have never heard of this Luke Robinson."

"I have." Lefty did his own fidgeting, although that may have been the hard wooden hospital chair. "He has a tendency to appear where he isn't expected."

"If you know Luke, then you know he would not hurt April. I don't think he means harm to any of the sleepers," Carolyn said.

April wasn't at all certain that a real person appearing in her dreams was completely safe, especially one who she had never met outside of dreams. After all, he was invading her mind, wasn't he? Except the dreams where he appeared were so strange and different from her normal worries. So perhaps she was invading his mind, a startling thought for April.

"But are you sure it is Luke?" Lefty asked.

"Not entirely. It could be a manifestation of April's experiences. Something that she's seen or read before," Carolyn admitted. "I almost prefer to think the man is a figment of April's imagination, a construct of her mind to deal with external problems."

"But you don't believe that?" April asked, hearing the clear uncertainty in Carolyn's voice.

Carolyn sighed. "I saw a person today who cast all my own suppositions into doubt." She hesitated and then added, "I have had other experiences as well, ones I cannot speak about. The explanation Harvey Walters offered me was neither logical nor rational. But it may be true. Luke Robinson is a resident of Arkham, as far as I know, but he is also known to a few as a resident of the Dreamlands. Literally a world beyond our own which is sometimes visited by dreamers."

"Oh, like how the Radio Man went to Venus," April said.

"Yeah," said Lefty. "It happens a lot in stories. Visiting other worlds, I mean. Although the Radio Man was transported by radio waves, not dreams."

"But other people go about in dreams," April said.

Lefty nodded.

Carolyn seemed to be a little shocked by their ready acceptance of the Dreamlands. But really, any reader would have encountered such a world if they liked *Tales from Nevermore* or the other pulps who specialized in uncanny stories.

"Will this help Nella? Mr Walters thought this was the best way for me to help her and the others," said April. She found Mr Walters a surprising man. She had expected someone pushy or dismissive, like some of the teachers who made school so miserable by spending all their time proving they were smarter than their students. But Mr Walters was much more like Mr Phipps, who once told her that she was a very bright girl with a real talent for art. She hadn't thought about her third-grade teacher for years. While the skinny and often nervous Mr Phipps was nothing like the rather solid and elderly Mr Walters, both of them had bolstered her courage with their casual praise.

"Harvey Walters often knows the correct answer. Much to my distress," Carolyn admitted. "I think if it is Luke Robinson, he may indeed help your friend. He may even lead you to her."

"But I know where Nella is," April said. "She's asleep in her bed."

"Her body is there. But if she is with Luke Robinson, then her spirit may be in the Dreamlands," Carolyn said. "Which is the illogical, irrational answer to why we cannot wake the sleepers."

April remembered the man in her dream shouting something about the Dreamlands. "But if I find Nella there, in these Dreamlands, then Luke can help her wake up?" April wanted to be very sure that she knew what she could accomplish if she was hypnotized.

"Yes. I hope so," Carolyn responded. "But it may not be that simple. Journeys into the Dreamlands can be terrifying."

April nodded, remembering the glass eye rolling along the silver path and the pursuit of giant ants. She tried not to think about the tentacled shadow looming over the tower.

"I won't lie to you. This can be a very difficult journey," Carolyn said. "But if we can find Luke, I believe it will help all the sleepers including your friend. But it is your choice. I can only promise I will do everything I can to keep you safe."

April wished people would stop talking about it being her choice. It was always easier if she could just do what somebody said she had to do. But wasn't she the one who kept saying that she wasn't a child? Perhaps being an adult meant making choices, even ones which worried her. If the man in the golden mask was a good man, and he could help Nella, then she had to speak to him.

As if he could read her thoughts, Lefty said, "Skids says Luke Robinson is an all right sort."

"Who?" chorused April and Carolyn.

Lefty rubbed one hand across his bald head. "Skids O'Toole. He's not exactly a shining character himself, but if he says a mug is a straight shooter, he means it."

As little as she knew of Skids, April trusted Lefty. He wouldn't let her be harmed. Nor, she realized, would Carolyn Fern. Mr Walters was right. She could depend on the people in this room. Not for any rational reason but because tonight was not a night for rational explanations. Tonight was a night to do whatever she could to help Nella and end the nightmares.

"I'll do it," April said. "Hypnotize me."

Carolyn seemed surprised by April's sudden decision. But Lefty only nodded and said, "I'll stay with you."

"Will this take long?" she asked Carolyn.

"Probably not. I prefer to keep the sessions short. Certainly for the first session, no more than thirty minutes." She turned to Lefty. "But I will ask you to wait outside. It's better that I have complete silence and no distractions in the room."

He nodded. "I'll go down to the truck and be back before you are done." April knew that meant he'd fetch a magazine to read.

"Maybe you can find Ollie," April suggested. "Let her know what's happening on Flotsam Street."

Lefty nodded as he slouched out of the room.

"He's a nice man," Carolyn offered.

"He's a friend," April said. "I'm lucky to know him."

"I think you are," Carolyn said. She went out the door and returned a few minutes later with a flickering old-fashioned oil lamp. "This room isn't ideal, but we can make this work. I'm going to turn off the overhead lights. Luckily they've been placing these lamps all over the hospital in case the power goes out."

Carolyn sat across the table from April, putting the lamp as far away from them as possible. In the flickering light, April saw their shadows grow on the wall beside them. Two women made into giants on the blank surface.

"Do you use a pocket watch?" April asked, remembering some of the stories that she read. "Are you going to swing it in front of me?"

Carolyn smiled. "Everyone asks that question. No watch, no props." She reached out her hands, placing them palm up on the table. "Put out your hands. Palms up."

April lay her own hands on the table as instructed. Carolyn placed her palms down on April's. Her clasp was firm and comforting.

"Don't be afraid," Carolyn said.

"I'm not," April replied and was a little surprised to realize it was true. "I trust you. You wouldn't send me to the Dreamlands without a way to return home. You wouldn't hurt me."

"Thank you. I always create a way for my patients to safely end the session." Carolyn squeezed April's hands.

"Remember," Carolyn continued. "No matter what you see, what you hear, you are with me. I won't let you go. You will leave this place as easily as counting to five. You will return just as easily by counting to five backward. You are entering your dream now." She stroked April's hands. "With each breath, you will journey toward Luke Robinson. I will count to five and you will find yourself again on the path to the tower. I will be with you, following you into your dream, helping you to stay safe and find the answers we need for Nella."

Carolyn's voice rose and fell in a soft, rhythmic cadence.

"Focus on my words." Carolyn's tone was low and steady. "Let your mind wander, let go of the here and now. One, two, three…"

April resisted at first, trying stubbornly to anchor herself to the reality of a plain room in a busy hospital. But the sounds outside in the corridor began to fade. Carolyn's voice tugged at her, a persistent tide washing away her continuing reluctance to return to the source of her nightmares. The lamplight flickered, the walls receded, and the shadow women turned to walk away, down a sandy path shining silver.

A sensation of floating overcame April as if she only watched the women from a far distant place. At the same time, she knew she was standing on the path as the two women became one woman, a small slight woman, a shadow of April's own self.

Then she felt the sand crunching under her feet. Above her hung loops of spiderwebs. Before her was a great tower and beyond the tower was another shadow, an inky blot across the sky, older and more immense than the stars.

April reached the end of the path. Unsurprised, she found herself once more confronted by the man in the golden mask. After all, Carolyn had told her that she would find him here. As before, he wore robes embroidered with strange angular symbols, all done in gold thread upon what looked like golden silk.

"Are you Luke Robinson?" she asked, just to be sure.

At first, he didn't answer. He seemed unnaturally still, as if he was watching or listening to something very far away. His eyes seemed almost lifeless, shadowed by the eyeholes of his mask.

April was about to ask again when a shudder ran through the man. The far-seeing eyes flashed and focused on her.

"You are not dreaming?" he said. "Can you speak to me?"

"I am being hypnotized," April replied. "So, yes to both of your questions."

The stiffness relaxed out of his shoulders. "Finally, a messenger. Quickly, tell me what is happening in Arkham!"

"But are you Luke Robinson?" asked April, wanting to be sure and feeling that he should answer her questions when she asked them. After all, she'd answered him.

"Yes!" His shout was sudden and abrupt. Then he paused. "I am sorry. You have come a long way, I think, and not by any road that you know. But the danger is so close. We must wake the sleepers."

"That is why I'm here," April said. "Harvey Walters told Carolyn Fern that you would know what to do. So she hypnotized me because I've seen you in my nightmares. But I haven't fallen asleep like all the others. They sent me to ask you, how do we wake the sleepers?"

As an explanation, it was a bit brief, April knew, and she hadn't even told Luke about the green umbrellas or the missing dogs or the Black Cave, all of which she felt oddly confident had something to do with the sleepers. The shadow April, as she was thinking of herself in this moment, seemed much braver than the April sitting back in the hospital office with Carolyn Fern. April was as distinctly aware of that part of herself, or her other self perhaps, as she was of the man in the elaborate robes standing before her. But this April, here and now, was feeling bold enough to tilt her chin up and ask again: "What do we do to wake people up?"

But Luke was fixated on something she said earlier. "You were hypnotized by Carolyn Fern?" he nearly shouted again. He seemed unusually upset for a man in a dream.

"Yes," said April. "She's with me now. She wants to speak to you." The last sentence slipped out as if April was repeating something being said to her over the telephone. Perhaps she was. Perhaps it was Carolyn who now asked, "Did you trap the sleepers in their dreams? How can we wake them?"

"No!" cried Luke. He made a pushing gesture as if he was

trying to shove April away, but he did not touch her. "You must leave here! You cannot let Carolyn Fern enter the Enchanted Woods."

"What?" The startled question which broke from her lips was all April. She knew her own squeak when she heard it.

"You must keep Carolyn Fern away. She is the danger," Luke Robinson repeated. "She is the spider who binds them all in her web."

CHAPTER TWENTY-SIX

Harvey barely heard his visitors depart. Obsessed with the drawings April had sketched on his notepad, he shoved aside the tray of abandoned cake slices and cooling coffee. Twisting around to the shelves, he began pulling down volumes he wanted.

Then Harvey shucked off his stiff shoes and slipped on his carpet slippers, his favorite part of every evening. Which is why he kept his carpet slippers under his desk despite Mrs Fox's regular attempts to move them to his bedroom. He wiggled his toes in comfort.

Harvey picked up a cup of lukewarm coffee, sipping it as he began to read. Sidetracked by an account of the Great Dreamer, the sleeping horror worshipped by the Ignoti, a splinter sect of the Amissa Peregrinorum, he searched out the account by Paschal. The man claimed to have met a surviving Ignoti in 1802 or 1803. The whole story of Paschal's adventure recalled the notes that Harvey had made while translating the little book that he bought at the French Hill auction. Harvey looked around his desk, but it contained only the papers and books that he'd just deposited on it.

Then he remembered Ira clearing off his desk when Lefty and his friend April arrived.

Wandering over to Ira's desk, Harvey found all his papers had been stacked neatly, corners all squared and aligned. Ira must have done it while listening to them discuss April's dreams.

But the book wasn't there. He was certain that he'd had it on his desk before dinner. It should be on Ira's desk if he didn't have it on his desk.

"Once you eliminate the impossible," said Harvey, quoting one of his favorite authors. "Except, of course, the impossible happens frequently in this city."

Where was the little volume that he purchased at the estate sale? In his head, he could see the scorched cover so clearly. Perhaps he'd stashed it away in his desk before dinner? He often put things away in odd places, according to Mrs Fox and Ira.

But two sorts through his desk drawers, including spreading half his papers on the floor, failed to yield the desired book. Nor could he find his notebook with his translations. Both were definitely missing.

"Hell's bells!" said Harvey, surveying his office again. Where could the books have gone?

He remembered adding both to his research stack shortly after Carolyn left. Distinctly remembered pursuing the pages of strange symbols and being caught again in contemplation of the meaning of the eye drawn at the end of the book. Yes, he had his notes and the book side by side when he showed the pages to Ira and discussed the familiar patterns of ritual and sacrifice. A return trip to Ira's desk confirmed neither the book nor his notebook were there.

Had the older book simply vanished?

It hadn't seemed like the sort of book to melt away on its own or to take his second favorite notebook with it. Harvey had encountered a few grimoires which slipped through time, disappearing and then appearing like a conjurer's pigeon. His smoke-stained oddity remained with him for years. In fact, he had forgotten about it until Ira had unearthed the book in one of his attacks of efficiency on the bookshelves.

Ira brought the book to Harvey's attention shortly after he began his job as assistant, perhaps even on his first day. He asked for translations of the odd French-Egyptian patois handwritten in the margins as well as certain passages of what appeared to be Greek, but Harvey finally recognized the language as a Macedonian variant.

The proposed system of augury and summoning using the entrails of a dog for the first ritual was particularly gruesome as Mrs Fox pointed out at dinner. But Harvey found it interesting that the writer claimed the two rituals protected a person from the power of the Giver of Answers Undreamt. Also how insistent the writer was that the rituals needed to be enacted in two separate places. Unusually specific, in fact, about the distance needed in time and geography before proceeding with the second larger sacrifice.

As with all such rituals, the two sacrifices were unnecessarily complicated. Harvey estimated at least three or four people were needed to coordinate the full rites. One to do the initial sacrifice and a few to do the second, because one person couldn't handle the second ritual alone. That rite involved a lot of dogs, eighty-one to be precise, and a couple of people. As Harvey said to Ira, any fool could slice up a single dog, but it took an extraordinary number of people to kill eighty-one dogs if you wanted to accomplish your goal in a reasonable amount of time.

Mrs Fox had looked particularly disgusted at this bit of information but had passed him a second helping of the creamed peas.

After that, Harvey left the dining room with Ira to help his visitors.

Harvey looked around his study again, playing out the scene in his mind. Lefty and April in the chairs facing his desk. Ira off in the corner, a single glass of wine by his elbow and all of Harvey's research stacked in front of him. The papers had still been there when Ira went to ring the hospital and inquire about Carolyn Fern's whereabouts.

They talked about the Black Cave, and the dogs found there, and the similarity to his recent translations seemed quite evident as he thought about it.

Then April and Lefty departed for the hospital. Harvey sat down to read Paschal. The Giver of Answers Undreamt sounded remarkably similar to the Great Dreamer of Paschal's Ignoti. Paschal also had drawn a wand of sallow used by the sect during a summoning. Suddenly distracted by a thought which had nothing to do with Ira or his missing book, Harvey bent the illustration in Paschal's journal toward the lamp. The wand looked so much like the shaft of the umbrella sketched by April.

"Ha!" said Harvey, his random thoughts now coalescing to a conclusion.

He turned to discuss this with Ira, but, of course, Ira wasn't in the study.

"Where is Ira?" Harvey asked the empty room. How strange that something which just happened should be so fuzzy in his mind. His adventures in the Black Cave forty years before remained so clear. He had seen the symbol of the Eye, as they called it in Rivertown. He even remembered Sol's grandfather, who had been about his age and a charmer of a smuggler, although unmarried and childless at the time. How life changed and the strangest people came back into your memories!

Harvey leaned back in his chair and tried again to reconstruct the events of the last hour. The doorbell rang, Ira left the study to answer the door, Lefty had introduced the nice young lady

April, who told him her story including Sol's tale of the Eye and drew the picture of the green umbrella on his best notepad, which reminded him of other symbols and Paschal.

Then Ira made a phone call to the hospital and escorted the visitors back out of the study.

Harvey's memories ended unhelpfully with searching the office for the books that he wanted after Ira left.

So he could not remember where Ira went after he left the study. Time to apply the basic principles of deduction. Where did Ira go? Well, obviously, he must have opened the front door and let the visitors out. But why hadn't Ira returned to the study after that? Was he still in the house? Had he gone home? How could Harvey have lost a young man who was nearly six feet tall as well as his book?

If he didn't have the answers, he knew who would. Gathering up the dessert dishes, Harvey left his office and headed into the kitchen where Mrs Fox was sipping a glass of wine. The dinner things were washed, dried, and put away. The dishes for breakfast were neatly stacked at one end of the kitchen table, all ready for Mrs Fox's return in the morning.

Harvey carried the tray of cake dishes and coffee cups to the sink and gave them a rinse. Cleaning up for himself would help avoid a confrontation about invading the space while Mrs Fox was working.

"Mrs Fox," said Harvey as he dried and placed the cake plates on the rack, "where did Ira go?"

"Ira?" Mrs Fox said. "I don't know. I just finished grinding the beans for your breakfast coffee."

"Mrs Fox, I have told you more than once that you should not grind the beans the day before. It is better to grind them just before you make the coffee." Harvey finished the cups and saucers. The coffee pot he left on the counter. Mrs Fox was particular on how teapots and coffee pots should be washed. It was apparently beyond his comprehension because she always told him that he did it wrong.

"Mr Walters, if I don't prepare the breakfast coffee now, you won't have breakfast within a half hour of my arrival," said Mrs Fox, who lived with the aunt of her former husband on the other side of town.

"If you would only come a little earlier," Harvey wheedled.

"I will not," Mrs Fox said firmly as she always did.

"I suppose breakfast could be served a little later," Harvey conceded, as he nearly always suggested.

"It could not." Mrs Fox fixed him with a stern look. "You last no more than fifteen minutes and then start grumbling about the world failing to function if you do not have your coffee on time."

Damn the woman, Harvey thought, she always wins this argument. But he knew better than to say it out loud.

"Now why are you in my kitchen telling me how to make breakfast?" Mrs Fox tended to forget who owned the house. Harvey did, too, at times. Certainly, they had an agreement that the kitchen was hers to organize as she wished, and the study was his to keep as untidy as he liked. All other rooms were of little interest to either of them and served their functions as needed.

She glanced at the cold pot of coffee remaining on the counter. "Did you want more coffee? I can reheat the pot."

"No," Harvey said with some regret as he liked his coffee hot at all hours of the day and night. "No, I want Ira. And he is nowhere in the house." Harvey remembered he actually hadn't looked in any other rooms. But Ira never went anywhere in the house except the study for his work and the dining room when he joined them for meals.

"Perhaps I should look in the dining room. He did ask for a third glass of wine at dinner." Harvey wondered if Ira had returned to the wine bottle or simply passed out from his unaccustomed drinking.

"I cleaned the dining room and put the wine bottle back in its cubby hole," said Mrs Fox, who had no objection to picking up an occasional bottle from a bootlegging friend, but also knew such bottles needed to be stashed out of sight during the day. "Ira wasn't there."

"He must have gone home." His conundrum resolved, Harvey decided to question Ira about the missing book in the morning. "Perhaps another small cup of coffee to tide me over until breakfast, dear Mrs Fox."

She shook her head but poured the coffee back into the pot on the stove to warm it. As Harvey went into the pantry to raid the cookie jar, Mrs Fox said, "The boiler is acting up again."

Harvey groaned and put the lid back on the cookie jar. He returned to the kitchen. He knew what came next.

"If you want hot water for your bath," Mrs Fox threatened.

"All you need to do is give it a small whack on the side with the pipe wrench," Harvey said, not at all hopeful that Mrs Fox would pick up the pipe wrench and descend into the basement.

"It's your house. Your boiler," said Mrs Fox who kept out of the basement six days out of seven. On the seventh day, she did the laundry in the basement and complained for the rest of the week about the washing tub and the hand-cranked wringer being at the bottom of the steep flight of basement stairs. She was adamant that while the kitchen was hers, the basement was Harvey's domain to rule and repair. She had been campaigning to build a laundry off the kitchen so she could avoid the stairs.

When a small inheritance made the purchase of the house and the employment of Mrs Fox possible, all of Harvey's colleagues congratulated him on achieving a comfortable retirement. Several even encouraged him to spend the money on a house and a housekeeper rather than adding to the piles of books in his rooms.

Despite the fact Harvey had no wish to ever stop his work. And renting an apartment had been much easier than dealing with the overly enthusiastic roses and the boiler. Harvey assumed his apartment building had some contraption for heating water. He just never had to go near it.

With a grumble, he picked up the pipe wrench where it sat in a place of honor by the kitchen door. Going outside, he grumbled more about the rain falling on his head as he made his way to the door leading to the basement. Then he cursed as the wet grass soaked his carpet slippers in less than a minute.

The double doors of the coal chute were closed as he passed them, but Harvey caught a faint glimmer of light along the cracks. Damning his thoughtlessness in leaving the electric light on after his last foray to battle the boiler, Harvey fumbled for the basement door next to the coal chute. It was unlocked, which was just as well as he had forgotten the key back in the kitchen. At least with the lights burning up electricity and his money, the stairs were well lit and he didn't have to fumble for the switch.

Because he was wearing his carpet slippers, Harvey made a slight squelch on the stairs but no other noise. Which meant Ira did not notice him as he descended. However, halfway down, Harvey had a very clear view of his assistant drawing grotesque angles and eldritch swirls around a sleeping dog.

Ira was crawling across the floor on his knees. He clutched a fragment of coal in one hand and Harvey's missing book in the other. Harvey watched in mild astonishment at his quick progress in rendering the complex design meant to beguile and draw forth ancient entities. Ira shuffled in a circular pattern around the dog. He drew the concentric spirals which mimicked the tentacles on the green umbrella. These shifted to become the pattern of the eye copied carefully from the book. Ira checked his drawing twice, muttering, rubbing out one line and replacing it with a bigger circle.

The two electric light bulbs hanging down from the ceiling sent Ira's shadow sprawling across the dirty marks that he had already made. Without surprise, Harvey noticed the symbols appeared to glow through the shadow. The book had mentioned such an effect, an impossible effect, but Sherlock never crossed the line between improbable and impossible which existed sometimes in Arkham. And, apparently, in Harvey's own basement.

"I never took you for a practitioner." Harvey advanced to the bottom of the stairs. He shifted his hold on the pipe wrench, curling his hand behind his back. No need to let Ira know that he carried a weapon. Some cultists were civilized beings, even rather dull, as Harvey knew from experience.

Others were too fond of blood and murder. And Harvey didn't like the look of the dog laid out in the center of his basement. He didn't know or care much about dogs, but the big German Shepherd was probably somebody's pet. He had a faint recollection of one of the neighbors telling him about how she had lost Fritzie earlier this week.

Ira nearly toppled over as he contorted his body to face Harvey. His face flushed. His eyes looked glazed and unfocused. Even a little drunk.

Augury and summoning through animal sacrifice was not a game for the squeamish. Harvey now understood the extra glasses of wine at dinner. It wasn't boredom. Ira had been fortifying himself for the last part of the ritual which Harvey had so helpfully translated for him earlier today.

What was certainly tiresome was that Ira then had the very bad manners to enact the sacrifice of a dog in nine parts in his basement. Which meant Harvey was going to have to do something about it, despite the fact his carpet slippers were soaking wet and he would much rather be drinking coffee and eating cookies upstairs.

"There is a great gulf between reading about something and actually doing it," Harvey said, hoping to distract Ira and stop this business before it became even messier. With some relief, he saw the dog take a large breath and let it out. The animal might be unconscious, but it wasn't dead yet.

Advancing across the floor, Harvey did his best to scuff the marks made with coal dust. Thank heavens Ira had not found the cans of paint in the corner of the basement. Coal could be washed away. And while there was a danger in disrupting the marks of such a spell, there was even greater danger in letting it be carried out and attracting a new occupant. Mrs Fox already complained enough about the basement. She would never do his laundry again if she encountered a demon or a demigod behind the mangle.

"Those books are never like cookbooks." Harvey kept his voice calm and his steps casual as he inched closer to Ira. So far, the lad seemed unable to process Harvey's appearance in the basement, simply swaying in place on his knees. "The writer assumes you know what you're doing. I noticed he or she never listed all the items needed. Like a cleaver to butcher the dog."

With a gargled cry, Ira started up. He dropped the coal and pulled a long silver carving knife out of his trousers. Harvey recognized the knife. It usually sat on his sideboard in the dining room.

"Ah, you found something." Harvey shifted a bit to the left and tightened his grip on the pipe wrench.

"The Unnamable Dreamer awakens." Ira sounded more than drunk. He seemed to be speaking to a large crowd visible only to himself. "We gain the answers undreamed and the powers unchecked. We will restore our family!"

If the crowd answered, Ira gave no sign of it. He swayed and waved the knife. "In blood and flood, the beginning ends. The sleepers succumb tonight!"

Recognizing the start of ritual nonsense when he heard it, Harvey dared another step closer to Ira. He concentrated on the knife, ignoring a spate of words now being babbled by his assistant. Did none of them ever read the part where the texts warned about how minds could be crushed by the mysterious and arcane prayers of the ancients? Harvey had long ago learned the art of not listening too closely to such stuff. He certainly never made the mistake of chanting it out loud.

Ira whirled in place, pointing the knife at where he probably imagined the compass points were. No, eight passes with the knife. Well, that meant it wasn't a simple east-west, north-south. With a ninth slash of empty air, Ira faced Harvey directly. For the first time, the younger man seemed to see him clearly. Ira's eyes narrowed. He raised the knife.

"I don't think my carving knife will work." Harvey shifted his feet into a stance taught to him long ago. "I haven't had it sharpened for ages. Mrs Fox complains every time we need to carve a roast chicken. You will never manage to quarter a dog, much less cut it into nine parts. Why nine, do you suppose?"

Ira shrieked, a scream of pure rage. He lunged at Harvey.

Harvey countered Ira's knife stroke with a feint that would have made his college fencing instructor proud. He also broke Ira's wrist. A pipe wrench was not a delicate weapon.

The knife clattered to the floor. Ira's screams rose to a new level of pain and anger. He came at Harvey with tooth and claw as he tried to tear out Harvey's throat with his teeth, a nearly impossible maneuver as Harvey could have told him. Especially when your opponent carries a pipe wrench and brings it down squarely on your head.

Ira dropped to the floor.

Like the dog in his basement, Harvey panted for a minute or two. Then he dropped to one knee and felt for Ira's pulse. To his relief, the young man was still alive. The disposal of bodies was not impossible in Arkham. He knew a few people. But Harvey would much rather call an ambulance.

He checked the dog next. It was indeed sleeping. A scratch behind the ears caused it to twitch but not awaken. Harvey hoped Ira used a mild sedative. With luck, he could send Fritzie home unharmed tomorrow. Or, more likely, Mrs Fox could do the errand for him.

Getting back up off his knees was almost a bigger struggle than his fight with Ira. Harvey cursed old age.

Then he looked around the basement. Other than the marks along the floor, which he could clean up with a wet mop, nothing seemed disturbed.

Ira lay nicely close to the foot of the stairs. Harvey could see an explanation forming easily. His assistant fell down the stairs chasing a lost dog. Poor man. Head trauma and possibly a broken wrist. Such a shame. He would phone for an ambulance as soon as the floor was clean.

The basement door opened. Mrs Fox called down to him, "I am going now. Is the boiler fixed?"

Harvey picked up the pipe wrench and banged it against the side of the boiler. It answered with its usual burbling hum.

"All fixed!" he shouted up to Mrs Fox. He heard the door close.

Harvey put down the wrench. He found a mop and bucket. As he cleaned the ghastly marks off his basement floor, he considered what he should do next. Things were growing worse, just as Lefty feared, but the rain was only a small part of it.

Ambulance first before Ira did something irritating like bleed to death in his basement. Then he would phone Carolyn Fern and warn her. Better yet, he would go to St Mary's. If she hypnotized April and managed to contact Luke Robinson, Harvey now had a very good idea what they would learn. They would need his knowledge as well.

Or he could enter the Dreamlands himself. Carolyn's preferred method of hypnosis wouldn't work for him, but he was fairly sure he knew another route. It might be faster to meet Luke and April there.

Dashing between the basement door and the kitchen, the steady downpour decided for him. Better to stay dry and comfortable at home than slosh across town in the worst rainstorm of the century.

Besides, he had wanted an excuse to try this particular spell for some time. If it did work the way the scroll promised, Luke Robinson wouldn't be the only person who could treat the Dreamlands as his personal playground.

Harvey made the phone calls needed. He waited patiently for the ambulance people to direct them to the unfortunate Ira still unconscious at the foot of the stairs. When the ambulance driver asked if he needed the dogcatcher, Harvey reassured them that the sleeping German Shepherd was a pet belonging to a neighbor.

"I have no idea how it got into my basement," said Harvey with no compunction about any untruths. He knew exactly who smuggled the dog into his basement, but Ira was unconscious and probably wouldn't admit to it anyway. "But it's a gentle dog, a neighbor's pet." The dog's collar stated his name was indeed Fritzie.

Fritzie was still asleep, although now comfortably arranged on an old wool blanket. Harvey found the blanket in a box of things to be donated whenever Mrs Fox found the time. He had considered, briefly, tucking something under Ira, too, but decided to leave him undisturbed on the cold concrete floor of the basement.

The unconscious Ira was strapped to a stretcher and carried out. After Harvey expressed his fears of flooding in the basement, the ambulance men also returned and took up Fritzie rolled in the blanket.

"Where should we put him?" asked one of the men.

"The kitchen would be best," answered Harvey. "My housekeeper likes dogs. She can feed Fritzie and return him to his owner tomorrow." Mrs Fox, Harvey knew, would recognize the dog immediately and, unlike himself, remember exactly which house had lost their pet.

Feeling tired in his bones, Harvey followed the men and dog up the basement stairs. After saying his thanks to the departing ambulance crew and checking Fritzie was comfortable in the warmest corner of the kitchen, he headed to his study.

Harvey poured himself a restorative glass of whiskey from the flask tucked in the hollowed out copy of Crowley's *Book of Lies*. Harvey had ripped the pages out long ago in a fit of frustration but kept the cover for some unknown reason. As a hiding place for his flask, he thought it more than appropriate.

Now ready to journey within to avoid the rain without, Harvey settled back in his favorite chair. The paper containing the spell rested lightly on his knee, but he hardly needed to read it. Long ago he memorized the words and that particular memory, unlike so many others, could not be lost. He closed his eyes and opened his mind to a voyage which Luke Robinson once warned him was deadly.

But, Harvey smirked to himself, what use was a long life if not to gamble it once in a while on a journey to the fabled cities contained within a nightmare.

CHAPTER TWENTY-SEVEN

As soon as Luke made his startling pronouncement about Carolyn Fern, April felt her connection break with Carolyn. She remained vaguely aware of her own body far away in St Mary's Hospital. Or was it far away? Wasn't she essentially in her body and in these strange Dreamlands? These thoughts made her head hurt, possibly in two places, so she pursued Luke as he strode back toward the tower.

"Wait," she called. "You have to help me! I am looking for my friends Nella and Sally. Are they here?"

Luke whirled around, his golden robes flaring in a dramatic circle around him. Nella would have been impressed. April was just impatient for an answer.

"There are dozens of dreamers all around us," he said, his arms making a broad sweep toward the tower and the surrounding woods. "I came here to lead them home through the Enchanted Woods. But every time" – he sounded as if he was grinding his teeth – "every time someone new arrives, I must begin again. You each manipulate this place to be what you expect. And your expectations are so strange."

Luke took a deep breath. He slowly and very deliberately

settled his golden robes so the cloth flowed around him in beautiful folds. He once again resembled a prince of some distant land as depicted in *Amazing Stories*. April hoped she would remember the picture he formed as she wanted to paint it later.

"If I can intercept dreamers early enough in their dream, I am able to send them home. Only there are too many now," Luke said. "I cannot reach them all before another dreamer arrives and undoes my work."

On the periphery of her vision, April saw the giant ants begin to assemble. Each bore a green umbrella to protect themselves from whatever gazed over the tower roof. She did not look up to see if it was still there. She knew it was. The weight of its vision remained a constant presence, as heavy as it had been in her nightmare earlier in the evening. Who dreamed the thing looming behind the tower? April did not want to meet that dreamer.

To distract herself from the tentacled shadow above, she asked, "So you were shouting at me in my dreams to make me leave?"

Luke looked a little closer at her. "No. I was trying to give you a message. You are different. You came here before."

"I don't know what you mean," April replied but she remembered her childhood dreams. This place did seem familiar.

"I think you are a dreamwalker," said Luke. "You go in and out of the Dreamlands as you please. The others were lured here through the powers invoked by meddlers in the mystic malfeasance."

"Well said, Luke. Mystic malfeasances are abounding these days. Wait until you hear about my evening." Harvey Walters appeared on the path. April recognized him with pleasure. He'd been so helpful and kind to her. She needed to find Nella and Sally as soon as possible. If it was a case of simply directing them to walk upon the silver path, as Luke suggested, she was sure her two close friends would follow her. For the others lost from Arkham, she didn't know what to do. She wished she could talk to Carolyn.

Despite Luke's warnings, she had seen how desperate Carolyn was to wake the dreamers and, regardless of her earlier fears, had a hard time believing Carolyn was responsible for their plight.

If only Carolyn could still talk to Luke directly! If only Luke would agree to talk to Carolyn!

Perhaps Mr Walters would be a better conduit between their world and Luke's. The professor's rumpled tweed suit and his crooked tie remained the same as when they had met only an hour ago. More surprisingly, his feet were clad in damp carpet slippers. April had no memory of his shoes. Most of the time, he had been sitting behind his desk. It was the detail and specificity of his wet slippers which convinced her that Mr Walters was actually there and not something conjured out of her mind like the ants.

Luke stopped whirling and pacing. "Harvey! How did you come here?"

"By spell, of course." Mr Walters looked pleased with himself.

"Why are you here, Harvey?" Luke seemed unable to believe his eyes. So much so that he removed his mask and revealed a well-featured man in his early thirties. If Nella was with her, she would have told April that he was movie star handsome.

Mr Walters didn't seem to notice Luke's clothes or attitude. He was far too busy admiring the scenery around him. "I came, my friend, because we have individuals in Arkham attempting to communicate with Cth…" Luke clapped one hand over Mr Walters' mouth.

The old man shook his head with anger. Luke removed his hand slowly.

"Do not speak its name." Luke carefully averted his gaze from whatever was looming over the tower.

"Oh, I doubt it would even notice me." Mr Walters took a quick glance upward and then looked away. "I rather think its gaze is turned elsewhere. In fact, I don't think it is actually here.

It's somewhere else, isn't it?" Then rather like a small boy taunting a playground bully, he chanted softly, "Cthulhu, Cthulhu."

April held her breath. Something about the name sent distinct shivers through her. But the shadow still remained at a distance, its vast eye roving the landscape beyond them.

"Perhaps you are right, Harvey," Luke said very slowly. "But the Ancient One's dreams cast a terrible shadow across the Dreamlands. Such things are hard to dispel."

"So we are occupying its dreams now, are we?" Mr Walters looked intrigued. "I always love Zhang Zhou's quandary. Are we all dreaming we are monsters or are the monsters dreaming that they are us? Although I think I would rather be a butterfly."

To April's eyes, Luke Robinson suddenly looked much younger and bone-weary. "No, we remain in the Dreamlands, but on the very boundary of its impossibilities near the Enchanted Woods. If more of the sleepers come here, then they might trap us forever in the dreams of the Ancient One." He gestured to the tower and the gathering ants. "Already so many are caught, like small insects in a web. I try to free them but more keep coming."

Luke stepped back and looked more carefully at Mr Walters. "You appear to be fading."

April also noticed this. The light was shining through Mr Walters, although the source of the light was unclear.

"Clearly this spell doesn't last forever," Mr Walters said. "Which means we need to come to a solution quickly. Then I'm back at my house, with a sleeping dog, and you're stuck here with…" He pointed with his thumb but did not look up at the giant monstrosity lurking behind the tower.

Apparently, like April, Mr Walters was beginning to feel the weight of the eye gazing down upon them. To distract herself, April looked instead at the ants gathering around them. There did seem to be more than she remembered from earlier dreams.

And a greater variety, too. Some were short. Some were broad. One wore a lovely flowered dress and fancy hat that reminded April of Mrs Hanover, the dress shop owner.

Luke made a sharp, brisk motion with his hand. Mr Walters appeared slightly more solid. "I can assist while the spell lasts," Luke said. "But the spell will end. I warned you it was dangerous. If you try to stay when you fade completely, it may become a permanent condition."

"What's a little danger? So thought influences the dream here?" Mr Walters looked as delighted as a kid on Christmas morning. Then he glanced down at his damp carpet slippers. "Those won't do," he said. The carpet slippers became stout boots that reminded April of the ones advertised in *Adventure* magazine for explorers.

"For some people, the manipulation of substance comes easily," Luke said, apparently ignoring the changes in footwear of the gentleman facing him. "For others, this malleability overwhelms them. Add the shadow of…" He paused, giving his own uneasy glance to the grotesque shape above.

"I'll call it the Ancient One too," Mr Walters suggested. "To spare your feelings."

"Then the minds of the dreamers are overcome and trapped here," Luke continued, ignoring Mr Walters' teasing interruption.

"So being a man with a powerful control over my own mind, I can think about something hard enough and it will exist. Like my boots." Mr Walters spun in a slow circle, taking in all the landscape around them. "I like those." He pointed to the giant ants bearing green umbrellas which now formed a solid line of watchers gathered around them. "Those appear to be your artistic imagination, Miss May."

April blushed. "I think they are my dream," she said. "I was reading about giant ants and seeing green umbrellas recently."

"Stories add significant detail to our dreams." Mr Walters surveyed the landscape. "No Carolyn? I expected her to be with you."

"She was. At least I could hear her asking questions. But now she's gone." April glanced at Luke. "He didn't want to talk to her." She tried not to sound accusing but she knew she sounded angry. The April in the Dreamlands was obviously more belligerent than regular April. She wondered how she would deal with the irritating Simon from the office if she found him here. Perhaps being this dream April had some advantages.

"I blocked Carolyn's ability to see or hear anyone in this place," Luke said. "Carolyn Fern cannot be trusted. She entangled many in this dreaming, like a spider at the center of a web, luring others to dream as well."

"Carolyn Fern is not part of any spider cult." Mr Walters slapped at the top of Luke's head in the way that April's Uncle Tito did to his sons when he disagreed with what the young men were saying. Luke dodged out of his way with a frown.

"Her treatments trapped twelve people in this dream. Together they form a powerful web of dreaming, catching even more like flies in a web," Luke said.

April didn't understand his answer. Luke talked like someone in *Tales from Nevermore*. In fact, she was starting to think Virgil Gray's stories weren't completely fiction. Which was a very frightening thought!

"Ridiculous! Carolyn would never try to trap someone in the Dreamlands," retorted Mr Walters. "She's a valiant and good woman. You know this. And she certainly didn't bring that into the Dreamlands." He nodded to the shadow lurking behind the tower.

"Perhaps Carolyn is being controlled unknowingly by the others," Luke conceded. "But still the danger remains. These dreamers must wake up. Carolyn's work prevents this!"

"So, did hypnotizing people start all this?" April asked, realizing her earlier fears might not have been so foolish after all. But she still remembered the feeling of safety and trust engendered by Carolyn as she started their hypnosis session. She could still sense the slender thread tying her to the hospital room and then she recalled something else. "But Carolyn tells everyone how to end their sessions. She always does this. She said so."

And April was certain if she started counting backward, she would wake up.

"Ah, that's a good point, April," said Mr Walters. "No, Carolyn was asked to treat people who were being driven into nightmares by the approach of something else. Something much bigger!" He glanced toward the tower again.

Luke frowned. "You think it is the Ancient One?"

April noticed Luke very carefully kept his eyes turned away from the shadow and did not speak the name of Cthulhu.

"Nightmares, storms, floods. If it is truly awake in the world, all these things herald its approach to Arkham. And Carolyn certainly didn't wake the Ancient One," Mr Walters said. "But there's someone else meddling too." Mr Walters looked down at his hands. A smoke-stained book appeared. He flipped it open to the last page. "If the chained sleepers dream the Ancient One's dream, then the power will descend safely upon the leaders of the group. That's what the final message in the book meant."

"What is that book?" asked Luke.

"A recipe book," said Mr Walters. "Containing one complicated recipe for siphoning off a god's power while it is busy elsewhere. Now, we have to ask ourselves, who are the cooks?"

"Are you saying the sleepers have something to do with that?" April almost glanced upward but restrained herself. "The thing?"

"At least twelve dreamers are being used by the cooks, for want of a better name, to drain this dream into our world. Clever idea,"

Mr Walters said, still staring at the book. "Keeps the cosmos as balanced as possible. They place dreamers inside the dream of a god, or rather the shadow of its dream here in the Dreamlands, to capture some of its power while not interfering with its actions in the waking world. Still highly dangerous and prone to apocalyptic outcomes. But such practitioners of magic never go beyond cause and effect to examine the longer term ramifications. Instant power and they're sure it will all work out somehow. But how did the Ancient One awaken in the first place?"

"The actions of others woke the Ancient One." Luke sounded very grim. "These manipulators of the dreamers seem to have followed after, rather like jackals in the wake of lions."

"Oh, supernatural scavengers? Hell's bells, of course there are." Mr Walters frowned. "Something this huge wouldn't wake up without giving off a surge of psychic power. Half of the world's mystics must be sitting up in bed and clutching their heads. Such a surge of power would be an invitation to certain unscrupulous magicians to manipulate the very fabric of reality. Suddenly we are knee deep in ritual sacrifices and dead dogs everywhere."

"Dead dogs?" April had been intrigued by the movements of the giant ants, who seemed to be growing more numerous, but was distracted by the change in direction of the conversation.

"Well, at least that was Ira's goal," said Mr Walters. "There is nothing so annoying as discovering your assistant trying to sacrifice a dog in your basement simply because nightmares are on the rise."

April gave a startled gasp of dismay at this pronouncement. "Did you save the dog?"

Mr Walters smiled at her. "Don't worry, Miss May, the dog is safe in my kitchen and will have a hero's breakfast tomorrow, courtesy of Mrs Fox. Ira is now removed from my home and may recover his wits eventually."

Luke looked confused. "What do canines have to do with the events occurring in the Dreamlands?" he asked.

"A rather nasty ceremony calling for the sacrifice of one dog in nine parts and a second ritual of nine times nine dogs done to death by drowning. Which would bring about the siphoning of the god's dream power as described in this book," Mr Walters said. "However, I don't see how the last ritual could be achieved without serious repercussions. Toss eighty-one dogs off a pier and somebody is bound to notice. And stop you before you are even halfway done. Besides, dogs can swim."

"Not if you have them trapped in the Black Cave," said April. The detachment of her shadow from herself back at the hospital continued to buoy her courage. She felt certain she now knew more than Luke. And was unafraid to say so. "Dogs have gone missing throughout Arkham. We've had dozens of lost dog ads placed with the newspaper."

"The symbol painted afresh in the Black Cave. The wands hidden in green umbrellas." Mr Walters looked almost exuberant. "Miss May, you are a genius! Of course the Black Cave would be the perfect place for a caster of unspeakable spells to perform a ritual drowning. Oh dear." He stopped.

"What is it?" April asked.

"The books specified nine times nine dogs plus one man and one woman. To perform the whole rite correctly. Have there been any ads for lost people?"

"No." April had a horrible thought. "Rex and Minnie went to my neighborhood, looking for a sea monster seen near the Black Cave. They never came back."

"That seems ominous. Who are Rex and Minnie?" Mr Walters asked. "The names sound familiar."

"Reporters at the *Arkham Advertiser*." April glanced at the giant ants. There were definitely more of them now. Their features were also changing, becoming more human in appearance, or she was growing used to being watched by enormous insects with parasols.

"Oh, I know. Minnie Klein wrote a rather clever piece on the drilled skulls last Halloween. Good photo too." Mr Walters thought for a while. "Purveyors of knowledge. Known to the community. Ties to many. Yes, that's exactly the sort who would be seen as excellent sacrifices."

"And Valentino!" April suddenly remembered Columbia insisting on taking the puppy.

"Who is Valentino?" The bewildered Luke sounded like a man who was being overcome by the conversation. Obviously he'd never sat at a boarding house table where a half dozen people related all the comings and goings of the day. Or grew up in a large family like April. She rather thought Luke seemed like an only child. Ted Nordby had been an only child who went to their school when she was younger. At times, Ted simply disappeared from the playground to avoid the long arguments between players on who had the next turn in whatever game ruled the day.

Luke probably wanted to vanissh too.

"Valentino is a poodle," April told him. "Columbia took possession of Valentino this evening. She's the woman with the green umbrella. At least one person with a green umbrella. Carolyn had the other."

Mr Walters appeared to have no problem following a long and complicated conversation. In fact, he looked like he was enjoying himself enormously, fastening his gaze on various parts of the landscape and chortling when it melted into a new shape or even small scuttling creatures.

"If Columbia is carrying a wand, then she is probably one of our supernatural scavengers, our jackals of the occult," Mr Walters said.

"If Carolyn also has a wand, then perhaps she may be one too." Luke seemed determined to make this point.

"Or Carolyn is being influenced by a wand," Mr Walters countered. "It's not unusual for practitioners to plant items on their victims. It's a very jackal thing to do, to steal strength from a fiercer predator."

"Like Tabaqui and Shere Khan?" asked April.

"Absolutely, Miss May. It's so pleasant to converse with a reader who knows her literature. Although, if Carolyn is a tiger, she is one who would use her strength for good. You know, Luke, magical jackals are a very good way to describe certain types of magic users. I may use it for my next paper." Mr Walters warmed to his theme and even settled himself down on a crumbling block of sandstone, which reshaped itself into a cozy armchair. "The remaining daughters of the Ignoti were said to form covens in England. They might have sailed to New England. Not all the witches settled in Salem. I wonder if this Columbia is a relative. Perhaps she and Ira are working together as jackals do."

"Well, Columbia is very good at files and billing." April couldn't see Columbia sacrificing people or dogs. It seemed very messy for Columbia and April said as much.

"Efficiency and organization might be a trait of this group," Mr Walters said. "They rather fail at the messy bits, to judge by my assistant Ira. But placing everyone in the Black Cave and letting the waters roll over man, woman, and dogs, well, that is a rather efficient way to do a mass sacrifice."

"It's horrible!" April cried. And also overwhelming. Once again, she felt too many problems were coming down on her. Nella trapped in sleep, the impending flood, the watery sacrifice of Valentino (to say nothing of Minnie and Rex), and larger than all the other problems, the gruesome tentacled monstrosity looming over them in the Dreamlands. At least that creature or god above them, as Luke and Mr Walters referred to it as both, was just a shadow of its own dreams and unlikely to ever be encountered in Arkham. She hoped.

Mr Walters looked thoughtful. "As I once was taught, problems are solvable if we tackle a bit at a time. If we can interrupt the ritual at the Black Cave, we may be able to scare the jackals off and save everyone there."

"You must return at once and do this," Luke said. "I will continue to try to send the dreamers home."

"I thought you said there were too many to send them home individually," April objected.

"While you have been talking, I had an idea," said Luke, but didn't elaborate. April wondered if he had thought of something or was just desperate to get rid of Mr Walters and her. Once again, she had the feeling that Luke just wanted to be alone in the Dreamlands. But Mr Walters' suggestion of dividing their problems into smaller, solvable parts was sensible, and, she had to admit, rather like what her mother would advise. She had come here to find Nella and Sally, so she would do that first. And worry about the rest once she found them.

"After I have sent the dreamers back, I will go to Ulthar. The cats may know how to deal with this dream of the Ancient One," Luke continued.

"Perhaps April could return to Arkham," said Mr Walters, who was starting to fade again. "I may still have a little time left. This is an absolutely unique chance to see the Dreamlands in the spirit, as it were. A trip to Ulthar? What an opportunity."

"No!" Luke began to pace in front of the line of ants, who swiveled their heads from side to side to track the agitated man. "The more who come here, the greater the threat of succumbing to the eternal dream. We must keep the Dreamlands stable. You must return to Arkham and stop the sacrifices." He waved his hands at Mr Walters and the old man faded more quickly. "I will deal with the dreamers."

"If you insist…" Mr Walters was nearly transparent. Then he was gone with a faint echo of the word "spoilsport" lingering in the air.

Luke ignored the comment, turning again to April. He motioned toward the shining silver path that she had followed to the tower. At that moment, he looked very much like the principal of her high school. Mr Smithers hadn't been as handsome as Luke, but he did like to point down the hallway while telling students to stop lingering and hurry to class. Mr Smithers liked a quiet school with the students all shut away behind closed classroom doors. He roamed the hallways in pursuit of order. Even this brief encounter gave April the impression that Luke also wanted less intruders and more peace in his world.

"You should go back now. Since you are still awake…"

"Not really, I am hypnotized," April said, thinking Luke had forgotten.

He made a face much like Mr Smithers when students spoke up. "You are not dreaming. You are in a state of trance. Others control their journey here through such trances and walking the path."

"Oh, do they?" April wondered why Mr Walters was able to disappear home from exactly where he stood. Perhaps because he used a spell. "But where are Nella and Sally? And the other people now asleep in Arkham. Are they all here?"

"Yes." Luke was pacing again. "Harvey and you have given me much to think about. But do not worry. I will force them to take the path toward the waking world."

The ants were gathering closer. Now April knew they were a product of her imagination, she found them less frightening. Many of the giant ants in *The Radio Man* stories had actually been very helpful to the hero. Certainly, any insect carrying an umbrella now seemed more harmless than menacing.

Luke was still talking. The ants seemed very interested in everything he was saying, leaning forward like an attentive audience.

"Journey home by the same path that you took to enter the Enchanted Woods. Tell them what you have learned. Warn Carolyn, but be wary. I am still not convinced she is unaware of her web. I will compel the other sleepers back to Arkham," Luke said.

April wondered exactly what he was going to do. The thought of turning around and going home seemed very tame. She wanted to find Nella and Sally before she left.

"Remember, be careful what you reveal to Carolyn Fern. She may mean well but dark forces surely have ensnared her," Luke repeated unnecessarily.

April paid no attention to the man in the glorious golden robes. Before her eyes, the giant ants were changing into people clutching green umbrellas, including one she knew very well. She brushed past Luke to embrace her dearest friend.

"Nella!" cried April. "I've found you!"

CHAPTER TWENTY-EIGHT

"April!" Nella squealed as she dropped her green umbrella and embraced her. "Where have you been? We will be late!"

In some confusion, April hugged her friend back. "Where are we going?"

As soon as she said it, April felt how wrong the question was. They were in the Dreamlands, not departing on some journey. Except she felt as if she was falling out of the Dreamlands and into a new place. New and not necessarily better. An incredible sense of wrongness swamped her senses.

"To Europe! But we need to run. We'll miss our boat. Oh, if only I could find the luggage!" Nella looked around with wild eyes. "Did we tip the porter? Is he taking it to our cabin? Oh, April, what will we do if we miss the boat?"

"Your friend is lost in her dream," Luke said behind her. "You must lead her out of it."

"How?" cried April, confused by Luke's voice as she could no longer see him or the tower, even though she spun in a complete circle. Only the tentacled shadow remained, dominating the pale pearlescent sky.

"Go into her nightmare and make her aware of her dream," said Luke. "I will help the others."

Even as he spoke, April found herself standing on the end of a horrible dirty pier. The smell of rotting fish swamped everything but a faint underlying odor of salt. It smelled exactly like the alleys in Rivertown and Northside. Poor and desperate, full of the stink of a river overwhelmed by the burning garbage and factory waste of the city that they were fleeing.

Looming above them was the steamship, the smoke funnels pointing like towers to the sky. April could barely look at the ship, but she was aware of the behemoth creaking at the end of its ropes.

The round portholes looked like a row of empty glass eyes peering from the rusted greenish-blue hull. No name was painted on the side. No crew waited to greet them. Pale lights draped along the boarding gangplank shifted and shimmered, reflected in the dim water below, both inviting and repelling at the same time.

"Nella," said April with great conviction, "we don't want to go there."

"But it's our dream." Nella dragged her by one arm, seeming unaware of the great gaping holes in the pier or the sinuous shapes swimming in the water underneath. "If we don't leave now, we never will. I'll be stuck behind a desk typing until I die!"

They reached the swaying gangplank leading to a large oval opening ringed with spiky protrusions. Beyond it, a red painted hallway led into the belly of the ship.

"Nella, come with me." April tried to coax her friend away from the gangplank. Just taking one step on it revealed a rough raspy texture that clung and scraped against their shoes. The shadowy entry ahead resembled a waiting mouth, ready to swallow up anyone foolish enough to enter it. "We will go to Paris later. But we need to return to the boarding house. This is just a nightmare."

The ship rumbled and shook. Below the water, great propellers began to turn, churning the sea into a bubbling froth of muddy water. Even though she was aware that she was visiting Nella's dream, April felt a terrible compulsion to hurry up the gangplank. She pulled harder at Nella. "Let's leave," she said, searching desperately for the shining path out of the dream.

Nella looked ready to burst into tears. "I wanted an adventure, but this is horrible. Why can't we have a nice adventure?"

"We can," April promised her friend. "But not here. We need to leave."

She pulled Nella off the gangplank and back onto the rotting pier. The gangplank rolled itself up into the ship with a sucking sound. April kept pushing and pulling, directing Nella away from the ship. She refused to look back but the shadows of the smokestacks falling across the pier began to writhe and change.

With some relief, April saw they had reached the shore.

"Oh, April, this is nicer," Nella said as they stepped off the pier and onto the sandy silver path winding around the tower. A great crowd of people still milled about the base of the tower, but Luke seemed to be organizing them into groups.

"Spiders," he called. "Fires. Falling rocks." At each proclamation, a few more shuffled into a loose line.

"Is this who you keep seeing in your dreams?" Nella asked. "He looks like a movie star, although rather old."

April stifled a giggle at Luke's appalled glance at Nella. "His name is Luke Robinson. He's trying to help."

"Help with what?" Nella asked, drifting slowly up the path, looking at the trees overarching it. She seemed oblivious to the tower and the looming shadow behind it. Dream Nella seemed much less energetic than Nella awake, and April found herself in the odd position of being the one in the lead.

"He's encouraging people to go home," April said. "We need to follow this path to leave."

Nella turned around. "But why would we want to leave?" she said. "It's nice here. Nobody cares what time you report to work. Nobody fusses at you about your typing."

"Nella, you don't want to stay here," April said. She was beginning to understand Luke's frustration. Imagine having to talk dozens of people out of their dreams! At least if they were pursued by their fears, they'd be more likely to want to leave.

Which, of course, April realized was what Luke was doing. He was organizing people into groups of what they feared most.

"Sheepdogs and sheep," she said.

Luke glanced over to her. "What?"

"I read that sheepdogs can control sheep when they act like wolves. Sheep will gather together and run together away from a wolf." The long article in *Adventure* magazine about living with shepherds in New Zealand was one of the better ones. Mostly because it concentrated on the dogs. "Sheepdogs can push a flock in the direction needed. One dog can control dozens of sheep that way."

Luke nodded. "I'm trying to do the same, but it takes considerable concentration."

"And you'll probably terrify half of them worse than before," April said. "Surely there's a better way to persuade people to leave than pursuing them with their fears. People aren't sheep. They are more likely to go in a dozen different directions rather than the way that you want."

"It's the only thing that's worked so far," Luke said.

"So you have been the one making their nightmares worse." April was very annoyed. After all he had said about Carolyn Fern and Mr Walters. Luke was creating nightmares to scare people out of the Dreamlands! He wasn't ending their dreams. He was making them so bad that people scared themselves awake.

"You dumped fish guts and blood on my friend Minnie," she said to Luke.

"I was helping her," he retorted. "I'm helping all of them."

"Actually, you are doing the opposite of helping me," said one of the dreamers, stepping away from the crowd. She was an older woman, tall and powerfully built. Long braids of brown hair, liberally streaked with gray, hung down her back. In one hand she held a slender wand of pale wood.

"Who are you?" said Luke.

"Augusta Palmer," the woman replied with a cold smile. "My sisters wrought a great work of magic to trap these dreamers here. We wouldn't want to waste their efforts, would we?"

CHAPTER TWENTY-NINE

Gripping April May's hands, Carolyn fought against despair. She had been so close to returning to the Enchanted Woods. Even though she had not entered the Dreamlands exactly as she had with Josephine Ruggles, she had been conscious of April's progress and conversation with Luke Robinson. Then suddenly she felt trapped in her own body, unaware of anything beyond the hospital room where she watched April's face change in a variety of expressions. Occasionally the young woman spoke. But her soft words were barely whispered and frustratingly fragmented, much as a sleeper might mutter in a dream.

Then April exclaimed very clearly, "Nella! I found you!"

Carolyn leaned toward April. "April!" she called. "Can you tell me about Nella? What do you see?"

But there was no response. Instead, April slid back into increasingly agitated murmurings. Real fear crossed her face as she stared blindly at something that Carolyn could not perceive. Carolyn shifted her fingers so they lay across the young woman's wrists. Her pulse was racing, almost abnormally fast.

This had gone on long enough, Carolyn decided. They could try again in the morning. For now, she needed to bring April out of the trance and learn what she could. Carolyn again shifted her hands, tapping gently on April's palms and speaking the sequence of words needed to end April's trance.

"You are leaving your dream behind." She stroked April's hands. "With each breath, you return to us. I will count to five. At five, you will be fully awake."

Carolyn counted slowly to five, with each number calling to April to make the journey back to her, but the shadows of terror continued to flicker across April's face. At five, April remained completely submerged in the dreaming hypnotic state that Carolyn both desired and dreaded for herself.

Two more attempts to wake April failed. Carolyn refused to surrender to despair. She had promised April that she would be safe.

Not since her sessions with Augusta Palmer had Carolyn felt so inadequate. She had completely failed in her responsibility to do no harm.

And with that thought, two sets of memories, both real and false, slid together. Carolyn knew exactly who Augusta Palmer was and where they had met. Not on a ship. The journey from London to New York happened six years ago, when Carolyn returned from an exciting and enlightening trip abroad. There had been no Augusta Palmer or Barbara on that voyage.

She had met both, and their sister Columbia, in Arkham Sanatorium. Where Augusta Palmer became Carolyn's greatest failure. Carolyn had failed to prevent Augusta from frightening the other doctors, frightening them so much, the doctors used the most extreme method available to them to silence Augusta. All because they feared the predictions of an ax murderer that Carolyn thought she could help.

Transferred from a Midwest asylum to Arkham Sanatorium only a few weeks ago, the woman's tragic history both intrigued and infuriated Carolyn. At the turn of the century, the spinster

Augusta Palmer murdered her stepmother in a case which earned her the nickname "the Lizzie Borden of the Midwest." Augusta claimed her actions were inspired by her ability to predict the future. Her sisters asked for leniency and the judge unexpectedly agreed. However, the method of murder was so extreme, a grisly dismemberment, that Augusta was sentenced to an insane asylum.

For nearly thirty years, Augusta was moved from one asylum to the next. She never stayed in any institution long, apparently because she predicted the future to both inmates and doctors. Further, her predictions were "horrific" and her conduct "abominable" (although what exactly she did was never specified). Death, destruction, and chaos were her obsession, according to one doctor.

Looking over the long list of brutal treatments used on the woman, Carolyn could not blame Augusta. In her pride, oh her stupid pride, she asked to be assigned to the case. Determined to help Augusta regain some measure of peace, Carolyn also wanted to demonstrate to her colleagues that even an ax murderer could be rehabilitated, using noninvasive methods such as hypnosis.

If some of the notes made about Augusta reminded her a little of the descriptions that doctors wrote about Josephine Ruggles, Carolyn still requested the case out of a desire to help the patient and not to further her own research.

"At least that's what you told yourself," said the elegant Augusta Palmer residing in her mind, mocking Carolyn's altruism. And now, facing the ruins of her own confidence and with dawning awareness of the harm done to so many, Carolyn knew she had indeed made a terrible mistake. Because Augusta and her two sisters were far more adept at mind control than Carolyn could ever be.

Calm, dignified, and reserved, Augusta arrived for her first session dressed in drab institutional robes, her long braids of brown hair hanging down her back. Twenty years of institutional living had drawn harsh lines in her face and streaks of gray in her hair, making her appear older than her sixty-three years, but her eyes were very bright and clear. Her gaze did not roam aimlessly around the room. Augusta looked directly at Carolyn.

"So," Augusta said, "you will be the instrument of my freedom and destruction. It will be interesting to see what comes first."

Her cold, knowing stare made it abundantly clear why so many doctors had called immediately for the most extreme treatments. Augusta was a frightening woman by sheer force of personality.

When Carolyn met with Augusta Palmer's sisters, Columbia and Barbara, she found terrifyingly cold calm decorum was a family trait. Somehow sessions in her office turned into conversations between the three with Carolyn unable to speak or move, trapped by them as easily as a mouse by a trio of cats. After every session, one of them looked at her and said, "Forget." And she did, layering false memories, like journeys at sea, over the truth of what happened.

"Oh," said Carolyn, staring wildly around the room at St Mary's. "They even stole my dream from me."

The pleasant office never belonged to Augusta. Carolyn had rented it a few weeks ago. She'd been so pleased when she saw her name finally painted in gold on the door. Carolyn even worked through the last weekend arranging her books on the shelves exactly the way that she wanted them.

Then came the final session on Saturday night, when she went like a lamb to Arkham Sanatorium after Barbara phoned her.

There she found the unconscious Augusta and a frantic staff unable to revive her with the glucose shots. The unnaturally calm Barbara requested her sister be transferred to St Mary's and Carolyn go with them.

Without uttering a single word of protest, Carolyn made the

journey. In the rush and confusion of admission, Roger had taken Barbara for one of the sanatorium's nurses.

Once in the hospital corridor, Barbara unfurled her umbrella indoors, lifting it over her head. Carolyn remembered staring at her, wondering if she knew the old adage about it being unlucky to open an umbrella inside.

"Oh, we never rely on luck," Barbara said even though Carolyn hadn't spoken out loud. "We always have Augusta to tell us exactly what will happen. She'll find it easier to control her passage to the Dreamlands from here. Now let's begin to collect the dreamers. We must do this quickly."

And after that?

After that, Carolyn apparently treated twelve patients believing she was occupying Augusta Palmer's office and Barbara was her secretary. Instead, she had been Barbara's puppet. She'd willingly subjected herself to injection after injection of her own sedative mix. No wonder the bottle had been nearly empty. In fact, in a desperate and forgotten attempt to save herself, she'd taken the bottle home and hidden it.

But nothing worked. Like a fool, she followed Barbara's directions on how to treat her patients.

With horror, Carolyn realized that she had sent them into a hypnotic state with suggestions to stay in the Dreamlands. She essentially had trapped all twelve of her patients, just as Roger originally feared.

"What have I done?" Carolyn said, tightening her grip on April May's hands. The young woman seemed calmer now, but her pulse still raced. Carolyn tried to focus on the moment and how she could help her. She had to bring April May back. She had to.

The rest could wait, must wait, until she had solved the problem before her.

A knock sounded on the office door. Before Carolyn could tell whoever it was to go away, Harvey Walters poked his head in.

"You may need my help," he said.

"Harvey," Carolyn replied with some force, "you have never spoken truer words."

Harvey turned and murmured to someone outside the door. Then he came into the office, carefully shutting the door behind him.

"Lefty wants to know if he can help, too," Harvey said. "Would you like him here?"

"It can't hurt." Carolyn gave a slight shrug without letting go of April's hands. As distracted and distressed as she was, she wasn't going to abandon the young woman in the Dreamlands. It seemed important to maintain physical contact.

Some idiot once wrote catharsis was a painful but welcome relief, that the gaining of insight and knowledge outweighed the agony. Carolyn rather feared she was the idiot who had written those arrogant words. Certainly, she would have given almost anything to have remained innocently ignorant of her mistakes. However, at this moment, she had no choice but to make a full confession and hope to repair the damage that she had done.

"Harvey, I've been an absolute fool," Carolyn said as April's friend Lefty came into the room. "Everything that I've done has made matters worse. I've sent twelve people into a deep trance state, which is holding them in the Dreamlands." Recollecting the scheming discussions between Columbia, Barbara, and Augusta, she added, "As unlikely as it sounds, my actions may be dragging even more people in Arkham into this forever nightmare. All at the instigation of Barbara Palmer and her sisters."

"My dear friend," said Harvey, "your actions might have impacted a dozen or so souls now safely housed in this hospital but they are not the cause of our troubles. You never even met

April's sleeping friends. The entire city is not falling asleep due to your admittedly grand skills at hypnosis. There's a terrible evil on the horizon. I fear that the Ancient One is causing both this contagion of sleep and the storms battering our homes. These Palmer sisters are simply taking advantage of the situation. Now I need to know exactly what they told you to do."

Carolyn told Harvey and Lefty about Barbara's directions on how to conduct her hypnosis sessions. The twelve patients sent to her had all been given a command, easily triggered by a telephone call, to fall into a deep sleep, to dream of a tower, and to not wake up.

"Just as the book instructed. With those twelve sleepers, a practiced bunch of witches such as the Palmers could spread a net to catch the power of a god's dream. Especially under our current conditions. But they are not the instigators of the nightmares," said Harvey. "The Palmers are simply magical jackals, following in the Ancient One's wake and snapping up scraps of power for themselves."

"So your assistant Ira Palmer?" Carolyn asked, suddenly remembering the slim young man who did resemble Augusta in some ways.

"Definitely one of them," said Harvey. "I wonder how he's related. Doesn't matter. I suspect he made most of the phone calls to entrap your sleepers... and on my line! Which makes me as complicit as you, Carolyn. I also handed Ira a great deal of information about certain rites and rituals which will make everything so much worse if we don't find the rest of the Palmer sisters and stop them."

"It seems to me that the first thing we need to do is wake up April," said Lefty with a worried glance at his friend. The young woman remained relaxed in her chair. Carolyn was relieved to see the look of sheer terror was gone, although April still made some worried mutterings.

"I've tried to bring her back," Carolyn admitted. "Nothing works."

"Perhaps you should enter the Dreamlands and tell her to come home," suggested Harvey.

"How?" Carolyn said.

"Send yourself there. You have done it before," Harvey said. "You are much stronger than you give yourself credit for."

"But I can't!" Carolyn said. "I failed. Just a few minutes ago, Luke blocked me from asking him questions. I cannot enter the Dreamlands."

"Luke threw me out too. Happens to the best of us," Harvey said. "But let's start over. Carolyn, please hypnotize yourself. I will give you a little push. Then Lefty and I will pull April's spirit forth with your help as a spirit guide."

Carolyn took a deep breath. Hadn't she told April that Harvey was often annoyingly right? She could do this. She could bring on the trance without the drug or the insidious Barbara. All she had to do was start counting backward, very slowly, from a hundred. But before she began, Harvey started to rearrange the chairs.

"Carolyn," Harvey said, "I have faith in you. You would never willingly harm any patient."

April had said something similar to her, Carolyn thought. "I trust you. You wouldn't hurt anyone," April had said.

And Carolyn finally remembered that they were right. She wouldn't simply send a dozen people into the Dreamlands without a way to bring them back.

"What are you doing, professor?" Lefty asked as Harvey moved the flickering oil lamp to the very center of the table. He placed himself on Carolyn's right side with Lefty between him and April.

"An old trick, but a good one. I haven't done one of these since... well, I don't remember the last time. Carolyn, give me your hand, and I'll take Lefty's hand. Lefty, you take April's hand when Carolyn releases it. Very nice. Carolyn, you keep holding April's other hand. I'll take Lefty's free hand. There we are! All in a circle!" Harvey sounded exactly like a kindergarten teacher who was very pleased with his pupils.

"Harvey Walters!" Carolyn said as she looked around the circle they formed. "Are you planning to conduct a seance in the middle of St Mary's Hospital?"

"Yes, I am." The old man grinned. "It would not be the first time. But we will call the spirits of the living tonight. We will help Luke Robinson wake the sleepers. Now, Carolyn, you go first, and we will follow."

Harvey's seance was absolutely ridiculous, absurdly mystical, and, given everything that had happened to her over the past week, the right thing to do! For once, Carolyn didn't even try to rationalize what would happen next. She just wanted it to happen as quickly as possible. For she intended to show Augusta Palmer that she was in control of her mind again.

Carolyn began to count backward from a hundred. Harvey chanted very softly, words that Carolyn could not make out, perhaps just a string of nonsense syllables. His voice faded away as the numbers dwindled and her mind became calm. The lamp dimmed. Before Carolyn was a steep flight of stairs leading to a silver path that she knew. She took the first step, then the next step, and another, and another, all in time with the count in her head, until she was gone from the hospital and finally walking through the Enchanted Woods.

CHAPTER THIRTY

April grabbed Nella's hand. Facing Augusta Palmer, she believed it was important to hang on to her friend. Something about the other woman reminded her of Columbia. Suddenly April felt strangely uncomfortable, as she had when she discussed Columbia's sisters. A feeling that she'd mis-stepped and this woman would unleash … what? How could a woman old enough to be her grandmother be such a terrible and certain threat? Augusta was standing alone, holding aloft a stick and doing nothing but staring at April with the same steady calm gaze as Columbia. It was exactly like the moment when Columbia asked for Valentino and April gave the puppy to her without a single argument.

But she wouldn't let Nella go. Not without a fight!

The slender shaft in Augusta's hand drew her eye. "Very good," purred Augusta. "Look at it carefully, remember what my sister's wand looked like and bring it here."

At first the surface appeared to be blank. But as Augusta rotated it, a swirling pattern emerged. Long tentacles and a single shining eye.

Stunned, April pulled away, dragging Nella back a few paces.

"Oh, very nice," said Augusta, twirling the wand. "I lost mine years ago when I was at the Ionia State Hospital. It feels good to have it back again. You have an excellent memory for designs. I'm not sure somebody else could have shaped it so well."

As with all compliments, April did not know what to say. This one paralyzed her more than most. Probably because she had a sinking feeling that Augusta with a wand was a very dangerous woman indeed.

"What are you doing?" said Luke, who had apparently recovered from his surprise.

"Magic," said Augusta with a shrug. "There's so much dreaming power here, just shed like the skin of a snake while the Ancient One stalks into the world."

At her pronouncement, April felt again the irrational fear evoked by the name of the monster. She shivered.

Augusta smiled and it was not a pleasant smile. But April noticed Augusta also was careful not to look directly at the thing which loomed over the tower. Perhaps she, too, feared attracting its attention.

"I knew a vast change was coming to Arkham," Augusta said. "In 1874, we lacked the monstrous power necessary for our spell's success. We tried to take advantage of the flood, but we needed a city engulfed in fear and nightmares to steal the power of these Dreamlands. We needed what is happening now! When I felt the world shiver in anticipation of an old god's awakening, I knew we had to return to Arkham. It's not easy making such a move when you're incarcerated in an insane asylum, but my sisters are clever women. Even my little half-brother Ira helped. And he's usually useless."

In another woman, Augusta Palmer's speech might have seemed like boasting or even gloating. But with her, it was simply a flat recitation of facts laid out for a relatively simple listener. Or at least a listener who Augusta considered well below her own intelligence.

Luke seemed equally unimpressed with Augusta. "You will leave here," he said, as shadows gathered around him in the shapes of spiders and snakes.

Augusta simply smirked at him. "Nearly thirty years in an insane asylum. Multiple asylums. There's nothing left to terrify me," she said. "I have seen it all in my waking hours. Your pale shadows of reality hold little terror in comparison."

The dreamers remained looking more like people than ants, but they still held the green umbrellas. At a gesture of the wand from Augusta, they formed a tight circle around her, lifting the umbrellas high to shade her from the gaze of the entity who still watched this dream landscape indifferently.

"Besides, I have all these lovely people to act as a shield between me and the Ancient One's dreams," said Augusta, who April noticed avoided saying Cthulhu's name out loud, much like Luke. "Also to be my protection against your creations." She smiled very coldly. "They'll even take any pain upon themselves created by our actions, the dear little sleepers. You did compare them to sheep, didn't you? So apt. And you have been so helpful in persuading them to act like lambs with your own actions."

Luke shouted back. "I didn't cause this. Carolyn Fern did."

"Carolyn Fern did what we told her to do. Hypnotized the twelve sleepers that our spell needed," Augusta said with a shrug. "The Ancient One pulled the rest of this crowd here. Its monstrous approach caused them to fall asleep. Its dream trapped them here. But it was you who persuaded all of those people to act like sheep, trying to think of ways to herd them out of the Dreamlands. I do thank you. Without your actions, it wouldn't be nearly so easy to harvest the Ancient One's dreams. You've given me so much more power than I expected."

Luke drew back from Augusta, now looking horrified. Augusta held out her empty hand and a single chocolate formed in her palm. She popped it in her mouth and ate it. One of the nearby dreamers cried out in pain. "A god's dream is so tasty. Even better than eating the dreams of doctors in the asylum. Still, this god's dreams contain a bit of mind-altering poison, too. Much better to have surrogates surrounding you to swallow the madness and the pain."

"You cannot consume its power!" Luke cried.

"No, not all of it, that would be too much for any witch to chew," Augusta agreed calmly. "But we can nibble a bit here and in Arkham. So much power! And the Ancient One will never know this old dream was taken by us as it consumes the waking world. That's our power after all. We're old women, eminently forgettable and thus easily able to steal from your dreams. Now if all you nice dreamers will gather a little closer…" Augusta gestured to the ant people surrounding her, drawing them tighter around her as they raised their umbrellas to shield her from the dream of Cthulhu.

April felt Nella tugging at her grasp, trying to go to the terrifying Augusta. She dug in her heels, determined to thwart the woman. Luke clenched his fists but seemed unable to act.

"If I strike her, she may hurt more and the harm may be permanent," he said to April.

As April considered running away, hoping she could pull Nella with her, she heard a shout come from the path behind them.

"But I remember you, Augusta Palmer. I remember your sisters Columbia and Barbara. I know what you did." The Carolyn Fern walking down the silver path resembled the Carolyn that April met the first time, a woman both calm and contained, able to see others clearly but with compassion. This indeed was the Carolyn that April admired.

Dressed in sensible clothes as she had been in the hospital, Carolyn did not look like a warrior. So April's imagination gave her an armored breastplate, like a painting of Joan of Arc. If she could imagine a wand for a witch, she could certainly dream protection for Carolyn.

Carolyn smiled briefly at April as if she knew where her armor came from. Then the level glance that Carolyn gave Augusta indicated she was ready to fight for the dreamers of Arkham. Her words confirmed it, to April's sudden relief.

"You have no right to interfere with these people's lives. You had no right to steal my dreams and memories from me," Carolyn said. "Let these people go."

Augusta stepped back, apparently startled by such a direct demand. "Do you think you can just command me and I'll obey?"

"Yes." Carolyn's calm voice didn't falter or change in tone. But something in the Dreamlands shifted, just a little, and April felt the landscape all around her quiver.

Luke started toward the two women. April clung to Nella, uncertain what Carolyn was trying to do. It was almost, but not quite, as if she was trying to hypnotize Augusta. Certainly, her voice contained an almost magnetic quality.

"Then tell me why I would do anything that you command, Doctor Fern." Augusta gave the last two words a terrible malevolence.

"You are the greatest sybil of this or any age. And you said that I was the instrument of your freedom," Carolyn said.

"And my destruction," Augusta added.

"Exactly. Take your freedom now. Return to your body. Find your sisters and leave Arkham," Carolyn commanded.

"Take the wand from her," April hissed, certain that if Augusta wanted her to create it, it meant something important to Augusta. And probably something bad.

"Yes," said Luke. "You can't let her keep it."

Carolyn nodded. She held out her hand for the wand. "If you give me the wand, we will let you leave."

"I'm not sure you can make me do anything." Augusta hadn't changed her position, but April saw her glance around as if looking for a way out.

"I can take away the dreamers surrounding you. Then there will be nothing protecting you from its gaze," Carolyn said. Like everyone else, she didn't look directly at the shadowy entity whose presence still weighed upon them all.

"You can't!" But Augusta didn't sound convinced.

If she could predict the future, April wondered if Augusta had seen this moment.

The former ants lowered their green umbrellas, no longer shading Augusta from the eye which now filled the sky like a terrible sun. The Dreamlands were changing, April realized, changing according to Carolyn's strong will in the same manner that Mr Walters had formed his boots out of his wet slippers.

And April thought she knew what was needed to scare Augusta away. So she tried to imagine the eye growing even larger, more menacing, and more focused on Augusta. She tried to make the dream of Cthulhu notice Augusta Palmer. Even as she concentrated on this, the terror evoked by Cthulhu's name sank deeper into her soul.

"Nobody ever does anything under hypnosis that they are not willing to do," said Carolyn. "I was not willing to hypnotize those twelve people without a way to call them back. So Barbara told me that it would be all right. All I had to do was count to five backward. Five, four, three ..."

Around her, the dreamers who had been ants and now resembled people from Arkham began to stir. They turned away from Augusta and started down the silver path away from the tower. Twelve took the lead, but the others began to follow them, as if pulled behind them by invisible threads.

Nella turned as well, pulling out of April's loosened grasp as April grappled with her fear. Nella called out, "Sally, Sally, wait for me! Are you going home?" April's friend ran down the path, catching up to the now visible Sally. Together they strode arm in arm down the path. Nella looked back over her shoulder. "April! Don't be late! We're going home."

"In a minute. Keep going, Nella, don't look back," April called after her, suddenly certain that they were safe but that she needed to remain to help Carolyn drive Augusta away. She tried to stand a little taller and tell herself that Cthulhu only cared about Augusta Palmer, that this was Augusta's nightmare, not her own.

Augusta glanced uneasily up at the sky. The eye stared directly at her.

"The dreamers are almost gone," Carolyn pointed out. Indeed, the figures heading down the path were already lost to sight in the Enchanted Woods. "Are you going to stay here and let its gaze fall upon you?" Luke stepped up, level with Carolyn.

For the first time, Augusta looked uncertain, then she shrugged. "Oh no, you are right. I do not want to attract its full attention. Even the attention of its forgotten dream." She tossed the wand to Carolyn. "Goodbye, Carolyn, I did enjoy our chats. Until we meet again."

She turned and strode away, a tall and confident woman, absolutely unforgettable.

Once Augusta was lost beneath the trees, Carolyn sagged, much to April's surprise. Perhaps Carolyn wasn't as in control as she appeared.

Luke moved closer to the two women. His golden robes no longer made him resemble a prince in a painting. Rather he seemed more ordinary to April's gaze. More human, she thought.

"That was very brave," Luke said to them. "She was uniquely powerful."

"Augusta is the most intelligent, calculating, and highly manipulative patient that I have ever had. And her sisters are exactly like her," Carolyn said. "I spent two weeks trapped in my office while they picked apart my brain and turned me inside out."

"But you remembered what to do," April said, coming closer and stroking Carolyn's arm the way she might comfort Nella on a bad day. "You saved everyone."

"I remembered how to do it because of you," Carolyn responded. "You told me that you trusted me to keep you safe. Well, I finally remembered I would never let anyone be trapped in a dream. That I would insist on a way to end it. You brought my memories back. Thank you."

For once, April knew exactly how to respond to a compliment. Smiling, she said, "I couldn't have helped Nella without you. It's over now, isn't it? Everyone will wake up?"

April risked a glance at the tower. To her relief, the eye was turned away from them and the entire grotesque shadow seemed diminished. Perhaps because of Augusta eating some of its power? Or was something else happening? She asked Luke and he also made a quick frowning examination.

"I think you are right. The Ancient One's dream is finally fading from the Dreamlands as it fully wakes," Luke said. "You should go home now. And take that with you." He nodded at the wand that Carolyn still held. "It's not safe for it to remain in the Dreamlands. Harvey will know what to do with it."

Carolyn nodded and thrust the wand in her pocket.

"Oh, yes," said April, suddenly remembering the earlier conversation with Mr Walters. "We need to find Columbia. And what is the other sister's name?"

"Barbara," said Carolyn, a little bemused as April dragged her down the path, following the returning dreamers of Arkham. As she expected, Luke watched them go with a definite look of relief. The man obviously wanted his solitude and now he had it again.

"Harvey warned us. Augusta's sisters are going to do something terrible to the dogs of Arkham. We have to save Valentino. And my friends Minnie and Rex. We need to return home now," April said, running as if she was trying to catch the trolley. Carolyn ran easily beside her, holding her hand, as the path wound its way through the Enchanted Woods. "We must go to the Black Cave."

"Start counting!" Carolyn panted beside her. "Five, four, three…"

"Two, one," chanted April, so happy to be finally free of the Dreamlands and opening her eyes in the hospital's plain meeting room. Where she was surprised to see a worried Lefty and a smiling Mr Walters.

"Back again and so soon!" Mr Walters said. "Well done, both of you! But we still have work to do."

CHAPTER THIRTY-ONE

No longer hypnotized, April was embarrassed to find herself clutching Carolyn's hand and Lefty's hand. "What are you doing here?" she said to Lefty.

"Harvey asked me to help," Lefty said, dropping her hand as quickly as she dropped his. But he gave her an awkward little hug around the shoulders.

"How are you, April?" Lefty asked.

"I'm fine," she whispered to him as Mr Walters began quizzing Carolyn on what had happened in the Dreamlands.

"When did he arrive?" April asked Lefty, nodding at the rumpled little professor.

"Just a few minutes ago." Lefty glanced at the wall clock.

"It didn't seem like a few minutes to me," April said, thinking about all she had gone through with Nella on the pier. As for the looming shadow cast over the Dreamlands by the creature Luke and Mr Walters called Cthulhu, April found she could not recall it clearly although she certainly remembered the fear it engendered.

"Dreamlands. Time distortion. Also, I had to call a cab to bring me across town after Luke sent me home," said Mr Walters, overhearing April's whispers to Lefty. "Fascinating effect but how are you, Carolyn?"

"You told me to believe in myself," Carolyn responded to Mr Walters. She reached into the pocket of her jacket and tossed a slender wand upon the table. It appeared as April had last seen it in the Dreamlands, carved with tentacles and a single staring eye. "It worked."

"You brought back a souvenir." Mr Walters twirled it in his hands.

"Yes, and I have no idea why." Carolyn looked at the wand with some disgust. "There's something very unsettling about it. Luke asked me to remove it from the Dreamlands."

"Powerful magic, I suspect. I would love to talk to your Augusta Palmer about her family history." Mr Walters pocketed the wand. "If you don't mind, I'll keep this."

"I'd be happy for you to take it. And this." Carolyn went across the room to fetch a damp green umbrella. Opening it slightly, she showed them the shaft of the umbrella carved in a manner similar to the wand. "This belonged to Barbara."

"Still does." After examining the umbrella, Mr Walters closed it tightly, hiding the shaft from view. "Clever way to conceal a wand or let you wander about in public with it in full view. If she gave the umbrella to you voluntarily, then it must have some ability to influence your actions."

"Barbara practically pushed it into my hands earlier," Carolyn recalled.

Mr Walters nodded. "A powerful charm then. Probably meant to direct you where she wanted you to go. And then draw you back to her."

"But what about Valentino? And Minnie?" April said, not at all interested in wands now she was truly back in Arkham. "We need to go to the Black Cave."

"What?" said Lefty, who looked as baffled as Luke had during their discussions in the Dreamlands.

"Minnie and Rex went to Rivertown and didn't come back," April told him. "Columbia has Valentino, but she means to drown all the dogs."

Lefty still looked confused.

"Ah!" said Mr Walters. "There are parts of the story that I need to tell you, Lefty. But April is correct, we must stop the sacrifices from taking place in the Black Cave." He pulled an old-fashioned pocket watch out of his pocket. "The river should not crest before dawn. At least that is what our magical jackals are expecting. The ritual works best at dawn. Since it's not even midnight, we have ample time left to confound them. But we should leave now."

"Harvey, be careful in how you approach Columbia and Barbara," Carolyn said. "You cannot threaten them or frighten them easily. Like Augusta, they are very intelligent and dangerous women."

"But you persuaded Augusta to leave the Dreamlands!" April said. To the others, she said, "Carolyn was so brave. She made Augusta give her that wand."

"Augusta left because we both made it far more unprofitable and unpleasant for her to stay. She may also have given me the wand because she had no further use for it. She always acts in her own self-interest. Nothing else. Only their own self-interest will motivate the Palmer sisters to do what you want."

"Interesting observations," said Harvey, "and helpful."

"Well," Carolyn said, "I am a psychologist and when not being hypnotized by a…"

"A magical jackal?" April suggested.

"Yes, that's the politest way to put it," Carolyn said. "When not being hypnotized by a magical jackal, I do recognize a trio of dangerous women when I meet them. And I was trapped in a room with them for nearly two weeks."

As they left the room discussing how best to proceed to the Black Cave, a doctor intercepted them.

"Carolyn! Thank goodness. We need you. Your patients are starting to wake up," he said.

"Roger, that is good news," she replied.

Although pleased to hear about the waking patients, April wanted to give her news to Lefty. "I found Nella. And Sally. I think everything will be fine now."

"I hope so," he said, but he sounded a bit gloomy. April refused to be anything but hopeful. All they had to do was rescue the dogs from the Black Cave and this strange adventure would finally be over. And she would spend the next day in bed, sleeping without dreams, she vowed.

The doctor was still preoccupied with describing the waking patients to Carolyn. "We need your help with them. Some are giddy, some are barely conscious, and one or two... well, almost screaming in fear. One woman claims she is a box of chocolates and in danger of being eaten," he said.

"Oh, no!" Carolyn said. "I'll come with you." Carolyn turned to Mr Walters. "Harvey, can you manage without me?"

"Of course, of course," he said. "Go help your patients. You might check on Ira Palmer and chain him to the bed if you can. Also Augusta, if she's still here."

As they hurried away, April heard the doctor say to Carolyn, "Chain them to the bed? What is he talking about?"

Outside the rain seemed less, or perhaps they had grown more used to it. Crammed together in the cab of Pequod, with Lefty driving, Mr Walters looking out the passenger window while talking and April squashed in the middle, they returned to Rivertown.

"It's going to take more than the three of us to remove so many dogs, and people, from the Black Cave," said Lefty.

"Perhaps they can walk out on their own feet or paws," said

Mr Walters. "Of course, if they sedate the dogs like Fritzie, that will be a problem."

"We need muscle," Lefty said.

"Perhaps," Mr Walters responded. "But the more people involved, the more things that could go wrong."

"Lefty," April suggested, "what about the Drowned Rats?"

"The Drowned Rats know the Black Cave better than anyone," she explained to Mr Walters. "And they like dogs." Or at least Joey had been upset by the idea of dozens of dogs drowning.

"Very well, where do we find these Drowned Rats?" Mr Walters asked.

"Schoffner's," Lefty grunted, turning the truck in the direction of the general store. April wished they could make a quick stop on Flotsam Street to check on Nella and Sally, but Mrs Garcia was there. If Nella and Sally needed help when they woke up, Mrs Garcia would know what to do. It had sounded like most of the patients at the hospital were fine, she told herself firmly, despite what she'd heard about the ones who needed Carolyn's help.

Arriving at Schoffner's, they found the crowd had grown larger since their last visit. There was barely room to squeeze by the cans of beans and stacks of cracker boxes. Mr Walters slid around one portly gentleman only to collide with a collection of brooms and mops. By the time April had disentangled him from those, Lefty had made it all the way to the potbelly stove.

"I need some help to search the Black Cave," said Lefty.

"We already cleared it," replied Sol, who was steaming slightly by the stove. An evening of sandbagging the neighborhood had left all of the Drowned Rats dripping wet.

"There's a couple of reporters gone missing. We think they are there," Lefty said. They'd decided in the truck to stick to the story of Minnie and Rex hunting a sea monster. Explaining about Columbia and Barbara would take too much time.

"If they are reporters, they should be able to nose their own way out," one of the Drowned Rats said, and the rest snickered.

"There are eighty-one dogs lost in the Black Cave," April spoke up and realized some of the brave April in the Dreamlands might have made it back to Arkham. "If we don't get them out, they'll all drown."

"Dogs?" Joey asked in a troubled voice. "Are you sure?"

"Yes. Minnie and Rex went looking for the sea monster, but they found the dogs. And they need our help to get them out before the river floods the cave." There, thought April, that sounded like a reasonable story but one which would move the Drowned Rats to action.

"If there's dogs, we should help them," Joey pronounced.

"April, we've been out in the rain for hours. Let everyone dry off a little," said Sol.

"So do I tell Genevieve that you let a bunch of dogs drown?" April stuck up her chin and stared Sol directly in the eye.

Sol winced. "When did you become so tough?" he muttered.

April smiled. "I am tough, aren't I?" she said. "It's been a long day. I'll tell you about it later."

Sol nodded, motioning to his damp and tired crew. "Grab your hats. One more trip to the Black Cave."

Mawmaw removed her corncob pipe from her mouth and said, "If there's that many dogs in the Black Cave, it sounds like the Palmer triplets up to their old tricks."

"Who?" said Mr Walters, his eyes lighting up.

"The Palmer triplets, the wickedest girls ever born in Rivertown. Their father moved the family west after 1874, but we haven't all forgotten about them," Mawmaw said.

"They're bad, bad luck," said the gaffer next to her, nodding his head with every word while still puffing on his pipe.

"Madam, I would love to talk to you–" said Harvey.

"But we have to go now!" interrupted April, who was beginning to realize that the professor was easily distracted at times.

The Drowned Rats piled into the back of Pequod while Lefty, April, and Mr Walters continued their conversation concerning what to do about Columbia and Barbara.

"There's nearly a dozen of us now," April said. "Won't they just run away?"

"Perhaps," Mr Walters said, pulling the wand out of his pocket and looking at it. "If they don't have anyone else with them. But we should be prepared for anything."

At the entrance to the Black Cave, two of the Drowned Rats recovered half a dozen lanterns concealed in a shallow cavity behind a crooked rock. The Rats passed these around with brisk efficiency. Lefty declined a lantern.

"I need to stay with the truck," he mumbled. But the agonized glances he cast at the Black Cave told another story.

Mr Walters seemed to understand. He clapped Lefty on the shoulder. "Keep an eye on the river for us. If it begins to go over the bank, hit your horn."

Lefty leaned on the horn's button and an earsplitting "aaaOOgah!" could be heard clearly over the rushing water of the Miskatonic. Then he reached under the seat and pulled out his Louisville Slugger. "Take it!" he said to April, thrusting it into her hands. Then more quietly, he said, "I can't go in there. Caves are my nightmare. The one I am afraid to dream."

April clutched the Slugger and her courage, summoning up the nerve to reassure her friend. "We have plenty of help with the Drowned Rats."

"And me," said Mr Walters, patting the wand from his pocket and taking a lamp from Joey.

"And Mr Walters," April said to Lefty. "We will be fine."

Sol organized them into a long line and led them into the Black Cave.

"They do know this terrain quite well," Mr Walters observed.

"Shh," said April.

Behind them, the Miskatonic River roared like a freight train. But it was still contained within its banks and Lefty would warn them if it rose too high. For now, the path was dry once they were inside the cave.

"I once met a man who walked all the way to Miskatonic University from this entrance," Mr Walters said. "He was in terrible shape when they found him in the steam tunnels."

"Shh," said Sol and April.

"Please, Mr Walters," said April, "be quiet."

"Do call me Harvey," he replied. "I feel by the end of this evening, we will all be friends. And calling me Mr Walters makes me feel ancient."

It felt odd to address a man as old as Mr Walters as Harvey, but April agreed, if only to keep him silent for a few more minutes.

Further in, the rocks grew larger. Strange outcroppings jutted down from the ceiling, and up from the floor, and even out of the walls. April recalled reading of such formations but couldn't remember which were stalagmites and which were stalactites.

The air became frosty and also unbearably close. A terrible feeling of being watched made April clutch the Slugger tighter, but she saw nothing except the bobbing lanterns carried by the Drowned Rats and Harvey.

The sound of the river faded but April still heard water dripping in the darkness beyond the lamps. Every now and then the lamps would illuminate a grotesque shape, almost animal in its outline, but when they drew closer it was only another boulder. There was an animal smell permeating the passage, though. The odor was sharp and unpleasant, worse than a stable. It smelled like too many dogs all crowded together.

Sol held up his lantern to illuminate the green painted Eye, the circle eerily luminescent above his head.

"We heard barking coming from there this morning," he said, pointing to a dark opening where little rivulets of water ran down the walls.

After spending a minute contemplating the glowing Eye, Harvey nodded and gestured them forward. He now placed one finger on his lips, which made Sol roll his eyes. But April was too tense to even smile.

The passage was narrow, forcing them to walk single-file down its length. With the broad backs of the Drowned Rats in front of her, April couldn't see the dogs at first. But she could hear them. Dozens of them, all whining and whimpering, with short little barks and long frantic howls.

Almost shouting to be heard above the dogs were the voices of two women.

"Ira should be done by now," said one, who April didn't recognize.

"Then he will be here soon with the poisoned meat," said the other, who April knew instantly was Columbia.

"I don't know why poisoned meat is necessary. It's an expense," said the first. April assumed this was Barbara, as it didn't sound like Augusta in the Dreamlands, although very similar.

"Because we cannot be sure the river will crest in time," Columbia said. "Especially without Augusta. And if the dogs live, then the spell won't work. Just like last time."

"The spell didn't give us any more magic because we lacked an ancient god overpowering the city with nightmares," said Barbara.

"The dogs drowned last time and it did give us a little jolt. I think Augusta is making too much of the Ancient One actually coming here. If anything, it's a reason to leave Arkham as soon as this is done," said Columbia.

"Ira says adding a man and a woman, human sacrifices, will make all the difference," said Barbara. "Now we will succeed."

Then April and her friends were through the passage and out into a large cavern. Two women were facing away from them, looking into the light of their own lanterns placed on a long low formation of stone which resembled a bench or table. It ran nearly the length of the cavern. On the end nearest to their group, April could make out the forms of two people gagged and tightly bound with rope.

"Minnie! And Rex!" she whispered to Joey, who was the Drowned Rat closer to her. He looked when she poked him with her elbow, but put his fingers to his lips and nodded at Harvey, who was edging around Sol for a better look at the arguing women.

Torn between pulling Harvey back and going immediately to Minnie, April took another glance around the cavern.

The other end of this stone ledge ended in a side chamber now walled off by a crude wooden fence, which was painted with odd triangles and circles, several dotted or interrupted with jagged lines, and all done in the same bright green paint as the Eye. Behind the fence were the dogs. April saw flashes of fur and heard them whimpering when Columbia banged the fence with her umbrella.

Suddenly April's fear melted as her anger flared up. How dare they threaten those innocent dogs? And Minnie? And Rex?

"Quiet," Columbia shouted, and an impression of something distinctly foul shivered through the cavern. The dogs fell silent.

"Better." Columbia turned to the woman at her side. "If the river does crest before Ira arrives, we might be trapped. Perhaps fifteen more minutes and then we leave. Augusta must have what she needs by now."

"Yes," said Barbara. "We should return to St Mary's before she wakes. It would be just like Augusta to leave us behind."

"Not if we remind Augusta how much she owes us," Columbia replied in a very cold voice.

"Besides, I want to retrieve my umbrella and the nice Dr Fern," said Barbara. "She's so very useful."

"I doubt you can hold the doctor much longer. There is a limit to how many times you can sedate and charm her," Columbia snapped. "Now where is Ira?"

Harvey stepped to the front of their slightly stunned crowd. Obviously, the Drowned Rats had never heard or dealt with anyone like Columbia and Barbara.

"Ira isn't coming. My apologies, ladies, but he is currently comatose at St Mary's Hospital." Harvey seemed less surprised than the rest of them to be holding such a civil if chilly conversation in a cavern far underground with a pair of sixty-three year old women. "Also, Ira failed to complete his part of the ritual. As did Augusta in the Dreamlands. So if your sacrifices here should siphon away a little power from the Ancient One, you will have no protection against its fearful attention. It will swat you like the mosquitoes that you are."

April gave a firm little nod behind him. There, that was telling them. "You let those dogs go!" she shouted. "And Minnie! And Rex!"

Columbia practically snarled. "All our work wasted and no more power than before. It is as bad as when Augusta axed step-mama." Then she turned to Barbara. "I told you Ira couldn't be trusted to do what he is told."

"Your son, madam?" Harvey asked Barbara. "Didn't you lean over the fence and ask me to employ him? When I was contemplating the roses on Sunday afternoon?"

"Our baby brother," Barbara replied.

"Half-brother!" Columbia said most emphatically.

"I had forgotten you until now," Harvey said. "A virtue of your umbrella, I suppose."

With Harvey distracting the two very evil old women, April

began to slide around the edge of the cave, angling toward where Minnie and Rex lay on a narrow stone shelf. Joey spotted her moving, and began to sidestep in her direction while never taking his eyes off Harvey arguing or discussing (hard to tell with Harvey) the umbrellas of the Palmer sisters.

"One of the umbrella's charms. So kind of you to do an old lady a favor, professor!" Barbara continued, ignoring her sister's interruption. "Father made us give the book back to the family who owned it. And then they lost it in a fire. So we were delighted you found it and translated it for Ira. Augusta saw you with it. Although we weren't sure exactly who you were until Sunday. Luckily Carolyn Fern kept a very complete address book. The minute Augusta spotted your name, she knew where to send Ira."

"Then you are the Palmer triplets?" Harvey continued, ignoring Barbara's taunting. April crept closer to Minnie, whose eyes were wide open and blinking frantically at her.

Columbia gripped her umbrella a little tighter. She narrowed her eyes. "You seem to know a great deal about us."

"Not nearly as much as I would like," said Harvey. "But the river is rising so I think it's time for you to go."

As Harvey talked, the Drowned Rats fanned out. April reached up and tugged on the ropes binding Minnie. Minnie gave a weak wiggle. The knots were damp and April couldn't undo them. So she leaned the bat against the ledge and grabbed for the gag binding Minnie's mouth. She nearly tore off a fingernail removing the gag from Minnie's mouth. Her friend sucked in a breath and said, "A monster! In the water."

April turned. Close to the stone ledge was a small puddle of water, probably a collection of the drips running down the walls. Despite the uncertain light of the lanterns, it appeared very shallow.

Columbia rapped the tip of her umbrella on the stone floor of the cavern. It gave off a hollow booming knock. "We have business here," she said. "You do not. Perhaps this will persuade you to go."

The puddle began to bubble and a long feathery tentacle, glowing blue, emerged from it. Then a second and a third.

Harvey looked intrigued. Everyone else drew back.

"Conjuring nightmares into our world?" Harvey muttered. "Interesting use of a wand. Manipulating the stuff of dreams. Dangerous, too."

All of the tentacles looked exactly like the "not a snake" April had seen in the alley. But now the body emerged, far too big to have actually been in the puddle, a round leathery sphere of a body with twisted fins. The head was a knob protuberance on the end with round wide eyes that looked straight up. It did look exactly like something that swam straight out of her nightmares into the cave.

"I am not a screamer," April muttered to bolster her courage as she took up the Louisville Slugger, moving to protect Minnie and the unconscious Rex.

The grotesque mix of fish and octopus started to float above the pond like a child's balloon. It drifted toward April. The Drowned Rats reacted with loud yells. They threw rocks plucked from the floor. A few bounced off the brown hide of the creature and it opened its mouth wide, displaying a double row of needle-like teeth.

"Go away!" shouted April, who decided being a shouter was different from being a screamer. She took up a batting stance, raising her hands holding the Louisville Slugger up to her shoulder, just as Lefty had shown her how he had batted with his beloved Slugger. She kept her eyes on the monstrosity drifting toward them. When it was only inches away from her face, she swung!

A cheer erupted from the Drowned Rats as the thing went sailing into the darkness at the far end of the cavern. A distinct splat was heard.

April bit back a moan as the force of the hit sent pains shooting through her arms. She'd never realized how hard it was to swing the Slugger. Lefty had made it look so easy when he demonstrated for her and Nella one day in the backyard.

"I can call more," Columbia warned.

But April had had enough. She whirled around and swung the bat at Columbia's umbrella. Taken by surprise, Columbia stumbled back. She raised up the umbrella, blocking April's hit.

Again, pains shot up April's arms, but this shock seemed more like bolts of electricity. Yet she swung a second time, overcome with fury that this horrible woman had eavesdropped on her, made her feel small, and now was threatening her friends. And planning to drown the dogs of Arkham!

With a quick twist of her wrist, Columbia deflected the blow. Another jab sent the Louisville Slugger spinning out of April's hands and rattling across the cave floor. Columbia raised the umbrella high and brought it down hard, aiming for April's head.

April flung up her left arm to protect her face. The umbrella smashed down on her forearm. The pain was excruciating, but April threw herself at Columbia.

Practically snarling, April tore the umbrella out of the startled Columbia's hands. Columbia stumbled and slipped in the puddle on the floor. Barbara caught her sister and shoved her upright.

April tried to twist the umbrella's handle off, but it wouldn't budge. So she reversed her hold and raised the umbrella above her head. With an enormous swing, she shattered the shaft against the stone ledge.

Despite the pain reverberating through her arm, April banged the umbrella again and again against the stone until it was a twisted wreck of green canvas, wire spokes, and splintered wood.

It was absolutely the most satisfying thing that April had ever done in her life. And she couldn't wait to tell Nella when she got home.

Columbia gave a short cry. "What a wicked girl you are," she said. Then with a cold little smile, she added, "I do think you can go far."

"If that's a compliment, thank you," April panted, hugging her left arm close to her body. The arm now felt like it was on fire. "And if it's not, I don't care."

The Drowned Rats and Harvey were staring at the disheveled April as if they'd never seen her before. Even Minnie, struggling to sit upright as Joey sliced at her ropes with his pocketknife, looked stunned.

An "Ahooogah!" could be faintly heard from the entrance of the Black Cave.

"That's Lefty," cried Sol. "The river is rising! The water must be over the banks."

Columbia turned her back on all of them. "Let us go," she said to her sister Barbara.

"What about my umbrella?" said Barbara.

"We'll find it later. You should never have given it to Carolyn Fern," Columbia scolded her sister as she pushed her away. The pair glared once over their shoulders at April and then stalked away down a long passageway.

Feeling utterly drained by the fight, April sat on the wet stone floor of the cavern, holding her aching arm close to her body. Harvey picked up the Louisville Slugger and came over to her.

He felt her arm gently but even that made April wince. "A bad sprain or perhaps a cracked bone," he pronounced. "Here, this will help." He pulled off Sally's scarf that April still had wound around her neck and turned it into a sling to hold her arm.

Sol was checking the exit that the Palmer sisters took. "That passage doesn't lead back to the river," he observed.

"Presumably they know another way out," said Harvey.

"Should we go after them?" Sol said.

"No," responded April, pulling herself up from the floor. "We need to get everyone out of here." Lefty was sounding the horn again. More water seemed to be collecting on the cave floor.

Sol pulled out a pocketknife, as did several of the other Drowned Rats. They took to sawing Minnie and Rex out of their ropes. April limped to the fence, which had a crude gate. Suddenly she felt like one giant bruise. The events of the day seemed to be imprinted in pain on her body.

A great many dogs huddled in the makeshift pen. Most were very young puppies.

"Oh, they can't all be lost dogs," she exclaimed.

"No," said Harvey, looking at the pack of dogs. "They probably bought most of them from farms or pet shops around the area. But eighty-one is a very large number. I suppose with such a short amount of time to prepare the sacrifice, they stole what they couldn't buy."

April looked at the panting pack. "How can we keep them all together?" she asked.

Harvey pulled the wand from his pocket. "This is made of dreams, quite literally," he said. "If it was the stuff of a dog's dream, what would it be?"

April thought for a minute. "Bacon?" she said, remembering how she lured Valentino with some. She searched among the dogs and found the poodle at the very front of the pack, looking delighted to see her, judging by the frantic wagging of its tail. "Oh, Valentino, I'm glad to see you too," she crooned, momentarily forgetting the pain in her arm.

"Bacon! Excellent idea." Harvey handed the wand to April. He kept hold of the Louisville Slugger. "Now please imagine bacon as enticing as possible. And walk slowly in front of the dogs when I let them out of the gate."

Why it worked April didn't understand. But it did work. Holding the wand in her good hand, she walked in front of the dogs. They trailed after her like the good puppies that they were, including the very tail-wagging Valentino, as they retraced their steps through the Black Cave.

The Drowned Rats carried Rex, who was still unconscious, and Minnie, who was barely conscious and rocking on her feet, back to Pequod.

Once they were clear of the Black Cave, April found the wand had become limp and greasy, much like a piece of uncooked bacon.

"Ugh," she said. "What do I do with it?"

"Throw it in the river," Harvey advised. "Running water is the best way to destroy such things. Although your method of beating the umbrella against a stone worked well too!"

So April dropped the wand into the river and watched the Miskatonic carry it away. The rain was still falling, and the water was definitely starting to lap over the top of the bank. Behind her came all the noise and confusion of loading eighty-one dogs, two barely conscious people, and all the Drowned Rats into the back of Pequod. Her arm throbbed but she felt almost peaceful and certainly ready to go home.

"What's happened? Where do we go now?" asked Lefty after he retrieved his Louisville Slugger from Harvey. Pequod was full of dogs and people. Luckily the rain had washed away most of the garbage smell, although all the people would soon smell like dogs.

"Rex needs a doctor, but we can't take a truckload of dogs to St Mary's," said April.

"Schoffner's," said Sol, leaning out from the back of the truck where he'd been organizing people and dogs into the now tight space. "We can sort things out there. Find someone to drive Rex and Minnie to St. Mary's."

"And take the dogs someplace safe," said Joey.

"I guess we can put them in the warehouse where we stashed the boats," said Sol, scratching the back of his head and trying to count the noses of the puppies.

"Are you sure there's only eighty-one?" he asked Harvey. "It seems like more."

"Just eighty-one," said Harvey.

"And you only need to take eighty," said April. "I'll take Valentino home with me." Mrs Garcia wouldn't throw out the poodle on such a night.

After they dropped Sol and all the rest at Schoffner's General Store, with many people exclaiming about the dogs and even one couple offering to take Rex and Minnie to the hospital, they went back into the cab of Pequod.

"Where now?" Lefty asked April and Harvey.

"Home!" said April with no hesitation. She wanted to see Nella and make sure she was safe. Sally, too. Valentino rested in her lap, although Harvey and Lefty fussed about her damaged arm. But she was unwilling to let the warm little body go. She needed the poodle for comfort and reassurance. Everyone was now convinced much of Rivertown would go under the water. People's homes and businesses would be destroyed, which was a greater terror than any nightmare.

"I'll go with you," said Harvey, contemplating the wet street. The old man had been very quiet on the drive to Schoffner's and was obviously still preoccupied.

So they returned to Flotsam Street.

CHAPTER THIRTY-TWO

When they reached Flotsam Street, April ran up the front steps with Lefty following, carrying Valentino in his arms. She shoved through the unlatched front door to discover Ollie hugging Sally in the front hall.

Ollie appeared nearly in tears as she clutched Sally and murmured, "Oh my dear, you are awake!"

Sally gave a soft laugh and patted Ollie on her back. "I had the oddest dreams," she said. "I was all tangled up in my knitting with half the town. Everyone was roped to me with multicolored yarn. Everyone but you."

"April!" Nella screamed from the stairs. She came running down with two suitcases under her arm. She dropped the bags next to a pile of bags in the hall.

"Nella!" April shouted.

Nella reached to hug her but pulled back when she saw April's arm in a sling. "What happened to you? Are you hurt?"

Ollie untangled herself from Sally, immediately becoming the nurse in charge, shifting Nella away to examine April's arm. "Bruised and sprained," she said. "But hopefully not broken."

"What are you doing here?" Bewildered, April glanced

around the foyer. She recognized one of the suitcases that Nella had been carrying. It was April's battered old suitcase that she'd brought to Arkham.

"I packed your things," said Nella. "Mrs Garcia said we needed to be ready to leave as soon as Lefty and you returned with the truck."

"But what's happening at St Mary's? What's happening here?" asked April, still struggling to figure out why Ollie was there and why there was a pile of suitcases in the hall. Yes, there had been talk of Rivertown flooding, but surely Flotsam Street was safe. They were practically on French Hill.

"Patients are recovering. A few are still asleep, but we've been able to wake most of them or they woke themselves up. I came home when I heard that Rivertown needed to evacuate. They say there's a huge wall of water headed our way!" Ollie turned to Nella.

"Is that a puppy?" Nella took Valentino from Lefty. She cuddled the little poodle and made an enormous fuss, just as April knew she would.

"Mrs Garcia, can we–" Nella began.

"We'll talk." Mrs Garcia followed Nella down the stairs. "Nella, take April's things out to the truck. She shouldn't strain her arm. And please find a leash for the dog." Mrs Garcia checked the knots on April's sling that Ollie had already tightened. Then she laid a hand gently on April's forehead. "Good, no fever. Now you must leave."

Bemused, April trailed after Mrs Garcia to the parlor. "But what about the other boarding houses? What will they do?"

"Mrs Alba is awake and has been using her phone. Cars and trucks are coming to take people away. The disaster is here, but it is better now that our girls are awake and you are home. Yes?"

"Yes," said April, not sure what Mrs Garcia was asking her but considering Nella and Sally were awake, some of their problems were solved. The Palmer sisters were probably gone. At least, she didn't expect to see Columbia at the *Arkham Advertiser* again. "It is better."

"Good," Mrs Garcia said. "Now, you sit still and do not strain the arm. You have done enough."

"Have I?" said April.

But Mrs Garcia was already off on an errand. So April waited and began to worry. Enough to question Harvey when he appeared in the parlor carrying Barbara's green umbrella.

"We left it in the cab," he said.

"I never want to see another umbrella in my life," replied April with some force.

Harvey gave her a rather sad smile.

"What worries me is what will appear next." Harvey looked out of the window at the rain falling past the streetlamps. Beyond their pale circles of light was utter darkness, a night without stars or moon.

"Professor, what is coming?" Lefty asked. He sounded tired and still depressed by his decision not to enter the Black Cave despite reassurances from Harvey and April that it had made no difference. Lefty had taken one glance at April's battered arm and shook his head at them in disagreement. "I should have done more," he said.

"Luke said what we were seeing in the Dreamlands was but a shadow cast by the entity." Harvey kept talking, although April was fairly sure he was speaking to himself and not really answering Lefty's question.

So she asked the question again, as specifically as she could. "Are you talking about Cthulhu?" The name echoed in her head, impossible to forget, like the giant eye staring down at her in the Dreamlands. It evoked a soul-deep terror that made no sense at all, not after what she'd accomplished.

Harvey turned away from the window and said very gently,

"Do not speak its name aloud again. I did so in the Dreamlands from bravado and foolishness, because I am an old man with no expectations of tomorrow beyond another cup of coffee." As he spoke, he twisted the umbrella round and round in his hands. "But you are a lovely young lady who should go to Paris and study art."

Pain and fatigue dulled April's fear but she knew Harvey was right about Cthulhu. She would never speak or write the Ancient One's true name again. Still, she felt Harvey intended to do something about it. April whispered, "What are you going to do next?"

But Harvey turned back to the window, lost in his contemplation of the night.

Before April could ask Harvey about his plans a second time, Mrs Garcia came into the parlor with a load of blankets. She set them next to the suitcases and other bags of small items that people wanted to take with them.

"There," she said, "everyone can wrap themselves up in these. It will help keep them dry."

"Where will we go?" Exhausted by all she'd seen and done in the Dreamlands and in the Black Cave, April was tempted to lie down on the pile of blankets. Let others make choices and be heroes now.

"You should go to my house," said Harvey. "There are plenty of rooms. Sometimes more than I think there should be. Mrs Fox has already ground the beans for the morning coffee. There's Fritzie, who will be delighted to share a blanket with Valentino."

"Good," said Mrs Garcia. She turned to Lefty. "You take Mr and Mrs Sullivan, Sally, Nella, Ollie, and April in the truck now."

"Mrs Garcia, aren't you coming with us?" April had a horrible feeling that if she left the house, she might never see Mrs Garcia again.

"I will see you later in the morning," she responded, obviously reading April's troubled thoughts.

"I'll be back as soon as possible," Lefty promised his landlady.

Mrs Garcia nodded. "The Drowned Rats are bringing more cars and trucks. We will organize the evacuation." By "we" they all knew she meant the efficient landladies of Flotsam Street.

Harvey handed his house key to April. "I expect Mrs Fox will be there by eight to make breakfast. But there's plenty of food in the pantry if you need something now. I recommend cookies for all. Jar is on the third shelf near the door."

"But where are you going?" Lefty echoed April's earlier worried question to the professor as they went outside. He carried two suitcases under each arm, slinging them with ease into the back of the truck.

Harvey looked down the street. Activity was evident at all the houses. People were beginning to assemble on porches with bags and bundles, waiting for the Drowned Rats to arrive with their caravan of cars and trucks. In the stillness of the night, the roar of the river sounded through the streets of Rivertown. The flood was finally coming. April now feared something else was coming with it.

"Returning to Schoffner's. I want to talk to Mawmaw. I need to know more about the Palmers," said Harvey. "Something terrible is slithering toward us. Those wicked women intend to take full advantage of the chaos. If they succeed, the flood will be the least of our worries. Actually, the flood is already the least dangerous event on the horizon." He started to say more but then shook his head. "Take care of your friends, Lefty. Get them to my house as quickly as possible. It should be the safest place in Arkham tomorrow."

"I'll come back for you as soon as I can," Lefty promised Harvey.

"Don't worry about me. I have an umbrella." Harvey smiled and opened the remaining green umbrella over his head.

April paused. The Sullivans were safely inside the cab. The rest of the tenants were climbing into the back of the truck, to be covered by tarps and blankets to protect them from the rain. Nella called to her.

"Take care of yourself, professor," April said.

"Harvey," the old man reminded her.

"Harvey," she repeated. Unable to say all the things that she wanted to say, April kissed his cheek. He felt like one more grandfather in her extended family.

"Farewell, and I mean it in every sense of the word," said Harvey. "Have an amazing life, April May. I highly recommend living marvelously."

"Come on," said Lefty, pulling her gently away, "we need to go." And more quietly, "Don't worry. I'll look after the professor. Even if I have to follow him into the Black Cave."

With Lefty's help, April scrambled into the truck-bed without jarring her arm. She huddled under a blanket next to Nella, who cradled Valentino on her lap.

"But Nella, how are you now?" April had to repeat her question as Nella was fussing over Valentino. She wondered if her friend remembered any of her time in the Dreamlands. April certainly did but she hoped the memories would fade.

"Me? Oh, I must have been sick," said Nella. "But I had such a long nap. Now I feel fine."

"Do you still want to go to Europe?" April asked, afraid that her friend's nightmare had ended their dreams of travel. She would be sorry if that was true. She believed Harvey was right. It was time to live as she wished. Perhaps she wouldn't succeed at everything, but she could start by studying art. Even if it was only learning how to draw ads.

"Oh, April, of course, I want to tour Europe. London! Paris! I cannot wait," Nella enthused. "Only perhaps we should save for a cabin on a very elegant ship. Have you seen the advertisements for the United States Lines? They promise comfort, courtesy, safety, and speed."

"Tell me more," said April as she finally relaxed against Nella's warm side. Lefty started up the truck and they began to roll away from Flotsam Street.

Across from them, Ollie had an arm slung around Sally.

"Oh," said Ollie. "I forgot. I have a message for you. From Carolyn Fern."

"Mmm?" April was nearly asleep, rocking with the motion of the truck.

"Yes, Carolyn said Augusta Palmer left St Mary's."

That woke April, and worried her, as the three Palmer sisters were definitely trouble. But there was an even greater terror coming if Harvey was right.

The lights of Flotsam Street receded as Pequod picked up speed. But April could still see Mrs Garcia standing in the doorway of her house, waving goodbye. Harvey Walters marched down the street away from them, holding the green umbrella high over his head. He looked absurdly old and vulnerable. April prayed that he would return home soon. She didn't want to lose this new friend.

"Are we safe now?" Nella asked as Pequod headed uphill, away from Rivertown and the rising Miskatonic.

"I hope so," April replied.

EPILOGUE

"Mr Googe?" Minnie Klein had searched through all the speakeasies of Arkham, which were crowded in the days following the flood. The circumstances surrounding the day of the flood, when the Miskatonic overflowed, left many rational adults convinced the only sane response to their memories could be found in drink, loud music, and dancing until dawn. The man sitting on a stool in the darkest corner of the bar resembled April's friend. But she wasn't sure.

This man had a thick stubble of gray beard obscuring the lower half of his face and sagged in his seat.

Still, he looked a lot like the man that she had seen on the bridge. Only even more haunted and sad.

So much had happened in the last few days. Minnie still dreamed about the horrible cave where she had been trapped with Rex and the dogs. The sound of the dripping water haunted her. As soon as she checked herself out of St Mary's, she had spent the day of the flood going everywhere, trying to document every moment with her camera. Then Lefty Googe and Harvey Walters barreled by her in a garbage truck toward something even she couldn't describe. It was as if she lost all words out of her head whenever she tried to think of what loomed before the truck, blotting out the sun.

"Monster," she said out loud. "Mr Googe, did you or did you not run a garbage truck into a monster?"

"Call me Lefty." He picked up the glass with perhaps an inch of beer left in it. He swigged the last of it but paid no more attention to her. This was one of the quieter speakeasies. No music or dancing. Just people huddled on chairs and stools, drinking to forget. April had begged her to start Lefty talking and get him away from places like this.

Minnie also had her own reasons for needing to track him down.

"Lefty," said Minnie, pulling out her notebook and pen. "Can you tell me in your own words what happened on the day of the flood?"

When he didn't respond, she added, "Please?"

"I can tell you." He tapped his empty glass with one finger.

Minnie nodded her understanding and signaled the bartender to fill it again. And to bring her a drink as well. After what she had seen…

Beer delivered to their table, Minnie waited. Sometimes silence was the best way to lure a person into talking. It worked.

"You want to know what happened during the flood?" Lefty looked at her with red-rimmed eyes. Every survivor had a flood story. All of them grist for the *Arkham Advertiser*'s giant presses, spitting out the news. But this story would be different. Minnie knew it in her bones. Because she had been there and what she had seen wasn't possible. Except April told her that it was. She also insisted her friend Lefty knew even more.

"Yes." Minnie wanted to know in the worst way what Lefty had experienced. It burned inside of her. The need to understand everything that she saw even when what she saw was impossible.

"I'll tell you what happened." Lefty's voice was picking up strength. He looked her straight in the eye and practically roared, "Harvey Walters was a goddamn hero! Here's to the finest man who ever lived." He raised his glass and chugged the beer. "You can print this in your newspaper. Harvey Walters saved us all!"

ACKNOWLEDGMENTS

Thank you to Erik Scott de Bie for the Cthoodle comments and all the rest of the Sunday CoW crew for cheering me on. I could not finish stories without Amanda, Catherine, Dawn, Erik, Gabrielle, and Nathan. You always remind me why being a writer is fun. The people at Aconyte remain my dream team. A special thanks is needed for everyone who worked on the magnificent *Welcome to Arkham* which so clearly lays out the neighborhoods near the Miskatonic River.

I fell in love with the idea of boarding houses while reading mysteries. A staple of early twentieth century fiction, real boarding houses were a great source of cheap housing for Americans as they moved from the country to the city.

The boarding house also gave women saddled with an aging house built for a large family and servants a way to monetize their only asset. My great-grandmother rented out rooms for teachers after the death of her husband left her with five stepchildren, a daughter of her own, and no other way to earn a living.

Single women in factory, office, and service jobs (the "Help Wanted – Female" was a legitimate ad category in the newspapers then) also found living in a boarding house stretched a salary. Of course, boarding houses often came with rules and regulations including paying extra for phone use. But as with all things American, who lived together varied greatly from town to town.

By the early twentieth century, writers figured out that the boarding house, which collected a number of unrelated people under one roof, would be a great place for murder, mayhem, and so on. My favorite writers of this genre came along toward the end of the boarding house era. Constance and Gwyneth Little took full advantage of the boarding house possibilities. I highly recommend seeking out their mysteries.

Insulin shock therapy was first practiced in the 1920s but didn't become a regular treatment in North American asylums until the 1930s. By the 1950s, the idea of inducing a brief coma to shock patients out of depression, addiction, and other forms of mental illness was seen as cruel and dangerous as well as ineffective.

Although cave exploration was a popular hobby, spelunking wasn't used broadly as a term until the 1940s. So Harvey is a little ahead of the times suggesting his group of cave explorers be called Fraternitas Speluncis.

April and Lefty were not alone in their love for the pulps. These popular magazines of the early twentieth century enjoyed broad circulation. Descendants of the dime novel and penny dreadfuls (depending on what side of the pond you are on), the pulps provided hundreds of writers an outlet for every conceivable type of story. Specific titles were dedicated to mysteries, science fiction and fantasy, Westerns, romance, or "weird fiction," which mixed a little of all categories with elements of horror. Printed on the cheapest possible paper, aka pulp, with colorful covers and promises of more adventures in the next issue, these magazines would remain popular for decades. A few titles, like *Weird Tales*, lasted past the pulp heyday.

Eventually the pulps would be replaced by the paperback novel. Imprints like Ace and Bantam picked up the 1920s stories, slapped new lurid covers on them, and sold them for 40 cents to a dollar in the 1960s and 1970s. Most of my 1920s pulp reading comes from those paperbacks collected from junk shops and, these days, online. The stories are just as strange and wonderful as you'd expect, including the giant sentient ants of the Radio Man series. Thanks to KDS for suggesting American writer Ralph Milne Farley.

The House of Dr Edwardes exists. If you're lucky enough to find a 1920s edition, the dust jacket art of the Hodder & Stoughton first edition is definitely weird fiction. As is this mystery set in an insane asylum. With apologies to the authors, the movie is much better than the book. Later editions, like my copy, bear the title *Spellbound* and often use images from Hitchcock's fantastic film on the dust jacket.

As always, this story was meant as a light-hearted adventure, not a history lesson, and any errors must be blamed on Cthulhu's interference.

I remain very thankful that the Seattle Public Library, despite suffering a devastating cyberware attack in May 2024, provided so many wonderful resources for research. Please support your local library. Thank you for reading to the very end of this book, too!

ABOUT THE AUTHOR

ROSEMARY JONES is the author of the *Arkham Horror* novels *Mask of Silver*, *The Deadly Grimoire*, and *The Bootlegger's Dance*. She is an ardent collector of children's books, and a fan of talkies and silent movies. Her other works include *Wrecker of Engines* (Cobalt City 20th Anniversary edition), *Dungeons & Dragons'* *Forgotten Realms* novels, numerous novellas, short stories, and collaborations.

rosemaryjones.com // x.com/rosemaryjones

ARKHAM HORROR
THE CARD GAME

THE DROWNED CITY
INVESTIGATOR & CAMPAIGN
EXPANSION
AVAILABLE NOW

ARKHAM HORROR™

Ancient forces muster in the gloom of Arkham.
Who will shine a light into the shadows?

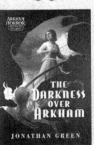

Explore riveting pulp adventure at
ACONYTEBOOKS.COM